FIRST TO FIGHT

Book One: The Empire's Corps
Book Two: No Worse Enemy
Book Three: When The Bough Breaks
Book Four: Semper Fi
Book Five: The Outcast
Book Six: To The Shores
Book Seven: Reality Check
Book Eight: Retreat Hell
Book Nine: The Thin Blue Line
Book Ten: Never Surrender
Book Eleven: First To Fight
Book Twelve: They Shall Not Pass
Book Thirteen: Culture Shock

FIRST TO FIGHT

CHRISTOPHER G. NUTTALL

The characters and events portrayed in this book are fictitious. Any similarity to real persons, living or dead, is coincidental and not intended by the author.

Text copyright © 2018 Christopher G. Nuttall
All rights reserved.
No part of this book may be reproduced, or stored in a retrieval system, or transmitted in any form or by any means, electronic, mechanical, photocopying, recording, or otherwise, without express written permission of the publisher.

ISBN-13: 9781983510038
ISBN-10: 1983510033

http://www.chrishanger.net
http://chrishanger.wordpress.com/
http://www.facebook.com/ChristopherGNuttall

All Comments Welcome!

PROLOGUE

The Empire did not believe in heroes.

This may seem odd to us, but the Grand Senate was very keen to promote the idea that no one - absolutely no one - stood head and shoulders above everyone else. The idea that someone might be deserving of extra praise was alien to it, an attitude that makes no sense unless you realise that a popular hero might serve as a rallying point for resistance to the Grand Senate and the government. Indeed, when someone *did* become a hero, their positions were quietly undermined; their reputations were called into question, their failures were publicised while their successes were quietly ignored and - if they failed to take the hint - they were often reassigned to somewhere nicely isolated.

The careers of Admiral Stockholm and Admiral Valentine serve, alas, as examples of the vicious jealousy shown by the Grand Senate towards anyone who dared to win unsanctioned admiration. Admiral Stockholm, who saved an entire sector from an insurgency that threatened to drag it out of the Empire's clutches, was punished for daring to succeed where others failed. Tame reporters were encouraged to ask questions about the disposition of the loot - with the obvious implication the Admiral had been looting himself - while his failure to achieve an impossible degree of perfection was held against him. By the time he resigned from the service, he was a broken man, worn down by fighting against a foe he could neither understand nor defeat.

Admiral Valentine, by contrast, knew very well which side his bread was buttered on. He served the Grand Senate loyally and, despite a lacklustre performance on Han, found himself assigned to Earth just prior to the Empire's collapse. Valentine was no hero; he may have been promoted as a military genius, but he commanded no loyalty from anyone outside his own family. He posed no threat to the Grand Senate, while Admiral Stockholm, given the right opportunity, could easily have become a rogue warlord, followed by his loyal officers.

Heroes, the Empire claimed, simply did not exist. The stars of stage and screen were not heroes; they were either promoted as figureheads for their staffs or portrayed as fools, cowards or criminals. Heroes from the past were deconstructed until their warts came to overshadow their successes. Captain Ian Macpherson, a noted naval hero during the Unification Wars, fought in seventy-one battles and won sixty-nine of them, a record unmatched before or since. However, most portrayals of Macpherson in the Empire focus on his relationship with his wife, including a strong allegation that he cheated on her. The simple fact that theirs was an arranged marriage, that they both had extra-marital partners, that they knew and understood what they were doing is simply ignored. Macpherson, dead and gone, is branded a villain in the eyes of the Empire's public.

It is easy, of course, to see *why* the Grand Senate was so distrusting of heroes. The Grand Senators lacked charisma, let alone the common touch that would allow them to win the love and admiration of the people they ruled. They were so detached from their subjects that they might as well have lived in another universe. A hero, on the other hand, who commanded respect and loyalty from his followers, was a deadly threat. Might Admiral Stockholm have taken his fleet to Earth and overthrown the Grand Senate? The Grand Senate did not command the loyalty it needed to secure its position - how could it? All it could do was systematically undermine anyone who might have posed a threat.

Like so much else, it was a policy that proved disastrous. As the Empire neared the point of final collapse, military officers in high places were paralysed by the fear of showing any independent volition of their own, or so resentful of the lack of appreciation that they were scheming to take advantage of the fall to establish their own empires. The emotional ties between the Empire and its military officers were broken, allowing room for strong-minded officers to forge ties of their own. In many ways, the post-Empire universe was a return to the age of heroes - and villains. A strong man in the right place, at the right time, could make the difference between the survival of civilisation or a collapse into barbarism.

Colonel Edward Stalker is one such hero.

I first met the Colonel when I was exiled from Earth, bare months before the Fall. He was and remains an impressive man, a Captain of Marines exiled himself (along with his marines) for daring to tell the Grand Senate the truth. In short order, Captain Stalker not only reasserted control over Avalon, but forged a lasting peace that laid the groundwork for the Commonwealth. Avalon may have been abandoned by the Empire - the message warning us that we were being left to our own devices arrived long after Earth itself had fallen - but Captain (now Colonel) Stalker never gave up. He led the growing power of Avalon against interstellar pirates, the military dictatorship of Admiral Singh and the threatening empire of Wolfbane. His life was not free of warts - no one is free of warts - but they never overshadowed his success.

It took me years to convince Colonel Stalker to write his autobiography. He was not enthusiastic about the project, if only because he didn't see himself as a hero or anything other than a marine trying to do his duty. I pushed as hard as I dared, reminding him that his story was an inspiration to the children of Avalon, to the men and women who lived in safety because of him and his marines. Even so, it was not until recently that I was able to convince him to put hand to keyboard and start outlining his early life and career.

I have changed none of the essence of this document, beyond inserting a handful of quotes and notes about the final days of the Empire. There are aspects, for various reasons, he chose to gloss over. As many of these aspects are covered in other works, I have not pressed the issue.

This, then, is the story of the forging of a Terran Marine - and a hero, even if he doesn't want the title. And it is that, I think, that makes him a true hero.

- Professor Leo Caesius, Avalon University, 46PE.

CHAPTER ONE

Marines are not born, I was told, but made. They were put through hell in Boot Camp, then a different kind of hell at the Slaughterhouse. Many fall by the wayside, but those who survive become part of a truly unique brotherhood.

-Professor Leo Caesius

When we rolled into the unnamed town - which we rapidly started calling Shithole, because no two factions could agree on a name - we were greeted in the manner we had come to expect. The women and children were hurried off the streets, while the young men glared at us, some of them waving weapons openly, daring us to emulate our predecessors in Shithole and try to confiscate them. Some of them spat, others made rude signs and a couple picked up rocks, as if they intended to hurl them at the AFVs. The machine gun whirred as it turned to point at the men, who stood their ground. I fingered my rifle and watched, feeling sweat running down my spine. It wasn't my first deployment, but it promised to be the most challenging.

"As you were," Sergeant Harris ordered. "They're not a threat."

I had my doubts. The waves of hatred and rage emitting from the men were practically a tangible force. They didn't want us anywhere near them, let alone trying to stop them from exterminating their rivals. Shithole had ten separate factions vying for control over the city and *all* of them, given half a chance, would happily rape, pillage and burn their way through the others. As far as I could tell, none of them were remotely decent people…

but then, war *does* tend to erode human decency. There's no point in telling people they should behave when war teaches us that nice guys finish last.

Five years of increasingly brutal civil war hadn't done anything for Shithole, which might have been a decent city once upon a time. The streets were cracked and broken, lined with piles of garbage that no one had bothered to clear up. I could have sworn I saw a handful of dead bodies lying amidst the pile, the remnants of a family that had been unlucky enough to live in a war zone. There was no way to know, now, whose side they'd been on, if they'd had a side in the first place. They might have been innocent victims or they might have been killed in revenge for an atrocity they'd committed. It didn't matter now, I thought, as I saw rats running away from the pile. Now, they were nothing more than dead bodies.

The buildings were pockmarked with bullet holes, their doors and windows heavily barricaded to provide a limited amount of protection for their inhabitants. A number of houses had clearly been knocked down, either deliberately to provide building material or blown up by their enemies. The taller buildings, skyscrapers that would have been impressive if I hadn't been born in the CityBlocks of Earth, looked deserted. One of them looked as though it had copped an HVM and, by some miracle, stayed upright. I wouldn't have cared to live there, if I'd had a choice. It looked as though a strong wind would send it crashing into a pile of rubble.

And we might knock it down ourselves, I thought, as the small convoy turned towards the Forward Operating Base. *A tall building could hide enemy snipers.*

I gritted my teeth as a dull explosion rolled over the city, followed by several gunshots. The Imperial Army detachment charged with securing the city hadn't done a very good job, according to the briefings; they'd rapidly managed to alienate all of the factions, even the ones that might have been happy to work with an outside force. I blamed it on the Rules of Engagement myself, rules written by people countless light years from Shithole. The soldiers had been ordered to show nothing, but strict neutrality…and to disarm the factions, as if removing weapons would somehow weaken the hatred pulsing through the city. It shouldn't have surprised anyone, least of all the soldiers, that *no one* dared risk being disarmed. The soldiers had promptly made themselves the enemies of everyone.

The Forward Operating Base looked utterly unwelcoming, even though it was - reasonably - safe. It was nothing more than a school that had been taken over by the soldiers, then turned into an armed camp. Strong prefabricated walls, topped with jagged glass and studded with murder holes, surrounded a large building, while a number of soldiers, radars and point-defence weapons were mounted on the roof. If the briefing hadn't already told me that the enemy had mortars and were willing to use them, I would have guessed from the presence of the point defence. But the soldiers had only made matters worse, thanks to the ROE, by not shooting back at the mortar teams. The planners who'd drawn up the ROE had worried that innocent civilians might be hurt.

I snorted, then disembarked with the rest of the platoon as soon as the convoy rolled through the gate. The soldiers looked tired and thoroughly demoralised, which really shouldn't have been a surprise. They *knew* they were being targeted, they *knew* they were vulnerable…and they *knew* that doing something to tighten up the defences would only get them in trouble with their superiors. Holding a city is hard enough at the best of times, but deliberately not taking basic precautions for political reasons only makes it impossible. The soldiers controlled only the territory under their guns and, sometimes, not even that. I was surprised the FOB had lasted as long as it had without someone smuggling a vehicle-borne IED through the gates and blowing it to hell.

"Get some rest," the Sergeant ordered, pointing towards one of the former classrooms. It looked better than the classrooms I'd seen on Earth, even though the tables and chairs were gone and the floor was covered with sleeping mats. "We're going out on patrol tomorrow."

The enemy, it seemed, recovered very quickly from the shock of our arrival and started to organise a proper welcome. I snapped awake hours later to the sound of mortar shells screaming towards the FOB, only to be picked off in mid-flight by the point defence. It might have seemed a pointless exercise, but the enemy knew that it wasn't *impossible* to overload the tracking radars and land a shell in the middle of the compound. The building itself had been strengthened, yet a lucky shot might kill a couple of us and convince our superiors to leave the factions to their mutual slaughter. And besides, it kept us awake. I might have grown used to only a few hours of sleep in Boot Camp, but it wasn't something I enjoyed. Tired marines made mistakes.

"Fuck it," Joker muttered. "This isn't funny, you know."

I shrugged. We'd trained for war endlessly, practicing in simulators and training grounds, but *this* was different. This time, real people could get hurt.

"Wake up, ladies," Sergeant Harris bellowed, crashing through the door. The rest of the platoon either sat up or jerked awake, depending on how well they'd managed to sleep through the welcoming barrage. "Stuff some crap down your throat, then grab your kit."

I nodded - salutes were forbidden in combat zones, with harsh punishment for anyone who dared - and reached for the MREs in my pack. The rations tasted better than anything I'd eaten in the Undercity, but I'd been told that complaining about them was an old marine tradition. I honestly hadn't understood why until I'd gone on leave for the first time. Joker crouched next to me and offered to swap one of his ration bars for one of mine. We made the trade, chewed rapidly, answered the call of nature and finally lined up in front of the sergeant, who eyed us all disapprovingly.

"1st Platoon is on QRF," he said, crossly. "2nd Platoon will take the first patrol, accompanying the old timers."

I felt a chill run down my spine. I was in 2nd Platoon.

The old hands met us as we assembled near the gates. There were four of them; Young, Benedict, Hobbes and Green. They looked less spruce than us, unsurprisingly; they'd been assigned to work with the army deployment here, instead of remaining with their regular companies. They *had* been intended to train the local soldiers, but apparently all attempts to set up a local militia to support the outsiders had floundered on political correctness and local realities, leaving them with little to do.

"Expect the wankers to test your determination as soon as they can," Young said. Wankers was an old term for enemy combatants, particularly those who didn't play by the rules. (As if there was any other kind, these days.) "Remember your training, watch your backs and don't let *any* of them come close to you. If you have to take prisoners, force them to strip. Better to walk someone through the streets naked than let them bring a bomb to you."

"Shit," Joker said.

The sickening feeling in my chest only got worse as we checked our weapons and body armour one final time, then advanced through the gates and out into bandit country. My hands felt sweaty as we slipped down the street, careful to give any piles of rubbish a wide berth. The enemy knew they couldn't face us - or even the soldiers - in open combat, so they resorted to all sorts of tricks to even the odds. Hiding an IED under a pile of debris and then detonating it when we passed was an old trick. I saw a couple of faces peeping at us from behind a curtain - were they reporting our progress to their superiors? - which vanished the moment I glanced at them. They had *looked* like kids, but that meant nothing. A kid could easily serve as a spy, his handlers banking on the fact we would be reluctant to shoot at them.

And if we did shoot a kid, I thought grimly, *we would only create a new rallying cry for the enemy.*

We turned the corner and strode towards a marketplace. I would have preferred to be somewhere - anywhere - else, but doctrine said it was important to convince the locals that we could go anywhere, at will, and there was nothing they could do to stop us. The locals scattered in front of us, the women hurrying out of sight while the menfolk looked ready to fight, if necessary. I didn't really blame them. They'd endured the attentions of a regiment more known for abusing the locals than fighting the enemy in the past, according to the briefing, and it would be a long time before any of them really trusted us. Stallkeepers eyed us warily as we passed, clearly expecting us to take what we wanted, but we had been warned not to take anything. If we wanted something, we'd been told, we had to pay for it.

The marketplace was a testament to human determination to survive, somehow. Everything was on sale, from meat (probably rat, but there was no way to know) to weapons and supplies smuggled in from outside the city. In a way, it was the only truly neutral ground in the city; I was mildly surprised the soldiers hadn't set up their base just inside the market. But then, there *were* weapons on display. We made a show of ignoring them as we reached the end of the market and headed down the next street. It looked cleaner than the others, which surprised me. In hindsight, it should also have worried me.

One of the wankers panicked and opened fire, a second before we walked right into the ambush. We snapped up our rifles and returned fire, putting several rounds through the windows to keep the snipers from continuing their attack, then ducked for cover and advanced, in fire teams, towards the house. It wasn't a big building, I noted absently as Joker prepared a charge to break down the door, but that wasn't reassuring. Our advantages were most pronounced in open battle, not close-quarter knife-fights. The enemy had worked hard to create a situation that maximised their advantages and minimised ours. Joker snapped the charge against the door, shouted a warning, then detonated the device. The doorway exploded inwards; I unhooked a grenade from my belt and threw it inside in one smooth motion, then followed up as soon as it detonated. Several wankers who had been lying in wait had been caught in the blast; I glanced at their bodies, then led the way through the house. Four other wankers made the mistake of running downstairs and straight into our waiting guns. We shot them down and advanced upstairs, checking the upper rooms one by one. The sniper who'd started the ambush was dead. There was no way to tell which of us had shot him.

The brief encounter expanded as the QRF arrived, then started setting up barricades to trap the insurgents. Determined to show that we would not be pushed around, we searched through a dozen houses, killing nine insurgents and capturing three more. I knew they'd go into our detention camps, rather than those run by the army or the local government, such as it was. Hopefully, we'd actually get some valuable intelligence out of them. Oddly, I no longer felt nervous. I was doing the job I'd trained to do.

It was nearly an hour before we heard the whimper.

The area was firmly under control, or so we believed. The prisoners had been dumped into an armoured van, the locals were being kept out and we were merely making a final sweep for anything we might have missed. We didn't - quite - relax, but we weren't expecting further trouble. The wankers hadn't expected such a vigorous response and, I thought, they were reconsidering their tactics. We were walking past an alleyway when I heard someone moaning in pain. It could have been a trap, but I couldn't simply leave it; I called it in, informing the sergeant of what we'd heard, then led the way down the alleyway. Joker followed, watching my back.

I stopped and stared in horror as the alleyway opened into a backyard. A young girl was bent over a dustbin, her long dress raised, while Young stood behind her, unbuttoning his fly and clearly preparing to have some fun. Hobbes held her arms firmly in place, his face consumed with an unholy lust. For seconds - it felt like hours - I just stared. We'd been taught, time and time again, that molesting the locals was not only stupid, but wrong. Marines were held to a higher code of conduct and anything that smacked of mistreating *anyone* would draw harsh punishment. And yet Young was preparing to commit rape…

"Get away from her," I snapped, levelling my rifle and aiming at his head. "Now!"

Young turned to look at me, then gave a sickly smile. "No one will miss the bitch," he said, as the girl's dress fell back to cover her legs. "You can have a go too, then we can dump her body and no one will ever know."

Horror and disbelief were rapidly replaced by anger. I knew, all too well, just how my sister had died.

"Keep your fucking hands where I can fucking see them," I ordered, snapping the laser rangefinder to visual. No one uses them in combat because the beam of light is visible in anything less than bright sunlight, revealing your position to the enemy, but they're useful for making an unmistakable threat. Beside me, Joker covered Hobbes. "You're a fucking…"

I got control of my anger, then muttered a command into the intercom. People passing the buck up the chain of command was one of the reasons the Imperial Army was so screwed up, but there were some matters that could only be handled by a superior officer. Captain Bilbo and Sergeant Harris arrived within moments, escorted by an entire fire team. Young and Hobbes were cuffed, stuffed into the van and driven back to the FOB. The girl was taken with them. We were told to join the rest of the QRF for the day, then report to Captain Bilbo when we returned to the

FOB. I wasn't looking forward to the discussion I knew we were going to have, but there was no choice.

"I understand you caught them in the middle of a rape," the Captain said. I honestly hadn't had much time to forge an impression of him, save for dedication and determination. "Do you believe we should press charges?"

"Yes, sir," I said. I fought down the bitter wave of emotion that, somehow, I had never managed to suppress. My sister's death had left scars I had never managed to lose. But that wasn't something I could say to him. "We have to show the locals that we're not above the law."

"Indeed," the Captain said. He keyed his intercom. "Come in!"

I turned…and blinked in surprise as Young, Hobbes and the girl stepped into the room. The two men were wearing their uniforms…and so was the girl. Hers marked her out as a Field Intelligence Officer.

Joker grabbed for the pistol at his belt. "Sir?"

I understood, suddenly. "It was a test, wasn't it?"

"Yes," Captain Bilbo said. "A test. And you passed with flying colours."

"Oh," I said.

I knew what he meant. We weren't training to become soldiers, any more than we were civil guardsmen or militiamen. We were training to become marines, members of the deadliest brotherhood in history. We *had* to live up to our own standards…and police those amongst our ranks who failed to keep faith with those who had died, serving as marines. And if that meant enduring a test so realistic that we forgot it was a test, it had to be done. I didn't like it, but I accepted it.

It would have been easy to fail. We could have told ourselves that keeping faith with our comrades was more important than an innocent girl's life and covered for them. But that wouldn't have kept faith with the *corps*. We'd have been binned - kicked out of training - and we would have deserved it.

"Thank you, sir," I said.

"Go back to your barracks," the Captain ordered. "You're on QRF tomorrow."

"Yes, sir," we said.

Chapter Two

The population of Earth, in the years before the Fall, was estimated as roughly eighty billion lives. (Just how accurate the estimate was is now impossible to tell.) It should not be surprising, therefore, that most of the population lived in the CityBlocks; towering constructions that held over a hundred thousand people apiece. Men and women were born within their CityBlocks and, unless they were lucky enough to escape, lived and died without ever leaving. It should be no great surprise that the lower levels of those blocks - the Undercity - fell into barbarism long before the Empire itself.

-Professor Leo Caesius

I was born in the Undercity.

If you were born on Avalon - or anywhere, really, outside the Core Worlds - you probably won't understand what that means. Imagine a transit barracks from Camelot, with a thousand tiny apartments for immigrants in search of employment and a new life, then scale it up until you get a rabbit warren composed of millions of apartments, each one playing host to a separate family, linked together by dim corridors and illuminated by flickering lights. Every so often, there's a school, an entertainment complex, a government office and not much else. Now imagine another such barracks built next to the first, and then a third barracks built on top of the first two…

It was not a pleasant place to live.

Truthfully, I have no idea who fathered me. My mother, like almost everyone else in the CityBlock, had no job and no particular hope of getting one. She only survived - and survived poorly - on the regular handout of rations, as ordered by the Grand Senate. As she received extra rations per child, it was perhaps no surprise that she managed to get pregnant several times, giving birth to five healthy children. None of us grew up with a father figure, not even when my mother was cohabiting with a man. They showed no interest in us for fear of being charged with our welfare.

I would like to claim we learned to look after each other, but the dog-eat-dog attitude of the Undercity ensured that we didn't. Trevor, my older brother, was a bully who'd learned that the only way to avoid being bullied was to be a bully himself. He was fond of saying, as he handed out beatings, that it was for my own good. The hell of it was that he had a point. If I hadn't been struggling with him, practically from the day I could walk unaided, I would have been eaten alive by school. Linda and Dare, my younger sister and brother, learned fast too. As soon as I was too strong to bully safely, Trevor switched his attentions to them. The only one of us children who escaped his attentions was Cindy, the baby.

In hindsight, of course, I was incredibly lucky to survive my childhood. The mortality rate in the Undercity was terrifyingly high and a child could die in so many ways. It wasn't uncommon for an ill child to be given bad medicine - someone in the assessment office missed the fact that the workers, in order to meet their quotas, had filled the capsules with powdered chalk instead of medicine - or simply to be killed by their parents or a random stranger. Or in an accident. The CityBlocks were immensely complex structures, keeping us all alive, yet by the time I was born they were already decaying. If a child went wandering in the wrong place, the child might well die.

It only got worse when I went to school, which was mandatory for kids from five to eighteen. Attendance might have been mandatory, of course, but learning something - anything - was not actually a requirement. The teachers had no power over us, which meant they were trapped in the sealed complexes with children who had learned that they could get away with almost anything, as long as they picked their targets carefully. If you showed a hint of weakness in an Undercity school, a hint that you couldn't stand up for yourself, you were targeted. And the teachers? They had no power. They couldn't do anything.

They tell me I'm a brave man. I've walked into firefights without showing a hint of hesitation, even though bullets were flying all around me. But I wouldn't willingly walk into an Undercity school and try to teach, not with the rules and regulations governing teachers and how they were supposed to relate to the kids. The merest suggestion that they'd hit a child, or spoken sharply to one, or made the grave mistake of telling them the truth, or hurting their delicate little feelings…well, let's just say it would destroy their lives. Teachers could be insulted, hurt or even killed by their charges and there was nothing anyone would do about it. I knew five teachers who left the school after being attacked, two of them in body bags.

I was lucky. I was strong enough to keep myself reasonably safe, thankfully, and Trevor's beatings had given me just enough empathy to refrain from picking on the weaker souls myself. By the time I was thirteen, I could actually read and write, which put me head and shoulders ahead of just about everyone else, and I had figured out that most of the classroom tests we were meant to do were pointless. I spent the time we were meant to be staring at a testing machine - I don't think I need to say that most of us goofed off - either doing nothing or reading from my datapad. There wasn't much else to do.

Matters only got worse as I matured. You can't imagine the horrors running through the schools as we grew interested in sex. Rape - in all of its horrific forms - was depressingly common, while the rapists were rarely - if ever - punished for their crimes. A smart girl would find a strong boy, someone capable of protecting her, and attach herself to him in exchange for protection. Others would hang around in gangs, trying to find strength and security in numbers. It rarely worked. There were hundreds of girls in my school on antidepressants, struggling to cope with the realities of helplessness, and countless others who chose suicide, rather than endure another moment of their hellish existence. When society starts to break down, it's always the women who get the worst of it.

Like everyone else, I wanted a way out, but how? My exam results were poor - I just wasn't a good test-taker - and I didn't have much hope of getting a place at Imperial University, no matter how much they lowered the standards. Nor did I have much patience, then and now, for bullshit... and Leo tells me that Imperial University was *full* of bullshit. As I turned sixteen, I knew there were only a handful of options awaiting me. I could go to the gangs and become yet another savage, I could try to raise a family to perpetuate the cycle or I could try to break out. But how?

It was sheer luck that led me to discover the marines. One of the teachers boasted constantly about his achievements in the military, as if it would impress or intimidate the barbarians he had to teach. Perhaps it would have done, if we hadn't been raised on a diet of ultra-violent movies that were both profoundly stupid and anti-military. The idea of him clowning around like the heroes of those movies struck us as absurd; we laughed at him, of course. But I grew interested in the military. Maybe I didn't have the qualifications to go to a colony world as anything other than an indentured colonist - a slave, in other words - but military experience might just offer me a chance to make my way in the world. I started to look up online resources, glancing through the different files on offer...

...And it didn't take me long to start sniffing bullshit.

The thing you have to understand - and you probably won't, if you were born on Avalon - is that the Empire's military was having a horrific recruitment crisis. It wasn't getting the sheer number of new bodies it needed, no matter how much it spent on propaganda. (The idea of giving soldiers respect and a living wage probably never occurred to them.) The kindest thing civilians on Earth said about the military was that it took idiots off the streets, gave them deadly weapons and pointed them at the enemies of civilisation on other worlds. By the time I started to look for prospective opportunities, there was a sheer mountain of bullshit about what the military would do for me...and, as I had learned in the cradle, anything that looks too good to be true probably is. It was only a reference on a datanet forum that led me to the marines.

Their site was different. The marines promised nothing to me personally, beyond a chance to make something of myself. Their site talked about being the best of the best, about fighting enemies on distant worlds...the more I read their blunt plain-spoken words, the more I liked it. There was no attempt to lure me in; indeed, if anything, their words were designed to repel anyone who couldn't stand the thought of seeing blood. The movies they showed me were live combat footage, not elaborate promises of keg parties and girls by the score. It looked harsh and unpleasant…but it still looked better than the Undercity. At least I'd be able to shoot back at my enemies.

At sixteen, I needed parental permission to enlist. My mother said no. My younger siblings needed me, she said, and my older brother might need me too. I grew frustrated and we exchanged harsh words; there was nothing to look forward to, I said, beyond finding a wife and starting a family of my own. Or, perhaps, impregnating a dozen different girls, secure in the knowledge that the state would take care of them. The argument ran backwards and forwards for hours, ending with my declaration that I could seek a special wavier from school - to signal my maturity - or simply wait until my next birthday. And, with that, I stormed out.

Trevor caught up with me an hour later. He wasn't too pleased.

"If you go into the military, you might die," he pointed out, curtly. "And for what?"

"A chance at a better life," I said. "What do we have to look forward to *here*?"

"I've made connections," Trevor said. "Why not join us?"

I groaned. Trevor had joined the Blades, one of the thousands upon thousands of gangs who controlled the Undercity. They were nasty; they fought each other for territory, or women, or what passed for honour among them…and, in the meantime, extorted payments from everyone unfortunate enough to live in the territory they controlled. Their primitive weapons - weapons were, of course, forbidden on Earth - should have been laughable, but their aggression and ruthlessness made them a threat to everyone. The police? Don't make me laugh. In some places, the gangs paid off the police force; in others, the gangs *were* the police.

And while Trevor might boast of his connections, I knew better. He might work his way to the top, but it was far more likely he'd end up dead in a pointless fight.

"It's pointless," I said. I hated the gangsters. Everyone did, but no one had the nerve to fight the bastards. No wonder so many young men, denied a healthy outlet for their aggression, set out to join them. "And I don't want to lie dead in a sanitation tube."

Trevor smirked. "You'd prefer to lie dead on an alien world?"

I shrugged. There was no point in talking to Trevor. He only saw the Undercity…and how best to make himself a major player. I knew he wouldn't care how many others got hurt, including his family, as long as he became a strong man. It was the only way to survive in the Undercity. But I just wanted to get out.

"What about Linda? Or Dare? Or Cindy?" Trevor asked. "Do you want to leave them here?"

"I could take them with me," I protested weakly. Linda was thirteen; Dare, at seven, was already showing signs of becoming a successful bully. Cindy, the baby, was barely old enough to walk. "I…"

"I don't *think* the military would be so glad to have you they'd provide accommodation for them too," Trevor said, sarcastically. "And what will they do without you?"

He showed no concern for them - or our mother - at all. And why not? The Undercity broke down parental bonds, convincing children they shouldn't listen to their parents on one hand and ensuring that parents had no power over their children on the other. Even *I* didn't think much of my mother; Trevor would happily have sold her - or our younger siblings - into slavery for money or power. It wasn't until much later that I learned how horrific - and unhealthy - such an attitude actually was.

Matters rested there for several weeks. I asked at school for a waiver, but I didn't have the money to pay the bribe and was told I'd have to wait. Trevor made several attempts to get me into the gangs, alternatively telling me how great it was or making veiled threats against my life. Linda, growing into womanhood, watched me fearfully. Trevor had told her that the only thing keeping her safe was my reputation - not his, for some unaccountable reason - and that it would be open season on her when I left. I asked him why he couldn't protect her himself and he said nothing, merely glared. Did it really matter so much to him that I joined the gangs?

I kept quiet and waited, patiently, for graduation. I'd be seventeen; I could join the military, if I wanted, or seek employment elsewhere. I spent the time reading more about the marines, and their role in the Empire, while trying to prepare myself as best as I could. The datanet offered all sorts of pieces of advice, some of it contradictory. I spent hours in the gym, trying to build up my muscles or running around the track as fast as I could. I'd never looked so fit, I told myself, as I looked in the mirror. I was *sure* the marines would take one look and beg me to join.

One week before graduation, all hell broke loose.

It was rare for us to have a family dinner. Our mother would get the rations from the local store, sell half of them to pay for her drug habit and leave the rest in the cupboards for when we felt peckish. There was never enough, really; it wasn't unknown for older siblings to steal food from their younger siblings. But Trevor was feeling full of himself for some reason and he'd actually paid for a *proper* dinner, one that tasted of something other than recycled cardboard. We were just sitting down to eat when the door unlocked and a stream of masked gangsters raged into the apartment. Trevor, it seemed, had alienated someone during his desperate struggle for power. That person - and I never found out who - had decided to nip this upstart challenger in the bud.

Resistance was futile, but I tried. I knocked one of them out before four more slammed me down and tied my hands and feet with duct tape. Trevor was slammed down too, despite his fearsome reputation. Dare, only seven, was thrown against the wall so hard that it cracked his skull. He died instantly, I hope. Linda and my mother were not so lucky. By the time they died, they'd been raped so savagely that death would have come for them anyway. And Trevor? I had to watch as they cut him open and bled him to death.

I don't know why they left me alive, when they'd finally finished their ghastly task. Perhaps they wanted someone to spread the word, just to make sure everyone *knew* they were bastards, or perhaps the drugs they were taking as they had their fun interfered with their thoughts. It took me hours to wriggle free and, when I stumbled over to the cot, I discovered that my baby sister was dead. They'd put a pillow over her head and…

My family was dead.

The Undercity doesn't encourage you to care. I knew people who had quite happily done horrific things to their families and gotten away with them. Trevor probably *would* have sold his younger sisters for power, if he'd been asked. And yet, I felt a pang as I stared down at their bodies. None of them had *asked* to be born, nor to grow up in hell. I forced myself to close their eyes, then step back from the bodies. There was nothing else I could do for them.

I knew there was no point in reporting the crime. No one would give a damn. It wasn't as if anyone in the Undercity had *friends*. Hell, I was sure the neighbours had heard the screams, but they'd done nothing. And I knew there was no point in trying for revenge. I didn't know who to target, let alone where to find them. All I could do was shower, change into something clean and search the apartment for money before leaving and closing the door, one final time. I have no doubt that our neighbours broke in the following day and took whatever they wanted, but I have no idea what happened to the bodies. They were probably carried to the nearest trash chute and dumped in.

Using some of Trevor's money, I boarded a tube and set off for the recruiting office. I was an orphan, without parents. There was no one to grant me permission to enlist - and no one who could object. Maybe the military would take me…

…Because, as I knew all too well, there was nowhere else to go.

Chapter
Three

I am often asked why so few civilians from Earth joined the military, even when it was clear the military would offer them a better life. To that, all I can say is that military service was not only roundly mocked on Earth, but also dismissed. There was, in their view, nothing and no one worth fighting for. The Grand Senate commanded neither respect nor loyalty.

-Professor Leo Caesius

I must have looked a sight on the tube as it progressed from the lower levels up to the more civilised sections of the CityBlock. Maybe I had showered, maybe I had changed my clothes, but my eyes were haunted and my fists were clenched. I was grimly aware of men eying me sharply and women inching away from me, as if I was a wolf who had come to prowl amongst the sheep. I think I hated the upper-blockers at that moment, hated them more intensely than Trevor or the men who'd destroyed my family; the upper-blockers had lives and opportunities few of us could even dream about. It wasn't until much later that I learned they had problems of their own.

It was a relief when I finally reached the recruiting stations. There were a handful of recruiting stations, most showing glamorous posters of men in uniform or starships performing immensely dangerous manoeuvres. The Imperial Navy, it seemed, was determined to milk the old line about all the nice girls liking spacers for as much as it could get, while the Imperial Army and Civil Guard talked about being all one could be. Only the marines were different, their office decorated with a simple picture of a marine in a muddy field. The sign on the door stated that the office was closed for the day, but it would be opening in a number of hours. I had nowhere else to go, so I sat down on the step and closed my eyes.

I must have dozed off, for the next thing I remember was a man peering down at me. He looked friendly enough, yet there was a *perceptiveness* in his gaze that bothered me at a very primal level. I had the impression - and nothing I saw later ever belied it - that he could see right through me. We stared at each other for a long moment, then I hastily stood and stepped aside, allowing him to open the office.

"I want to enlist," I said.

He gave me a look that was neither welcoming nor unfriendly. I felt an unaccustomed pit in my stomach as he looked me up and down, then beckoned me to step into the office. Inside, it was dark and bland, almost Spartan. The walls were bare, save for a single rank chart and a couple of medals. I assumed, in the absence of other evidence, that they belonged to the man who'd met me. He sat down behind a desk and pointed me to a chair, then tapped a terminal keyboard. The system came to life with a contented hum.

"I am Recruiting Sergeant Muhammad Bakker," he said, shortly. "Before we begin, there is one piece of advice I want you to bear in mind at all times. Never - ever - try to lie to me."

"I won't," I said.

Somehow, I doubted Bakker would be fooled if I tried to lie. There was something in the way he moved that spoke of an easy confidence, a self-certainty so strong that it had no need to justify itself. I'd met men with more muscles, men who looked more intimidating…and none of them had seemed so *capable*. I wished, with a sudden bitter intensity, that some of our teachers had had that attitude. Our schools might have actually been worth something.

"Good," Bakker said. He took my ID card and ran it through the scanner, then shrugged when no obvious red flags appeared. "Tell me why you want to join the marines."

I swallowed. I had my reasons, but how could I put them into words?

"Because I want to be something more," I said, finally. "Because… because I don't want to remain stuck in the Undercity."

Bakker lifted his eyebrows. "And you feel the marines can offer you that chance?"

"Yes, sir," I said. The *sir* just slipped out automatically. His attitude commanded respect, even from an Undercity brat. "I don't want to go back there."

His eyebrows lifted again. "Is this one of those enlistments when the recruit wants to be shipped out at once?"

"Yes, sir," I said.

"Explain," he ordered.

I did, starting with my pathetic education and ending with the death of my family. Bakker listened, saying nothing, as I went through the whole story, his face utterly expressionless. I cursed myself mentally, wondering if I should have worked harder at school. Maybe if I'd had better grades, no matter how pointless, he might have enlisted me on the spot.

"I see," Bakker said, when I had finished. "Do you have a criminal record?"

"No, sir," I said.

"Very good," he said. He glanced at his terminal. "Piss-poor academic standing, young man."

"The tests are useless, sir," I said. His eyebrows rose, once again. "All they do is test how well you can swallow, then spit back the material. I forgot everything I was taught as soon as the test was over."

"How true," Bakker agreed. He gave me a considering look. "Can you read?"

"Yes, sir," I said, irked. It wasn't a stupid question - I doubted that more than ten percent of the Undercity's inhabitants could even recite the alphabet - but it was annoying. "I mastered reading at a very early age."

He took a datapad from a drawer, tapped a switch and passed it to me. "Read this out loud."

I glanced down at the datapad, then started to read. "I, insert your own name here, agree to submit myself for testing in line with the Military Readiness and Accountability Act," I said. "I understand that data collected…"

Bakker held up a hand. "Finish it silently, then summarise it for me."

I felt sweat prickling down my back as I finished reading the document. "It says…it says that some of these tests can only be given with prior permission," I said, carefully. "And that I'm not allowed to be offended by the results."

"Press your finger against the reader, if you agree," Bakker said, tonelessly. It was obvious that he considered the whole procedure to be bullshit. "If you don't agree, get out that door."

"I agree," I said. I hesitated, then asked. "Why do we have to do this?"

"Because you're about to undergo a set of aptitude tests," Bakker said, as he rose to his feet and walked around the desk. He didn't make any attempt to loom over me, yet I still couldn't help feeling intimidated. "By law, those tests can only be given with permission, as testing all children and teenagers is deemed unfair. They will hopefully suggest your general suitability for the corps and what, if any, role you may be suited for."

I didn't understand what I was being told until much later. Aptitude tests measure both developed intelligence and how a person may react, if put into a number of different situations. They could be used to separate a prospective computer expert from a prospective janitor and, as such, were considered unfair by the educational community. It wouldn't do, they said, to tell a teenager that he or she wasn't suited to be anything more than a cleaner or garbage disposal man. It would only undermine their self-confidence.

"You clearly didn't take the standardised tests seriously," Bakker said. He led me through a hidden door and into another room. It was empty, save for a computer sitting on a desk and a water dispenser placed against the wall. "This test? You *need* to take it seriously. Give each question serious consideration before you answer, if there's time."

I blinked. "If there's time?"

"Some of these questions have a time limit," Bakker said. He sat down in front of the computer, then took me through a couple of sample questions. "Even the others, the ones without a formal time limit…we *will* be measuring just how long you take to answer them."

He rose, motioning for me to sit down. "Feel free to take water from the dispenser, if you like," he added. "Touch the keyboard when you're ready to start."

I stared at the computer, bracing myself, then tapped the switch. The first question blinked up in front of me. *Dave is smarter than Devon. Who is stupider?* I stared at it for a moment, then worked out that Devon was the stupider one of the pair. There was nothing to tell me if I was right or wrong, merely the next question. The first set were along the same lines, testing my ability to comprehend what I was seeing; the next set were far more complex. I found myself sweating again as I answered them to the best of my ability, growing increasingly convinced that I was failing badly. My food-deprived mind was starting to hurt and hurt badly. By the time the series of questions finally came to an end, I was half-expecting to be unceremoniously booted out of the office. Instead, Bakker returned and beckoned me through yet another door.

"I need to evaluate your results," he said.

He passed me a ration bar and a bottle of juice, then motioned for me to sit and wait. I had the feeling it was another test, so I sat quietly and ate my ration bar slowly, savouring every morsel. It tasted far better than the crud we'd been given in the Undercity. Bakker sat on the other side of the room, tapping away at his datapad. It felt like hours before he finally looked up at me and smiled, rather cruelly.

"You'll be pleased to know you meet the minimum necessary requirements for Boot Camp," he said. "Do you still want to go?"

"Yes, sir," I said. "How well did I do?"

"You met the minimum requirements," Bakker repeated, shortly. It wasn't until much later that I learned I'd been placed in the top percentile. "Have you finished your meal?"

"Yes, sir," I said.

"Stand against the wall," he ordered. "I need to take measurements, as well as a blood sample. If you took any drugs prior to coming here, this is your one chance to tell me."

"I didn't, sir," I said.

"You'd be amazed at just how many idiots think they can fool a blood test," Bakker said, as he picked up an injector tube. I refused to show any sign of unease as he pressed it against my arm, withdrawing a small sample of blood. "Do you have anything you want to confess to me now?"

"No, sir," I said.

"Good," Bakker said. He put the blood sample in a machine I didn't recognise, then measured my height and weight manually. "Decent enough, I suppose. You really need to put a bit more weight on, but they'll take care of that at Boot Camp."

He turned back to the machine, then nodded. "Your blood sample seems to be clear," he added. "Do you have any allergies that you know about? Any medical problems? Any genetic enhancement in the family?"

"No, sir," I said. Getting ill could be the kiss of death in the Undercity. "If there was any enhancement, I don't know about it."

Bakker frowned. "There are some traces of hackwork in your blood, but that's true of most residents of Earth these days," he said. "It shouldn't be a problem, as it isn't flagging up any warning signs. Boot Camp will do a full work-up, if necessary, but I don't think it will stand in your way."

"Thank you, sir," I said, relieved. "Hackwork?"

"Genetic engineering to fix a hereditary problem," Bakker said, shortly. "Your distant ancestors might have had a problem with hay fever, for example, and they might have spliced a modification into your DNA to ensure their descendants didn't have the same problem."

He met my eyes. "Your test results, both physical and mental, show that you can proceed forward from here," he added, changing the subject. "You may quit at any time, but you have to *tell* us you quit. If you decide not to show up for the shuttle flight, you will be listed as a deserter and probably arrested. It may also be counted against you if you wish to sign up for another branch of the military - and there will *not* be a second chance to join us. We don't want quitters. Do you understand me?"

"Yes, sir," I said.

"There's a scheduled shuttle flight from here to Boot Camp tomorrow, then another two weeks from now," Bakker said. "You may, if you wish, leave on the second shuttle, but it's unlikely I can offer you a later seat."

"I'll leave tomorrow," I said.

Bakker lifted his eyebrows, yet again. "You don't want a chance to think about it?"

"No, sir," I said. I could live on the streets for a night, if necessary, but not for two weeks, not when I had almost no money with me. "There's nothing left for me here."

"Very well," Bakker said. He reached for another datapad and placed it in front of me. "I want you to read this carefully, then sign it. That will put you in the system as a recruit."

I read through it, page by page. There wasn't much; it was just a note that I was old enough to enlist, that I understood what I was doing and that I accepted the risk of death, either in combat or in a training accident. Bakker kept an eye on me as I read the last paragraph twice, then placed my finger against the reader to sign it. He smiled, took the reader back and held out a hand. I shook it, feeling committed. And I *was* committed.

"This is a rough outline of the training schedule and a list of regulations for Boot Camp," he said, holding out a set of papers. "I suggest, very strongly, that you spend the rest of the day reading through them and committing the details to memory. Here" - he passed me a card - "is the emergency number, which you may ring at any time if you wish to quit. Your temporary recruit number is printed at the top; don't bother to memorise it because you won't keep it past the day you arrive at Boot Camp. Quote it if you wish to quit so they know who you are."

"I won't quit," I said.

Bakker gave me a nasty smile. "If I had a credit for every prospective recruit who told me that and then quit, I'd have enough money to afford my own starship," he said. "And some of them did *better* on the tests than you."

I swallowed.

"Your shuttle will be departing from Admiral Nimitz Military Spaceport at 1700 tomorrow," Bakker continued. "Here is your travel warrant, which includes a flight from here to the spaceport, and permission to stay in a recruit hostel on the complex. It's free, but I strongly advise you to remember that everything you do may be counted against you."

I took the piece of cardboard, then placed it carefully into my pocket. "Thank you," I said, sincerely. "Do you…do you have any pieces of advice?"

"I have plenty," Bakker said. "But most of them won't mean anything to you until it's too late."

He looked me in the eye. "There's a list of what you can take in the paperwork," he said, after a moment. "Don't worry about clothing, as that will be supplied, and *don't* take anything illegal. If you have anything with you that *isn't* on the list, dump it before you get on the shuttle. And don't go out partying after you reach the hostel, no matter what invites you get from your fellows. A high alcohol count in your blood when you enter Boot Camp will be enough to get you in deep shit."

"Yes, sir," I said. I honestly hadn't had a drinking habit, not after one of my stepfathers had shown me just how far a man could fall when he was hooked on booze. "I won't drink."

Bakker smiled. "The only other piece of advice I will give you is this," he added. "At Boot Camp - and the Slaughterhouse - *everything* is a test. You will be watched and evaluated constantly by men who have already seen the elephant. They will contrive a hundred situations where you will be tested on everything from combat skills to moral grounding, just to see how you react. You will find yourself pushed to the limits, because they will prefer to break you in training rather than have you break in the field."

That was, if anything, an understatement. But I didn't realise it until later.

"You can get a flight from here at any time up to 2200," Bakker warned. "But I'd suggest you leave now."

I nodded. There was no way I wanted to spend too much time in the upper-block. As soon as he dismissed me, with a set of paperwork and dire warnings about what would happen if I didn't read it all, I hurried up to the airport on the top of the CityBlock and boarded a flight to the military spaceport. It wasn't a pleasant experience - I had never flown before - but I forced myself to endure it. I was quite certain there would be a great deal more flying in the marines.

And, as soon as I found the hostel and was given a room, I sat down and started to shake. My family was gone, my old life was wiped from existence…and I was entering a whole new world. The spaceport alone looked very different from anything I'd seen before; hell, I'd never seen the sky in my entire life, until now. And tomorrow I was going to leave Earth forever…

I recalled my family one last time, then forced myself to put the memory in a box. There was no point in dwelling on the past, not when the bitter pain and helplessness would drag me down into madness. It was time to look to the future.

CHAPTER FOUR

> Mars is the oldest settled world in human space - and one of the very few to ever be terraformed completely. Indeed, Mars was settled for so long that many people are unsure if humanity was born on Mars or Earth. However, despite its proximity to Earth, Mars has a far smaller population. Its combination of harsh environment, natives who dislike immigrants from Earth, and low gravity sees to that.
>
> -Professor Leo Caesius

I was not, of course, the only prospective marine who boarded the shuttle to Mars. There were thirty of us, twenty-seven boys and three girls. The latter attracted my attention more than I care to admit; one of them looked muscular, glaring defiantly at any of the boys who dared look at her for longer than a second, while the other two had the edgy brittleness I'd seen at school, the face of a woman who was trying to carry on despite everything that had happened to her. I didn't speak to them, or any of the boys; none of us spoke, save for a couple of friends who'd signed up together. We were too lost in our own thoughts to socialise as the shuttle made its way to Mars.

It was my first shuttle flight and, alas, my first brush with the agoraphobia that bedevilled so many Earthers who left Earth, searching for a new home among the stars. The sheer wide open *vastness* of interplanetary space was so different from the endless rabbit warrens of the Undercity that I almost cowered into my seat, before forcing myself to look out of the porthole as the shuttle left Earth. It had been bad enough on the aircraft, but this was far - far - worse. I couldn't help feeling that I was all alone, even though I was on a shuttle with twenty-nine other recruits. By the time the shuttle finally started its descent to Mars, I was torn between a desire to face my fears and a primal urge to hide. It was something I knew I would have to overcome.

Welcome to Mars, I thought, as the shuttle dropped towards the red-green orb. *And welcome to hell.*

The windows went black as we descended, preventing us from seeing anything as we flew down to Boot Camp Olympus Mons. It was, I learned later, the core marine training facility for Sector 001, accommodating recruits from Earth, Terra Nova and most of the original Core Worlds. But for the moment, all I could do was brace myself as the shuttle dropped to the ground and landed with a heavy thump on a shuttlepad. Moments later, we were ordered off the shuttle and onto a landing strip. A dark-skinned man wearing a white uniform was standing there, glaring at us as if we had personally offended him. I took one look and felt utterly intimidated.

"Welcome to Boot Camp Olympus Mons," he growled. His accent was odd, but understandable. "Do any of you want to quit now and save time?"

His gaze raked our line, but none of us spoke.

"The shuttle will be staying here for two hours," he said, after a moment. "If any of you want to quit, you can get back on the shuttle and go home, no questions asked. There's no shame in admitting you don't have the guts to do something. However, we are over three hundred miles from the nearest settlement. If you head off into the badlands, the chances of you making it to safety are very remote - and, in the unlikely event of you surviving, you will promptly be arrested for being a deserter. I strongly advise you, if you feel like quitting, to do it the proper way. There is no shame, again, in admitting you cannot make it through basic training."

He waited, again, then cleared his throat loudly. "I am Sergeant (Recruit Processing) Darren Cobb. It is my job to get you through this day, nothing else. Tomorrow, you will meet the Drill Instructors who will have the task of breaking you down and turning you into marines. Until then, do as you're told and you might just survive the day. Follow me."

I winced inwardly - I wasn't the only one - and followed him as he led us towards a large building at the far side of the shuttlefield. The mountains in the distance were red, but covered with flecks of green; the air was hot and humid, warm enough to send sweat pouring down my backside. Cobb shouted encouragement at us as we half-ran into the building, then stopped in front of a set of doors, each one numbered and topped with a bright red light. I couldn't help thinking that it looked very much like a doctor's waiting room.

"Halt," Cobb bellowed. He pointed a hand towards the doors. "When the red light above the door goes green, I want one of you recruits to walk through the door. Ladies, you will take door one. Everyone else, take doors two to seven."

The lights turned green. We started forward.

"One at a time," Cobb reminded us, sharply. He jabbed fingers at six of us men, pointing them towards the doors. "The rest of you, *wait*."

I waited, feeling the heat in the room steadily starting to rise, until the lights turned green again. There was no sign of the men who'd already gone forward. Cobb pointed to six more men, including me, and motioned us forward. I sighed, braced myself as best as I could, and walked through the door. Inside, there was a large table, a plastic box placed on top of it, and a grim-faced woman standing behind it.

"Undress," she ordered. "Place everything you brought with you into this box, including your clothes. You'll be leaving this room as naked as the day you were born."

I blinked. "Naked?"

"Are you deaf?" She asked, nastily. "Undress and place everything you brought with you into this box."

I swore under my breath - I had never liked being naked - and did as I was told. Her gaze showed no interest in me, but I still felt exposed as I removed my underwear, folded it neatly and placed it into the box. The handful of items I'd brought with me followed; she looked me up and down, perhaps checking to make sure I wasn't carrying anything in my hands, then snapped the box closed.

"You can claim this back the day you leave Boot Camp," she informed me, as she jabbed a finger at the far door. "Go through that door."

I obeyed, feeling cold as the door opened. This one led to a doctor's room, with a man wearing a white coat standing next to an examination table. I gritted my teeth, expecting to be poked and prodded mercilessly, but he merely took another blood sample, examined my teeth and ran a scanner over my eyes. I couldn't help wondering why the regular medical check-ups at school couldn't be so simple, although I suspected I knew the truth. There was so great a risk of being sued that *every* test had to be done, even if they were complete wastes of time.

"Healthy enough," the doctor grunted. He pressed an injector against my neck and pushed the trigger before I could object. I felt a sudden sting as…*something*…was shot into my bloodstream. "It is unlikely you will suffer any side effects from the injection, but if you feel unwell over the next week inform your Drill Instructor at once. It will not be held against you."

"Oh," I said. "And what is the injection?"

"Broad-spectrum vaccine," the doctor explained, curtly. "It will protect you against most diseases known to exist, along with a number that were created in laboratories."

He looked me up and down, then pointed to yet another door. "Go."

I went. The next room held a barber's chair and a young man standing there, holding an electric razor. I suppressed my fear at the thought of anyone holding a sharp instrument next to my throat, then sat down. There was a buzzing sound, a handful of passes and most of my blond-brown hair fell to the floor. He held a mirror in front of me and…

"Shit," I muttered.

I'd kept my hair short, if only to keep bullies from having something to grab when we were fighting, but the barber had shaved it so close to the scalp that there was barely any left. I touched it, then looked at my face in the mirror for the second time. If I hadn't known who I was, I might have doubted it at that moment. I looked completely different.

"They all say something like that," the barber said. He pointed at another far door. "Don't worry, it does grow back. And then I shave it again."

I rubbed my scalp as I walked into yet another room. This one held a set of shelves crammed with clothing, managed by an older man who looked tired. I thought I understood how he felt, if all he had to do was hand out clothing to the recruits. He held out a set of clothes for me, then pointed to a bench. I took them and started to get dressed. The uniform - I couldn't help feeling a tingle of excitement - fitted surprisingly well.

"Make sure you use this marker to mark your clothes," the man said, holding out a black pen. "You really don't want to get it mixed up with everyone else's clothes."

I nodded, then took the pen and wrote my name on everything. He watched me for a long moment, then held out the jacket. I took it, pulled it over my head and glanced into the mirror hanging from the wall. I looked *very* different. The green uniform made me looked like a real soldier, not just a recruit. Maybe I would have been mistaken for one, if I hadn't slouched. The red bands around the shoulders were a bit of a giveaway too.

"Take this bag and check the contents," the man ordered. "There's a masterlist at the top."

The bag felt lighter than I'd expected. Inside, there was a spare jacket and trousers, five pairs of pants and socks and a small cleaning kit. I shuddered - clearly, we were expected to clean our own clothes - and checked everything against the list. It was complete. The man nodded wordlessly, passed me a pair of shoes and then pointed to the final door. Outside, there was another large waiting room, with a handful of recruits standing outside. A sergeant was watching them, his rugged face unreadable. I couldn't help thinking, as I joined them, that we looked identical. Hell, it took me a moment to spot the girl who'd gone through the doors first. Without her hair, she looked surprisingly masculine.

Cobb appeared from a side door as soon as the remainder of the recruits had joined us, then led the way out of the building and back into the open air. I followed, feeling sweaty once again as we half-ran towards the next building. It was a relief to step back into the air-conditioned chamber, which was crammed with chairs set facing a large podium. Half of us moved immediately to sit down...

"And what," Cobb demanded, "do you think you're doing?"

He went on before any of us could answer. "This is Boot Camp, not a pathetic school on your pathetic planet," he continued. "You will only sit when you are *told* to sit."

There was a long pause. "Once the other recruits arrive, you will be addressed, here and now, by the commandant of this camp," he warned. "When I tell you to sit, you will sit; when he enters, you will rise to your feet until he tells you to sit. If you are lucky, this will be the last time you meet him until the day you graduate. Place your bags under the seats, then sit."

I sat, relieved. Cobb watched us all through dark eyes, firing off a question from time to time, always aimed at a different recruit. Some of the questions were understandable, others puzzled me. I did my best to answer them mentally, hoping I would get one of the understandable questions. There didn't seem to be any point in asking what instrument a recruit would play, if he could afford it. Even now, I'm still not sure I see the logic.

"Stalker," Cobb snapped. I did my best not to cringe. "You have a grenade. Where do you want your buddies to be when you throw it?"

"Under cover," I said, at once. "Or behind me."

"Behind you," Cobb repeated. "Are you trying to be funny, Stalker?"

"No, sir," I said, hastily.

"You don't call me *sir*," Cobb said. His voice hardened. "I am a *Sergeant*. As the old saying goes, I *work* for a living. You will address me as *Sergeant*."

"Yes, *Sergeant*," I said.

I caught myself before I could point out that Bakker hadn't objected. But then, he *had* been trying to convince me to join. Cobb…had me in his clutches, as long as I didn't quit. And I was damned if I was going to quit.

"And relying on your body to shield your comrade from a grenade is unwise, Stalker," Cobb added, nastily. I have no idea why he singled me out. "The blast could easily kill both of you."

He paused as the door opened, revealing a tall man wearing a dark uniform and a number of medals. A gold badge - the Rifleman's Tab - glittered prominently on his collar. I rose to my feet hastily, followed by the other recruits. There were over a hundred of us now. I later discovered that most of them had actually come from the edge of the Core Worlds, rather than Earth itself. There were eighty billion people on Earth, or so I was told, and yet only thirty of us had left for Boot Camp.

"Be seated," the newcomer ordered. His voice was crisp, precise; there wasn't a hint of doubt in his words. But there wasn't a sense of *threat*, either. He was deliberately presenting a fatherly image to us. It would have meant more to me if I'd *had* a father. "I am Commandant Paul VanGundy, CO Boot Camp Olympus Mons."

He paused, then spoke on. "In the Marine Corps, we have a tradition we call Nice Day and Hell Week. *This* is Nice Day. We bring you to Boot Camp, we check your medical condition, we give you this little talk" - he smiled, rather thinly - "and we generally get all our ducks in order before the end of the day. Hell Week…is your first real introduction to Boot Camp. It is no exaggeration to say that we lose around half of our prospective recruits within the first three to four days as they find themselves unable to cope.

"We don't promise you anything, but blood, sweat, tears and the simple awareness that it is all worthwhile. Those of you who make it through the course will have your chance to go on to the Slaughterhouse, to become part of the finest fighting brotherhood in human history, or to take up a high position in the army, if that is your wish. I can honestly tell you that I have been a marine for over forty years and I have never regretted sticking with it, even though there were times when I seriously thought about walking away.

"We are, in many ways, the ones who hold the Empire together. We are the first responders, when a crisis blows up. We have crushed countless warlords, saved the lives of millions of civilians and helped them to rebuild their worlds. We rush from crisis to crisis, putting out fires, and we love it; when we retire, we take our expertise to colony worlds and help the settlers establish themselves. We simply do not know how to quit.

"It will not be easy. These six months will be the hardest thing you have ever done. Many of you will quit; others, I'm afraid, will die in training. Some of you will complete Boot Camp and choose to transfer into the regulars, rather than go to the Slaughterhouse. But I promise you that it will all be worthwhile. I look forward to the day I shake your hands as you graduate…wherever you go, afterwards. Good luck."

He nodded to us, then strode out of the room.

The rest of the day passed in a blur. Cobb took us into another room, administered the oath and organised our pay. The marines, it turned out, had their own bank; our salaries were paid directly into those accounts for as long as we served, which could then be transferred to another bank after we retired.

"Anything you need will be issued to you," Cobb informed us, as we were shown the sole shop on the base. "If you want anything else, it will be charged to your account…if, of course, you can convince your Drill Instructor that you need it."

He showed us a handful of other locations, ending with the first set of recruit barracks. They were large, crammed with bunks; the toilets - heads, we learned to call them - were at the far end. I couldn't help noticing that all the female recruits had been taken off somewhere; I learned, later, that they were kept strictly segregated from the males until they passed the first two waypoints. By the time I was told I could flop into bed, after a dinner composed of ration bars and juice, I was utterly exhausted…and yet, in a way, happy. I'd been nervous, and I hadn't liked parts of it, but I could endure six months if necessary…

In hindsight, of course, that was just laughable.

CHAPTER FIVE

> The concept of discipline was largely unknown to the children of Earth, in the final years of the Empire. They were not forced to learn, let alone develop the skills they needed; the only form of discipline they could rely on was self-discipline and that was extremely hard to develop. For them, going to Boot Camp - even a relatively mild Boot Camp - would be a complete culture shock.
>
> -Professor Leo Caesius

"GET OUT OF BED! GET DRESSED! GET OUTSIDE! MOVE IT!"

I jerked awake, my head spinning. Where was I? Who was shouting?

"GET UP, GET DRESSED, GET OUT," the voice repeated. "MOVE IT, RECRUITS!

I rolled out of my bunk, grabbed for my uniform and pulled it on as fast as I could. All around me, the other recruits were doing the same, banging and crashing into one another as they hurried towards the door, pulling their jackets over their heads as they ran. Someone grunted in pain as they tripped and fell, two more tripping over the prone body and landing on top of the poor bastard. The voice kept bellowing orders, practically dragging us out into the darkness. It wasn't quite pitch dark outside, but it was dark enough to keep us disoriented.

"LINE UP," the voice bellowed. "FEET ON THE YELLOW FOOTPRINTS!"

In my dazed state, it took me a moment to see the yellow footprints on the ground, glowing slightly in the darkness. We ran forward, the voice growing more and more impatient as the last of us scurried out of the barracks, and rested our feet on the footprints. I would later learn that these were to help us stand at attention, but for the moment all I could do was wonder in horror just what I'd managed to get myself into. This wasn't anything like the last couple of days! I cursed myself for a fool for thinking it could be anything else.

The lights came on, throwing the entire scene into sharp relief. Three men stood in front of us, wearing Smoky the Bear Hats. (No, I don't know who Smoky the Bear was, but his name lives on with us.) I'd thought that Bakker and Cobb were intimidating, but these two were far - far - worse. Their faces were set in expressions that promised pain, their eyes seeming to peer straight into our very souls, while their bodies were staggeringly muscular. I had never seen anyone so tough, not even among the gangs. They struck me as men who would dominate anywhere they chose to live.

"I am Drill Instructor Douglas Bainbridge, Top Hat," the leader said, in a *slightly* more normal tone of voice. "To my left is Drill Instructor Scott Nordstrom, Black Hat; to my right, Drill Instructor Alan Johnson, Hard Hat. Our mission is to train each and every one of you to become a Terran Marine. Starting now, you will treat me and every other marine you meet with the highest respect. Do you understand me?"

There was a ragged chorus of understanding.

"In future, you will answer YES SIR or NO SIR," he said. "Do you understand me?"

"Yes, sir," we said.

"Louder than that," he ordered. "Again!"

"YES, SIR," we screamed.

"Better," Bainbridge said, grudgingly. "This course is designed to separate those who can handle it from those who can't. If you want to quit, raise your hand and say so. We will dismiss you from the training platoon, arrange shipping back to wherever you come from and wave goodbye without regret. There's no shame in admitting you can't handle it. It might even be easier to give up now."

He gave us all a sardonic look, daring us to quit. "The three of us will be with you at all hours of the day," he added. "We will accept nothing less than the best from you; in return, we will treat you with firmness, fairness, dignity and compassion. If you feel that you have been abused by any of us, you are *expected* to take the complaint to the base commandant. Do you understand me?"

"YES, SIR," we bellowed.

"I didn't quite hear that," Bainbridge said, cocking his head as though he was deaf. "Again!"

"YES, SIR," we bellowed.

"There are four ways you can leave this place," he said. He made a show of ticking them off his fingers as he spoke. "You can quit. You can die. You can commit an offense against the Imperial Code of Military Justice and get booted out. Or you can graduate and go on to a long and successful career in the military. We will be covering the Imperial Code of Military Justice every day until you can memorise all fifty of the headshots that will kill your career, but for the moment all you need to know is that you must obey orders from seniors such as myself without hesitation. Do you understand me?"

"YES, SIR," we shouted.

"Good," Bainbridge said. He looked from recruit to recruit. "For the moment, you are all part of Recruit Training Company OM4574, Platoon 2. Do *not* forget those details unless you are reassigned to another unit. If asked, you are expected to shout out the number without hesitation. Do you understand me?"

"YES, SIR," we bellowed. My throat was started to get sore.

Bainbridge didn't look as though he cared. "From now on, you will talk about yourself in the third person," he said. "You will refer to yourselves as 'this recruit.' You" - he pointed at a young man I didn't know - "where were you born?"

"I was born on…"

"I? I?" Bainbridge demanded. He didn't move, but the atmosphere suddenly became a great deal more intimidating. "I?"

The recruit stumbled backwards, clearly terrified.

"No, keep your feet on the footsteps," Bainbridge ordered. "Try again!"

"YES, SIR," the recruit bellowed. He took a breath. "This recruit was born in Rowdy Yates Block, Earth."

"Better," Bainbridge said. His eyes swept the row, looking for a second victim, and I found myself praying he didn't choose me. No such luck. "You" - he jabbed his finger at me - "where were you born?"

I had to swallow before I could answer. "This recruit was born in Jackson King Block, Earth," I said.

Bainbridge eyed me for a long moment - it took all I had to stand my ground - then moved to the next victim. I watched, feeling suddenly hungry, as he checked with five more recruits, telling one of them off for getting it wrong after watching four others getting it right. The other Drill Instructors watched us, their eyes following our every movement. They hadn't said a word and yet I was far too aware of their presence. It was almost like sharing a room with Trevor again…

…And yet, none of them gave a damn about me.

"I'm sure we're all feeling cold right now," Bainbridge said, as he returned to his position in front of us. "You see that building over there? That's where they're serving the slop that will keep you warm and healthy while we break you down and build you up again. When I blow the whistle, I want you to run over to the building and line up outside the door. Do you understand me?"

"YES, SIR," we bellowed.

Bainbridge smirked, then blew the whistle. We turned towards the building and ran, rapidly falling into a disorganised mass. The three Drill Instructors ran behind us, shouting encouragement; we rapidly discovered that the building was further away than it seemed. By the time we reached the door, we were sweating buckets and gasping for breath. None of the Drill Instructors even seemed to be winded. I fought for breath as Bainbridge eyed us darkly, then made another show of consulting his watch.

"Over fifteen minutes to run one and a half miles," he sneered. He gave the recruits who had finished last a sharp look. "Pathetic. Absolutely pathetic. And to think you're going to be ruining *my* corps."

I swallowed, again. I hadn't finished last, not by any means, but I knew I hadn't done anything like as well as the Drill Instructors. Several of us glared at the slower runners, as if they were to blame for the delay, then straightened up as the Drill Instructors eyed us warningly.

"This is the Chow Hall," Bainbridge said, raising his voice slightly. "Inside, you will take one plate from the pile, one serving of food from the cooks, one glass of juice from the dispenser and finally take a seat at the nearest table. You will *not* eat or drink anything until I permit you to eat. Do you understand me?"

"YES, SIR," we stammered.

"Shout louder," Bainbridge ordered. "Again!"

"YES, SIR," we bellowed, somehow.

"Inside," Bainbridge ordered.

I wasn't sure what to expect from the Chow Hall, but it turned out to resemble a school dining room. The only real difference was that there weren't any armoured bars protecting the cooks from the students, although I rather doubted anyone on the base would dare pick a fight with the cooks. All the material I'd read insisted that all marines, even logistics staff, were riflemen first, having passed both Boot Camp and the Slaughterhouse. I took a plate, received a serving of food from the cook and took a glass of juice before sitting down. The food didn't *look* very appetizing, but it smelled heavenly.

Bainbridge watched us all closely, snapping and snarling at anyone who even *looked* as though they were going to start eating. The other Drill Instructors got their own meals and sat down at the table, but Bainbridge neither ate nor sat. Instead, he strode up and down, eying us nastily. He didn't even give us permission to eat when the last of the recruits sat down and waited, nervously.

"You may eat," he said, finally.

I grabbed for my spoon and started to dig into the slop.

"Wait," Bainbridge snapped. "Haven't you forgotten something?"

I swore. I wasn't the only one.

"YES, SIR," we bellowed.

"Good," Bainbridge said. "Eat."

The food had the same consistency as porridge, but tasted better. It wasn't until later that I learned that it was seeded with various compounds to boost our energy levels, develop our muscles and enhance our appetites. We ate in silence, listening to Bainbridge telling us more about the Marine Corps and the standards we would be expected to uphold, if we made it through another week of Boot Camp. I looked from face to face as he advised us not to get too close to anyone, not until Hell Week was over. It wasn't uncommon, apparently, for Hell Week to convince half the recruits to raise the white flag and quit. I wondered, at the time, how many of my fellows had homes to go back to, if they left. There was nowhere for *me* to go.

We had just finished when the door opened and a second platoon entered, led by another Drill Instructor. I stared at them; they wore the same uniform as we did, but they held themselves like *real* soldiers, not children playacting at being men. They walked in step, they carried actual weapons…and there was something about them, a confidence, that I knew none of us showed. Bainbridge let us study them in silence for a long moment - I later learned that absolutely nothing in Boot Camp, including that meeting, happens by coincidence - and then bellowed for us to rise to our feet. We looked like a bunch of slobs compared to the older platoon.

"And just *what*," Bainbridge demanded, "do you think you are doing?"

He eyed a recruit darkly, while the rest of us were silently grateful he wasn't looking at us.

"Sir…ah…this recruit is saving food," the recruit said. He reminded me of myself, a little, or perhaps of the boys at school who were hounded away from the dining hall at lunchtime and never had enough to eat. "This recruit couldn't eat everything on his plate."

"There is no need to save food," Bainbridge snapped. His voice softened, just slightly. "And when you see the medic, tell him about it."

He looked us up and down, then led us out of the door and back into the morning air. It felt warmer now, although the sun had barely peeked over the horizon. Mars, I later discovered, had one hell of a greenhouse effect, something designed to trap what little heat the planet received in the atmosphere. For the moment, all that mattered was that it felt warmer, but I had the uneasy feeling that it was going to get warmer still.

"This time, we are going to *march* back to the barracks," Bainbridge informed us. "Line up in a single column, then follow the recruit in front of you."

It wasn't anything like as easy as it sounded, I discovered. Our first attempt at marching forward in unison proved to be an embarrassing disaster. Bainbridge and his fellows ran up and down, snapping and snarling at us, until we were shuffling forward, putting one foot forward and then the other. It was hard to hold back the tendency to move faster, or to accidentally walk into the person in front, but we managed it - eventually. Bainbridge chanted a drill march - a cadence - as he took the lead, walking us slowly back to the barracks. I found myself joining in the singing as we marched and I wasn't the only one.

"Get inside, stuff all your crap in your bags and get back out here," Bainbridge ordered, shortly.

"YES, SIR," we bellowed.

We were learning, I told myself, as I recovered my bag from the locker and hurried back out of the barracks. The Drill Instructors pointed me towards the yellow footprints, waiting for the others; Bainbridge strode up and down, glowering at the latecomers, then finally waved us all forward into line when we were done.

"If you need anything you left behind," he informed us, "it will be coming out of your pay."

He paused as I frantically tried to remember if I'd left anything behind. I didn't *think* I had, but what if I was wrong? I had only the vaguest idea of just how much the items in the bag *cost*…and, in truth, I wasn't sure how much free cash I'd have. It wasn't unknown for employers on Earth to withhold over seventy percent of the money they were meant to pay their employees, just to meet taxes or to keep them dependent. I hadn't realised - yet - that the Marine Corps didn't work that way.

"Follow me," Bainbridge ordered, when that had sunk in. "One, two; one, two; one, two…"

It felt like hours of marching, winding our way through a series of buildings that looked depressingly identical, before we reached another set of barracks. Bainbridge stopped outside, then looked us up and down. We did our best to look back at him, but very few of us could meet his gaze.

"These are your barracks now," he said. His voice was very calm. "Most of you will be staying here until you complete Phase Two Recruit Training, whereupon you will be moved to new accommodation. *You* will be responsible for keeping *your* sleeping quarters in shape. They will be inspected every morning, after reveille. Anyone who fails to keep his bunk in shape will be given a hefty dose of Incentive Training. Do you understand me?"

"YES, SIR," we bellowed.

He led us into the barracks and pointed towards the nearest bunk. "The last occupants of these barracks did it up for you," he snarled, in a tone that suggested *he* thought we should have started from scratch. "Note just how it has been done, because that's what we want to see every day. The showers and toilets are to be cleaned once a day too and the floor is to be swept - we expect you to sort out your own rota for cleaning. You'll find cleaning equipment in the cupboard."

I swallowed. I'd been a teenage boy. Okay, I wasn't as bad as some of the assholes from school who would deliberately make a mess, just to force someone to clean it up, but I'd still been pretty messy. My mother had never tried to get us to do chores, or clean the apartment; I honestly didn't know where to begin. And, judging from some of the looks, nor did most of my fellow recruits.

"One of us will be sleeping there, every night," Bainbridge continued, pointing to a bunk by the door. "After Hell Week, one of you will also take watch every night. Should you notice any problems with your fellow recruits, we expect you to bring it to us. Homesickness is not uncommon among new recruits. Later, there may be depression, even suicidal thoughts."

I wasn't impressed. Why would I want to go home?

"Place your bags in the lockers, then meet me back outside," Bainbridge ordered. "If any of you need to go to the head" - the toilets - "go now."

The locker was barely large enough for my bag, but I managed to put it inside and check out the showers and toilets before going back outside. They were communal - there was no such thing as communal showers and toilets on Earth, for fear of lawsuits - and the thought of either stripping naked or having a shit in front of my new comrades was appalling. But it was clear I had no choice. None of us did.

I can endure, I told myself, as I stepped back into the warm air. *Whatever they throw at me, I can endure.*

"Now," Bainbridge said, in a sweet voice that fooled absolutely no one. "Who wants to learn how to do a push-up?"

CHAPTER SIX

Everything in Boot Camp is meant to be a teachable moment, even if it's nothing more than a lesson in what not to do.

-Professor Leo Caesius

We lost our first recruit later that day.

I never knew his name. In truth, I barely remember him as anything other than the wimp who opened the floodgates. There's a certain reluctance among humans to be the *first* to do anything, be it the first to put up one's hand or the first to quit military training. But once someone actually takes that first step, others follow. We had been told, time and time again, that there was no shame in quitting - and there was some truth to it - but at the same time we needed to develop the stubbornness *not* to quit. The reluctance to be the first might have saved many of us from quitting within the first few days of Boot Camp.

"When you do something *mildly* stupid," Bainbridge told us, as soon as we gathered outside the barracks, "you will be given push-ups to do. This serves as both a punishment to remind you of your own stupidity and a chance to do more exercise, which will help you to develop more upper body strength. You will not be expected to do many push-ups now, but as you progress you will be given more and more to do every day."

He dropped to the ground, rested briefly on his chest and then used his arms to push his entire body upwards. I watched, doubtfully, as he lowered himself until his chest was *almost* touching the ground, then pushed himself back up again. It didn't seem to cost him any effort at all.

"You are not to allow your body to return to the ground until you have finished," Bainbridge said, without standing up. "As you can see" - he lowered himself to the ground; Nordstrom blew a whistle, making us all jump - "we will be watching and we will add more push-ups for you to do, just to make sure you get the right amount of exercise."

He jumped to his feet, then smiled at us. "Spread out," he ordered, "then lie down on the ground."

I scowled as I fell to my knees, then rested on the hard ground. I'd gotten them wrong, back when I'd been trying to make myself stronger; I'd lowered my body to the ground every time, rather than just at the end. I had a feeling I was going to find it hard to *keep* my body in the air, no matter how hard I tried. Bainbridge glanced from recruit to recruit, then motioned for us to lift up our bodies. It felt easy at first, resting on my hands, but the longer I kept my body in the air the harder it grew. The aches and pains were surprisingly strong.

"Lower yourself, gently," Bainbridge ordered. "Do *not* touch the ground."

I tried. It wasn't easy, but somehow I managed to hold my chest an inch above the ground. I heard the whistle blow, again, as some unlucky recruit was caught resting his chest on the ground; I felt a flicker of sympathy, which I ruthlessly suppressed. My arms were aching badly now; it was almost a relief when I was ordered to lift my body again, even though the aches and pains were getting worse. Bainbridge ordered us to lower ourselves again, then rise; the whistle blew, several times, as others failed to follow orders. By the time we had stumbled through ten push-ups, I felt as though my arms were on the verge of breaking. It looked as though others felt the same.

"Only nine of you managed to follow orders and keep your chests off the ground," Bainbridge said, in a disgusted tone. I couldn't help a flicker of pleasure at being one of the few who'd made it, even though I knew it had been a damn close shave. "Let's try that again, shall we?"

There was a collective groan as we fell back to the ground and stumbled through another ten push-ups. This time, I managed to get through five before I lost control and fell to the ground. The whistle blew - my face went red with shame - and somehow I started again, plodding through the remaining five push-ups. I doubted the Drill Instructors would be pleased, really. But they'd sighted another target.

"Recruit," Nordstrom snapped, pointing at a young man who couldn't have been any older than myself. "Did you only do *one* push-up before parking your chest on the ground?"

The recruit looked terrified. "No, sir," he said, weakly. "I…"

Nordstrom purpled. "I? I?"

There was a nasty pause. "I quit," the recruit said, finally. "I want to go home."

Some of us sniggered. Bainbridge shot us all a dark look and we shut up, instantly.

"Very well," Nordstrom said. His voice dripped honey and battery acid. "A wise decision, if I may say so. Walk to the administrative building over there and report to the front desk. They'll send you home."

I watched the former recruit go before we were sucked back into more physical training. A day? No, not even a day; I wasn't sure of the time, but I knew it couldn't be later than 1100. He'd gone through Nice Day, but Hell Week had defeated him. I wondered just what would happen when he got home, if he had a home to go to, then pushed the thought to the back of my mind. Later, I would be glad that that person wouldn't be behind me when I went to war.

"See how easy it is to quit?" Bainbridge asked. "Anyone else want to go now?"

There was an awkward pause. No one said a word. I tried to avoid rubbing my arms as the Drill Instructors looked at us, then started to show us more exercises. Some of them were easy enough, others were far more complicated; the stretching exercises, in particular, seemed designed to tear our limbs from their sockets. I puzzled over them as we were put through our paces, then ordered to take another run to the Chow Hall and back.

"There are fifty headshots - criminal acts - you can commit that will get you kicked out of Boot Camp," Bainbridge informed us, as we ran. "These include insubordination, use of drugs, tobacco and alcohol, possession and/or consumption of food outside designated eating periods, possession of any contraband, failure to perform duties as assigned to you by lawful authority, being absent without leave and, last, but far from least, fraternisation. To repeat; any of those offences will get you a punishment that may range from summarily discharged to court martial and execution. You will have those offences read to you every day, along with the definition of each offence. You will have no excuse for committing any of them!"

"Fraternisation," Nordstrom said. He was talking and running, but he didn't sound even remotely winded. "Sexual contact with a marine, marine recruit, marine auxiliary or marine consultant. Punishment: immediate discharge from the corps. You may request a court martial, if you wish, but a court martial can heap additional punishment on you if it feels you have no acceptable excuse."

I glanced at the recruits running beside me. They were all male: hot, sweaty, smelly and tired. It didn't seem likely that I'd come to see *any* of them as potential conquests, assuming I'd have the energy. The files I'd read told me that we'd be worked to death every day, then woken up after seven hours of sleep to do it all over again. It wasn't until later that I learned just how badly sexual integration had damaged the Imperial Army when the discipline to enforce regulations against fraternisation had faltered. The Marine Corps was determined not to allow it to undermine its fighting power.

The day started to blur into a haze as we worked our way through a long program of exercises, running, more exercises and yet more running. I rapidly realised that Bainbridge hadn't been kidding about using push-ups as punishment; every little mistake, no matter how minor, was greeted with an order to do an immediate ten push-ups. Nordstrom watched us closely, snapping orders to repeat the entire ten push-ups if a single one was dropped. We lost two more recruits after lunch, when one gave up in the middle of a push-up and the other tried to throw a punch at Nordstrom. The Drill Instructor caught his arm and asked if he wanted to quit. It wasn't until later that I realised it was a mercy. Legally, the recruit could have been put in front of a court martial for attempting to strike a superior officer.

By the time we staggered back into barracks, we were tired, cranky and utterly drained…but it didn't end. The Drill Instructors lined us up in front of the showers and demonstrated how to use them, one by one. I couldn't believe it when they told us we were expected to wash by numbers - heads, then arms, then legs, etc - but they were insistent. Somehow, I forgot my embarrassment as we were marched through a hasty shower, then were guided towards our bunks. I noted that several of the other recruits clearly intended to go to the head after the rest of us were fast asleep. It was hard to blame them. I knew, all too well, what could happen to people at school who were caught in the toilets by the bullies.

"If you wish to make a head call," Bainbridge informed us, once we had all showered and changed into a fresh set of underwear, "you must ask permission from the watch officer. It doesn't matter how urgent it is; request permission from the officer before leaving your bunk. For the moment, that's the Drill Instructor on duty."

He pointed to the bunks, then strode back towards the front of the building. "Lights will dim in ten minutes," he added. "After that, anyone moving around without permission will be in deep shit."

I believed him. Hastily, I scrambled into my bunk and closed my eyes. It had been hard sleeping in a crowded barracks last night, but this time I fell asleep almost at once. My entire body was sore after running hundreds of miles - it certainly *felt* like hundreds of miles - and I was dreading the rest of Hell Week. It would be easy to quit, I knew, but where would I go if they sent me home? I had the feeling that begging for mercy wouldn't get me anywhere - and even if it did, what could they do? Perhaps they could send me to a colony world…

…But I still wouldn't have any stake, no money to buy land. Maybe I'd be better than an indent, but not - alas - by much.

It felt like seconds had passed before Bainbridge started shouting at us, again. I'd been too tired to realise - and I *should* have realised - that we would be woken up in bare hours and driven back out to the training field. I jerked out of bed - my body felt stiff and unfamiliar - and groped for my uniform, cursing under my breath. Hell Week wasn't called Hell Week because some asshole had wanted to make it sound bad. Someone literally fell out of bed with a crash, then picked himself up just before Nordstrom stamped over to check he was alive and well. I barely had time to notice before we were headed back outside, where the sun was just peeking over the horizon. The Drill Instructors looked disgustingly fresh and eager as they looked us up and down, then started to point out all the problems with our uniforms.

"We expect you to be out, in future, within five minutes," Bainbridge said, once he had finished telling us off for a number of minor problems, including - in one case - forgetting to don underwear. I honestly don't know, even today, just how Bainbridge *knew* the poor recruit was going commando. "Those of you who don't get out in time will be doing *more* push-ups. Now drop and give me twenty."

"YES, SIR," we bellowed, somehow.

We dropped and, somehow, stumbled through the push-ups, even though our bodies were aching from the previous day. Oddly, the heavy exercise helped me feel better, as if my body was slowly becoming accustomed to the new workload. The Drill Instructors paced around, bawling out anyone who dared let their chests touch the ground, then assigned a whole series of new exercises, followed by a run to the Chow Hall. This time, there were two platoons already there, waiting in line to be served. None of us dared to try to cut in line ahead of them, not when they looked nastier than any of the gangsters on Earth. It would be weeks, if not months, before we looked like them.

As soon as we had eaten, we marched around the field, chanting the latest cadence. This time, we didn't have *quite* so many problems, although Bainbridge kept varying the speed to keep us alert. I found it harder and harder to think clearly as we paused for breath, then stepped into an obstacle course. Some of the wooden frames looked easy - we rapidly learned that that was deceptive - and others looked impossible to understand, let alone complete. The netting under the high wire structures chilled me to the bone.

"This is the Phase One Obstacle Course," Bainbridge informed us. "Each of you will be expected to master each and every one of these structures by the time you proceed to Phase Two. Should you fall off" - he waved at the netting - "it will be counted as a fail. Do you understand me?"

"YES, SIR," we screamed.

I'll say one thing for the Drill Instructors. They never asked us to do anything they couldn't or wouldn't do for themselves. Bainbridge walked up to the first structure, clambered up a wooden wall that looked unbeatable, then waved to us from the top. Nordstrom, following him, showed us how to find handholds and make our way slowly up the wall. Johnston stood at the back, watching us all. We advanced forward, one by one, and tried to climb the wood while Nordstrom offered advice and instructions. It was tricky as hell to clamber up without looking down, but somehow we made it. I think it would have been easier if I hadn't made the mistake of looking down.

"Don't look down, you fucking idiot," Nordstrom called. He was right, of course. "There's no safety wire holding you in place."

The next structure had a rope I was meant to clamber along to reach the other side. It gave me trouble; I barely made it three or four steps along before I lost my grip and plummeted into the safety netting. Johnston helped me out, then pointed me back to the end of the line and offered some valuable pieces of advice. I honestly wasn't sure if I *needed* to learn how to clamber along a rope, but I later learned it was a very useful skill. Besides, another recruit - who had been having problems after three successive tries - quit in disgust.

"This one is particularly interesting," Bainbridge said, as we walked up to a large metal barrel. It was surrounded by a square marked out with string that was anchored firmly to the ground. I didn't understand what I was seeing; the string, barely a couple of inches off the ground, was hardly high enough to keep anyone from reaching the barrel. A coil of rope had been placed just outside the square. "And - this time - we are not going to show you what to do in advance."

I eyed him, torn between nervousness and puzzlement. Everything else had seemed obvious, but this was odd. Were we meant to jump over the barrel? I didn't see how.

"A convoy of vehicles is running short of fuel," Bainbridge informed us. "The intrepid flyboys have dropped a barrel of fuel for you, but they managed to put it in the middle of a minefield. If you put a foot into that patch of ground" - he pointed to the square - "you will be blown to smithereens and the fuel will explode. All you have to do is get the barrel out of the square without putting a foot into the field."

I stared. How the hell were we meant to do that? I could just reach the barrel, if I stretched, but I couldn't hope to pick it up. If someone was on the other side…no, we'd break our wrists if we tried. They wouldn't have given us an impossible task, would they? There had to be a solution, but what?

"We could try to pick our way through the minefield," a recruit offered.

"Bang," Nordstrom said, coolly. "You're dead. Drop and give me twenty."

"Can we set up a pipe?" Another recruit asked. "Drain the barrel without moving it?"

Nordstrom smirked. "With what?"

I looked back at the coil of rope. They wouldn't have left it there by accident, would they?

"Here," I said, as everything fell into place. I picked up the rope and uncoiled it. "Wrap the rope around the lid, then use it to lift up the barrel and get it to the edge of the square without touching the ground."

"Try," Nordstrom said.

It was the hardest thing I'd done so far. I'd never seen myself as a leader and getting everyone organised wasn't easy, but somehow we managed to lift up the barrel and manoeuvre it to the edge of the square and over the line. Bainbridge congratulated us briefly, just enough to make me flush with pleasure, then mustered us for the march back to the barracks.

"It isn't enough to fight," he said, as we started to march. "You have to be prepared to solve problems too."

CHAPTER SEVEN

The Terran Marine Corps has a strict cap placed on manpower, thanks to the Grand Senate's paranoia. Therefore, every marine has to be trained extensively to ensure that he or she is as adaptable as possible. Marines are expected to be capable of making a silk purse out of a sow's ear, if you will excuse the metaphor, at a moment's notice.

-Professor Leo Caesius

The remainder of Hell Week passed in a blur.

There were endless exercises, forced marches, constant tests of our mental agility and an infinite number of push-ups. We worked our way through the obstacle course, time and time again, and learned to swim in the pool, dire warnings ringing in our ears that there would be far nastier water tests in the future. I had never learned to swim - I'd honestly never seen the value - until I entered Boot Camp, an oversight I rapidly came to regret. Perhaps it would have been easier to master the skill if I'd started as a child…

…But, given just what happened in swimming pools, perhaps I should be relieved I hadn't.

The Drill Instructors watched us constantly, but they seemed to have different roles. Bainbridge, the Top Hat, played the strict father; Nordstrom, the Black Hat, was the disciplinarian; Johnston, the Hard Hat, seemed to be the technical expert, always there to offer advice on how to complete a task…if, of course, we needed to ask. It was hard to *like* any of them, but we were definitely starting to *respect* them. We wouldn't have made it through Hell Week if they hadn't been pushing us along - and, I realised later, helping to separate those who couldn't get much further from those who could. By the time Hell Week was officially at an end, the platoon had lost half of its recruits and was merged with another platoon to keep the number up.

"I don't know what they're putting in the water on Earth," Bainbridge sneered. "We have bugger-all recruits from that shithole these days and hardly any last the first week."

He was right. I discovered, later, that Earth produced the smallest number of military recruits in the Empire, even though it had easily the largest population. Even the Imperial Navy - widely regarded as a cushy billet by everyone else - recruited only a few thousand Earthers every year. There were even calls to abandon recruiting on Earth altogether, although they never came to anything. The manpower crisis was just too acute to turn down *any* prospective source of new recruits.

I understood, but it took me a long time to articulate it. Earth's population, thanks to a combination of social engineering and emigration, was effectively divided into two subsets: sheep and wolves. The sheep couldn't lift a hand to defend themselves, let alone defend others; the wolves, the gangsters, were more interested in preying on the sheep than defending them against other wolves. Even the smarter gangsters, the ones bright enough to realise the dangers of killing the geese that laid the golden eggs, weren't really interested in spreading security. They were just interested in their share of the booty. There were only a handful of sheepdogs in Earth's entire population and most of them chose to immigrate to new worlds rather than stay on Earth.

Does that sound absurd? Consider this - on Earth, there was no right of self-defence. Beat the tar out of someone who threatened your family and you might wind up in deep shit yourself. It was a great deal easier for the police to pick on the lone defender than try to take on the might of the gangs. Or, if you lived in the Undercity, you'd just make a whole string of new and deadly enemies who would stop at nothing to make a horrific example out of you, just to keep resistance from spreading. And, if you thought you could better yourself, it wouldn't be long before taxes and regulations defeated you. How could I blame anyone for fleeing Earth?

There was no real let-up, of course, just because we'd passed Hell Week. I honestly don't think the Drill Instructors respected us *that* much more, although we had survived a test intended to weed out the quitters from those who just wouldn't quit. All that changed, I think, is that we developed a little more confidence in ourselves. We'd survived the first test and we could go further. And yes, we were doing more and more push-ups too.

With the recruits more settled, I actually started to get to know my squad. (A recruit training company has three platoons, each one approximating thirty to forty recruits, which are further divided into squads of ten recruits each.) The later exercises we were given were deliberately designed to force us to work together, even if we didn't *like* each other. There is no 'I' in 'team,' as Bainbridge pointed out. Each of us had different strengths and weaknesses, which was perhaps unsurprising. There were only four recruits from Earth in my platoon and I was the only Earther in my squad.

Joker rapidly became my best friend in the squad, even though we had very little in common beyond being human, male and marine recruits. He was a thin lanky young man, a year older than me, who kept cracking jokes at the worst possible moment. Apparently, he had an older brother in the corps who told him that Drill Instructors appreciated recruits who tried to show that they had a sense of humour. He was somewhat lacking in *common* sense as it seemed to me that the Drill Instructors only used it as an excuse to pile more push-ups on him, but that wasn't necessarily a bad thing. Thanks to the intensive physical training, we were all developing more muscles than any of us had ever enjoyed in our lives.

(I knew his name. Of course I knew his name - I knew all of them, by the time we completed Phase One. But, as God is my witness, I honestly can't *remember* any of them. I only remember the nicknames - some complementary, some insulting - they earned.)

Professor was an odd one, a student at Imperial University who'd quit for an undisclosed reason and joined the marines. I didn't think much of him at first, but after he completed Hell Week it was clear that he might be weaker than the rest of us, yet he had an icy determination to keep going no matter what the Drill Instructors heaped on him. He was easily the best-educated of the platoon and later, when we completed Phase Two, he was one of the recruits tapped to help with educating the other recruits. When he started, he was slightly overweight - not enough to put him in the special platoon, just enough to be noticeable - but that flab was replaced by muscle soon enough. It was just a shame they made him wear a pair of dorky glasses. He didn't have a hope of being laid while wearing them.

Posh, in some ways, was even stranger. He didn't talk about his life at first and it was only when we pressed, after sharing some of our own stories, that he confessed. His father was a relative of a Grand Senator, which placed him solidly in the upper class; he'd grown up on Island One, a giant space habitat orbiting Terra Nova. But, for some reason, he'd grown disenchanted with the aristocracy and chosen to join the marines. I later found out that his father expected him to help shape the Marine Corps in the future, a difficult task for anyone who didn't graduate Boot Camp. Luckily, by the time Posh *did* graduate, he'd absorbed enough of the marine ethos to keep him from becoming a major problem. It wasn't until *much* later that I understood why he'd wanted to leave.

Thug was a simpler case. A short man who had shaved his head long before entering Boot Camp, he'd grown up on Terra Nova in one of the slums surrounding Landing City. He liked to fight and, after a run-in with the law that had put him in front of a judge, he'd chosen military service instead of being exiled to a distant colony world. I was surprised the marines had taken him, but I had to admit he was a good man to have on your side. He wasn't the sharpest knife in the drawer, yet he never stopped coming.

Bandit had a similar story, in a way. He'd been a dealer on New Washington when a deal had turned sour, leaving him running for his life - and straight into the recruiting office. By his own admission, he'd nearly been rejected and he'd been given a strong warning, before he'd been shipped to Boot Camp, that the charges against him would be resurrected if he stepped away from the straight and narrow. I'd met too many people like him before - Trevor had been fond of bragging about his connections - to like him, at least at first, but if the corps wanted to give him a second chance it was none of my business. Besides, he had a devious mind and no reluctance to use it.

But it was Viper who bothered me.

He was a reject, someone held back from completing the first phase of training. The Drill Instructors added him to the platoon shortly after Hell Week, informing us that he knew most of what we had to learn and we might find him useful. They were wrong, I figured; Viper might have mastered some of the skills we hadn't - yet - but he moaned and whined about everything. I honestly didn't understand why he didn't quit. A month or two of recruit training, we'd been told, could be parlayed into a better deal, if one wanted to go to a colony world. God knew we'd already picked up enough discipline - it was astonishing how motivational push-ups and the threat of more push-ups could be - to actually make something of ourselves, if we left. But Viper seemed reluctant to either stay or go.

It might not have bothered me so much if we hadn't been in constant competition. My squad was in competition with the rest of the platoon, the platoon was in competition with the rest of the company and the company is in competition with any other companies on the base, if they're at the same level. (Mind you, if a junior company outshot a senior company, their Drill Instructors would engage in achingly polite gloating at the officer's club.) It didn't take us long to realise that Viper was a weak link. He did the bare minimum to pass each test and each of us, even Professor, rapidly started to surpass him.

"Maybe he's just a loser," Thug snarled. "He's not even trying!"

I nodded in agreement. I'd seen people like Viper on Earth, people who knew they had no hope of anything in their future, but I didn't think it could be tolerated in the corps. They just drifted through life, doing nothing. Most of them were on some kind of medication because it was easier for the state to drug them than admit their lives were utterly meaningless…and there was no hope of meaningful reform. They spent their lives in front of the viewer, watching the latest programs. Why not? They had nothing to live for.

But Viper was a marine recruit. His lassitude, for want of a better word, wasn't just dragging him down (we could have ignored it, if that were the case). He was dragging us down with him. We were sinking down the competition tables within the platoon and we knew - we just knew - that it wouldn't be long before the Drill Instructors started to 'counsel' us to do better…with push-ups, of course. But how could we do better when we had Viper pulling us down?

"Go talk to him," Professor said, looking at me. "He might listen to you."

I was tempted to ask *why me*, but I already knew the answer. The Drill Instructors praised those who took the lead, who saw a problem and leapt to grapple with it. I'd done that once and been rewarded; now, we *all* tried to take the lead, except Viper. And besides, overall, I had the best scores in the entire squad. Thug was better at some tests, Professor was better at others, but I had the best overall score. (I was third in the entire platoon.)

That night, Viper made a head call. I followed him as soon as he entered the chamber. This wasn't uncommon; we'd all grown used to sharing a communal toilet, even if the jokes had to be heard to be believed. (And the less said about the stench the better.)

"Tell me something," I said. I'd rehearsed the moment as best as I could, in my head, but now the time had come I decided to go with my instincts. "Why the fuck are you dragging us all down?"

Viper stared at me, sullenly. "They held me back."

I felt a flicker of pure rage. We'd been told that if we really had to have it out with one another, we could do it in the field with fighting sticks. Picking fights inside the barracks was strictly forbidden. The best we could hope for, if we were caught, was a long session of Intensive Training. But I wanted to slap some sense into him before it was too late.

It was all I could do to keep my voice down, but I really didn't want to alert Johnston. "So you're holding *us* back?"

I gritted my teeth. "They didn't hold the rest of your squad back," I pointed out. I didn't actually know it for sure, but I had a feeling that Viper was the only person who'd been held back. He was definitely the only one who'd joined the platoon. "Why would they hold the rest of us back, when the time comes, if the only one who's a real problem is *you*?"

It was, I later learned, one of the weaknesses of the training program. A person could quit, or commit one of the headshots, but they couldn't be dismissed without good cause. The Drill Instructors had plenty of ways to urge someone to quit, yet they couldn't *force* them to take that step. As long as Viper met the bare minimal requirements, it was impossible to do more than keep holding him back until he got the hint.

"I don't care," Viper said.

"Well, you fucking should," I snapped. "Every fucking day, we go out into the exercise grounds and fucking depend on each and every fucking one of us to do our fucking share!"

Viper smirked. "Do you get a credit for every time you swear?"

I clenched my fists. Maybe he'd had extra training, but I could take him. I was *sure* I could take him…

…And then what? Burn up my career just to take down his?

"Tell me something," I said. "There isn't a person in the platoon who doesn't know you're a fucking loser. What do you think is going to happen when you get out there in the pit and face all of us? Either shape the fuck up or quit. You can go to the Drills now and quit. No one will think any less of you."

Viper's eyes flashed. "Do you think I want to be here?"

That, I have to admit, stunned me. Who in their right mind would go to Boot Camp if they didn't *want* to go to Boot Camp? Even Posh, despite his background, freely admitted he'd hoped for a military career. Hell, it wasn't as if it was *difficult* to get into the Civil Guard - although, if the Drill Instructors were telling the truth, Viper was probably overqualified on the grounds he could string more than two words together into a reasonably coherent statement.

"If you don't want to be here, then quit," I snarled. I didn't want to hear a sob story. I'd heard enough of them on Earth. Viper had more opportunities than I'd ever had and if he didn't want to make use of them…well, that was his problem, not mine. "Go to the Drill Instructors and quit! But don't keep fucking things up for us!"

I turned and strode back to my bunk, cursing him under my breath. We were supposed to get somewhere between seven to eight hours of sleep each night, but the Drill Instructors had a nasty habit of sometimes waking us up early, just to see who would snap. I was just closing my eyes when Viper stalked past me and climbed into his own bunk. He didn't look happy…I wondered, suddenly, if it was a mistake to sleep so close to him. But there was a Drill Instructor at the far end of the room…

In hindsight, maybe we should have complained about Viper. He wasn't physically weak, unlike Professor, or mentally challenged; he was deliberately not giving us his all. There were no excuses for his conduct - and besides, he'd had over two months of training before being held back. But none of us really wanted to go sneaking to the Drill Instructors, not when the situation was so sensitive. Bitching about our fellows might not make any of us look very good.

And, when Viper started to shape up, I told myself that our little talk had actually worked and maybe we'd actually get some use out of him. Maybe the thought of being completely isolated, of being completely alienated from the rest of the squad, had convinced him to put his own problems aside. I liked to think I'd made a very real difference…

But that too was a mistake.

CHAPTER EIGHT

It is difficult to exaggerate just how stressful recruit training can actually be. The typical Core Worlds recruit may never have been away from home before, let alone had to rely on a band of complete strangers. Drill Instructors are trained to watch for signs of trouble, but many teenagers and young adults from Earth are skilled at hiding their feelings. A minor problem, therefore, can become a great deal more dangerous before it is exposed.

-Professor Leo Caesius

"Well," Doctor Jenna Amundsen said, as I entered the examination room. "How are you feeling?"

Odd, I thought. The doctor wasn't the prettiest woman I'd ever seen, but it was the first time I'd seen a woman for three weeks. *I look at you and I feel nothing.*

I wasn't stupid enough to say that out loud, of course. "This recruit is fine," I said. Regular medical check-ups were part of our training, but we resented them hugely. "No problems at all."

"Glad to hear it," the doctor said. "Take off your clothes, then lie down on the table."

"Yes, sir," I said, automatically. 'Sir' seemed to be the default term of address for both male and female superiors. "How long will this take?"

"As long as it takes," Jenna said, giving me a sympathetic smile. "I'll be a quick as I can."

I sighed inwardly as I removed my uniform. In theory, we were entitled to half an hour of free time each day, but in practice we rarely got to make any real use of it. There was reading to do, exercises to catch up on…and the Drill Instructors kept us hopping. I'd heard that some of the recruits were complaining loudly about not having time to write home, something that would have annoyed me too if I'd had anyone to write to. As soon as I was naked, I clambered up onto the table and lay down. Oddly, I no longer felt nervous at being naked in front of anyone, even a doctor.

"You had the last set of injections the day you entered Boot Camp," the doctor said, poking and prodding at my growing muscles. "Did you notice any ill effects?"

"No, sir," I said.

"Good," the doctor said. "It's very rare that anyone gets any effect at all, but it needs to be watched."

I nodded, curtly. Malingering was not encouraged, unsurprisingly, but we had been warned not to conceal *any* health condition from the Drill Instructors. Better safe than sorry, they said, although few of us would have dared to malinger. If the medics believed you were malingering, you were doomed when you were sent back to the platoon. Even Viper, for all his faults, wouldn't have claimed to be ill unless he could prove it.

She prodded my chest, then nodded to herself. "No problems with breathing? Or muscular problems?"

"Just aches and pains as we push ourselves forwards," I said. "Pain is weakness leaving the body."

"In some ways," Jenna agreed. It was one of Bainbridge's favourite sayings. He said it at least four times a day, normally while supervising our push-ups. "On the other hand, everyone has limits and we need to make sure you're not crossing yours."

She poked me one final time, then ordered me to roll over. I did as I was told, then shivered as her hands walked down my back and upper legs. There was nothing remotely erotic about it, just a sense that she was checking my development against a file stored in her head. I sat up as soon as she was done, then watched as she produced a device that looked like a large gun and placed it on the table next to me. It looked silly, in a way, as if it were a ray gun from a bad movie, but somehow I found it ominous.

"You appear to be developing within acceptable limits," Jenna said. "You're cleared to proceed to the next stage of training."

I breathed a sigh of relief. "Thank you."

"You're welcome," she said, giving me a faint smile. "I'm afraid I have to inject the side of your neck, now. This may sting a little."

She picked up the gun-like device and held it against my neck before I could object, then pulled the trigger. There was a stab of pain, as if someone had jabbed my skin with a pin, which faded rapidly as she pulled the device away from me. When I touched the skin, I felt an odd lump just below the surface. It felt as if she'd stuck something in me.

"It shouldn't cause you any problems," Jenna said. "The pain should be gone within an hour, but if it gets worse or reoccurs inform your Drill Instructor at once. This can be quite serious, if something goes badly wrong."

I swallowed. "What did you do to me...ah, to this recruit?"

"The Drill Instructors will explain tonight," Jenna said. She nodded towards a chair on the other side of the room. "Sit there and open your mouth."

I eyed her warily, then obeyed. Jenna sat down next to me and peered into my mouth, using a small device to shine a spotlight into the darkened recesses of my teeth. I suddenly wished I'd had time to brush my teeth before the appointment, or something to make my breath smell better; I cringed in embarrassment at the thought of her smelling the remains of the ration bars we'd been given for dinner. Jenna didn't say anything; she merely inspected my mouth, then nodded curtly to herself.

"No change from the last report," she said. "Have you been having problems with your teeth?"

"No, sir," I said. "I believe this recruit was vaccinated against tooth decay."

"The vaccines aren't always effective, not the ones on Earth," Jenna warned. "There hasn't been any genuinely comprehensive program of vaccination for centuries, recruit."

She shrugged. "Still, there doesn't seem to be any problem," she added. Her face curved into a mischievous smile. "If you have a few knocked out in the pit, we can replace them within hours.

"This recruit was told that anything that wasn't immediately fatal could be fixed," I said. "Is that actually true?"

Jenna made a show of considering it. "Minor injuries, yes; we can heal those at once," she said, slowly. "Anything more serious…yes, we can heal it, but you would need time to recover and you might find yourself recycled back to an earlier training cycle. I've known marines who had their legs blown off and replaced. They returned to duty, eventually, but it took them months to get used to their new limbs. We can pretty much replace everything, save for the brain."

I smiled. "Could you grow me a whole new body?"

"Technically, yes; legally, no," Jenna said. "We can grow you a new pair of arms or legs, if necessary, but growing a full-body clone to serve as a walking transplant is illegal. You'd be killing your genetic brother just so you could have his body. There are brain transplants, occasionally, but they rely on having a suitable donor."

"And they're rare," I guessed.

"Of course," Jenna said. She took another blood sample as she spoke, then dropped it in the analyser. "Would you die so that someone else can have your body?"

"This recruit has seen flicks where that happens," I said. The analyser bleeped, reporting that I was clean of forbidden drugs. "It never ends well."

"No, it doesn't," Jenna agreed. She removed the tube from the analyser and dropped it into a metal container. "Get dressed, recruit, and inform the Drill Instructors that they can send the next one in."

"Yes, sir," I said. I'd forgotten I was naked. "Nothing to worry about, then?"

"You're healthy and fit," Jenna said. "Try not to get injured when you start martial arts training."

I nodded, then finished dressing and headed out the hatch. The rest of the platoon was supposed to be in the barracks, but I wasn't surprised to see half of them outside, performing various exercises as they were supervised by the Drill Instructors. Johnston was watching Viper with dark eyes, shouting encouragement as the recruit worked his way through a series of push-ups. It didn't look as if either of them was having fun. I reported to Bainbridge, who promptly ordered me to do another fifty push-ups. They were *very* good at finding excuses for punishment exercises.

"All right, ladies," he said, half an hour (and innumerable push-ups) later. "Line up, single file!"

We snapped to attention. The Drill Instructors had somehow managed to become more and more critical as the days went by, snapping at us for something they would have let pass a week earlier. I'd found myself checking and rechecking the bunk every day, just to make sure there wasn't something they could use as an excuse for more punishment exercises. And yet, no matter how hard I tried, there was always something they could use. If I hadn't thought it was all worthwhile - and there was nowhere else to go - I would have quit in disgust.

"I trust you all have a pain in the neck now," he said. "Is there any of you who *wasn't* given an injection into the neck?"

There was a long pause. No one spoke.

"Stand to attention, recruit," Bainbridge bellowed. Professor had made the mistake of scratching the side of his neck. "It won't come out no matter how much you stroke it!"

We would have sniggered, but we knew better. Bainbridge wouldn't hesitate to punish anyone who showed amusement at another person getting in trouble, no matter how funny it was. We were meant to be a team, after all, and laughing at our fellows wouldn't build a sense of camaraderie. Or so we had been told.

"You have been implanted," Bainbridge continued, in a slightly quieter voice. "I'll spare your innocent minds the technical details, recruits; all you really have to know is that the implant will, when queried, send out a pulse reporting your location to the base's sensors. If you manage to get lost on the track, we can and we will find you - or your body. There are recruits, men and women just like you, who have been swept away by sudden downpours on the training grounds. Their lives were lost, but their bodies were recovered and buried with full honours."

He paused, his features shifting into something more intimidating. "Headshot Fifty," he added, coldly. "Accessing the implants and using them to cheat on the training field."

I swallowed. None of us liked being reminded of the headshots, the offences that could get us kicked out of Boot Camp, but the Drill Instructors did so frequently. Headshot Fifty hadn't made much sense to me at the time, although I hadn't had the nerve to ask the Drill Instructors to clarify. What implants? But I understood now.

"You will be working with all manner of devices intended to make enemy lives miserable," Bainbridge said, after a long moment. "Some of those devices - which we will go over in greater detail later - are designed to track radio signals. You can, if you felt like cheating, use them to track your fellows on the training field. Why do we not permit you to try?"

He looked from face to face, then pointed a finger at Thug. "Explain."

Thug hesitated. "This recruit thinks it would be cheating," he said. "It wouldn't be fair."

"And yet I have told you that if you're not cheating, you're not trying," Bainbridge said. He looked from face to face again, then pointed a finger at Professor. "Why is this particular brand of cheating not allowed?"

Professor frowned. "This recruit thinks that the enemy, in a real combat situation, will not have implanted troops, sir."

"Correct," Bainbridge said. He scowled at us all. "You cannot assume the enemy will be kind enough to broadcast his location to the entire universe. Our opponents know that emitting any form of betraying energy leads to certain death. The Imperial Navy is good at tracking morons on the ground and dropping rocks on their heads. I will not allow you to develop the lazy habit of tracking your fellows when the fog of war will envelop any actual deployment. Do you understand me?"

"YES, SIR," we bellowed.

He was right, of course. Most of my career, prior to Avalon, was spent on worlds where we could call in fire support from the Imperial Navy, if necessary. Our enemies were good - very good - at hiding from prying eyes, knowing that a moment of weakness would spell doom. Even without the starships, drones could track radio messages and call in long-range strikes from field artillery. The enemy would know to be very careful.

"It will be a long time before you're able to cheat in such a fashion," Bainbridge added, "but you will *not* have a chance to get into bad habits.

Anyone who does will be summarily removed from Boot Camp and tossed back into the civilian population. Do you understand me?"

"YES, SIR," we bellowed, again.

"Good," Bainbridge said. He glanced at his watch. "We should *just* have time for a run over to the Chow Hall and back before Lights Out."

A few weeks ago, I would have groaned out loud at the thought. Now…I just started to run, pacing myself as best as I could. The throbbing in my neck had faded completely, leaving me feeling…happy. I knew it wouldn't last - the Drill Instructors kept upping the pressure, pushing us to step past our previous limits - but for the moment I felt good. We reached the Chow Hall, slapped our hands against the wall as instructed, then started running back again, right into the barracks. Nordstrom, standing just inside the door, pointed us at the shower and supervised as we washed ourselves, then climbed into bed.

"Stalker," he growled. "You're on first watch."

I did groan this time, which earned me a warning look. Being on watch meant that I would have to stay awake for four hours, then snatch a bare three to four hours of sleep before it was time to get up and do our early morning callisthenics. I had no idea how the Drill Instructors picked the watch candidates - we weren't allowed to set a rota for ourselves - but it wasn't going to be fun. I sighed, picked up one of the books we'd been assigned to read in our *copious* spare time and sat down by the door.

"Hard luck, mate," Joker called.

"Silence," Nordstrom growled. "Lights Out."

I flicked a switch and the lights went dim, save for the one over my head. The Drill Instructors were *never* gentle, but they reserved particular wrath for anyone who fell asleep on watch. It could spell death, they'd warned, if someone fell asleep while they were watching for enemy infiltrators. I'd seen Joker and Thug being berated for falling asleep and I had no intention of having it happen to me. I was midway through the latest chapter when I heard someone moaning in fear, as if they were having a nightmare.

Bracing myself, I rose to my feet. Some of the first recruits, back when we'd just arrived at Boot Camp, had been homesick, something that had puzzled me until I'd learned that they actually came from decent homes.

A handful had quit within the week; the remainder had learned to adapt, to cope with being so far from their families. I slipped down past the rows of sleeping recruits, wondering who was making the noise. Viper? No, it was Professor. He jerked awake as I approached.

"It's all right," I said, very quietly. If he woke everyone else up, he'd rapidly become even less popular than Viper. "What's the matter?"

"Just a nightmare," he said, rubbing the side of his neck. "I'm sorry."

I frowned. "Are you in pain?"

Professor shook his head. I thought it was genuine, although I didn't think any of us would admit to suffering if there was any alternative. The last thing we wanted was a reputation for being unable to handle pain, even if we were visibly injured. And yet, there were ways to cope with pain. He could make a visit to the medics, they could check him out…

"It was just a nightmare," he said, keeping his voice low. "Probably that slop we were eating for lunch."

I had to smile, although I didn't believe him. We joked that the cooks served us crap to save time, but the truth was that it was better than anything I'd eaten for the last ten years on Earth. And it did help us to build up our muscles. Besides, we were always too tired for nightmares. I honestly couldn't recall dreaming, even once, since entering Boot Camp.

"You have to be tougher than you look," I said, with a smile. "I just go out like a light when my head hits the pillow."

Professor gave me a wan smile. "Just don't tell the Drills."

"I won't," I promised. I probably should have asked what he was dreaming about, but I didn't want to know. "Go back to sleep. I'll see you in the morning."

I watched him close his eyes, then walked back to the seat at the front. Nordstrom was standing there, his eyes expressionless. I waited for a moment, wondering if he was going to either compliment me - unlikely - or tell me I'd overstepped my bounds. Instead, he pointed a finger at the chair, ordering me to sit. I saluted - we'd spent weeks mastering how to salute - and sat. By the time he woke up the second watch officer, I was engrossed in the book.

"Get some sleep, Stalker," Nordstrom growled. "Morning will come soon enough."

He was right, of course.

Chapter Nine

The use of tracking implants was - and remains - one of the most controversial aspects of social control in the Empire, particularly in the years leading up to its fall. There were strong movements to give everyone an implant, in the name of public safety, that would make it impossible for anyone to develop a political movement without being tracked, monitored and eventually arrested. Indeed, a number of CityBlocks trialled mass implantation programs that helped to accelerate their social breakdown.

-Professor Leo Caesius

"Well," Nordstrom said, as soon as we had marched through the camp and into a whole new section. A large circle was drawn on the ground, with the Drill Instructor standing in the middle of it. "This is the day you've been dreaming of since you first arrived. This is the day you get to actually *hit* a Drill Instructor without repercussion."

I shared a glance with Joker. Hitting a superior officer - which was effectively everyone in the camp - was one of the headshots. I'd seen a couple of recruits throw the first punch, then get dragged off to the commandant for immediate dismissal. The idea of actually being allowed to take a swing at one of them was tempting, yet we knew them too well by now. I doubted I could beat *any* of them on my best day.

"There is no such thing as a dangerous weapon," Nordstrom continued, calmly. "There are only dangerous men. A man carrying the most deadly weapon in the universe is harmless, if he lacks the will and skill to use his weapon. But an unarmed man who knows how to use his body to best advantage is very dangerous. You, if you still want to complete the course, will be expected to become *very* dangerous men."

He smiled, coldly. "The Marine Corps has its own particular fighting style - the disrespectful call it Semper Fu - which draws from a hundred other fighting styles. By the time you graduate, you will hold a tan belt - at the very least - in Semper Fu. If you go to the Slaughterhouse, you will require a black belt to graduate. We will hold you back as long as necessary to make sure you have the right qualifications before you go onto active service."

There was a long chilling pause. "Before we go any further," he added, "does anyone want to take a crack at me? A free shot at a Drill Instructor - and an automatic pass if you actually manage to knock me down. Anyone want to take me up on it?"

I shook my head firmly. Nothing in Boot Camp was easy…and while I trusted the Drill Instructors to honour their offer of an automatic pass, I doubted anyone could actually win the prize. Nordstrom was the toughest man I'd ever met.

"Come on," Nordstrom said. His gaze swept our ranks, challengingly. "You can't get kicked out here, if you slam a fist into my jaw."

Thug lumbered forward, looking pleased. Nordstrom smiled at him, then waved him into the circle. "I should add, for the benefit of everyone else, that it's an automatic fifty push-ups for anyone who steps into the circle without being invited," he said. "Only the contestants are allowed inside until the match is over."

He nodded to Thug, who lunged forward and threw a punch. Nordstrom, moving so quickly I could barely follow his movements, caught his arm, yanked it forward and sent him falling to the ground. I heard Thug grunt in pain as he landed on the hard surface, then gasp as Nordstrom sat on his back and smirked at us.

"Aggressive enough, but a complete lack of proper training," Nordstrom said, addressing Thug. "Not too hard a combination to beat."

He looked up. "Anyone else?"

I was still reeling, mentally. It had happened so *quickly*. Someone like Thug would have been intimidating as hell, in the Undercity; he'd been taken down so fast I hadn't even seen what had happened. Nordstrom stood, helped Thug to his feet and muttered something I couldn't hear in his ear, before pushing him back towards the rest of us. I silently gave him some respect, if only for having the guts to *try*. No one else had dared take the Drill Instructor up on his offer.

"You should always focus on taking the offensive," Nordstrom said, as Johnston stepped forward and halted at the edge of the circle. "Trying to go on the defensive is asking for trouble, unless you are *very* certain of your own supremacy."

He didn't say it out loud, but the implication was easy to see. *He'd* been confident he could best Thug without doing him a serious injury. And he hadn't even thrown a single blow at his enemy.

"We will now demonstrate something more complex," Nordstrom said. He waved Johnston into the circle, then smiled savagely. "Watch carefully."

Johnston lunged forward; Nordstrom ducked back, then feinted himself with a handful of quick jabs. Johnston threw a punch of his own, then followed it up with a kick aimed right at Nordstrom's balls. Nordstrom hopped backwards quickly, but Johnston followed up with a blow aimed right at his throat. No matter what Nordstrom did, he couldn't take the offensive again. Johnston landed a blow that sent Nordstrom reeling back and falling to the ground. It wasn't until later that I realised just how carefully the entire thing had been choreographed.

"I lost the chance to take the offensive," Nordstrom said, as he picked himself up. I'd known people who would be completely humiliated by such a public loss, but Nordstrom took it in stride. "As long as my opponent was beating on me, I had no opportunity to strike back and take the offensive for myself. To tamely accept such a loss is to accept eventual defeat! You will learn to reverse such a disaster as quickly as possible."

He paused, then blew a whistle. A line of recruits - all from the platoon above us - walked into the section, looking tough. We'd improved a great deal, I knew, but they were still heads and shoulders above us. Their Drill Instructors didn't look any tougher…I looked at the older recruits and frowned, inwardly, at the nasty expressions on their faces. They knew what was coming, even if we didn't. And they were looking forward to it.

Joker elbowed me. "We have to fight them?"

"Line up, single file," Nordstrom bellowed. "I want one recruit from my platoon facing one recruit from the other platoon!"

I exchanged looks with Joker as two tough-looking men marched over to stand in front of us, resting their hands on their hips. They had the same sense of easy confidence I'd seen in the older marines, although it was ruined by the air of grim anticipation I could sense pulsing off them in waves. They were *definitely* looking forward to what was coming.

"My platoon," Nordstrom said. "Lock your hands behind your heads! Tense your muscles! Keep them there until ordered otherwise!"

"YES, SIR," we bellowed.

"Today's lesson is on how to *take* blows," Nordstrom said. "*Strike!*"

I had no time to react - as if there was anything I could have done - before the recruit facing me lunged forward and stabbed a fist into my gut. Pain. Lots of pain. It was all I could do to keep my hands locked as he drew back and struck me again, this time in the upper chest. I gagged, almost losing my lunch; somehow - and I have no idea how - I kept my hands in place. Judging from Nordstrom's snapped orders, others hadn't.

"I believe I told you to keep your hands in place," he thundered. Despite the pain, I turned my head and realised that Viper was in deep shit. "You were *not* permitted to block the blow."

"Yes, sir," Viper said, tonelessly. "This recruit allowed his training to guide him."

Nordstrom gave him a nasty look. "Drop and give me fifty," he ordered. "Everyone else who moved their hands can join him."

"You too, Harris," the unfamiliar Drill Instructor said. "This isn't a place to work out old grudges."

"That must be his old platoon," Joker muttered to me.

I nodded. The pain was fading, but slowly; very slowly. I couldn't help wondering if I'd cracked a rib, something that might well be a death sentence in the Undercity. Jenna had told me that almost everything could be fixed, but why would anyone spend money on saving *my* life? It wasn't as if anyone really gave a damn about Undercity rats...

"Change your partners," Nordstrom ordered, once the punishments were over. "And prepare to do it again."

We were all aching and sore by the time the first session was over and, unfortunately, burning with hatred for the other platoon. Luckily, the second session covered how to block punches; Nordstrom and Johnston demonstrated them, one by one, before calling in the second platoon once again. We still couldn't hit them back, but at least we could try and deflect their blows before we were hit. None of them gave us any mercy; later, I realised they hadn't been shown mercy either, back when they'd been in the first phase. It was a great relief when we were taught how to punch, kick and take the offensive, even though it took weeks before any of us managed to beat them in open combat.

"It is time to introduce you to one of our favourite games," Nordstrom said, two weeks after we started unarmed combat training. "You'll notice the circle on the ground?"

We nodded in unison. Nordstrom had called our attention to it regularly, both for demonstrating moves to us and reminding us - time and time again - that we weren't allowed to cross the line without permission. I assumed it was something more than merely a line delineating the combat zone, but he hadn't elaborated. Now...

"The rules of Circle are quite simple," Nordstrom said. "Two marines enter; the victor is the one who either flattens his opponent or forces him out of the circle. Would anyone try to hazard a guess as to why we have *that* victory condition?"

I decided to gamble and raised my hand. "Sir," I said, when he nodded. "This recruit thinks that it exists to keep us aware of our surroundings."

"Correct, recruit," Nordstrom said. "It is quite possible for someone who is winning to accidentally cross the circle and lose the match. You can be beaten in the game by your own carelessness...and, alas, you can be beaten in real life that way too. Would you care to take a guess how?"

There was a pause. None of us dared to try to answer.

"There have been incidents where someone has accidentally put a hole through a habitation dome on an asteroid," Nordstrom said. "Or somehow managed to vent the shuttlebay, throwing themselves and their comrades into space. One *very* elaborate trap for marines involved filling the air with explosive gas, then waiting for some idiot to pull a trigger. You *must* remain aware of your surroundings at all times."

He beckoned to Johnston, who strode back into the circle and nodded, curtly, to his opponent. Nordstrom ran forward; Johnston stepped to one side and stuck out a foot, sending Nordstrom flying forward and out of the circle. He picked himself off the ground and turned to face us, his expression unreadable.

"That was a depressingly easy victory for him," he said, shortly. "I expect you to do better."

The Drill Instructors ran through two more demonstrations before we were allowed a chance to enter the circle. The first time, Nordstrom allowed Johnston to literally *push* him out of the circle; the second time, Nordstrom did *something* and threw Johnston over the line, dropping him to the ground just past it. As soon as Johnston picked himself up again, they divided us back up into pairs. I was not best pleased to find myself paired with Viper.

"Go," Nordstrom ordered.

I watched Viper closely for a second - Nordstrom had talked about learning to read one's opponent, but I hadn't managed it - before advancing forward, carefully. Viper *had* had two months of extra training, after all; I knew I shouldn't take him lightly. But the moment I crashed into him, he jumped backwards and over the line. It was so blatant it took me a moment to understand what he'd done.

Nordstrom blew the whistle, angrily. "Do you actually *intend* to learn how to fight or are you just being stupid, recruit?"

I felt a hot flush of rage. I'd won - but he'd practically handed me the victory on a silver platter. Didn't he give a damn? I wanted to hurt him… somehow, I managed to keep myself calm as Joker was ordered into the circle beside me. Friend or no friend, I knew *Joker* wouldn't go easy on me. And I was right. I was a little stronger than him, but he was fast and managed to land a number of punches before I knocked him to the ground and landed on top of him. He kept struggling right up until I put my hand on his throat and the whistle blew.

"You should have ended that quicker," Nordstrom snapped. He jabbed a finger at Professor and Posh. "You're up."

It was an interesting match, I decided, as the two oddballs squared off. Posh seemed to be more aggressive, but Professor was definitely more of a thinker. They both sparred carefully, rather than risk over-committing themselves; it was only when Nordstrom cleared his throat loudly that Posh jumped forward and slammed right into Professor. The ensuring struggle sent them both rolling over the line.

"Draw," Nordstrom said. "Learn to focus your anger and beat the crap out of your enemy."

I scowled. I'd hated the first part of the training, but if I hadn't been taught how to take a punch Joker would have had me on the ground within seconds. I watched several other matches, then scowled inwardly as I was urged back into the circle. Viper was facing me again, his face impassive. I glared at him - what the fuck was his problem? - and lunged forward. This time, Viper blocked my punch and threw one back of his own. I realised, too late, that I'd underestimated him; his fist slammed into my jaw, knocking me over backwards. He lunged forward; I brought up my legs and kicked him in the chest as hard as I could. I pulled myself upright as he staggered back, then slammed a fist into his chest, sending him falling down. It would have been easy to shove him over the line, but I wanted him to hurt.

The whistle blew. I threw another punch....

...And a hand caught mine.

"Stop," Nordstrom ordered. He jerked a hand towards the edge of the training ground. "One hundred push-ups, now."

I flushed, embarrassed. I'd allowed my anger and hate to overwhelm me, instead of stopping the second the whistle blew. Nordstrom could have given me a far worse punishment and we both knew it. I stumbled out of the circle, did my push-ups despite the pain, and thought dire thoughts about Viper and his attitude problem. Maybe the beating I'd given him would force him to quit.

The training grew harder as the weeks turned into months. We had already been introduced to sticks; now, we were introduced to knives - the feared KA-BAR - and a dozen other weapons, including some I hadn't seen outside bad martial arts movies. I hadn't known there were actual uses for swords, throwing stars and whips, but the Drill Instructors were insistent that we needed to know the basics. We were advancing, slowly but surely, towards weapons mastery. *Anything* could be a weapon…

…And we were meant to be able to use it as one, without thinking.

It was Joker who asked the question that was on all of our minds. "Sir," he said, "this recruit would like to know why we train with swords when we'll have guns and our enemies will have guns too."

I expected Nordstrom to demand a hundred push-ups. Instead, he gave the question serious consideration.

"There are two answers to that question, recruit," Nordstrom said. "The first is that we are training you to be dangerous men and for that you need to develop an instinctive understanding of all manner of weapons. To become dependent on one weapon, even one as dangerous as a gun, can undermine you when you lose that weapon.

"But the second answer is that you may not always have a gun," he added. "Or you may find a gun a hindrance rather than a help. There are plenty of situations - hostage rescue, for example - when you may not want to start firing off guns at random. Killing an unwary man on watch is *so* much easier if you use a knife, because then there's no noise to wake up his comrades."

He shrugged. "And shooting someone to wound only works in the flicks. It's a lot easier to interrogate someone you've beaten into a pulp than shot, even if you *thought* you weren't shooting to kill. Is that answer satisfactory?"

"Yes, sir," Joker said.

I took Nordstrom's words to heart; indeed, I think we all did. Our weapons were tools, nothing more or less; it was our attitudes and training that made us dangerous. I'd wondered why were weren't started on guns earlier, but now I thought I understood. We needed the right attitude before we handled guns for the first time or we'd become convinced that our weapons made us invincible.

And that, I learned later, explained a great deal about the Civil Guard. They thought their weapons made them gods…

…And they were always wrong.

CHAPTER
TEN

The Empire had an unthinking horror of guns in private hands. There was no shortage of justifications - guns were dangerous, guns enabled crime, guns brought out the worst in people - but they all boiled down to a simple desire to keep power out of the hands of commoners. Guns might be turned against criminals, yet they could also be turned against tax men, corrupt policemen and the bureaucracy. It was vanishingly rare for anyone from the Core Worlds to see a gun, let alone use it…

…This did absolutely nothing for social safety, of course. By the time I left Earth, violent crime was still on the increase.

-Professor Leo Caesius

Our first visit to the Shooting Range was the first time we encountered another training officer, outside the trio of Drill Instructors. Firearms Instructor Dexter Guptill was a tough-looking man, wearing a set of light body armour and webbing rather than the normal instructor uniform. We stopped outside the building long enough to let him inspect us, then followed him into the building. Inside, there were a set of tables, with a metal case resting on each one. Our names were already written on top of the cases.

"Find your table, then stand behind it," Guptill ordered coolly, as he strode to the front of the room. "Like your teachers on Earth, I have to instruct you; unlike your teachers from Earth, I have the power to evict you without warning, if you misbehave. That will result in you being recycled, at the very least. You have been warned."

He tapped a switch, activating a projector. "Four absolute rules of firearms safety," he stated, as a list appeared behind him. "One: a weapon is always loaded until proved otherwise. Two: *do not* point the gun at anything you do not want to hit. If you think the gun is unloaded, see rule one. Three: keep your finger off the trigger until you are ready to fire. This is the most important rule; in my experience, violators are responsible for nearly all cases of Negligent Discharge. Again, keep rule one in mind. Four: identify your target and its surroundings. Do *not* shoot at anything you have not positively identified."

There was a pause. "If I catch any of you violating these rules from this moment on, you will be doing hundreds of push-ups," he warned. "If you make a *habit* of violating these rules, I will assert my authority as Firearms Instructor and Range Safety Officer to get you dismissed from Boot Camp. I have neither the time nor the patience to deal with idiots who blatantly ignore rules intended to ensure both their safety and the safety of everyone around them.

"For the record, the punishment for a Negligent Discharge - either a blank or a live round - that injures no one is a major fine and a black mark in your record," he added. "If you *do* injure someone, you will be in deep shit.

"Forget all the crap you might have picked up from the flicks. This is the real world. If you go into this with the wrong attitude, you are likely to get yourself or someone else seriously hurt - or dead."

I swallowed. I'd been looking forward to weapons training, but his warnings chilled me to the bone. How many accidents had there been in the movies? I'd seen millions of people gunned down, blood and gore splattering everywhere…was it really like that?

"Open the cases," Guptill ordered. "Do *not* touch anything inside."

I unclipped the case and stared down at the two shiny weapons, both fresh off the production line. One was a pistol, large enough to be intimidating; the other was a rifle, gleaming faintly under the light. My name was engraved into the metal, along with a pair of serial numbers I assumed they used to identify the weapons if they fell out of my hands. I wanted to touch them suddenly, with a passion I hadn't felt since my first girlfriend had taken off her dress in front of me, but I held back. There was no real chance of sneaking a feel without being caught.

"These are standard issue weapons," Guptill informed us. "The pistol is a SIW-32, carrying a magazine of nine rounds of ammunition, or cartridges; the rifle is a MAG-47, capable of switching from single-shot to automatic with the flick of a switch. From this moment on, you will be expected to carry these weapons with you at all times, proffering them for inspection upon demand. You will clean them - religiously - every day. Take care of your weapon and it will take good care of you."

He held up a pistol of his own. "Your Drill Instructors - and myself - will ask for your weapons," he said. "When we do, you expose the chamber like so" - he opened the action to demonstrate - "to prove that the gun is unloaded, then you hold it out, careful not to point the barrel at anyone. Your Drill Instructor will be furious if you point the weapon at him. When he has finished his inspection, he will pass it back to you in the same manner. If the weapon is dirty, or shows signs of having been abused, you will be in deep shit."

"You are also expected to call us out if we do pass it back to you in any other way," Bainbridge added, from the back of the room.

I groaned, inwardly. Another bloody test!

"You'll find a cleaning set in the case," Guptill said. "Take it out, then *carefully* remove the pistol and check it isn't loaded."

I hesitated, then reached for the pistol, feeling…conflicted. Part of me was nervous at the very idea of touching a weapon, even though I'd spent the last few weeks training on everything from knives to throwing stars and staffs. It felt almost as if I were touching a spider…the others, save for Viper, seemed to be having the same problem. But then, he would be repeating the class. I opened the chamber, checked there wasn't anything inside, then locked the chamber open and placed the pistol on the table, pointed well away from anyone else.

"Shit," Joker said. Something clattered out of his pistol and hit the floor with a sound that made us all jump. "Sir…"

"You found one of the training rounds," Guptill said. "Is the weapon empty?"

Joker looked hesitant. "This recruit thinks so…"

"Not good enough," Guptill said. He strode over to Joker's table, then demonstrated how to clear the chamber and check there were no rounds left in the magazine. "Be sure, recruit. Check with me if you don't understand what you're doing."

I watched closely, then checked my own gun. The magazine was empty. Guptill nodded in approval, then strode back to the front of the room. "Watch carefully," he said, picking up his pistol and holding it out to prove it was empty. "You take the gun apart like this, piece by piece, and then you clean it carefully…"

The gun was a remarkably simple design, I realised, as we worked our way through it. Guptill was a patient teacher, more patient than any of the Drill Instructors, although that could have been because he was used to working with deadly weapons and recruits who had already had several weeks of training. I took the weapon apart, then put it back together; Guptill inspected our work, corrected our mistakes and told us to do it again and again, until we were perfect. The thought of doing the same thing every day was irritating…

But you already do plenty of repetitive things every day, my own thoughts pointed out, sarcastically. *What's one more*?

"Very good, for the moment," Guptill told us. "Now, the rifle is a slightly more complex beast, but quite simple once you get the hang of it…"

It was definitely harder, I decided, as we took the rifles apart, cleaned them for the first time and then put them back together. Guptill told us that the best marines could field-strip and reassemble their weapons in under a minute, but none of us believed him until he took Professor's weapon and showed us exactly how it was done. He didn't seem surprised at the question; he merely proved his point and then moved on.

"You will not be issued any ammunition until you complete the first two phases of training," Guptill said, once we thought we knew what we were doing. "You *will*, however, be carrying exercise magazines, as you will be using them when you start putting everything together for the first time. You can find those magazines at the bottom of the case, marked with a pink line. Take them out and put them on the table."

He waited until we were done, then showed us how to load them into the guns. "These behave like real ammunition in all, but one respect," he said. "They shoot harmless beams of laser light instead of lethal bullets. As you can see" - he pulled the trigger; there was a loud bang and a beam of red light shot out of the gun - "the beam can be switched from visible to invisible with the touch of a button. On exercise, you will be wearing suits that will automatically register a hit, should someone manage to tag you. You will be declared dead and marched off the field."

I smiled. We'd heard enough about field exercises to know we wanted to try one. It sounded like fun, from what the older platoon had said. We'd even seen them going back to their barracks once or twice, covered in mud but grinning from ear to ear.

"They also produce a loud noise, should you have a Negligent Discharge," he added. He tapped the gun, which emitted another loud bang. "This noise *will* be heard and you *will* be yelled at by your Drill Instructors. And, as I said, there will be a fine and a black mark."

He paused. "Now, I will take the first squad into the range itself," he said. "The rest of you; sit here, read the papers in your case and practice taking the weapons apart. Any questions?"

"Yes, sir," Posh said. "This recruit was wondering if we were allowed to keep the weapons."

"Should you graduate Boot Camp, you will be allowed to keep the weapon," Guptill said. "I suggest you check out the firearms laws before you pick a final destination. Civilians in the Core Worlds tend to get nervous around guns. A colony world, however, will be quite happy to have you *and* your weapon."

He raised his fist. "First squad, with me," he ordered. "Bring both your weapons, chambers open."

I rose, carefully carrying both weapons. Guptill watched us carefully, then led us through a metal door into an antechamber. Two large crates of ammunition sat on a table, sealed with a solid lock. Guptill opened the first one, then produced his pistol and held it open for inspection.

"You'll notice that these are dummy rounds," he said. "The pink line around the bullet signifies the lack of charge. You could pull the trigger all day and nothing would happen, but in all other respects they are identical to standard-issue rounds. As you can see…"

I watched, closely, as he demonstrated how to load the magazine with bullets, then insert it into the pistol. "The safety should be on right up until the moment you are ready to fire," he said, showing us how to click it on and off. "The weapon *cannot* fire as long as the safety is on. Point towards your target and pull the trigger" - he pulled the trigger; there was a click and the cartridge was ejected from the chamber - "and then keep firing. If you get a dud and the round refuses to fire, snap the chamber open and eject the cartridge. Don't worry about it hitting the floor. It takes a solid smack to fire a bullet. Any questions?"

"Yes," Professor said. "If something is coming backwards…"

"The cartridge," Guptill said.

Professor nodded. "Is that dangerous?"

"Probably not to you," Guptill said. "You're going to be wearing eye goggles - well, you're already wearing birth control glasses so it shouldn't be a problem - and earmuffs. But, just to give you a warning…"

He leaned forward. "I was assigned to teach a bunch of women to shoot, a couple of years ago," he explained. "They weren't soldiers, you see; they'd been assigned to serve on some shit-tip of a planet where attacks on offworlders were depressingly common. I gave them pistols and ammunition, then took them onto the range. It might have worked very well if one of them hadn't been wearing a very low-cut shirt. And the cartridge landed right between her tits."

I snickered. I wasn't the only one.

"So she drops the pistol, screaming her head off, and starts trying to get the cartridge out of her cleavage," Guptill continued. "It might seem funny now, but the poor bitch was quite badly burned…the moral of the story is to listen to me when I tell you something, even if it's merely an order to wear something that will protect you."

He shrugged. "I shall be issuing live ammunition once we're inside the range," he added. "I expect you to treat it with the respect it deserves."

We nodded, hastily.

"Take a set of earmuffs and goggles, unless you're already protected," Guptill ordered, once he'd finished telling us how to stand. "Make sure your ears are completely covered."

He checked our protections, then beckoned us through another metal door. This chamber was larger, with a handful of paper targets hanging from the ceiling at the far end. A red line had been painted on the ground, with a warning saying DO NOT CROSS THIS LINE. Guptill walked forward as the door closed, then raised his voice. I was mildly discomforted to discover that I could still hear him through the earmuffs.

"I'm putting a rest here so you can lean on it to take your first shots," he said. "Stalker, you're up first. The rest of you, stay back and watch carefully."

I blinked - if he'd wanted someone to do well, Viper might have been the better choice - and then stepped up to the rest. Guptill passed me a set of rounds, each one glinting gold under the light; I felt my fingers shaking as I took them, one by one, and carefully slotted them into the magazine. It was simple enough, yet I was slow…I had the feeling we'd be doing a great deal of practice with dummy ammunition…

"Keep your hand away from the hammer," Guptill warned. "Point it at your target and then pull the trigger slowly."

I peered down towards the target - a simple set of bull's-eyes - and pulled the trigger. It didn't go off. For a crazy moment, I wondered if he'd given me dummy ammunition, then I realised I'd forgotten to take off the safety. I clicked it off - my hands felt sweaty, all of a sudden - and pulled the trigger a second time. There was a loud bang - I jumped, despite the ear muffs - and a small hole appeared in the paper target. Something rattled down by my feet. I glanced down and saw the cartridge spinning to a stop.

"You'll be sweeping those up later," Guptill warned. "Go on. Fire off the rest of the magazine."

I pulled the trigger several times, slowly gaining in confidence. I didn't quite manage to hit dead centre, but I wasn't doing badly. The final bullet proved to be a dud; I panicked, for a second, then cleared the chamber and discovered there was no more ammunition. I slipped the safety back on, opened the chamber and held the gun out for inspection.

"Good enough," Guptill said. He pointed to the wall, then called Joker forward. "Wait there."

We rapidly formed a line and went through the shooting exercise three times, before Guptill finally called a halt and detailed us to pick up the cartridges and dump them in the recycling boxes. None of us were entirely confident about picking them up after the horror story, but it turned out they cooled very quickly. Guptill entertained us with a story about how the Marine Corps had sent a team to the Imperial Army's sharpshooting contest and walked away with all the prizes.

"We don't have to account for each and every piece of ammunition fired," he explained, when we asked him how this had been achieved. "How many bullets did you fire?"

I tried to calculate it in my head. There were ten of us, the gun could hold nine rounds at a time and we'd each had three turns at shooting…

"Two hundred and seventy," Professor said. Trust him to have the advantage when it came to calculation. "More or less…"

"Close enough," Guptill agreed. "The Imperial Army expects its NCOs to fill in a form for each round of ammunition they requisition, even if they don't use it. And then, they wonder why their sergeants find it so much easier not to have live-fire practice at all."

He cleared his throat. "Back to the classroom, recruits," he added. "You have papers to read."

I didn't believe him at the time, not about the Imperial Army. But, if anything, he understated the case. All marines have to be riflemen first, and ideally they have to have experience of combat, but it's possible to rise quite high within the army without ever seeing the elephant. And then you lose track of what is actually important and what can be safely ignored…

And that, perhaps, explained just what went wrong with the Empire.

CHAPTER ELEVEN

> As hard as it may seem to believe, Ed is also understating the case. One could make a valid case that it was bureaucracy, not the Grand Senate, the Secessionists or anyone else, who actually killed the Empire. If a crowd is only as smart as the stupidest person in it, a bureaucracy is pretty much a brain-dead beast. On one hand, someone could survive a screw-up if that person could demonstrate that they'd followed procedure; on the other hand, someone using common sense could easily be fired.
>
> -Professor Leo Caesius

It really was astonishing, I discovered as we moved through phase one, just how much information the Drill Instructors crammed into our heads. Every day started with inspection, then we did callisthenics, unarmed combat training, firearms training and water training…and then we were introduced to everything from basic medical treatment to survival in the wilderness. By the time we reached the first waypoint, the first set of exams to determine if we could proceed into phase two, we felt as if information was leaking out of our ears.

The Drill Instructors did not, of course, let up. Things they would have let slide at the beginning were now the cause of endless push-ups, while they were happy - sometimes - to let us learn from painful experience. I managed to slice my finger while firing a pistol when the slide rocketed backwards, teaching me a sharp lesson about holding weapons carefully. It might have been smaller than my hand, making it difficult to fire properly, but that was no excuse. The medics healed it up at once, yet I never forgot. None of us did.

"Marines are *thinkers*," Bainbridge bellowed, after we completed the shooting and unarmed combat tests. I'd mastered the art of shooting at stationary targets, although their favourite trick for when one of us was getting a little overconfident was to have us shoot at moving targets instead, which was a great deal harder. "*Why* are we thinkers?"

He jabbed a finger at Thug. "This recruit thinks it is because marines" - we'd been seriously ticked off for calling ourselves marines - "have to fight with less than most, more than most."

"True," Bainbridge agreed. "There hasn't been a battle in the last two centuries where marine units have not been outnumbered at least ten to one. Sometimes, we have been backed up by the regulars; mostly, it's just us, surrounded on all sides by the enemy. We have to learn to make the most of what we have."

He paused. "These exams will measure your intellectual development" - he spoke the words as if they were a curse - "and determine if you are allowed to proceed to the next phase or held back to join the newcomers. These are not the pointless exams you might be familiar with from school. I shall be severely displeased if I have any reason to think you are not giving your all.

"You will be shown to a private room inside the examination building. You will sit down in front of the computer - paper and pencils have also been provided - and answer all the questions as best as you can. You will not attempt to leave the room without an escort; if you need to take a piss, there's a bucket at the rear. When you have finished, we will be alerted and you will be collected and taken down to the training grounds. We will make some good use of your time while the remainder of the platoon are completing their exams."

I nodded, inwardly. Exams at school had been pointless - and, when we were finished, we were expected to just sit quietly and wait for everyone else. Needless to say, we hadn't done anything of the sort; I would have been surprised if *anyone* did very well on the exams, or even managed to finish them when there was no punishment for failure. But here…

there wasn't one of us who would defy the Drill Instructors, not when they could assign us hundreds of push-ups.

Bainbridge scowled at us all. "Do you understand me?"

"YES, SIR," we shouted.

"Inside," he ordered.

We walked into the building, past a desk manned by a grim-faced woman wearing a green uniform, and down a long corridor. Our names were already written on the doors; I waved goodbye to Joker, when I found mine, and pushed it open carefully. Inside, there was a computer terminal - like the one I'd taken the aptitude tests on, back on Earth - and a small selection of papers and pencils. A water bottle stood next to it, full and sealed. I knew from experience that we were expected to keep hydrated at all times and there might be some hard questions if I didn't. Shaking my head, I sat down and braced myself, then tapped the switch to start the tests. Moments later, the first question flashed up in front of me, a repeat - almost - of the original aptitude test. I worked my way through the questions, one by one, then stopped as a far more complex question popped up.

"You have proof that your superior officer has been stealing supplies from the logistics centre and selling them on the black market," I read out loud, parsing out every word. "Do you report him, confront him or ignore him?"

It was a tricky question. There wouldn't have been any real doubt at all in the Undercity. A superior officer could be a deadly enemy - and he would be believed, not you, if you happened to report him. Besides, *his* superiors might be in on the racket too. But in the marines…

I agonised for long seconds. Would it be better to report him, in line with the instructions to uphold the ideals of the Marine Corps, or to ignore him, on the grounds that I would be snitching on my superior? Who knew which way the chips would fall? But if I was to be a marine, as I had been told often enough, I had to put the interests of the corps ahead of my personal interests. I'd report him…and handle whatever consequences came my way, when they came. I tapped the answer into the machine, then read the next question. It looked to run along the same lines, but had a far more complex problem. I answered as best as I could, silently praying I never had to face such a problem in real life. It would be damaging no matter what I did.

The third question threw me for a long moment. "You have discovered that two of your platoon mates are having a sexual relationship," I read. "Do you report them, confront them or ignore them?"

I swore under my breath. This was worse than the first question. Loyalty to one's superiors was important, but loyalty to one's platoon was *vital*. Did I betray them, thus undermining the glue holding us together, or ignore their affair, even though it too would be damaging to the platoon? I knew - I thought I knew - the regulations. Sexual affairs between marines were absolutely forbidden, with discharge the mildest punishment laid down in the books. And yet…

"I'd have to report them, if I couldn't talk them out of it," I muttered. Personally, I would have been astonished if anyone had had the *energy* for a sexual affair, not when we staggered into bunks each day feeling utterly shattered. "What else could I do?"

It was a relief to discover that the next set of questions were tactical, focused around a number of scenarios the marines had encountered over the years.

"A marine platoon has taken up residence in a small village," I read, "and has orders to defend the residents against enemy raiders. Two people in the town are dickers - watching everything the platoon does and reporting them to the enemy. Identify these people from the profiles and state your reasons."

I groaned as I read through the seventy profiles. The village seemed tiny compared to a CityBlock (nowhere else had the population density of a CityBlock) but there were still enough residents to make it hard to guess at the enemy agents. I was tempted to blame the policeman - the police on Earth were hopelessly corrupt - but the file indicated that he'd been a decent man, despite his limitations. It wasn't until I started looking at the relationships between the villages that one of the dickers jumped right out at me. He was a complete stranger, as far as I could tell. There were *no* ties between him and the rest of the villagers.

"Gotcha," I said.

My good mood didn't last. Who was the *other* dicker? The schoolmaster? No, in my experience schoolmasters and teachers were too cowardly to do anything that might require taking a stand. A housewife? No, the enemy seemed to think that women should remain pregnant, barefoot and in the kitchen...although, if that were the case, having a housewife as a spy would seem unthinkable. Someone we'd offended somehow...

I glanced back through the files and smiled. One of the villagers had had his daughter molested by the platoon's predecessors. He had an entirely understandable motive to want a little revenge. It was an unfamiliar attitude to me - there were few fathers on Earth who could or would stand up for their children - but it made sense. I tagged him as the second dicker and moved on.

It felt like hours before I reached the final question and the exam came to an end. The door clicked invitingly, offering me the chance to leave, but I knew better than to step through until the Drill Instructors arrived. Instead, I drank the rest of the water and enjoyed an unaccustomed moment of sheer relaxation. Johnston arrived, just after I'd finished, and beckoned me through the door. I wanted to ask how well I'd done, as he led me down to the training grounds, but I knew I'd find out soon enough. Instead, I joined Joker in running laps around the field.

"Bet Viper gets held back again," Joker muttered. Once, running several miles - even pacing ourselves, as we had been taught to do - would have left us both gasping for breath. Now, it felt easy. "We'd finally be rid of him."

I nodded in agreement. Everyone else was pulling their weight, to the best of their ability, but not Viper. He should have been stronger than Professor, smarter than Thug - he'd had an entire month of training - yet he was still only doing the bare minimum. It held us back in anything requiring teamwork, putting us at the bottom of the ranking system. I knew it was only a matter of time before the Drill Instructors 'counselled' us to do better or someone took a swing at Viper outside the unarmed combat pit.

"Just think of the poor bastards who'll get him next," Joker added. "Maybe we should have given him a thumping after Lights Out."

"Better not," I said. "The Drills would kill us."

Joker frowned, but nodded reluctantly. One of the recruits - not in my squad, thankfully - had started to bully someone he thought wasn't doing very well. Nordstrom had picked him up, *carried* him out of the barracks and then...well, I don't know what happened next, but we never saw the bully again. (We joked that Nordstrom had eaten the bastard and we half-believed it.) His victim might have started slowly, but he was doing very well now.

The whistle blew as the last of the recruits was escorted out of the examination hall. We were marched down to the shooting range, where we fired off several hundred more rounds from our rifles in our endless quest for accuracy. Guptill had taken to posting our scores on the walls, pushing the squad into competition with the rest of the platoon and the platoon into competition with the senior platoons. The seniors *should* be well ahead of us; Guptill had told us, mischievously, that if we happened to beat them in a shooting match, they would be in deep shit with their Drill Instructors. It was remarkably motivating.

"Pick up your brass, recruit," Guptill snapped. Somehow, I wasn't surprised to discover that it was Viper in trouble. Again. He must not have done well on the exams. "You don't want to spend your free hour cleaning this place, do you?"

"No, sir," Viper said.

He bent over and started to pick up the shells, one by one. I watched for a moment, then turned my attention back to the rifle and checked my sights, again. Guptill had a habit of adjusting our sights, just to force us to reset them every time we fired. It was a useful thing to learn, although I rather preferred the laser rangefinder. But the Drill Instructors had explained, at some length, that we couldn't rely on being able to use them in the field.

"Laser rangefinders are not new pieces of technology," Bainbridge had explained. "They have been in use for longer than the Phase Drive. A *smart* enemy could protect their installations with sensors intended to *detect* laser beams, even beams invisible to the naked eye, and call down artillery fire on your position. Or even just shoot back in your general direction."

I frowned, remembering. We'd been told not to shoot off the whole magazine at once, as the odds of hitting something were surprisingly low, but there were times in the field when it came in handy. If nothing else, spraying and praying in the enemy's direction would force them to duck, upsetting them enough to let you get off a more accurate shot. Or so we hoped.

As soon as we had finished cleaning the range, we were marched back outside and back down to the barracks. Somewhat to my disappointment, Viper was still with us, alone and isolated as always. I might have felt sorry for him, if he'd tried; I wouldn't have cared if he hadn't wanted to talk with us, if he had pulled his weight. But he wasn't even trying…

Professor was weak, when he started, I thought, as we lined up in front of the Drill Instructors. *But he worked hard and overcame his weaknesses.*

"You have all completed your exams," Bainbridge said. "I trust you enjoyed yourselves?"

"NO, SIR," we shouted.

"Good," Bainbridge said. "You all passed the first set of tests. We will be talking to some of you individually about your answers, over the next couple of days, but the important detail is that you passed. You haven't managed to *quite* embarrass us."

We cheered, loudly. None of us would have dared to *deliberately* embarrass the Drill Instructors. We might have been the freshman platoon, the maggots who only just got off the shuttle, but we were trying. Even *Viper* had passed…my heart sank as I realised we were going to have to put up with him for at least another month or two. Unless he quit, of course, but I had the impression that quitting (for him) was worse than being recycled. I knew how he felt, yet surely he could put in more effort?

"You are expected to review the details of the *next* phase of training this evening, in your free hour," Bainbridge continued. "You will not be expected to make up any exercise routines this evening, unless you want to make your way to the shooting range and fire off some more rounds. Guptill will be on duty until 2000; report to him, draw ammunition and blow some targets away."

It was a tiny reward, by civilian standards, but it meant a hell of a lot to us. If nothing else, it was a quiet acknowledgement that we'd proved ourselves competent to handle our weapons without three Drill Instructors looming over our shoulders at all times. An hour of actual free time…? I agonised backwards and forwards over what I'd do with it, once I'd read through the details of phase two. (I knew better than to think we hadn't been *ordered* to read the details.) It wasn't as if I had anyone to write to…

"One other thing," Bainbridge said, softly. I tensed. A soft voice meant trouble. "Next week, there will be a new intake platoon, a new set of maggots. You will be expected to assist in training them, as your seniors assisted you. Be professional or spend hours working it off in the pit."

"I'm going to be writing to my family," Joker said, as we relaxed. "Tell them all about passing the first waypoint."

I grinned, despite feeling alone. We were one step closer to becoming marines - and, perhaps, we would never be civilians again. Not really. Even if I went back now, I wouldn't be a true civilian. The learned helplessness that had overshadowed my life on Earth was gone.

"I don't have anyone to write to," I confessed. "You guys are my family now."

"Then write to one of us," Joker said. "Dear Joker; today I did five hundred push-ups and thought myself lucky. Your friend, Stalker."

Professor leaned over. "No friends or family at all?"

"My family is dead," I said, tartly. The idea of writing to anyone else back home was absurd, really. I had never had any real friends, nor - unlike several of the recruits - had I left a girl behind, waiting for me. (Most of those girls moved on before the recruits finished Boot Camp.) "I have no one else at all."

"Well, at least you have us," Joker said. He smirked. "I suppose you could always write to my sister. I'd have to beat the crap out of you for *daring* to write to my sister, of course, but you could write to her."

"Oh, shut up," I said.

Chapter Twelve

The sensation of being isolated from one's family and friends is one of the most difficult problems to overcome at Boot Camp. A recruit may write to his family, if he has time, but he will almost certainly not be able to call them in real-time or record video messages for them; he certainly won't be allowed to receive them. This helps to break the links between civilian and military life - recruits are only expected to meet their families after they graduate, thus keeping their training firmly in place - but it also leads to homesickness, depression and other psychological problems. It is quite rare for a recruit to not feel at least a flicker of homesickness during his first week, no matter what the Drill Instructors do.

-Professor Leo Caesius

I couldn't help a thrill of anticipation as we marched away from the maggot training grounds - where we had been training for the last month - and into the field training ground. We might be wearing webbing that would sound the alert if we were hit, we might be slipping and sliding our way through the muddy ground, but I still felt excited. And why not? We were going to have a chance to put all of our training to the test for the first time.

"Welcome to Hellhole," Bainbridge announced, as we marched past the border fence. "You can go anywhere inside the border, but trying to cross the border without authorisation will be considered cheating. And *no*, you're *not* allowed to shove someone over the border. This is a realistic combat training exercise, not an scaled-up version of Circle."

He led us on a long march that took us right through Hellhole (actually, quite a few training grounds were called Hellhole, Shithole or some other less than pleasant designation). It was a small village, just like the one discussed in the exams, surrounded by woodland and - thankfully - completely deserted. We inspected some of the buildings and discovered that the engineers had made them look *very* realistic, even including clothes in the drawers and food in the fridges. The surrounding landscape looked odd; there were small streams running through the village - and bridges allowing people to cross from the road to their homes - and plenty of hedges and bushes. Birds flew through the air and small animals rustled through the undergrowth, disturbed by our presence. I couldn't help feeling nervous when I saw them, even though I was sure they were harmless; rats and cockroaches infested some of the CityBlocks, spreading diseases throughout the complex. They'd told us that small animals could be eaten - and we *would* be eating them, when we started to test our survival training on long overnight marches - but I wasn't looking forward to it.

Bainbridge kept up a running commentary as we crossed the wider river on one side of the village, pointing out details that seemed completely irrelevant to us. It wasn't until we actually began that I realised the village had been carefully designed to provide plenty of training opportunities, if we were prepared to take advantage of them. The river, for example, might make an ideal place to slow an enemy advance…if, of course, the enemy didn't try to ford the river away from the village. And we could hide in the canals, if we wished; our bodies would be largely invulnerable if the enemy couldn't see them to take aim.

"The only objective here is to eliminate your opponents," Bainbridge said. "Any hits will be considered lethal; your webbing will start to flash red as soon as it records a hit and your training packs will be disarmed. The victors will be the squad that has even a *single* remaining member, as long as the other two squads have been eliminated. Do you understand me?"

"YES, SIR," we bellowed.

"Good," Bainbridge said. "As soon as you are hit, walk out of the training ground and cross the border. Do not do *anything* to assist your comrades, as you are counted as dead; make your way around to the entrance and wait there. Failure to follow these orders will result in intensive punishment. You will *not* get the opportunity to cheat on a real battlefield."

And I thought that if we weren't cheating, we weren't trying, I thought, a little resentfully. I wasn't fool enough to ask that out loud. He had a point; in a real battle, a wounded or dead marine wouldn't be able to point to the enemy positions or anything else that might be helpful. Stretching the rules was one thing, breaking them outright was quite another.

"Squad One will deploy from the north," Bainbridge said. "Squad Two will deploy from the west. Squad Three will deploy from the east. Remember, the objective is not to take and hold territory, but to eliminate one's enemies. Staying where you are in the hopes the enemy will come to you is just plain stupid."

And might cost us the chance to win, I thought. We'd been taught, time and time again, to take the offensive. *But if we stayed where we started, we might see One and Three eliminate each other before we intervened and wiped out the victor.*

I kept those thoughts to myself as Bainbridge smirked. "If the exercise is declared terminated, which is signalled through a red flare, return to the entrance at once," he added, darkly. "There isn't a time limit, I'm afraid, but you really don't want to bore us."

I winced, inwardly, as Johnston marched us around to the western flag, marking our start point. We'd have to crawl through the forest to reach the village, like Squad Three, while Squad One would have to cross the river. The Drill Instructor said nothing as we had a brief discussion about tactics; Three might make it to the village at the same time as us, while One would have very real problems. They'd have to cross on the sole bridge, or swim, or find a place to ford the river.

"We could always ford the river ourselves and take One up the butt," Posh offered. "Everyone is going to try to go to the village, aren't they?"

"There's too little cover," I countered. The trees wouldn't stop real bullets - I'd seen machine guns at work - but the lasers we used for training would be stopped. We could get away with using *very* flimsy cover. "We'd be caught out in the open."

"So will One, if they try to get across the river," Joker said. "They practically *have* to get to the village faster than everyone else."

I recalled what I'd seen of the village's layout. "If we try to secure the bridge, Three will take *us* in the back," I pointed out. "What if we sneak up to the edge of the treeline and wait there?"

"They might be able to take the village and turn it into a strongpoint," Professor said.

"If the village is clear," Posh said, "we advance forward and secure it for ourselves. If not, we can pick around the edges and weaken them, piece by piece."

I groaned inwardly as the last minutes ticked away. If we'd had real weapons - rifles, machine guns, grenades - the village might become a liability, rather than an asset. But with training lasers, whoever got to the village first would have a very definite advantage. One might need to get across the river before anyone else could set up a defence line, but us - and Three - needed to get to the village. Anything else risked certain defeat.

We hammered out a basic plan - Viper said nothing, of course - just before a flare burst over the foliage. It was time to move. I dropped low, as I had been trained, and took point, advancing towards and through the forest. It didn't seem likely that someone had jumped the gun and started before the flare gave the signal, but it *was* possible. Would Johnston have stopped us sneaking through the forest or would he have applauded us for showing cunning in the face of the enemy? I pushed that thought to the back of my mind as I kept moving forward, peering through the trees. Was that something moving ahead of me…?

I almost pulled the trigger as a shape moved, right in front of me. The small grey creature - I learned later it was called a squirrel - ran up the side of a tree and vanished, while I nearly had a heart attack. I had never seen anything quite like it…I somehow managed to calm my beating heart and continue the advance. Suddenly, sooner than I'd expected, the first houses came into view. They looked…nice, and empty. I'd honestly never seen anything like them on Earth.

Bracing myself, I dropped to the ground and peered towards the river. There was no sign of movement, but that meant nothing. One and Three had the same training we had, after all, and they'd know to keep low as they advanced. It was much - much - easier to spot someone running forward, standing up. I almost gave the go-ahead signal, then froze as I saw four shapes advancing towards the river. Moments later, I heard the sound of shooting.

Joker crawled up next to me. "One must have run into Three," he said.

I nodded in agreement, then signalled the squad forward. One, trapped on the wrong side of the river, had decided to gamble. They'd surrendered stealth in favour of speed, running towards the bridge as if the devil himself was after them. I suspected, from what I was seeing, that Three had intended to secure the village and run right into One. It was a stroke of luck for us, I decided, as I passed orders using hand signals. If we were lucky, One and Three would weaken themselves significantly before we took a hand.

And then Viper opened fire. I saw two recruits - both from Three, I thought - flash red as his lasers struck them, but the remainder dropped to the ground and returned fire in our direction. The laser beams were invisible - bullets are invisible in flight too, no matter what you see in the flicks - yet we knew they were there. I returned fire myself, trying to take out as many of the enemy as possible, but it was stalemate. We were unable to advance.

"You fucking idiot," Joker swore at Viper. "You…"

"Take Professor and Thug and move to the right," I said. Maybe I wasn't formally in charge - Johnston hadn't designated anyone to serve as commander - but *someone* had to do it. "Posh, Bandit and I will move to the left. Everyone else stays here and lays down covering fire."

"Gotcha," Joker said.

Another round of shooting broke out as one of the enemy took possession of a house and turned it into a makeshift strongpoint. Smartass's webbing flashed red as he copped a hit; he swore loudly, rose to his feet and stamped off towards the exit. I half-hoped he'd find a way to signal to us, yet I knew not to expect it. Greater love hath no man for his friends who lays down his life in their defence, but asking someone to endure a chewing out from the Drill Instructors and umpteen thousand push-ups is a bit much. Besides, trying to cheat so openly would only get him a black mark on his record.

"Go," I said.

The stay-behind group, including Viper, laid down covering fire with enthusiasm as the two flanking parties set off, hoping to get better firing positions. It was probably more intimidating to have real bullets cracking through the air, smashing into branches and trees, but for the moment we weren't allowed to use live ammunition in exercises. I kept my head low as I crawled forward, somehow no longer concerned about the mud staining my uniform; I wondered, vaguely, if it blocked the webbing, then decided it wasn't worth the risk of trying to test it. Maybe I could send Viper forward instead…

I smirked as I saw a group of wet recruits sneaking forward - One must have had a back-up plan, either swimming or fording the river - then nodded to Posh and Bandit. We opened fire as one, catching them in a deadly crossfire. I heard a number of swearwords I'd never heard before as their webbing flashed red, forcing them to stand up and head towards the entrance; I smirked nastily, then turned to crawl into the nearest house. Bandit followed me, but made the mistake of allowing himself to be seen inside the house; someone saw him through the window and took a shot at him before he could get down. His webbing flashed red and he had to leave.

Stalemate, I thought, as we took up firing positions. The house provided protection, but we couldn't hope to cover every angle of approach. I'd made the mistake of losing track of the rest of the squad. For all I knew, Posh and I were the last ones still active. *Now what?*

"We can't stay here," Posh muttered. "They can get in from any angle…"

He was rapidly proved correct. One of the enemy recruits had a far more tactical brain than myself. His comrades forced us to keep our heads down while he scaled the side of the house and sneaked in through one of the upper windows. We didn't hear a thing over the noise of the rifles before he opened fire from the rear and hit Posh in the back. I rolled over, half-convinced that he'd been shot through the window, too late. My webbing flashed red a moment later, taking me out of the game.

"Fuck," I said.

I exchanged irked looks with Posh, then walked out of the house and back towards the entrance. A couple of recruits shot at me, which was pointless, but then they had to be sure I was genuinely out of the match.

(Or maybe they were just rubbing it in.) I tried to see Joker and the others, yet I saw nothing until I reached the entrance. Viper was standing there, slightly apart from the others, while Smartass was doing push-ups under Bainbridge's watchful eye. I guessed he hadn't waited until we were back in the barracks before trying to tell Viper *precisely* what he thought of him.

It was nearly half an hour before Bainbridge finally declared us the victors - Joker and his team, it seemed, had managed to eliminate everyone left after the knife-edge battle. I cheered them as loudly as anyone else as they emerged from the woods, swinging their hips in a manner that would probably have invited a kick anywhere else. Bainbridge glanced down at a terminal in his hand, then coolly started to outline all of our mistakes. Three had run forward too fast, One had tried to be clever and Two - us - had made the mistake of splitting up into three separate forces, none of which could assist the others. In the end, Joker and his two comrades had won only by sheer luck.

"If there had been only two squads, it might have made things more interesting," Bainbridge said. "Did any of you consider a prospective alliance?"

I shook my head. I'd assumed we weren't allowed to make alliances… although, now I thought about it, I recalled it had never been specifically forbidden. Gangs on Earth had made alliances all the time, even though none of them had lasted very long. Why *couldn't* we have tried to make an agreement with One? Or Three?

They would have stabbed us in the back as soon as we beat the other squad, I thought. *Or we would have stabbed* them *in the back.*

"There are times when you will have to make short-term alliances with factions already on the ground," Bainbridge said, shortly. "Of course, *this* time we deliberately made it harder for you to talk before it was time to start shooting. Next time…well, let's see what happens, shall we?"

We went through the whole exercise several times more before we were marched back to the Chow Hall for dinner. It was a fun experience, although it was also some pretty serious training; we learned the advantages of taking cover, of maintaining a distance, of everything else we'd need to know by the time the bullets started flying. By the time we entered the Chow Hall, we were tired and yet happy…

Joker poked me as a new set of recruits entered the hall. "Look at them, Stalker," he said. "Did you ever see such a line of boobs?"

I stared. They wore the same uniforms…but they were utterly out of shape. They stumbled along instead of marching, they looked fearful and ill-prepared…they looked like we must have done, only a month or so ago. I felt a flicker of disgust at their dishevelled appearance, wondering how their Drill Instructors refrained from tearing off their heads and pissing down their necks…

"We probably looked worse than that," I said. One of the recruits even had his belt on the wrong way round. Another had forgotten to apply shaving cream the previous night. I dreaded to *think* what I would have been called, at inspection, if I'd looked so scruffy. "They've only just started."

"Bainbridge would have booted us out if we looked like them," Joker said. It was an article of faith among each of the training platoons that *they* had the roughest, the toughest, the all-around nastiest Drill Instructor. "And Nordstrom would have kicked our asses."

"Probably," I agreed. "And if we're not careful, we'll probably be recycled back to join them."

CHAPTER THIRTEEN

> There's a very old saying that basically boils down to 'hard training, easy mission; easy training, hard mission.' The Marine Corps works hard to make training as realistic as possible, deliberately slanting the deck against the new recruits. In theory, this assists the recruits to handle the (presumably) easier missions they will undertake as qualified marines. However, it is impossible to prepare for all contingencies…
>
> -Professor Leo Caesius

My first sight of the aircraft did not inspire confidence.

Indeed, I hadn't really *seen* a proper aircraft, outside flicks, for my entire life. The airbus that had flown me to the spaceport on Earth was an antigravity craft; the shuttle that had taken me to Mars was a spacecraft. I believed, from what I'd been taught at school, that aircraft had been banned on Earth years ago for polluting the atmosphere, something I learned later was a minor attempt to come to grips with the ecological collapse that had rendered large parts of the planet uninhabitable. The craft in front of me looked as though it was on its last legs, within bare minutes of falling apart. I really *didn't* want to climb inside.

I had no choice, of course.

"Before you graduate," Bainbridge informed us, "you will have to qualify for a jumper badge from both atmosphere and orbit. This, your very first jump, will be made from this aircraft and you will be expected to do nothing, beyond jumping out of the plane. The parachutes are completely automatic, crammed with" - he spat - "*civilian*-grade safety features. If something happens to the main parachute, the secondary parachute will unfurl instead; if something happens to the secondary parachute, an automated antigravity system will come online and save your worthless hides. There are *civilians* who do this for fun, every day, so you lot should have no trouble at all."

I swallowed. "There are people who do this for *fun*?"

"I used to jump from low orbit," Posh said. He didn't sound as though he was boasting, although it was pretty obvious that it was a rich man's sport. "It's great fun provided you handle it properly."

Viper threw me a nasty sneer. "What's the matter, Stalker? Having doubts?"

I was, of course, but I was damned if I would admit it to him. Viper was growing worse and it was all I could do to convince Joker and the others not to arrange a nasty accident. It didn't help that *someone* had given him a push in the shower, which had given Viper a black eye and the rest of us an extra hour of punishment exercises. I honestly felt like giving up on him; perhaps, if we all complained to the Drill Instructors, we could have him removed from the squad. He was nothing more than a load.

"Silence," Bainbridge bellowed. He glared us into submission, then continued. "The jumpmaster will check your parachutes before you step up to the hatch, but you will not be pushed out into the air. If you are unable to take that step, recruits, there's no shame in admitting it. Parachute diving has defeated bigger and stronger men than yourselves in the past. Just step back from the edge, sit down on the bench and wait for the plane to return to the ground."

It wasn't a pleasant thought. On one hand, the whole concept of falling from an aircraft towards the ground was utterly fucking terrifying. But on the other hand, I didn't want to fail, not like this. No one would make fun of me for being unable to take the jump; they wouldn't have to, not when I would be recycled back to phase one if I didn't quit. I'd torment myself more than anyone else possibly could.

"Pick up and don your chutes," Bainbridge ordered. "Once you have checked them, check your partner's chute and then proceed to the plane."

"Don't worry," Posh said, very quietly. "I pissed my pants the first time I took a dive too."

I glowered at him, then checked his parachute. It looked good, as far as I could tell; I later learned the parachutes genuinely *were* civilian models, slightly modified. Later, we'd start training on standard military-grade parachutes, designed to open at low attitude. A mistake with one of *those* could send us slamming into the ground before we had a hope of recovery.

They even told us to leave our rifles behind, I thought. We still carried our pistols, but we'd been told to leave the rifles in our storage lockers. It was unusual - and worrying. Normally, *not* carrying one's rifle was a serious offense, punished with dozens of push-ups. For us to be told to leave them behind…*They must be worried about losing them.*

Bainbridge wasn't leaving anything up to the jumpmaster. He checked our chutes as we filed past him and onto the plane. Compared to the shuttle, it was barren; it took me a moment to realise that we were meant to sit against the bulkheads (not an easy task with our chutes) and wait for takeoff. There were no windows, something I found oddly reassuring, even though others clearly found it claustrophobic. A large hologram of a pretty woman appeared the moment the hatches were banged closed and started to run through a safety lecture, but almost none of us paid attention. We were too busy contemplating what was to come.

The engines started, sending shivers running through the aircraft. I braced myself, unsure of what to expect, as the aircraft started to move, then surged forward so hard I grabbed hold of the handles and held on for dear life. It tilted sharply, then roared into the sky; I felt my ears pop as it wobbled from side to side, climbing rapidly. I couldn't help thinking that God was angry with us for daring to fly, slapping gusts of wind against the aircraft. Later, of course, I learned that Mars had uncomfortably strong turbulence in the upper atmosphere. But it still beat flying through a hurricane.

"You will not be expected to guide your descent," Bainbridge said. He ignored the sound of someone being sick at the back. "All you have to do is take a step out of the aircraft and drop like a stone."

I wished he hadn't said that. The butterflies in my stomach were mating and producing little baby butterflies. I told myself that it was fine, that I was wearing a civilian parachute, that civilians would bitch like anything if something went wrong…and yet, it was hard to even think about standing up and walking to the hatch. The deck was shaking so badly - the aircraft shuddered every three minutes, as if someone was timing the turbulence - that I wasn't sure *anyone* could stand up without losing his balance moments later.

"There's no ground-fire," Nordstrom added. "Nothing reaching up to swat you from the air, just…a safe and easy descent to the ground. You'll be back in barracks before you know it."

"And there's no shame in declining to jump," Johnston concluded. He seemed to have forgotten that he was meant to be one of the disciplinarians. "You can sit back down and no one will think any less of you."

The hatch opened with an almighty *bang*. It was hard to see much, from where I was sitting, but I could hear the sound of the wind rushing past as the aircraft entered the jump zone. The jumpmaster stood, carefully hooked himself onto the plane, then peered out into the atmosphere. He was hanging bare millimetres from a lethal fall, linked only by a line thinner than a piece of string, yet he seemed completely calm. And he wasn't even wearing a parachute!

"All right," he called. "Who's up first?"

Nordstrom stepped up to the hatch and jumped. It was so quick that I barely saw it. He'd just jumped and vanished! The jumpmaster made a thumbs up sign, then nodded to Bainbridge, who jabbed a finger at the first victim. Focus, an older recruit from Squad One, stood, shuffled towards the hatch and perched on the edge of oblivion. I watched, unable to take my eyes off him, as he toppled forwards…

The jumpmaster caught him. "Jump out, don't fall," he ordered. "Try again?"

Focus gave him a nasty look - rather ungratefully, I felt - and leapt into the atmosphere. The jumpmaster watched him, gave another thumbs up, then nodded. Bainbridge chose a second jumper, then a third; he was stabbing at us at random, rather than letting us form lines or jump out by squads. I think he was trying to make it easier on us, but I didn't feel very reassured. It might have been better if we had done it by lines…

My body didn't want to move when Bainbridge pointed at me. It was all I could do to stand up, to walk forward; I hadn't been this nervous when I walked into the unarmed combat pit for the first time. But then,

I hadn't really known what to expect. Here, I knew all too well. I took my place behind Hope and watched as first Totem, then Hope stepped up to the hatch and jumped into the air. Moments later, their parachutes blossomed into life, slowing their falls. I already knew, from the safety briefing, that the men on the ground would find them at once and get them back to the waiting room. They'd also have a chance to change their pants, if necessary.

"You're up," the jumpmaster shouted.

I could barely hear him over the wind. It was hard, incredibly hard, to inch up to the hatch and stare down towards the landing zone, far below. I had known, intellectually, that planets were big, yet now I grasped it emotionally for the first time. Mars is only half the size of Earth, but there's no such thing as a 'small' planet. The landscape spread out below me was terrifyingly huge.

"Jump," the Jumpmaster ordered.

I hesitated, completely frozen. I wanted to dive back into the plane, to hide from the vast landscape below me, to surrender to my fears. My mind was already coming up with excuses; I'd been born in the CityBlocks, I'd been taught to fear open spaces, I had nothing to be ashamed of…I could go…go where?

I threw myself forward in an undignified tumble. Gravity asserted itself at once and I plummeted down, straight towards the landing zone. I felt hot liquid in my pants as I lost control of my bladder, convinced - at a very primal level - that I was about to die. And then there was a terrifying jerk and my fall slowed, rapidly. When I glanced upwards, I saw the orange parachute safely deployed above my head.

I will not be beaten by this, I told myself. I might have pissed my pants, but I'd done it. I'd survived the urge to just give up, to put my tail between my legs and go home. But then, I had no home to go back to. Would it have been easier to quit if I'd had somewhere to go? I didn't want to know. Instead, I made myself a silent promise. *I will not be beaten at all.*

The descent became almost relaxing as I slowly grew used to the wide open landscape. It was almost a shock when the ground came up and I landed, the parachute falling around me as I touched down. I untangled myself from the backpack, crawled out from under the canopy and looked around. The jump zone was in the middle of a grassy plain, covered with the red weed that gave Mars its breathable atmosphere. I started to fold up the parachute, as per instructions, as I saw the aircar racing towards me. The ground crews had been waiting for us.

"You made it," Hope called. We might have been in different squads - and bitter enemies on the training grounds - but we were united today. "That was fun, wasn't it?"

I scowled. "I need to change my pants," I grumbled. There was no point in trying to hide it, not when there was a visible stain running down my legs. "Where do we go to do that?"

"There's spare uniforms in the base," the driver assured me. "You'll be fine."

Only three of us, it seemed, refused to make the jump. They were taken back down in the plane, then hurried off by the Drill Instructors and - by the time we returned to barracks - their bunks had already been stripped bare. We never saw them again, although I later learned that one of them had gone on to be a military policeman and another had become a surprisingly successful Civil Guardsman. Boot Camp was so intensive that the other military branches were quite happy to take our rejects, provided they quit rather than broke one of the rules and were kicked out. It was one of the ways the marines quietly gained influence over the other services.

"Congratulations," Bainbridge said, as we gathered after a quick change of clothes. I wasn't the only one who'd had an unfortunate accident on the way down. "You have just endured the most terrifying experience in Boot Camp until we start practicing in zero-gee. Now…all you have to do is get up there and do it again."

He wasn't kidding. We jumped four more times, each time using a different model of parachute. I rapidly learned the difference between army-issue and marine-issue, although it wasn't until Nordstrom explained it to us after our landing that I understood just what I was seeing. An army parachutist using an automatic parachute would often have it deploy too soon, slowing his fall and exposing him to enemy fire from the ground; a marine would fall like a rock until the last possible moment, whereupon he would pull the cord and deploy his parachute. It was safer, in the sense the enemy would have less time to take aim, but dangerous, if the cord wasn't pulled in time. A parachutist might slam into the ground before slowing his fall and die…

That was how we lost Ace.

I hadn't known him well, not really. He was one of the shining stars of Squad One; a recruit from a background that actually prepared him rather well for the marines. I certainly don't think he showed any hesitation when jumping out for the first time; even Viper, our snake in the grass, had managed to leap from the plane. And I have no idea just why he failed to deploy his parachute in time. All I know is that he hit the ground at terrifying speed and died.

We saw his body, afterwards. It looked surprisingly intact - most of us had seen plenty of violence, physical or sexual, on the flicks - but it was dead. Ace had been handsome, I supposed; now, he was just a broken sack of bones. It took time for us to realise that this could have happened to *any* of us, that our training wasn't completely safe, that we could die before we graduated and saw the enemy. Like so much else, we knew it and yet we didn't quite believe. We were a sombre group of recruits that night, completely subdued. Even Viper looked pale and wan before Lights Out.

There was a small ceremony for him the following evening, after we had completed our daily exercises and training schedule. All of the training platoons gathered in the great hall and listened, silently, as Bainbridge spoke about Ace. I hadn't known he'd been born to a family on Shaddock, or that life there was so hard that the planet's major export was *people*, or that Ace had had four parents and seven siblings. It sounded like a happy group marriage to me, one designed to provide a safety net for children who could lose their biological parents at any moment. He had had something I'd lacked until I joined the marines…

…And yet, when he'd started to look for a career, he'd chosen to join too.

"We do our best to eliminate accidents, but there is always a certain level of risk," Bainbridge said, after he had finished the brief eulogy. Ace had asked that his body be shipped home, if he died during training, and the corps would honour his request. "You should all understand, now at least, just how dangerous this can be. Training will go on, of course, if you wish to continue. If not, speak to one of us and we will see to your separation from the corps."

I understood what we were being told, even if Bainbridge didn't say it outright. If we thought it was suddenly too dangerous to proceed, we could quit. The corps didn't want to keep anyone against their will, not when it needed men who would never quit. I could have left…

…But I didn't.

Life was cheap in the Undercity, before the end; I'd known children who had died before reaching their teens and adults who had been casually murdered by the gangs. My own family had been killed in a spasm of gang violence. And yet, Ace's death affected me more than any of those. Perhaps it was because he had been trying, unlike so many others, to become part of something greater than himself, or perhaps it was because he'd had true promise, promise that had been smashed along with his life. I mourned him as well as I could, then carried on. It was all I could do.

I never learned to love parachute jumps, not even after completing hundreds of them as part of basic training. But I learned to endure, to continue despite my fear…

…And not, whatever happened, to allow fear to slow me down.

CHAPTER FOURTEEN

The downside of 'realistic' military training is the prospect of an accidental death - or several, if something goes badly wrong. Marine recruits have suffered a number of ghastly fates, ranging from drowning to depressurisation, but the corps has gone on. Safety is important, it insists, yet realism is also important. The Civil Guard safety record, during basic training, is far more impressive…a fact that only looks good when seen in isolation. On deployment, marines - quite simply - do far better than anyone else.

-Professor Leo Caesius

They worked us hard for days after the accident.

I think they wanted to keep us from having time to brood and they were probably right. Ace had been a good recruit, one of the best. His death proved that *anyone* could die in training. We shot off thousands of rounds, marched hundreds of miles, beat the crap out of the younger platoon (and had the crap beaten out of us by the older platoons) and generally did our best to get over any lingering trauma caused by the death. By the time we were marched into the doctor's office for another round of injections, two more of us had quit and the rest were feeling pushed to their limits.

"You will be pleased to know that higher authority has deemed you worthy of more investment," Bainbridge said, as we rubbed our arms after the injections. "It will take several weeks for it to bed in, but you are now capable of eating a wide range of foodstuffs without suffering any ill effects. You will be able to eat grass, if necessary, while you are on deployment. It does have its limits, of course, but it makes it easier to support a marine detachment on the far side of the Empire."

He went on about it in great and tedious detail. As I understood it at the time, there were plants that simply couldn't be eaten without ill effects, even if they did include some of the vital necessities of life. The injections would suppress the bad reactions, allowing us to eat them. They did have the great disadvantage of forcing our bodies to expel anything completely useless faster than normal, something that might be inconvenient in a combat zone, but I've yet to discover anything that didn't have disadvantages, no matter what the eggheads said.

"So basically we're always going to swallow instead of spit," Joker muttered.

"Shut up," I muttered back.

I wasn't quiet enough. Bainbridge, as I may have mentioned, had abnormally sharp ears.

"Are you interrupting me?" He asked, in a polite tone that sent chills down our spines. "Is there something more important than my words exciting you?"

"No, sir," we said, hastily.

"Drop and give me fifty," he ordered, then continued as we dropped to the ground. "There *will* be some adverse effects from these injections, so you will spend the next couple of days on light duty. The time will not be wasted, however. You will attend the first lecture from a guest professor this evening."

He was right, unfortunately. Most of us, including me, spent the day retching, although none of us actually threw up. *Light* duties consisted of more training and exercises than we'd done during Hell Week - it says a lot about how far we'd come that we took it in our stride - while they watched us carefully for more serious reactions. Joker had the worst of it, I think; he stumbled to his knees in the middle of a training run, dry-retching until I thought he was going to be genuinely sick. I helped him to his feet and ran with him until we reached the finishing line; oddly, none of the Drill Instructors berated us for coming in last. They must have been more worried than they let on.

That evening, after chow, we were herded into the briefing hall and told to sit down and relax. I couldn't help feeling as if I were going back to school, although I think I would have learned a great deal more if school had been run like Boot Camp. It probably couldn't have been, though. Recruits like us selected ourselves; we were in Boot Camp because we *wanted* to be in Boot Camp. Historically, conscript armies haven't had the motivation or training of volunteer armies and I saw no reason why it would be different for us. Marine training, as elaborate as it is, can only work when someone willingly places themselves into Boot Camp and submits to the Drill Instructors. I could have quit at any moment…

…But I couldn't quit school.

Professor Sidney Baldwin struck me, at the time, as an odd duck. It wasn't until much later that I learned he was a typical marine academic. Marines are thinkers - *that* had been hammered into our heads time and time again - and perhaps it wasn't too surprising that some of us went back to the academic world to earn degrees. It was rare for a marine, serving or retired, to go to one of the big universities, but there *was* a War College on the Slaughterhouse and several smaller universities where freedom of thought was considered more than lip service to an unattainable ideal. I hadn't heard anything good about university in the Undercity, yet the War College sounded like fun. But I never had a chance to go.

"This is not a test," Baldwin said. Unlike the teachers at school, he didn't have to shout - or beg - for silence. None of us would have dared pass notes, throw paper aeroplanes or bully our comrades anywhere near the Drill Instructors. And even if they hadn't been seated in the back, we wouldn't have done it anyway. "You can go to sleep, if you like, and I won't care."

Hah, I thought. *Baldwin* might not have cared, but the Drill Instructors certainly would. And besides, I doubted they'd be wasting our time. What Baldwin told us would probably relate to some aspect of our training, perhaps something just far enough away to give us an opportunity to forget before we needed it. I was starting to learn how they operated by now.

"Tonight, I'm going to talk about *trust*," Baldwin continued. "Who do you trust?"

He smiled at us all, then went on. "Trust is the glue that binds society together," he said, briskly. "If you are able to trust someone to keep their word, you can rely on them; if you can't, you *cannot* rely on them. By now, I believe most of you will have learned that you have to rely on your comrades to get through Boot Camp. Can you *trust* them?"

I nodded, slowly. I didn't trust Viper, but I trusted the others. Two months of intensive training had broken down the barriers between us as we were forced to work together. Some of the tests were simply impossible to pass unless we worked together.

"A cynic might assert that trust is based on being able to *get* someone for *breaking* trust," Baldwin continued. "It would be more accurate to say that trust is based on reputation. A person who breaks trust, for whatever reason, is unlikely to be trusted in future. This is so true that a person who might have a good *reason* to break trust is still going to be tainted."

He took a breath. "In early human societies, trust only really existed between families. It was possible to trust your parents, or your siblings, but not someone outside them. Later, as societies became more sophisticated, trust extended to one's social group. It became possible to trust someone who shared your race, or religion, yet not someone who didn't. This happened because the group tended to exclude or punish anyone who broke trust.

"You will discover, if you graduate, that that applies to us too. A marine is far more trustworthy, you will believe, than anyone else."

I frowned. No one in their right mind trusted *anyone* in the Undercity, not even their own family. I'd known that Trevor would happily sell out the rest of us, if it made him wealthy and powerful. Others had sold their siblings to the gangs, or preyed on their schoolmates, or raped and murdered their partners. To put your life in someone else's hands was asking for trouble. But I'd learned differently at Boot Camp.

"The development of certain human societies reflected the development of trust," Baldwin said. "Societies that managed to forge trusted links became wealthy and powerful; societies that didn't, for whatever reason, tended to stagnate. For example, aristocrats were willing to make and honour promises to other aristocrats, but not to honour promises made to those they considered their inferiors. By breaking those promises, often made for tactical advantage, they proved *themselves* to be untrustworthy, which undermined the very basis of their society and eventually led to their destruction. The true test of a society lay in how it would handle the issue of trust between different groups. This eventually led to the development of contract law and neutral courts."

He smiled, rather humourlessly. "A contract, at base, is an agreement between two people," he continued. "I could sign a contract with you to provide a service, in exchange for payment, and - on that level - there would be very little difference between a written contract and a verbal agreement. The importance of contract law, however, lies in the fact that there would be an enforcement mechanism. Should I fail to uphold my side of the contract, you could take me to court.

"It is difficult to exaggerate the importance of this development. Historically, humans tended to support their own tribe, even when their comrade was clearly in the wrong. An outsider could be cheated at will, which placed limits on just how far trust - and hence society - could spread. The development of legal courts that looked at contracts - and only the contracts, instead of other factors - allowed trust to expand beyond a given group. It was this trust that allowed for the development of far more complicated - and enduring - societies."

I had a feeling he was right, although it was hard to put it into words. There hadn't been anything *permanent* in the Undercity. The gangs were held together by the strongest, who lost their positions when they were challenged and beaten by their rivals. Nor did anyone place any faith in the courts, or schools, or doctors…there had been no trust. And who in their right mind would have trusted *anyone*? It was always wise to keep one eye on the door, just in case it might be time to make a run for it.

"So you might ask," Baldwin said, "why is society so fucked up today?"

There were some chuckles. He waited for us to finish, then went on.

"It didn't take long for the new system of contract law - the system that binds the Empire together - to get undermined," he warned. "A very basic contract, like the one I suggested earlier, might be no more than a single page. However, a contract detailing something vastly more complex might run to hundreds of pages, which no human could hope to read, let alone comprehend. There might even be a section that completely invalidated the rest of the contract, or insisted on one party meeting impossible conditions to cancel the contract, or even honest confusion about the measuring system. I have seen legal cases where one party clung to a single section of the contract, while the other pointed to a different section or started arguing about the precise meaning of several words.

"Furthermore, the courts themselves tended to become undermined. Money talked. So did political influence. Right now, contracts between colony worlds and interstellar corporations tend to have a clause stipulating that any disputes between the two parties have to be settled in the Galactic Supreme Court, which is based on Earth. The corporations, which have a vast amount of influence on Earth, are therefore able to influence the Galactic Supreme Court to rule in their favour. And, as these rulings give a legal basis for military intervention if necessary, the decisions are often enforced. It isn't unknown for a corporation to deliberately provoke an incident just so they can get military support."

He peered down at us for a long moment. "It is no exaggeration to suggest that there is no trust in the Empire today," he stated, bluntly. "And many of the problems you will have to deal with come from that lack of trust.

"No one in their right mind would expect the Galactic Supreme Court to rule in favour of a colony world, when that colony world is facing a major corporation. Nor would anyone expect the Grand Senate to do anything about the situation. A corporation can even convince the Grand Senate, the source of all authority and power within the Empire, to make a ruling that places legal authority over a colony world into the hands of a corporation, if there is the tiniest of fig leaves to justify it. And then they act all surprised when the colonists rebel, when they decide they would prefer to fight rather than bend over for the corporations."

I nodded in understanding. No one would have expected anything more in the Undercity. A person with power and influence would use that power and influence to get more, at least until they grew old and were replaced by someone even nastier. The corporations had the same issue, on a much larger scale; the only major difference, as far as I could tell, was that people actually *rebelled* against them. It took me years to realise that the gangs had been up close and personal in the Undercity, while the corporations were often a distant threat.

"Humans do not appreciate acts of blatant unfairness," Baldwin noted. "A colonist who is emotionally invested in his farm will not like losing it because someone thousands of light years away has made a decision. He will fight - and so will hundreds of others. A person who faces legal discrimination on a regular basis will rapidly lose all respect for the law - and why should he respect it, when it is biased against him? Their unwillingness to submit to outside arbitration will eventually lead to social collapse. Indeed, I was once on a planet where the victors in a legal dispute would always be the ones who laid on the biggest feast for the outsiders. Would you be surprised to hear that their opponents often refused to accept the rulings against them?"

There was another point right there, I noted silently. No one in the Undercity had been emotionally invested in anything. We had been given the apartment, rather than paying for it ourselves; we were given prizes at school, even if we hadn't earned them. Finding a partner, having children...even they were stripped of all feeling. But if someone had mocked my time at Boot Camp, I would have been furious. Because, in the end, I'd worked hard to get as far as I had. We'd *all* worked hard.

"You will discover, as you start your careers, that the marine corps is one of the few institutions left to hold any public trust," Baldwin added. "Despite those awful flicks, despite the fact we're summoned to deal with problems caused by political misjudgements, we are still trusted. We are regarded as being tough, but fair. We must struggle, constantly, to live up to the trust they place in us."

I nodded. We'd been told there were lines we must never cross, regardless of the situation. It was a far cry from the Undercity, where there had been *no* lines, but I understood. A reputation for looting, raping and burning our way through civilian towns would undermine their trust in us at terrifying speed. We'd wind up as just another bunch of thugs, as unreliable as the Civil Guard.

"That won't be easy," Baldwin concluded. His voice was suddenly very cold. "Once, the Empire was held together by trust, by faith in its government. Now, there is no trust and no faith in government, or the courts, or the military. Most of the problems you will have to tackle are *caused*, directly or indirectly, by that lack of faith. There may come a time when the weight of that distrust pulls the Empire down around our ears."

That was, in hindsight, the first time I heard a suggestion that the Empire was falling apart. It wasn't something I wanted to hear, not really. I *liked* the thought of being able to go somewhere else, somewhere better. But, the more I came to grapple with the realities of Empire, the more I realised that Baldwin had - if anything - understated the case. No one trusted anyone…

…And, because of it, the Empire was gravely weakened.

Everywhere might end up like the Undercity, I thought. It was a terrifying prospect. No law…nothing, but the rule of the strong, forever. Gangs taking territory, only to lose it again when their leaders died or their enemies made common cause long enough to prune them back, with countless civilians caught in the middle. *Everything we built might be lost.*

It wasn't a comforting thought.

From then onwards, we were given one lecture a week, covering dozens of different subjects that touched on future issues. We looked forward to them, because they were a chance to sit down and relax; they also made us think, for the first time, of just what it was like to operate in the midst of a civilian population. It wasn't something we'd encountered in the simulations. We'd only had to worry about defeating the other squads without being defeated ourselves.

Naturally, that changed shortly afterwards.

CHAPTER FIFTEEN

If anything, as Colonel Stalker noted, Professor Baldwin understated the problem. The lack of trust was everywhere. No one trusted the law courts, true, but no one trusted the schools, or the universities, or the media, or anything else. Indeed, education was so badly out of shape because teachers weren't trusted to use their common sense. Instead, they were expected to follow a specific learning plan, even when the plan didn't fit the situation. A teacher who tried to do otherwise, who taught the kids the truth, could expect to be fired in short order.

-Professor Leo Caesius

"All right," Nordstrom said, when we had assembled at the RV point. "It's time for something a *little* more challenging."

We winced, inwardly. Weeks of training had introduced us to everything from simulated IEDs to simulated mortar fire. We'd learned, very rapidly, how to lay traps for the enemy and, at the same time, what to watch for when advancing towards the enemy position. It hadn't been easy. I'd lost my 'life' during one particularly embarrassing exercise when I'd located a poorly-hidden sensor, only to discover - too late - that some smartass on the other side had placed an IED underneath, just waiting for someone to come along and try to take the sensor. Nordstrom had been *quite* sarcastic about the whole affair.

"A gang of terrorist scumbags have taken over the local village," Nordstrom continued, darkly. "Your task is to liberate the village, free the hostages and capture or kill as many of the terrorists as possible. There are no other units in the vicinity, so everything rests on you."

No artillery, I thought, sourly. Not that I *wanted* to pound the village into bedrock - that would kill hostages and terrorists alike - but it would have been nice to know that some big guns were on hand. *And we won't have any specialised snipers either.*

Nordstrom looked us up and down. "Viper will be in command, this time," he said. "Try not to fuck up."

He took a step backwards, making it clear that he was now nothing more than an observer. I cursed under my breath as Viper unfurled the map and peered down at the village; we'd all been given opportunities to command, but none of us particularly trusted Viper. How could we? I suppose that was what Baldwin had meant, when he'd talked about how the loss of trust undermined society. Our lack of trust in him made him an ineffective commander at best, an outright failure at worst.

"This is how we're going to do it," he said, pointing to the map. "Joker and Stalker have the best eyes, so I want you to crawl to here" - he tapped a location on the map - "and observe the village from a distance. Locate the terrorists and report back to me. The rest of us will proceed to here" - another location, closer to the village - "and make more detailed plans based on their reports."

I glanced at the map, making sure I knew where to go. Our first exercises in map-reading had taught us precisely why one of the most dangerous things in the world is a junior officer with a map - we got rather badly lost, which led to more sarcasm from the Drill Instructors - but we'd managed to get a great deal better with practice. In theory, Viper was right; the position he'd selected should allow us to peer down at the village without being seen, provided we approached with care. There shouldn't be any villagers in the fields, not if they were being held hostage, but smart terrorists would watch for approaching trouble.

And as the terrorists are being played by a senior platoon, I thought, *they'd know the tricks and the terrain already.*

"It doesn't sound like a bad plan," Joker muttered, as we slipped away from the platoon. "I expected something worse."

I frowned. Viper hadn't done badly, so far, but I still didn't trust him. I kept that thought to myself as we approached the fields, keeping low, then started to crawl up the hill overlooking the village. There were no sensors watching for trouble, as far as we could tell, but we took precautions anyway. It wasn't until we were halfway up the hill that we ran straight into a watching terrorist, half-hidden under a bush. We blinked at him for a second, then charged before he could raise his gun. We didn't dare shoot him - the sound would have alerted his friends - so we crashed into him, battering the bastard to the ground. He fought back viciously until Joker pushed his unopened Ka-Bar into his neck.

"You're dead, asshole," he muttered.

"Fuck it," the 'terrorist' muttered back.

I keyed my radio. "Viper, Stalker," I said, subvocalising the words so they couldn't be overhead by anyone without access to the radio net. "One tango located and neutralised; I say again, one tango located and neutralised. Proceeding."

There was a pause before he replied. "Did he get an alert out?"

"Unknown, but probably not," I said. "Proceeding."

Viper, thankfully, didn't ask anything else as we reached the ridge and peered down at the village. It was, I'd been assured, a typical farming hamlet; a general store, a church, a school, a handful of houses and very little else. I wouldn't have considered it particularly important, but I supposed the locals thought it the centre of their universe. We peered down, searching for targets, and saw nothing. The entire village looked deserted.

I frowned. "Could they have moved the hostages *out* of the village?"

"It wasn't included in the briefing," Joker pointed out.

That meant nothing, I knew. Briefings covered the bare facts and little else; sometimes, the facts were wrong, just to keep us on our toes. If I'd been taking hostages, I might have considered moving them elsewhere, just to make life interesting for any would-be rescuers. But then, it would really depend on my long-term objectives. Just what did the terrorists actually *want*?

Something *moved*. I tensed as I saw someone sneaking through the village, carrying a rifle in one hand. It *had* to be one of the terrorists.

We'd been told that some terrorists were downright idiotic - videos of bomb-making classes blowing themselves up had made us all laugh - but it wasn't something to take for granted. I peered down at him, watching closely as he walked over to the school. Two more armed men appeared, both looking grim. If there were others, they had to be inside the building.

Unless they're turning the place into a fortress, I thought. Given our lack of heavy weapons, they could slow us down considerably if they decided to fight for every building. *But do they have the numbers to do that?*

I keyed my radio, again. "Viper, Stalker; the tangos appear to have occupied the schoolhouse. I say again, the tangos appear to have occupied the schoolhouse. No other buildings appear to be occupied. I say again, no other buildings appear to be occupied."

"As far as we can tell," Joker added.

"Understood, Stalker," Viper said. "Numbers?"

"Three living tangos," I said. "If there are others…"

Viper cut me off. "Remain in place; I say again, remain in place," he said. "We're moving to launch position now."

I scowled as the connection broke, then peered down at the hillside. It wouldn't be easy to get down to the village from where we were, at least not without being seen. I looked for a prospective route that might give us at least some cover, but saw nothing. We'd have to sneak back the way we came, then around the village to have any hope at all of getting close without being detected.

"Fourth tango," Joker whispered. "On the church roof."

"Shit," I muttered. "Call it in."

Joker did so, just as two more terrorists emerged from the schoolhouse. I hastily tried to estimate how many terrorists - and hostages - might be hidden in the building, but gave up when I realised it was impossible. Growing up in the Undercity had left me with a skewed idea of just how many people could be fitted into a tiny apartment and my first estimates had always been an order of magnitude too high. There were six terrorists now, not counting the one we'd killed. God alone knew if there were any others.

And my estimates for how many villagers there are might be off too, I thought, grimly. *There can't be more than a hundred people in the village.*

Actually, there were probably a great deal less. Most people in the Undercity were either sheep or wolves; the former would offer no resistance to terrorists, the latter would probably be dead by now, having flung themselves on their tormentors. But villagers on a colony world? They might well know how to use weapons, or have the nerve to defend themselves…I contemplated what my life might have been like, if I'd grown up in such a place, then pushed the thought aside as the squad appeared at the edge of the village, moving forward in a careful manner. Something was nagging at my mind, but I wasn't sure what it was… something worrying.

"Tangos one, two and three are still outside the schoolhouse," I warned, keying my radio. "Tangos four and five are advancing towards our position; tango six is on top of the church."

"They may be coming to relieve the moron we killed," Joker muttered. "Or to check on him. He didn't have a visible radio, but that means nothing."

I cursed under my breath. We'd been told a little about human augmentation, which ranged from implanted weapons to enhanced muscles and cyborg modifications that allowed humans to survive in space without protective garments. If a terrorist happened to have an implanted radio…it wasn't something I would care to have, but it might come in handy, under the right circumstances. Or what if there had been some kind of signal the dead terrorist was meant to send that had been missed?

"Understood," Viper said. "Remain in place, but avoid contact."

Joker blinked. "Avoid contact?"

I shared his astonishment. If the terrorists came up the hillside, they'd stumble over us no matter what we did. There was no way we could both remain in place and avoid contact! My mouth dropped open as I realised, finally, what was bothering me about the advance. The squad wasn't moving forward organically; it was being directed, with Viper pulling the strings. He wasn't leaving any room for the point men to take advantage of unexpected opportunities or to react to any surprises.

"They'll be on us in minutes," I said. If there had been just one terrorist, we might have jumped him, but two were depressingly even odds. "We need to leave or engage them as soon as they come closer."

"Do *not* engage," Viper ordered. Down below, the terrorists had started walking up the hillside. "When we engage..."

It became academic before he could finish the sentence. Tango six had spotted the advancing squad and opened fire, alerting his comrades. I swore, then opened fire myself, picking off both tangos four and five. Tangos one and two had started to run towards the squad; tango three had jumped back into the schoolhouse. I knew it wouldn't be long before they started killing hostages, if they hadn't already.

"Take out six," I ordered, sharply. Joker was a better shot that me, even though I hated to admit it. "Viper, Stalker; get in quickly, now!"

"Countermand," Viper snapped. "We need to get all our people into the village!"

"*This isn't the time for a fucking debate*," I snapped back. On paper, there was nothing wrong with what he was doing, but time had just run out! We needed to save the remainder of the hostages before it was too late. "Get the point men forward..."

"Don't argue with me," Viper thundered. "Get..."

He was drowned out by a sudden burst of shooting from one of the buildings. I swore out loud as the point men came under heavy fire. They hadn't taken the time to check for traps, even though they should have *known* to take precautions. Viper barked orders no one heeded as the advance came apart, Professor hurling a grenade into the building seconds before a burst of fire sent him tumbling to the ground. The shooting stopped, too late. A flash of light marked the destruction of the schoolhouse...

"Exercise terminated," Nordstrom said, over the communications network. It looked as though we weren't going to have a chance to exterminate the remaining terrorists, even though it would be pointless. "I say again, exercise terminated."

"I'm going to fucking kill him," Joker snarled, as he picked himself up. "What sort of stupid fucking idiot would come up with a half-assed plan like that?"

I found it hard to disagree as we walked back down the hillside and back to the RV point, where Viper was surrounded by a handful of angry-looking recruits. It reminded me of school, when one of the unpopular kids was lynched and beaten to death; Viper looked torn between defending himself and keeping his mouth firmly shut. If the Drill Instructors hadn't been there, I think the whole issue would have been settled through violence.

"*That* was one of the worst showings I have ever seen in my long career," Nordstrom said, coldly. "Seven recruits killed, along with twenty-five hostages. A *complete* failure by any reasonable standard."

I swallowed. We'd been told that accidents happened during hostage rescue missions and, sometimes, the hostages were killed by the people trying to save them. But this time, the terrorists had had a plan to kill all the hostages and, thanks to Viper, had been given time to hit the switch before it was too late. If it had happened in reality, I had a feeling there would be an inquest and possibly a court martial. Viper had screwed up badly…and, as it wasn't the first time we'd gone through such an exercise, he hadn't learned from earlier screw-ups.

"So tell me," Nordstrom said. "What went wrong?"

He glowered at Viper, who paled. "This recruit's plan didn't work," he said, slowly. At least he was willing to admit it had been *his* plan. "*That's* what went wrong."

"How true," Nordstrom agreed. "And *why* didn't the plan work?"

"Because the enemy saw us coming," Viper said.

"True, but *very* incomplete," Nordstrom said. His voice was very cold. "You committed two separate cardinal sins, recruit. The first was that you assumed your enemy was stupid. The second was that you clung to the plan even when it fell apart."

He paused, significantly. "Your plan wasn't a bad one, but it failed to take account of a sudden change in conditions. You intended to assault the schoolhouse from three different directions, after getting your people in place. However, the enemy had both spotters watching for your approach and a pre-prepared ambush. You discovered the former, thanks to your observers" - he nodded at Joker and me - "and yet you failed to adjust your plan. The latter could have been discovered with a more careful approach, giving you a chance to back off without alerting the enemy."

"Stalker and Joker already killed a terrorist," Viper protested.

"Which wasn't an immediate problem," Nordstrom said. "You would have had time to decide on a new approach before the terrorists realised they were missing someone."

He paused, his expression darkening. "At that point, the whole idea was sinking fast. Your original plan was dead in the water. You could have ordered a rush at the schoolhouse, using grenades to clear the buildings as you rushed past them, if you had thought it wasn't worth the risk of backing off and finding a new angle of approach. Instead, you hesitated and kept following the plan until it was far too late. It cost you the mission and far too many lives."

I swallowed. It hadn't been my fault, but I still felt as though I'd failed.

"These missions are never easy," Nordstrom said. "We shall be doing it again and again, until you understand just how to balance planning and on-the-fly improvising. Do you understand me?"

"YES, SIR," we bellowed.

"Good," Nordstrom said. He made a show of checking his watch. "Seeing we still have another hour before chow, we might as well spend it on the training field. There are some exercises that will remind you, once again, of the value of teamwork..."

"Perhaps he's a plant," Professor muttered, later that night. Our free hour wasn't, thanks to an order to go through everything that had gone wrong and work out how we could have done better. "They put him here deliberately to see how we react to him."

"Or perhaps he needs a beating," Thug suggested. It was odd how he and Professor had become friends, but they'd learned to rely on each other - and, of course, the rest of us. "He just got us killed!"

"Only in a simulation," Posh pointed out.

"That didn't save *me* from being bawled out for accidentally shooting Smartass in the back," Joker snapped. "We're supposed to treat these as if they were *real*."

"Maybe we should all complain," Professor said. "It could be one of those tricks where we *have* to report someone."

"Or be taken for snitches," Thug growled. "If we're supposed to be a team, and we are, how can we betray him?"

"There's a difference between betraying someone who works hard to be part of a team and someone who manifestly isn't interested," Professor offered.

"Give it until the next set of exams," I suggested. We'd been warned that the second set would be harder than the first. "If he doesn't improve, we can complain as a body."

"Or have another word with him," Thug said, cracking his knuckles. "I think this has gone far too far."

CHAPTER SIXTEEN

> Loyalty, of course, depends upon loyalty. A person who is not shown loyalty will not feel any great urge to offer it himself. This, of course, explains why so many institutions in the Empire were crumbling to dust; the best and brightest workers felt underappreciated, so they kept their ideas to themselves or sought better opportunities elsewhere. Ironically, the one place where loyalty was actually rewarded - the bureaucracy - was the one place where it was actively harmful…
> —Professor Leo Caesius

The written exams for the second phase were harder than the first, but - thanks to endless cramming - I didn't have many problems with them. But I was dreading - really dreading - the practical exam. It would be the hardest thing I'd ever done (at least until the *next* hardest thing I'd ever done came along.)

"All right, ladies," Bainbridge said. "Pay attention, because I'm going to tell you this once and only once."

He glowered at us all. "You will be taken up in an airplane and parachuted down to a location within Kirkwood," he continued. Kirkwood was a vast wilderness to the north of Boot Camp, where we'd gone for survival training. "Your mission, should you choose to accept it, is to make your way through Kirkwood to the RV point. The good news is that you will have a standard emergency pack with you; the bad news is that a team of dedicated hunters will be after you. Should they catch you before you reach the RV point and safety, you will be taken to a POW camp and interrogated. They will do everything in their power to make you give up the piece of sensitive information" - he held up a set of folded envelopes - "that you will be carrying. I don't think I need to add that you will fail if you tell them anything more than the basics."

There was a long pause. I felt sick.

"You will be completely on your own from the moment you're launched out of the plane," he warned. "In the unlikely event of you stumbling across one of your comrades, you are not allowed to stay together. Give each other the finger and then move on or you will be counted as a failure. You will also be given a dedicated emergency transponder, just in case you run into trouble. Using it will mean another automatic failure unless you have a *very* good excuse. Any questions?"

"Yes, sir," Professor said. "This recruit would like to know if there's a *reason* we can't stay together?"

"Because this is a solo test," Bainbridge said. "If we had the time, each of you would be sent in completely alone. However, Kirkwood is large enough to minimise the odds of you running into each other accidentally. Any other questions?"

I frowned. Perhaps we could…but it was a bad idea. They'd be tracking us through the implants, I was sure, and they'd know if we stayed together. And if we were being chased, two people would be easier to track than one.

Thug held up a hand. "This recruit would like to know how long we have to complete the exercise?"

"It shouldn't take more than a day for you to escape, unless you get lost," Bainbridge said. "If you're not back in two days, we might just start getting worried."

There was an uncomfortable pause.

"The hunters will be dispatched from their base at the same moment you are booted out of the airplane," Bainbridge warned, after it was clear that no one else had any questions. "You will, at best, have twenty minutes to make yourselves scarce before they arrive at your landing site and start hunting. I suggest you remember the basics and put some distance between yourself and the landing site before it's too late."

He took a breath. "The aircraft will depart in thirty minutes," he concluded. "Be there or fail."

"This should be fun," Joker said, as he checked his survival pack. "I could stay ahead of them long enough to escape."

I nodded, but I still felt sick. Countless hours of survival training hadn't made me feel *much* better about walking through the countryside, even though I'd grown up trying to slip through dark corridors where gangsters could easily be lurking, waiting for me. The jungle that made up much of Kirkwood was terrifying, on a very primal level. Joker, who'd had much more experience of open spaces, didn't seem so scared.

"See you on the far side," I said. My survival pack, as per orders, held a small collection of ration bars, a bottle of water and a map and compass. It was lucky my map-reading skills had improved or I would have been in deep shit. "Have a good one."

"You too, mate," Joker said. We headed for the plane, silently preparing ourselves for the ordeal to come. "You too."

Bainbridge greeted us when we reached the plane. "This is your piece of information," he ordered, passing us each an envelope. "Open it, read it, then give it back to me."

I glanced at the envelope, then opened it carefully. Inside, there was a single sheet of paper, with a single line of text. THE PEN OF MY AUNT IS IN THE GARDEN. I blinked in astonishment - I'd expected something different, perhaps information on military operations - but it did make a certain kind of sense. The nonsensical phase was easy to remember and, naturally, hard to forget. I shivered, again, as I recalled the training I'd been given on resisting interrogation. Did they know what they were trying to get me to say? Or were they merely planning to interrogate me until I coughed up the truth?

"That's funny," Joker said. "Why…?"

"That piece of information is yours and yours alone," Bainbridge said, curtly. "Do not share it with anyone else."

"Yes, sir," I said. I put the paper back in the envelope, then passed it to him. The pen of my aunt was in the garden. I wouldn't forget. "When do we leave?"

He gave me an evil look. "Now."

The skies were darkening rapidly as the pilot took the plane into the air, the airframe shuddering so much I was sure we were going to have a *real* accident. Humans had learned a great deal about terraforming since Mars had been colonised over two thousand years ago - it wasn't uncommon for Mars-like worlds to be terraformed within a century - but Mars still had ghastly storms that sprang up from time to time. I had an unfortunate feeling it was going to start raining badly and, as long as it happened after I landed, that was fine by me. Visibility would be down to almost nothing, giving me more opportunity to hide.

"Stalker," the jumpmaster bellowed. I had never warmed to him. He seemed to have a nose for sniffing fear and a sadistic urge to exploit it. "You're up!"

"Good luck," Joker called.

I waved, then jumped out of the plane and plummeted down towards the forest canopy. The skies looked eerie, a dark blue that suggested the clouds were crammed full of water. It struck me that I was in very deep shit if the rain started to fall while I was still in the air - I had no idea what would happen if the rain started to hammer the chute - but there was no time to do anything, but pray. I pulled the cord at the right moment and braced myself as I fell into the canopy. I wasn't sure what would happen if my chute wound up hanging from a tree either, apart from the hunting team laughing their asses off when they finally found me...

The skies opened bare minutes after I hit the ground. I scooped up the parachute, packed it into my bag and stumbled away from the landing zone, knowing I didn't have much time before the hunters gave chase. Water splashed down around me, running down through the trees; I headed downwards, despite the risks. It would be harder for them to pick up on my trail. I was drenched within seconds, soaked to the skin; by the time I reached an overhang I could use for shelter, it seemed rather pointless. Thunder roared overhead as I pulled the map out of my pocket - luckily, it was waterproof - and checked the compass. I wasn't *quite* sure where I was, but if I kept walking southwards I would eventually cross the river. That would take me down to a place where the river divided into two branches, which would tell me where to leave the river and keep walking south. Or so I hoped. There was no way I could read the skies, given how overcast it was; if I was so far wrong that I couldn't find the river, I was hopelessly lost. Gritting my teeth, I returned the map to my pocket and started to walk.

It felt like hours before the rain finally came to a halt. I allowed myself a moment of relief, then walked with more caution. The rain hadn't just made visibility a joke, it had covered up my movements and hidden any noise I might make. Now, they could hear me if I stepped on a twig or did something equally stupid. I listened as carefully as I could, but I couldn't hear anything that was remotely human. Insects were buzzing through the trees, birds were flying high overhead and small animals were jumping through the undergrowth. I blinked as the skies cleared and sunlight came pouring down, then kept moving as the temperature began to rise. It wasn't long before I was hot, sweaty and uncomfortable. I seriously considered taking off my uniform, before deciding that a modicum of comfort wasn't worth giving up the camouflage. A naked man would be much easier to catch.

I pulled a ration bar from my survival pack when I felt a hunger pang and chewed it slowly, without stopping. The ground had dried rapidly, forcing me to pick my way forward with extreme care to avoid leaving marks. I thought briefly about reversing my boots, to make it look as though I was headed in the other direction, then dismissed it as a tactic that only worked in bad novels and worse flicks. Besides, I couldn't do anything of the sort unless I walked backwards and then I'd only walk into something.

Something *moved* behind me. I froze, then turned; I saw nothing, but for a second I heard a snatch of someone whispering. I dropped low, crawling forward on my belly as fast as I could. How the hell had they caught up with me so fast? Did they have a tracking dog with them? I'd heard about K9 units, but I'd never seen one…a dog? How did one evade a dog's nose? There were chemicals one could use, yet I didn't have any of them. Water? Water might work, but I wasn't sure just how far I was from the river. I glanced at the compass, just to make sure I was going in the right direction, then kept moving. From time to time, I heard noises behind me, but they didn't seem to be getting closer. Maybe I was imagining them…?

Or maybe they're driving me into a trap, I thought. I had no intention of surrendering quietly when they found me, if they did. Maybe I hadn't been allowed weapons, but I still had my fists. *If there's someone ahead of me...*

I cursed, mentally, as the temperature grew hotter. We hadn't been told just how many men were attached to the hunting unit, but I could guess. Assuming the upper platoons were the same as ours, there were nine squads...and ten of us, parachuted into Kirkwood. That suggested each hunting squad had eight men - and, perhaps, radios. Maybe they were trying to coordinate a pincer, slowly tightening the noose around me. Gritting my teeth, I turned and crawled to the side for several minutes, then returned to walking south. It shouldn't be long until the river...

It still managed to surprise me when I walked into it. I had never seen a river on Earth and the handful of rivers I'd seen on Mars had been orderly, designed to serve as training grounds. *This* river had burst its banks; I could see trees poking up from the water as it poured onwards, down to the sea. I heard someone or something behind me, again; cursing, I splashed forward and into the water, allowing it to carry me down towards the distant fork. If I *was* being hunted by dogs, they'd have some problems tracking me once I was in the water.

I could have enjoyed the water, even though my uniform rapidly became waterlogged - again - and I had to grab hold of a branch to ensure I stayed afloat. Swimming in the pool was a chore, not a hobby; the water training we'd endured had been savage, leading to at least two recruits quitting when they almost drowned. I honestly couldn't understand why some people swam for fun. Now, though, I thought I understood. It was almost relaxing...hell, I almost fell asleep before I saw the fork in the river and swam ashore. I checked my compass, walked south long enough to be out of sight, then rechecked the map before starting my walk once again.

The temperature kept rising, drying me out. I paused to eat another ration bar and take a drink of water, then kept moving. Tiny insects buzzed around me; I tried to swat at them, then gave up and endured their attentions as best as I could. I'd never seen anything like them on Earth (I later learned some idiot had introduced creatures called mosquitoes to Mars). I kept an eye on my compass as the trees hedged closer - I could have sworn they were moving, if I hadn't known it was impossible - trying to make sure I was on the right route. It would be easy to accidentally lose my bearings and turn east or west. I picked a way through the trees carefully, freezing in place as I heard something crashing through the branches. Moments later, a large animal came into view and peered at me with dark beady eyes.

I stared. *A deer?* I'd only ever seen cartoon deer, portrayed as sweet animals in flicks about the evils of hunting for food. Not that that had impressed everyone, in the Undercity. Rats might be disgusting creatures, but there were people who raised them for food, just to have a change from ration bars. The deer staring at me didn't look remotely sweet or harmless. It was pointing its horns at me in a decidedly threatening manner. I reached for the Ka-Bar, cursing the flat ban on guns. Killing the creature before it killed me might be difficult.

Maybe it recognised the threat. It turned on its heels and gambolled away into the distance.

I watched it go, then resumed my walk. We'd been told we might have to catch, butcher and eat wild animals, but it wasn't something I'd had to do yet. It wasn't something I was looking forward to. Besides, taking the time to kill and eat the deer would probably have given the hunters enough time to catch up with me. *That* would have been more than a little annoying.

Someone probably introduced a lot of different animals here, I thought, as I kept moving onwards. *They must have been out of their minds.*

I'd read, somewhere, that the original settlers had tried to transfer breeding populations of just about everything from Earth to Mars, even though not everything had actually managed to last long on the planet's surface. Earth itself was a polluted mess that only harboured the toughest and least pleasant of creatures, including the Undercity's dwellers. There were even people who believed the Undercity was literally populated by sub-humans, creatures created by incestuous breeding and exposure to random mutagenic compounds dumped by one corporation or another. They seemed to assume we were so different we couldn't even breed with normal humans.

There was no truth in that at all, as far as I know. Sure, some of us had genetic modifications running through our DNA, yet we were still human. And incest was very - very- rare, even though the gangs happily broke all the other taboos. But it didn't stop people being idiots.

It was another hour before I finally saw the flag, fluttering over the RV point. I allowed myself a sign of relief - I'd made it - then ran forward. If there was still someone after me, I'd be ahead of them…I heard something, all of a sudden, and swore out loud as I reached the flag. Four men emerged from the trees, wearing camouflage uniforms. They'd been very close and I hadn't even realised they were there.

"I win," I said, although I wasn't sure if that was actually true. They'd been so close that part of me wondered if they'd *let* me reach the flag before showing themselves. I didn't think they'd be punished if we escaped, not when this wasn't part of the endless competition. "I beat you…"

They dogpiled me. I barely had a moment to react before I was on the ground, one of them pounding his fists into my side while another grabbed at my hands and a third covered my mouth with his hand. I bit him, of course, and kicked out at the others, but it wasn't enough to win the fight. They were just too strong and experienced for me to beat. I grunted as something cold and metallic was pushed against my head…

…And I plunged headfirst into darkness.

CHAPTER SEVENTEEN

> Officially, captured personnel are expected to give nothing more than their name, rank and serial number. However, for reasons expounded elsewhere, the Empire rarely regarded any of its prisoners as legitimate combatants - and, unsurprisingly, its enemies tended to do the same. POWs could therefore expect everything from immediate death to torture, if they refused to talk. Marine corps training, therefore, is designed to prepare a marine for an unpleasant experience, should he fall into enemy hands.
>
> -Professor Leo Caesius

When I woke up, I was naked, cuffed and trapped in a dark cell.

Those bastards, I thought, as I looked around. There was nothing in view, save for dark walls and a solid metal door. *I got to the goddamned flag*!

I tested the cuffs carefully, just in case, but no amount of pulling or tugging would budge them in the slightest. We'd been taught to look for weaknesses - cuffs linked to pipes that could be broken, for example, or broken bottles that could be used to slice through ropes - yet there was nothing useful in sight. Grimly, I resigned myself to the fact that I was a prisoner - and that I was at their mercy. We'd also been warned that no one even bothered to pay lip service, these days, to decent treatment for POWs.

"The Empire has a habit of treating its prisoners badly," Bainbridge had said. It had all been theoretical at the time. "They have no hesitation in returning the favour."

It wasn't a pleasant thought. The gangs had used torture on Earth just to illustrate that they were in charge. I'd seen a woman who'd had her teeth knocked out, just to keep her from biting, and a man who'd been hamstrung to teach him a lesson. I have no idea what happened to the woman, but the man had died shortly afterwards. Suicide…or someone taking advantage of an easy target? I honestly don't know. Whoever held me prisoner wouldn't do anything too drastic, would they? It was a test…and yet, people had been killed or injured in Boot Camp. That too wasn't a pleasant thought.

I frowned as I heard something in the distance, someone screaming in pain, begging for mercy. It was terrifyingly realistic. Chills ran down my spine as I realised the speaker was pleading, but his pleas were intermingled by screams as…*something*…was done to him. I tugged at the cuffs again, feeling panic howling at the back of my mind. All my training was meaningless if I could barely move, if I couldn't fight back. They could do *anything* to me…

…And there was nothing I could do about it.

There was a clunk as the door opened, revealing a masked man. I looked up at him, then glanced down, trying to appear submissive. Interrogators liked to feel as though they were in control, I'd been told, and it cost me nothing to play along. The tiny piece of nonsensical information danced through my mind suddenly, reminding me just what they wanted. I could spit it out right away and save us both some time. And yet, I was too goddamned stubborn to consider the possibility for long. I didn't want to give up at the first hurdle.

"You are our prisoner," the masked man said. "This place is hundreds of miles from any possible help. You will *not* be rescued. The only way you're going to leave this room is through cooperating with me. Do you know what I'm saying?"

Fuck you, I thought, but I kept my mouth firmly closed. Trying to match wits with an interrogator was a losing game, according to the Drill Instructors. They were skilled at using the tiniest cracks in one's defences to probe through and extract information. *I don't care what you're saying.*

The masked man shrugged. "You'll starve soon enough," he predicted. "There's nothing to gain by resisting us."

Of course there's something to gain, I thought. *I want to pass!*

He reached down and lifted my chin so I was staring into his eyes. The mask covered everything else, wiping all traces of individuality from his face. We'd been told that most interrogators liked to hide their identities; this one, it seemed, was no different. They had a habit of being shot while trying to escape. Sure, whoever captured them *might* have been told they were needed alive, but *no one* liked interrogators. And there was a distant possibility that one's comrades had been interrogated by the prisoner.

"There really isn't any hope," he said, gently. "Give up now and no harm will come to you."

I refused to show any trace of unease at his touch. It was funny; I hadn't felt so uneasy when I'd been taught how to take a punch, even though the blows had *hurt*. He allowed his fingers to trail over my face, then drew back as I prepared to try to bite him. It would have been futile defiance, but I wanted to do something - anything - to strike back.

He's trying to make you feel uncomfortable, I reminded myself. I'd heard horror stories of what happened to marines - and soldiers, and civil guardsmen - who fell into enemy hands. Beatings were the least of it. *And he's succeeding.*

His voice hardened. "Name, rank and serial number," he ordered. "Now."

I'd been told I could give those up as soon as I was taken prisoner, if I wished. In a civilised society, my captors would let my comrades know I was a prisoner and - perhaps - arrange an exchange. But I was determined to keep them to myself as long as possible. If nothing else, stubbornness would probably make me look good.

I shook my head, but said nothing.

"You'll think differently soon," he warned. "Enjoy your stay in darkness."

He strode out of the room, closing the door behind him. The light went out a second later, plunging me into pitch darkness. It didn't scare me *that* much - I'd grown up in the Undercity after all, where power cuts were common - but I had to admit it made me uneasy. I had known what to expect in the Undercity, while here…anything could be lurking in the darkness. Cold logic reminded me that I had seen the cell, that I knew no one could hope to slip inside without being heard, yet the darkness still worked its way into my mind. If the intent was to weaken my resolve I had to admit that it was working.

They knew where I was going, I thought, trying to distract myself. *All they had to do was lie in wait for me.*

It wasn't something I'd considered, back when they'd dumped me into Kirkwood. Had the hunters actually given chase at all? Had I imagined the ones behind me? Or had there been several teams, one for each of us, including one that had staked out the RV point and waited to see who'd come along? Who had they been? An upper platoon, being tested on its hunting skills as much as we were on our evasion skills? Or a dedicated unit, one that had nothing to prove by catching us?

I'd always had a good sense of time passing, but I'd lost track by the time the door opened and *someone* stepped into the room. I could hear the bastard breathing, yet I couldn't see a thing in the pitch darkness. The room's acoustics were playing merry hell with my ears; there were times I thought he was walking around me and times when I was half-convinced he was leaning against the wall, presumably watching me through enhanced eyes or night-vision gear. And there was nothing I could do about it…I heard the door open and bang closed for the second time, yet I had no idea if he was still there or not. Maybe, just maybe, I should call out…

No, I told myself, firmly. *That's what they want you to do.*

The lights came on again, so brightly I clenched my eyes shut. When I opened them again, I found myself staring at two masked men. I thought one of them was the man who had spoken to me earlier, but it was hard to be sure. Their loose clothes concealed almost everything that might have identified them. One of them was holding out a plate of warm food, the kind of meal I'd rarely seen before Boot Camp and never since leaving for Mars; the other was carrying a bottle of water and a pair of glasses.

"You're bound to be hungry," one of the men said. I mentally dubbed him Food; his companion, Water. "Tell us what we want to know and you can eat."

I salivated. I *was* hungry and, no matter *what* they put in the rations they served us, it didn't smell as good as a proper meal. There was chicken

- *real* chicken - potatoes and gravy. I wanted it. Oh God, I wanted it. It would have been easy just to surrender, just to give up my information. It wasn't as though it was *really* important. Who gave a damn about the pen of my aunt being in the garden anyway, apart from a particularly dunderheaded language teacher? I could have told them everything…

"Fuck you," I said, before I could stop myself.

Food shrugged. "You must be thirsty too," he said. "Would you like a drink?"

I glowered at him, cursing my slip under my breath. Water knelt down, placed the glasses on the floor and filled them both with water. Food smiled, then picked up the fork and speared a piece of chicken, sniffing it before holding it out, under my nose. The smell was almost heavenly. I could have eaten it all day.

"Just tell us the information," he said. "Tell us and you can eat whatever you want."

It would taste like ashes in my mouth, I thought, morbidly.

He swallowed the piece of chicken, then slowly ate the rest of the food in front of me, taunting me. I wanted to look away, but I couldn't; the urge to just start spitting out the words was terrifyingly strong. He finished the plate, took one of the glasses of water and drank it slowly, his eyes never leaving me. I think I hated him even more than Viper at that moment, even though I *knew* I wasn't being fair. He was just doing his job.

"It won't get any better from now on," he warned. "You might as well give up now."

I glowered at him. He shrugged and carried the plate out of the room. Water followed him, closing the door loudly. An instant later, I plunged back into darkness, taunted by the smell of food. He was right about one thing, I told myself in a vain attempt to keep my thoughts away from my growling stomach. It wasn't going to get any easier from now on. They'd be forced to use less pleasant methods, if such a thing were possible, to get the information out of me. I heard a faint hiss in the distance and realised, in horror, that I was being gassed. My head swam…

…When I awoke, I was lying on a table, my hands and feet firmly strapped down. Four masked men were surrounding me, their eyes dark with frustrated anger. I gritted my teeth as they spun the table around, then tilted it downwards and straight into a tray of water. There was almost no time to realise what was coming before my head was immersed in foul-tasting liquid. I gagged, then choked, feeling utterly helpless for the first time since I'd entered Boot Camp. Something struck my chest and I vomited; I knew, with absolute certainty, that I was going to die before the table shifted again, bringing my head out of the water. I struggled vainly against the restraints, my heartbeat pounding so loudly I was sure the entire world could hear it. Were they mad? Were they actually trying to get me killed?

"Tell us the information," one of the men ordered.

I coughed, spitting up water and vomit, then shook my head firmly. They didn't like that; two of the men came forward and started raining blows on my body. Pain surged through me and I knew it would have broken me, if I hadn't been taught how to take punches. They stopped after a long moment, then attached a handful of devices to my arms. Seconds later, I felt my hands start to twitch in pain. It wasn't a pleasant sensation - I later learned they were stimulating the nerves in my wrists - and it grew worse with each repetition. My hands seemed to be practically moving on their own.

"Tell us what we want to know and the pain will stop," another man said. He sounded calm and reasonable, as if he were on my side. I wanted to believe it, but I knew better. "There really is no point in trying to resist."

I closed my eyes as they started to beat on me again, then swung the table back around and shoved my head back into the water. This time, it was even less pleasant, but I managed to take a gulp of air before the water enveloped me. Maybe it was a mistake - my chest already hurt badly - yet it let me feel as though I had some control. They pulled me out after a minute, then sat me upright and shouted questions at me. Most of them seemed to be completely immaterial, to say nothing of irreverent. What did *I* know about the current favourite in the gladiatorial games?

They're trying to confuse you, my thoughts warned me. *And it's working*.

I gritted my teeth and endured as best as I could. They kept shouting questions, then hitting me when I refused to answer. Words hovered on my lips - maybe the pain would end, if I talked - but I was too stubborn. I had come too far to simply give up. But they were getting frustrated too. I tasted blood in my mouth after one of them slapped me across the face.

"We cannot attempt to tell you when you should talk," Bainbridge had said. "Everyone has their breaking point. You will not know yours until it is too late."

I clung to his words - and my determination to make him proud of me - as the interrogators closed in again. This time, they were holding a blowtorch; I stared in numb horror as they held it in front of my eyes, just so I could see what it was, and then lowered it until it was pointed right at my balls. The heat rose rapidly; I knew, beyond a shadow of a doubt, that they were going to mutilate me. I'd heard horror stories, but…

What if this isn't a test? My thoughts asked. *What if you've actually been captured by the enemy?*

"Talk," the interrogator said. "Tell us what we want to know."

I tried to cringe backwards, but there was simply no room to move. They could move the flame forward any moment they liked. I looked into his eyes and saw…nothing; no sense of concern, no sense of enjoyment. He was a sociopath, someone who would do whatever was necessary to make me talk. I had no doubt of it. In some ways, he was more terrifying than any of the sadists who'd ruled the gangs with iron hands. He would never lose sight of his goal.

But I was damned if I was giving in.

"Fuck you," I said, again.

There was a stab of pain, then blackness. When it cleared, I was lying in a bed.

"Congratulations," Bainbridge said.

I stared at him numbly, then sat upright and lifted the covers. My unmentionables were still there, still unmentionable. My body ached, but no worse than it had done after the forced marches, or the unarmed combat training sessions, or any of the other exercises we'd done to prepare ourselves for war. There was no sign of any bruises.

"You kept quiet despite the pain," he said, as I sat upright. "You passed with flying colours."

I wanted to hit him. Only the certainty that he'd kick my ass, then throw me out of Boot Camp held me back. Nordstrom had repeated his challenge - a chance to actually *hit* a Drill Instructor without punishment - at every unarmed combat session, but so far no one had actually managed to land a punch.

"Thank you, sir," I said. "I…"

He *must* have been in a good mood. I only got fifty push-ups for saying 'I'.

I tried again. "This recruit would like to know how far they were prepared to go?"

Bainbridge gave me a sarcastic look. "Do you really believe that *real* terrorists wouldn't go much further to extract information?"

I shook my head.

"Then you should really understand that we had to push you as far as we could without causing permanent damage," Bainbridge added, sternly. "No one would have faulted you for trying to dribble out the information, or even for breaking after they started getting physical."

That wasn't true. *I* would have faulted myself.

Bainbridge studied me for a long moment. "And one other thing? Don't compare notes with your fellow recruits."

"Yes, sir," I said. "Did we all pass?"

"You all did very well," he said.

I learned, later, that all of us passed the basic requirements. We'd either flatly refused to talk or misled the interrogators. No *wonder* Bainbridge was in such a good mood. Indeed, he was in such a good mood that he let me have an extra hour in bed before I was sent back to barracks. A small thing, perhaps, but in Boot Camp…

…Well, let's just say it was worth its weight in gold.

CHAPTER EIGHTEEN

> One might ask, as many do, why the marine recruits weren't subjected to any form of chemical interrogation. There are, after all, no shortage of drugs designed for interrogation purposes. However, marines - and many other military personnel - are given special enhancements to render such drugs either harmless or lethal. Smart interrogators know better than to risk using them.
>
> -Professor Leo Caesius

The third phase of Boot Camp was, in many ways, the best.

It's hard to explain why, at least to a civilian. We were still being pushed hard, we were still being punished with innumerable push-ups - I'm sure Nordstrom invented a few new numbers just so he could inflict them on us - and there was still a very real danger that some of us would quit. But, at the same time, we had earned a considerable amount of respect from the Drill Instructors. I won't say they were gentler, because they would probably come back from the grave to kick my ass if I did, but they were *slightly* more patient with us.

And that wasn't the only thing. Having decided we were worth the investment, they started offering us other treatments. Professor's eyesight - so bad he wore the dreaded Birth Control Glasses - was corrected in a short, but expensive operation. He looked odd after three months of seeing him with his glasses, but I had to admit it would make his life easier. I'd been wondering how he intended to serve in combat while wearing a pair of spectacles that made him a spectacle. Others received their own treatments; I received a handful of DNA modifications that removed some of the hackwork inflicted on my ancestors and added a handful of new enhancements. I did ask if they could compare my DNA to the Empire's master database, in hopes of identifying my father, but there were no matches. The half-assed fantasy I'd had of discovering my father had been a marine - or something I could respect - vanished like a snowflake in hell.

The downside was that we were expected to assist with the newer recruits, something I think we would have preferred to avoid. We weren't, of course, given a choice in the matter. I enjoyed some of it - playing hunter while the newer recruits played prey - was fun, but I disliked other parts of it. I hadn't expected to *loathe* the new recruits when I laid eyes on them, as part of their unarmed combat training, nor did I expect the chaos when one of *their* Drill Instructors started to bark orders and we obeyed without thinking. Bainbridge was *very* sarcastic about *that* little mishap.

It was an open secret - we heard it from someone in the fourth phase - that the Drill Instructors were evaluating us, now that we had proved we had staying power. Some of us would go to the Slaughterhouse, some of us would go to auxiliary units…and some of us, alas, would be directed towards the Imperial Army. It seemed a fate worse than death, as far as we were concerned; we'd heard so much crap about the regulars from the Drill Instructors that we took it as an article of faith that the Imperial Army was a pool for losers. Hell, we'd been told more than once that when the army was on the hunt, the safest people in the region were the targets. They just couldn't shoot for toffee.

(That was, of course, a base libel. But we believed it at the time.)

The most fun part of the whole phase, however, was the introduction to military vehicles. I didn't know how to drive - very few people on Earth knew how to drive, when the lucky few who owned aircars had to submit them to traffic control - but I learned quickly. It helped that the Empire believed firmly in standardising everything; if someone happened to master a military jeep, it was fairly simple to scale up to a Landshark Main Battle Tank. Yes, the steering *was* a little more complex; the basic principles, however, were still the same. We started with basic vehicles, then moved all the way up to AFVs and tanks. It was unlikely we'd be using them, we were told, but one never knew. Besides, it was good for our confidence.

"You are only expected to know the basics," Bainbridge told us, after we'd driven a dozen Hammerhead tanks around the exercise grounds. The Hammerhead was a light tank, designed to provide mobile firepower; they were definitely more nimble than the Landsharks, allowing us to take them into places a Landshark couldn't go without smashing its way through buildings and streets alike. "The experienced crews will be far more capable than you."

We didn't believe him, of course, until the instructors took a tank out onto the field and really let themselves have fun. I'd never believed a tank could move so sharply and fire so accurately, not until I'd seen the results of thousands of hours of practice. The Imperial Army wasn't keen on allowing anyone to practice - again, every requisition of ammunition and supplies had to be accounted for - but the tankers had their ways of getting around the system. Given a chance, they would be formidable foes.

"You should never assume that a tank is an unbeatable opponent," Bainbridge explained, as we learned their weaknesses as well as their strengths. "A tank can dominate the battlefield, but a smart enemy can still disable it."

He was right, we discovered, as we worked our way through more realistic exercises. A company of tanks could crush resistance, but they couldn't hold the ground; that, it seemed, was still the task of the infantry. There was no shortage of wars in history, we were told, where the tanks were cut off from their support and overwhelmed. Learning how to work *with* the tanks - and aircraft, assault helicopters and orbiting starships - was a complicated task, but we managed it. None of us wanted to give up now.

It was Viper, oddly enough, who asked the question we were all thinking about.

"Sir," he said, as we made our way back to the barracks, "this recruit would like to know why our technology is so primitive."

Bainbridge lifted an eyebrow. "You think our technology is *primitive*?"

"This recruit has seen aircars and hover trucks, armoured combat suits and antigravity lifters," Viper said, refusing to be cowed. He was still a malingerer, but he *had* made it into phase three. "There shouldn't be any need to use tracked vehicles that are largely identical to the designs used a thousand years ago."

"An interesting question," Bainbridge said. He studied Viper for a long moment, then explained. "Yes, it is well within our capabilities to produce more advanced weapons and vehicles. You will discover, as you go on to later courses, that there *are* more advanced weapons and yes, you will be trained on them. However, such weapons have their limitations. Would you care to suggest what those might be?"

Viper hesitated, then shook his head.

Bainbridge tapped the rifle he carried, slung over his shoulder. "At its core, this weapon is very - very - simple," he said. "A dunderhead can learn how to use it; more importantly, perhaps, he can learn how to *maintain* it. You can pour a great deal of abuse on the MAG-47 and it will continue to take good care of you."

I smiled, inwardly. We'd had a handful of incidents where a weapon was dropped and the Drill Instructors had gone ballistic. None of the weapons had actually been *damaged*, but that hadn't stopped them from tearing us new assholes. We'd had to recite the Rifleman's Creed hundreds of times, while stripping our rifles down and rebuilding them, just to make sure the lesson sunk in.

"If you break a component beyond repair," Bainbridge continued, "you can replace it with one from another rifle. Or, for that matter, one can be sourced from a mobile support ship, one of the handful of starships we use to support our deployments. If worst came to worst, a civilian-grade fabricator could be used to put one together, if you overrode the safety features designed to keep people from churning out weapons. The rounds you fire off, too, are achingly easy to produce. Even a mobile support ship can churn out hundreds of thousands within a day.

"That's true, too, of most of our *simple* vehicles. You can repair a jeep, or a tank, relatively easily, provided you have the spare parts on hand. Again, sourcing them isn't exactly difficult. A stage-two colony world shouldn't have any difficulty producing replacements if necessary. None of the hours you spent practicing were wasted; you should have no difficulty carrying out necessary repairs. You may, of course, discover that the entire vehicle is beyond repair, but that would require a significant level of damage."

He paused. "But something more complex, even something as simple as a hover tank or aircar, can be a right bastard to repair while on deployment. A relatively simple problem would force the crew to send the vehicle all the way back to the repair yards, which would render it completely useless until it was sent back again. Something as minor as a flaw in the antigravity system would reduce your mobile firepower quite considerably. The more complex a system, the easier it is to break down and the harder it is to repair on the spot. A sniper rifle, capable of picking off a target three kilometres away, can break down quite easily and be a right pain in the ass to repair."

There was a second pause as his words sank in. "There is no shortage of systems that are, on paper, far superior to everything we use in the field," he said. "Sometimes, someone comes up with something that is actually usable, so we work it into our deployments; more often, the systems have major problems that only show up when a bunch of marines - or terrorists - start looking for flaws. There was a device, once, that monitored the number of humans in a given zone. It looked brilliant until, one day, it started screaming about how there was a *billion* enemy soldiers advancing on the command post. Someone had pissed on it and that was the result."

He gave a rather thin smile. "A brand-new command and control system gets hacked...and the enemy uses it to call down fire from orbit on our positions. A brilliant new encryption program ends the requirement for microburst transmissions...apart from the minor detail that the *reason* we use microbursts is to avoid giving the enemy targeting information on a plate. A new piece of body armour is damn near indestructible, but anyone who wears it will overheat so rapidly that they'd be useless for anything within minutes..."

"Not that that's the only problem," he said, dryly. "If I had a credit for every time a new system went over-budget and ended up costing the taxpayer twice as much, I'd have enough money to buy my own planet."

I stuck up a hand. "Why do people keep *buying* them?"

Bainbridge laughed. "Politics," he said. He spoke the word as if it were a curse. "Stalker. What makes the universe go round?"

"Power, sir," I said. The Undercity was a perfect example of just how power could be used to shape the world. Those with power would use it to take whatever they wanted, including money; those with money but without power would have to either hide it or lose it. "Not even money comes close."

"Correct," Bainbridge said. "You can look up the details later, if you like, but the military budget is one of the biggest slush funds in creation. Everyone wants a share of that money, so they use their power to force the military to buy expensive new weapons systems it doesn't need, weapons systems which might not work in any case. Someone at the top of the heap is unlikely to give a damn about our lives when there's billions upon billions of credits at stake."

He shrugged. "That's why the marine corps fights so hard to keep control of procurement," he added. "Given half a chance, we would find our MAGs replaced by pieces of crap that, if we're lucky, will fire a couple of rounds before breaking into pieces of biodegradable plastic."

Joker coughed. "It can't be that bad, sir."

"Go look up the Shrunken Tree massacre, when you have time," Bainbridge ordered. "The short version of the story is that some corporation wanted trace elements in the trees, which happened to be defended by a tribe armed with nothing more dangerous than spears."

I scowled, inwardly. We'd been told, time and time again, that there were no dangerous weapons, only dangerous men. A man with a spear, a man willing to use it, was potentially *much* more dangerous than a man with a gun. We'd been taught not to dismiss someone because he was unarmed…

"The regiment dispatched to deal with the tribe, either by convincing them to move or simply exterminating them, had the latest in modern weapons," Bainbridge continued. "Their rifles had been tested extensively under laboratory conditions. They had everything from air support to orbiting starships, ready to provide additional firepower if necessary. There should have been a very quick massacre, ending the whole affair."

"Once they stole the tribe's resources," Professor said.

Bainbridge nodded. "It turned out that no one had tested the rifles in tropical conditions," he said. "The regiment's NCOs couldn't be arsed doing the paperwork necessary to get a few hundred rounds of ammunition to shoot off before they actually went to war, which sounds really bad until you realise that they would have had to ask for each round separately. A handful of rounds in such conditions caused the rifles to fail, if the bearer was lucky. I believe a number of rifles actually exploded. The tribe lost around fifty people, according to the classified after-action report, but they slaughtered the entire regiment."

"Shit," Joker said.

Viper looked shocked. "Surely we would have *heard* about it…"

"The whole affair was hushed up, of course," Bainbridge said. "Do you think that any of those investigative reporters actually *investigate*? Even if they did, their editors would kill any story that might threaten their fat paychecks. There were dark rumours, of course, but there are always rumours. The colonel in command of the regiment took most of the blame, as he was safely dead, even though there was nothing particularly wrong with his battle plan or early deployments. If his weapons had worked, everything would have gone just fine."

"Except for the locals," Professor muttered. "What *happened* to them?"

"Another regiment was sent, eventually," Bainbridge said. "I believe they were moved to a place well away from the trees. And the hell of the whole affair, a few years later, was that they found another way to get the trace elements they wanted, without having to get thousands of men killed. Not that their lords and masters actually gave a damn."

He cleared his throat. "You'll find yourself in places where yes, you are expected to enforce injustice," he added. "If you can't handle it, now is probably a good time to quit."

It was a warning that stayed with me for the rest of my life. The exercises had forced us to grapple with some problems - was it a wise idea to lock up every male in a city, just to keep them from posing a threat? - that underlined the whole issue. How far were we meant to go if we *were* expected to enforce injustice? What would I do, I asked myself, if I *was* ordered to force people to move, just because they were living on top of natural resources someone else wanted?

There was a part of me that said it didn't matter. I'd never seen any real justice in the Undercity. The strong had ruled with iron fists; the weak did as they were told, or they were punished. Why should I sympathise with people when no sympathy had ever been shown to me? But, at the same time, two wrongs didn't make a right. I didn't have the right to kill anyone who tried to kill me…

…And yet, did I have the right to kill the men who'd killed my family?

The question nagged at my mind as we worked our way through phase three. We dealt with actors playing corporate managers, local insurgent leaders and countless civilians, caught helplessly in the middle. Some of them were greedy, some clearly wanted power, but all too many of them were nothing more than victims. They weren't any better than I'd been in the Undercity.

"We're at least *trying* to do good," Professor said, when I discussed it with him. "Aren't we?"

"I don't know," I said. I'd grappled with the question for days without finding an answer. "What makes us any better than gang enforcers?"

"We don't loot, rape or kill," Posh pointed out. We'd all heard horror stories about the civil guard. They'd enter a town which had a handful of insurgents and, by the time they left, everyone in the town would be insurgents. "*That* makes us better than them."

"We clear away the insurgents," Viper said. There was a bitterness in his tone that surprised me. He still wasn't really one of us, but he was doing better. "And yet, when they're gone, we find that we have cleared the way for exploiters."

"We clear up messes," Professor said. "They don't send us in to crack heads…"

"Messes that they create for themselves," Viper said. "In the end, there's no real difference."

I hoped, desperately, that he was wrong.

CHAPTER NINETEEN

> Viper was not wrong, in a way, to state that the marines cleaned up messes, messes caused by bad government, corporate mismanagement or naked exploitation. It is quite true that many of the brushfire wars that weakened the Empire, prior to Han and the Fall of Earth, wouldn't have happened if the Grand Senate had told the corporations to treat the locals with something resembling decency. (There were some decent corporate rats, but most of them believed that they earned more credit by serving their corporation's immediate interests than trying to build up a long-term relationship.) However, as sickening as it may seem, such involvement did tend to create improvement…of which Avalon is a prime example.
>
> -Professor Leo Caesius

It felt like almost no time at all had passed from the day we entered phase three and the day we commenced the exams for entering phase four. I know we did a great deal of work, combining our older exercises with newer ones, but I honestly can't remember most of them. It was overshadowed, far too much, by everything that happened on the third day of the exams.

"All right, maggots," Bainbridge said. He'd been increasingly cranky with us as the exams started, although none of us were sure why. We suspected we weren't doing as well as the previous platoon and *their* Drill Instructor was rubbing it in a little. "The mission is as follows. An enemy regiment is on the move to Wander Gap, where it will attempt to punch through and down into our heartland. Your mission is to get a blocking force in place before it's too late. The bad news is that your trucks are short on fuel."

I cursed mentally as I recollected the map. Wander Gap was quite a slog away, assuming that we drove…and, it seemed, we couldn't. Two days of manoeuvring around the landscape in our trucks had left us with severely depleted fuel. Getting into place wouldn't be *that* hard - we'd mastered forced marching by now - but getting there with enough weapons to do more than slow up the enemy would be a little harder. I didn't want to get there in time to have our asses kicked by a heavily-armed opposition force.

"Stalker," Bainbridge snapped. "You're in command."

Shit, I thought. *Now what? The clock is ticking…*

I pushed the thought aside as hard as I could as the rest of the squad gathered around me, waiting for orders. We'd swapped commanding officers so often that we'd all had a turn in the hot seat…something I wouldn't have minded, if I hadn't been the guy in charge during the exam. I might end up less popular than Viper if I fucked up.

"Joker, Professor, get me a count of how much fuel we have left," I snapped. Maybe, just maybe, we could pile everything into one or two of the trucks. Transferring fuel from one vehicle to another was a pain in the ass, but it could be done. "Everyone else, get ready to start unloading the trucks."

I unfolded the map as everyone went to work and checked my earlier conclusions. The shortest way to Wander Gap was up a mountain path; the map, unfortunately, made it clear that there was no way we'd get a truck up it without a minor disaster. I'd have to send the trucks - if we *had* working trucks - the long way round. If we'd had enough fuel, it would have been pathetically easy. As it was, the Drill Instructors had timed it perfectly.

"Not much, sir," Professor reported back. His thoughts had evidently been running along the same lines. "We can get one truck to Wander Gap, but we'd have to drain the others completely dry."

"Do it," I ordered. I checked the map again, then sighed. "Take *Bongo*" - yes, we'd named our trucks - "and transfer the contents of *Booger*, then drive it all to the gap."

"Yes, sir," Professor said.

"Keep Posh with you," I added. Professor couldn't handle everything alone. "The rest of us will march up to the gap."

I called everyone back, then started to bark orders. "I want everyone carrying a heavy weapon or helping to carry an ammunition pallet," I bellowed. "We need to empty the trucks as much as possible before start the march."

Viper stuck up a hand. "Shouldn't we leave a rearguard?"

Someone to watch the remaining trucks, he meant. It wasn't actually a bad idea, but there were only thirty of us. Bainbridge had put the entire training platoon in the field and I had a feeling we'd need all of them to close the gap. I fought the temptation to leave him there - it *was* a tempting thought - then shook my head.

"I'll call in for someone to pick them up, if we can strip them bare," I said. I had a feeling the AAR would call my judgement into question, but I just didn't have the manpower to deal with everything. "Depending on the time, we may send someone back once we're in the gap."

"Coward," someone muttered.

Viper spun around, fists raised. "What was that?"

"Silence," I bellowed. Viper hadn't been coping well with teamwork, which hadn't endeared him to everyone else. I was mildly surprised he'd made it into phase three. "Grab your load and get ready to march!"

I hadn't exactly been weak in the Undercity, for which I will be forever grateful, but I hadn't known what strength was until I'd spent two months in Boot Camp. All of us, including Viper, were solidly muscular now, used to carrying immense combat loads. I checked the recruits assigned to carrying heavy ammunition boxes, then picked up a rucksack I *knew* I would never have been able to lift as a teenager. As soon as we were all loaded up, we started our march.

It wasn't easy. The pathway was thoroughly treacherous; I nearly lost my footing twice and others were just as unfortunate. If the enemy had a scout watching us, or a drone hovering high overhead, we were probably under observation. Once they stopped laughing, they'd call in an airstrike. I looked up, knowing it was futile, then shook my head as sweat kept running down my back. If they *were* watching us, it was unlikely I'd see anything until the first bomb fell on our heads and by then it would be far too late.

There was a crashing sound behind me. I spun around, almost losing my footing, and paled as one of the ammunition boxes crashed to the ground. Marine-grade mortar shells are relatively safe, but 'safe' has many separate meanings in the military. If one of those shells blew, they'd all blow…and we'd all be blown to bits. I had a feeling that Bainbridge, who was tagging along in the rear, would survive - I had a hard time believing that *anything* could kill him - but the rest of us would be dead.

"That was your fucking fault," Joker snarled at Viper, who'd evidently slipped and fallen. "Watch where you're fucking going!"

"You keep fucking pushing me," Viper snapped back. "This isn't a fucking parade ground…"

"Shut up, the pair of you," I shouted. I wasn't surprised that *someone* had lost their footing while carrying the boxes - it took four men to carry them safely - and it probably wasn't Viper's fault. "We don't have time for a squabble."

"He's not pulling his weight," Joker said, angrily. Friend or no friend, we were all getting short-tempered as the day grew hotter. "We keep pushing him forward because he's a fucking slowcoach."

"I don't care," I said, gathering myself. We were carting live ammunition around, not blanks or training rounds. "We're running short on time and we have to keep moving."

I briefly considered giving Viper my pack and taking his place myself, but I had a feeling Viper would just fall behind. He consistently came in at the back on route marches or training runs, save for the escape and evasion course. Like me, he'd reached the flag before getting nabbed, which made me suspect the whole exercise had been rigged and *none* of us had had a hope of avoiding the experience of being a POW.

"Keep moving," I repeated, looking directly at Viper. "We do not have time to waste."

I kept my eyes on Viper, willing him to understand. There was no way I was going to lose the exercise because of him. If he caused any more problems, I was going to take him behind a tree and settle the matter with my fists. He must have read *something* in my gaze because he picked up his handle and started to walk, slowly but surely. I met Joker's eyes for a long moment, then turned and continued to walk myself.

"We should have walked along the road," Viper said, as we kept going. "It would have been a damn sight easier."

"And slower," Smartass commented. "We might not have gotten there in time."

"Then we should have sent a squad in the truck and got them into place first," Viper snapped.

"And you didn't think of it," Joker hissed. "Or did you intend to land Stalker in the shit?"

"Shut up," I said. Maybe Viper had a point…and if he'd suggested it at the time, I would have happily stolen the idea. It would have its problems - a single squad might not be enough to hold the gap - but it might have been worth trying. "There's nothing to do now but endure it."

Viper kept muttering until we finally reached the gap, despite increasingly angry remarks from the other three porters. I did my best to ignore him as I looked at the gap, a narrow road running through the mountains. If the enemy had trucks, or even light tanks, they would have to come at us single-file, giving us plenty of opportunity to tear hell out of them. I'd have given the task to light infantry instead; hell, for all I knew, that was what the enemy intended to do. Sending tanks along the road, when there were so many trees to provide cover, was asking for trouble.

"Get the machine guns into the trees," I ordered, as I considered the situation. The enemy would have a chance, at least, to impale themselves on my weapons. "Once the truck arrives" - I didn't dare call Professor to check on his progress, not when the enemy would know to listen for microburst transmissions - "get the trees further down the road felled, just to slow them down a little. The five best shots in the platoon are to set up sniper nests; I want one of them armed with a laser pointer, so mortar shells can be guided onto their targets."

The problem was I didn't know where the *enemy* was - and, as Bainbridge had told us often enough, war is a democracy. The enemy gets a vote. I could have used the crew-portable mortars (the only people who say carrying mortars is easy are people who have never done it) to hit a target within five kilometres, but I had no way of knowing if the enemy was already within range. I contemplated possibilities for a long moment, then ordered Joker to move the mortar crews downrange so they were well out of sight, but ready to engage the enemy.

You'll have to keep them ready to move, I reminded myself. The enemy might have mortars of their own - and radars that could track a shell back to its launch point, then open fire on the guns. We trained against hard opposition just so our actual missions seemed easy. *Who knows what they're planning for me.*

I unfurled the map and studied it, thinking hard. The enemy lines - officially - were several kilometres from the mountains. In practice, the so-called front line was a nebulous, shifting term of convenience. They might have rushed forward, intent on getting to the gap before we could respond, or they might have planned on the assumption we'd be too quick off the mark and they'd have to force the gap.

It was nearly ten minutes before the truck came into view. I allowed myself a moment of relief as Professor jumped out and waved, then hastily started unloading the remainder of our supplies. Joker and the others hurried to join him, grabbing tools that could be used to rig up mines and booby traps. I took a certain amount of sadistic pleasure in giving Viper the job of setting a handful up. None of us *liked* messing with explosive traps, even when using proper explosives instead of makeshift bombs; if Viper intended to moan and groan, he could at least do it while doing something useful.

"Sneak, I want you to get up the mountain," I ordered. Sneak was from squad one, a man with an inhuman talent for sneaking around. Apparently, he'd been the only person from squad one to make it to the flag before getting scooped up anyway. "When the enemy come into view, use the torches to flash an alert."

"Yes, sir," Sneak said.

"Pity you can't send Viper up there," Joker muttered.

I shrugged. Maybe Viper *would* be better operating on his own. He wasn't a team player, but he seemed to do all right on solo tests. If I'd thought I could trust him to handle the task, I would have sent him. I briefly considered sending him back to the remaining trucks, then dismissed it. After he'd planted the traps, I could find him something else to do.

Time wore on, slowly. We waited, impatiently, for the enemy to come into view. Where were they? I looked at the map again and again, reassuring myself that I wasn't wrong, that there simply wasn't any other way they could take if they wished to bring an armoured force through the mountains. Hell, I'd have had my doubts about taking tanks along the road; a Hammerhead would seriously damage the road and a Landshark would probably ruin it for everyone else. There's a reason we have tank transporters when we want to move tanks from place to place.

I doubted myself, time and time again. Maybe they were sneaking up on us - the gap *was* an obvious place for an ambush, after all. *I* sure as hell wouldn't drive along it at full speed without making damn sure it was clear first. Or maybe they had decided to give the gap a wide berth after all, even if it put them miles out of their way. Or maybe they had seen us in place and decided not to push it. I wouldn't have cared to tangle with a carefully-laid ambush, if I had a choice, and calling in an airstrike would mess up the road. Or…

A burst of gunfire shocked me out of my thoughts. Were they here?

Viper was standing near one of his emplaced traps, holding his rifle. The remains of a small forest creature were lying on the ground, smoking slightly. I jumped up and ran down to him, feeling raw anger twisting in my gut. This was it. Plant or no plant, I was going to knock some sense into him if it was the last thing I did.

"You fucking idiot," I bellowed. Everyone for a dozen miles had probably heard the shots, even if we were in the middle of a war zone. If the enemy hadn't known where we were beforehand, they sure as hell knew now. "Are you trying to get us all killed!"

Viper glared up at me, furiously. His hands tightened on his gun.

"Enough," I snapped. "You're relieved. You can go to the Drills and quit or we'll all go to them and demand your removal."

Viper lifted his rifle and pointed it at me. I jumped aside - my reflexes had been honed by endless practice - as he pulled the trigger, sending a hail of bullets into the trees. Someone shouted behind me as I twisted and lunged at him, knocking the barrel into the sky. There was another burst of gunfire as he fell backwards, with me on top of him. I was too angry to care as we struggled for supremacy. I was a better fighter, but Viper seemed to have snapped completely. It was like grappling with a lunatic who didn't give a damn how much he was hurt, as long as he hurt you.

"Hold him down," Bainbridge snarled.

I was trying! The rifle went flying into the underbrush as Viper let go of it. Moments later, we had him on his front and his hands caught behind him. He still struggled, even when Bainbridge tied his hands; he kept struggling until the Drill Instructor pressed an injector tube against his neck.

"ENDEX," Bainbridge said, keying his radio. "I say again, ENDEX."

I stared. We had been told, time and time again, that exercises didn't stop because someone had been injured or killed. Bainbridge had the authority to cancel anything at any time he liked, but it was rarely used. Now...

"Get everything packed up," he ordered, tartly. He scooped Viper's unconscious body up and placed it over his shoulder. "We'll be going straight back to barracks."

"Yes, sir," I said.

"Make sure you put all the live ammunition under lock and key," Bainbridge added, after a moment. "One snapper may set off others."

I swallowed. "Yes, sir."

"Fuck me," Joker said. "What the fuck got into him?"

"I don't know," I admitted. I'd been wrong. Viper couldn't have been a plant, not when he'd come within a hairsbreadth of shooting me with live bullets. I knew the Drill Instructors were tough, but they weren't mad. "I really don't know."

Chapter Twenty

> The marines, it should be noticed, have a lower rate of suicides or lethal 'accidents' than any of the other military services, but that doesn't mean they are entirely absent. A recruit who has failed to blend into his squad and feels, in consequence, alone and entirely abandoned, may find himself feeling suicidal. Drill Instructors are trained to watch for potential suicide risks, but the fundamental ethos of Boot Camp - that it is the desire to succeed that counts, rather than anything else - goes against most suicide prevention strategies.
>
> -Professor Leo Caesius

It was a very silent group that packed up and made its way back to barracks, where we were told to remain until we received further orders. A Drill Instructor I didn't know arrived shortly afterwards, taking over the task of supervising us while Bainbridge and the others went…where? I knew from bitter experience that people on Earth played musical chairs to evade the blame, but somehow I couldn't see any of the Drill Instructors I knew trying to avoid their share of responsibility. And yet, how was it their fault?

I was still mulling it over when another officer I didn't recognise arrived and spoke, very briefly, to the Drill Instructor.

"Stalker," the instructor said. "Captain Giovanni will escort you to the Commandant's office."

"Yes, sir," I said.

I had never been anywhere near the administrative block since my arrival at Boot Camp. None of us had, unless we were getting kicked out for breaking one rule or another; it was closed and sealed, access only possible if accompanied by a senior officer. Captain Giovanni led me through the gate, past a set of dull buildings that were completely sealed, and up to a large building at the centre of the camp. A man wearing a dark blue uniform was standing guard outside, eying everyone who went by. He gave me a long considering look before I was led past him and into the building.

"An inquest has been organised at very short notice," Captain Giovanni informed me, as we entered a small antechamber. I couldn't help feeling as though I was going to see the headmaster, although no headmaster I'd ever met had the power to order my removal from school. "The Commandant and a couple of other officers will ask you questions, which I advise you to answer to the best of your ability. You are not - yet - in any trouble, but if you wish one of the Drill Instructors to accompany you…"

"No, thank you," I said, quickly. Was I in trouble? It seemed quite likely. "What are they going to ask?"

"Questions," Captain Giovanni said. Either he was needling me or he honestly didn't know *what* they would ask. "Like I said, answer them to the best of your ability."

I swallowed, then reminded myself that I was a marine recruit who'd completed two phases of Boot Camp and was on the verge of completing a third, if my career hadn't just hit something made of hullmetal. Captain Giovanni looked me up and down, then rapped on a door loudly enough to make me jump. It swung open a moment later, revealing a bare room and a table, with three men sitting behind it. I recognised the Commandant from his welcoming speech - it felt like decades ago - but the other two were unfamiliar. A fourth chair was on my side of the table, with a glass of water resting in front of it.

"Recruit," the Commandant said. I snapped to attention. "Be seated."

I sat, carefully.

"We have some questions about what happened today," the Commandant said, once I was seated. My mouth felt terrifyingly dry and

I was far too aware of Captain Giovanni, standing behind me. "Answer them and our follow-up questions as best as you can, please."

"Yes, sir," I said.

"Very good," the Commandant said. "Describe for us, in your own words, just what happened today."

I swallowed, then began. The Commandant's face was completely expressionless as I described the problem with Viper, his decision to fire at a small animal and then his murderous attack on me. In hindsight, I should have sent him back to the trucks or done something - anything - else, although I wasn't sure what. It had never been in my power to remove him from Boot Camp.

"This recruit - Viper - was apparently a problem for quite some time," the Commandant said. "Why didn't you complain to the Drill Instructors?"

"Because we thought that there was no point in complaining, sir," I said. "Some of us suspected he was a plant, someone to force us to learn how to deal with him, while others believed that complaining would make us all look bad. We assumed he would be recycled after the phase three exams."

"Hardly a wise assumption," one of the unfamiliar men said. "Teamwork is considered important, recruit. His attitude might have cost you your chance at a pass. He might not have been the only one forced to redo phase three."

"Yes, sir," I said. In hindsight…but hindsight was always clearer than foresight. I'd screwed up; we'd *all* screwed up. "We should have complained."

"It's never easy to tell what might be considered a valid complaint," the Commandant observed, coldly. I shivered, but I had the feeling it was his companion who was being told off. "Recruits aren't expected to evaluate one another at this stage of their training."

The other unfamiliar man looked at me. "Regardless, recruit, what was your impression of Viper?"

I took a breath. "I don't think he wanted to be here, sir," I said. He wore no rank badges, but if he was here, sitting at the table, he had to be important. "He did the bare minimum to pass each exam, scraping through by the skin of his teeth. His contribution to teamwork was pathetic. I think he wanted to quit, but didn't quite dare. That's why some of us believed him to be a plant."

"It's a flaw in the system," the Commandant acknowledged. "We try to find people with the sheer bloody-minded determination to keep going, then nurture them. We're not allowed to reject anyone who has the grit to carry on."

I said nothing. I'd been told that the marines were quite informal - none of them had anything to prove to their fellows - but I wasn't a marine, not yet. The Commandant could blight my career with a word, if he wished. I wasn't sure I agreed with him either, something I kept firmly to myself. Viper had been a danger and he should have been removed from the platoon well before he pointed a gun at me and pulled the trigger.

"Given Viper's behaviour," one of the unfamiliar officers said, "do you believe he was on drugs? Or any other form of influence?"

"No, sir," I said. "Where would he have gotten them?"

It *was* an absurd question, as far as I could tell. Boot Camp was completely sealed off from the outside world. There were no packages in and out, only electronic messages that passed through the censor before being distributed to the recruits. Viper couldn't have gotten his hands on anything more dangerous than light painkillers...and even those would have been recorded, if he'd requested them from the medics. There was, quite simply, no way to get drugs into Boot Camp.

And even if he had managed to get them through the first hurdle, I thought, recalling the day I'd stripped naked upon entering Boot Camp, *he would have used them all by now, surely.*

"Some criminals can be quite inventive," the Commandant muttered, sardonically. He cleared his throat. "In hindsight, is there anything you wish you'd done differently?"

"I wish I'd complained about him, sir," I said, honestly. I had a feeling that there was no point in wishing he'd gone back to the trucks instead. "We could all have lodged a complaint."

"Maybe you should have done," the Commandant agreed. "There are some people who, through no fault of their own, never quite fit in here. Viper, however, does not fall into that category. He should have had the wisdom to quit."

"Yes, sir," I said.

"I'm afraid I'm going to have to ask you to remain in a side room until the inquest is over," the Commandant said, after a moment. "Do you have anything else you want to tell us?"

"No, sir," I said. Was I in trouble? I didn't know. "I..."

I stopped myself. The Commandant smiled.

"You may speak freely," he said.

"Sir," I said. "What is going to happen to him?"

"That depends on what we determine over the next few hours," the Commandant said. He nodded to Captain Giovanni. "Escort the recruit to the waiting room, please."

"Yes, sir," Captain Giovanni said.

I saluted, then allowed him to lead me through a maze of corridors and into a small room. It reminded me of the hostel, back on Earth; a bed, a small computer terminal and little else. I checked the terminal as soon as he left me alone and discovered, not entirely to my surprise, that it was locked out of the main system. The only files I could access were a handful of manuals, mainly centred around administrative procedures. Cursing under my breath, I started to read them anyway. The door might not be locked, but I knew better than to wander.

Bainbridge came for me two hours later. "Stalker," he said, as he opened the door. "Come with me."

"Yes, sir," I said.

"You have been found personally blameless," Bainbridge said, as we walked. "There was some disagreement over the question of what precisely you should have done, if you should have reported him to us, but they understood that you wouldn't have found it easy."

"Thank you, sir," I said.

"But you should have brought it to us," Bainbridge added. "We might have told you to shut up and soldier, but we might also have taken you seriously."

I wasn't so sure. The Drill Instructors had taught us to hate shirkers and malingerers - and recruits who grumbled incessantly. Viper had definitely fitted the bill, but at the same time *we* might have done, if we had bitched about him to our superiors. Yes, they *might* have taken us seriously - we *had* completed phase one and two, after all - or they might have chosen to override our concerns.

"Yes, sir," I said, instead. "Can this recruit ask a question?"

"Yes," Bainbridge said.

"Viper," I said. "What will happen to him?"

"It would depend, I imagine," Bainbridge said. "He will be dismissed from Boot Camp, certainly. Given the nature of his offense, he may be jailed or dumped on a penal colony, although he *might* be able to request indenture instead. His training would be quite useful on a colony world."

"Poor colonists," I said, without thinking.

"Don't underestimate them," Bainbridge said. "Many of the folks who left Earth and the Core World are self-selected for grit, determination and bloody-mindedness. Why do you *think* we find most of our recruits there?"

I hadn't thought about it at all, to be honest. It wasn't something I was going to tell him, either. And yet it was true; Earthers might be used to the government taking care of them - badly - but colonists knew they had no one to rely on, apart from themselves. Viper's training wouldn't make him a wolf among sheep, not on the colonies. He'd either find a place for himself or wind up dead.

"Yes, sir," I said. I hesitated, then asked another question. "Why was he caught between wanting to quit and being unable to quit? I thought *any* of us could quit."

Bainbridge gave me a thin smile. "And if I told you, recruit, that the answer to that question would cost you two hundred push-ups, would you pay?"

"Yes, sir," I said. I hadn't done anything like enough push-ups for the day anyway. "I would."

I wondered, just for a second, if he'd been expecting me to say no. But he was merely composing his thoughts.

"We do look into the background of our recruits, Stalker," he said. "Mainly, we look for criminal records, histories of substance abuse and other factors that might allow us to decline a particular application. Viper had no criminal record, nor did he have a history of drug abuse. But he did have a father who had political ambitions. A marine, perhaps someone who'd worked his way up the ranks, might be quite useful to him."

I frowned in puzzlement. The idea of a father actually raising his children was largely alien to me. God knew *my* father hadn't stuck around for my birth, let alone my childhood. I found myself torn between envy and an odd kind of sympathy. The Undercity had few decent fathers, but it had far too many adults who'd abused their children. It was hard to imagine Viper having a decent father.

"We get quite a few recruits who are pushed into the corps by their families," Bainbridge added. "Many of them are less than committed to the corps and quit before they reach the Slaughterhouse. Others find themselves absorbed into the marines and lose whatever tendency they might have had to put politics ahead of everything else. But Viper, it seemed, could neither let go of his father's ambitions for him nor concede defeat and quit. He was, as you said, forever torn between the desire to quit and the inability to quit."

"I don't understand," I admitted.

"His father would have disowned Viper if he had quit," Bainbridge said. "And he would probably have been disowned if he'd blended into the corps, losing whatever inclination he might have had to do whatever his father wanted. He never realised, I think, that the corps would have taken care of him. The brotherhood you and your comrades founded would have absorbed him too, if he had been willing to let go of his individuality. A shame, really. He had talents that might have been useful."

In truth, I still didn't understand. It wasn't until much later that I understood.

The Terran Marine Corps says that every man is a rifleman first. You cannot serve in the marines, or wield tactical authority, without passing through Boot Camp and the Slaughterhouse. Sure, we had auxiliaries who performed good and necessary work - starship driving, for example - but they never held authority. Our senior officers were all men who had seen the elephant; hell, we rotated officers between desk jobs and actual deployments on a regular scale, which was more than any other branch of the military did. It made sure they never lost track of what was important. Or, for that matter, of the simple fact that a plan which looked good on paper might be disastrous if tried in real life.

Every other branch had problems with uniformed politicians. It was staggeringly easy for the aristocracy to get its children into military academies, then ensure they graduated with high honours and took up commands without a day of actual experience. This, more than anything else, explains why there were so many problems with the army and navy. General Mendham, who was the overall CO on Moderato, was promoted to captain the day he left the academy…and spent most of his career doing staff work (or, more likely, getting someone *else* to do the staff work.) It might have needed doing, but it didn't prepare him for the task of pacifying an entire planet.

We walked back into the barracks and Bainbridge called us all to attention.

"You will be retaking the exams, starting tomorrow," he said, without preamble. I breathed a sigh of relief; I'd feared we would have to repeat phase three right from the start. "There will not, I'm afraid, be any credit based on your previous attempt. However, Viper's conduct will not be held against you."

"Thank god," Professor said.

"Fifty push-ups," Bainbridge said, tartly. He scowled at me, as if I'd personally offended him in some manner. "And Stalker, you owe me two hundred push-ups."

"Yes, sir," I said.

"One moment, both of you," Bainbridge added. He looked us over, one by one. "It is rare for someone to crack up in Boot Camp, particularly in phase three. We are normally very good at isolating recruits who pose a danger to themselves or others. In this case, we screwed the pooch, for which we apologise. It could have ended very badly."

I nodded, inwardly. If I'd moved a fraction slower, I would have ended up dead. I might have been wearing body armour, but it wouldn't have been enough to stop rifle bullets at close range. We designed our rounds to punch through body armour, after all. The enemy tended to wear armour too, if they could source it.

"If you have problems in future, you may come to us about them," he continued. "We will take them seriously."

I had my doubts, but they might well have been misplaced. We'd all learned a harsh lesson in the dangers of leaving problems to fester; in hindsight, perhaps we should have forced him to quit. Or isolated him... but that would have gotten us all in deep shit. Some of the tests couldn't be passed without the entire squad working together.

"Make sure you get plenty of rest, after chow," Bainbridge concluded. He gave us all an evil smile, promising blood, sweat, tears and pain. "You're going to need it."

He was right, of course. They plunged us straight back into the exams the following day, as if they wanted us to bury our fears in activity. And it worked. I never forgot Viper, or the inquest, but it didn't overshadow my thoughts...

Oh, and we aced the exams too.

CHAPTER
TWENTY-ONE

Stalker was not in trouble, when he was summoned to the inquest. The important matter, as far as the corps was concerned, was establishing precisely what had happened and why before making recommendations to higher authority. As it happened, Viper was dishonourably discharged from Boot Camp for numerous Headshots and offered a flat choice between being indentured on a colony world and immediate transport to the nearest penal colony. He chose indenture.

His ultimate fate is not recorded.

-Professor Leo Caesius

"You know," Joker said. "I *could* introduce you to my sister."

I shook my head. Joker's family had travelled to Mars for the pleasure of watching us march out as Boot Camp graduates, trapped midway between civilian and marine. We were no longer civilians - we had reached a point where we were guaranteed positions in the military - but we weren't marines either. Some of us, we knew, wouldn't be going on to the Slaughterhouse, even though we had completed Boot Camp. Phase four had made that far too clear.

"I think she wouldn't like me," I said. We'd bullshitted about girls in the barracks - although most of us had come to believe that girls simply didn't exist - but it was clear that we came from very different worlds. The Undercity was no place to develop manners for talking to women. "You go have fun with your family. I'll be fine."

Joker shot me a concerned look, then nodded slowly. "Make sure you do *something* with your leave, when you get it," he said. "If I'm around, we'll go hit the bars together."

I sighed, inwardly, as he headed towards his waiting family. Being on parade had been surreal. On one hand, I'd made it through Boot Camp, but on the other it was a grim reminder that my family was dead. I doubted they would have travelled to Mars just to watch me graduate in any case - the corps paid for family tickets - but it would have been nice to see them again. It wasn't going to happen, unless there *was* life after death. My father was an enigma, but the rest of my family was dead.

It felt strange to walk back towards the barracks, now largely empty. Most of the recruits - the ones with families - were going to Wells, where they would have a chance to catch up with their relatives and tell lies about Boot Camp. A handful of others had requested permission to travel to their homeworlds, which had been granted. I couldn't help wondering if that would be held against them, later. But there was no way to know.

The barracks felt abandoned, almost, as I stepped through the door. Those of us who were staying in the barracks, at least until we knew where we were going, had been told we could stay for as long as we liked, but it still felt odd, as if I were a butterfly climbing back into the cocoon. It was a *recruit* barracks, after all, and I was no longer a recruit. I peered down at the badge I'd been given for completing Boot Camp and sighed to myself. It was hard to deny that I no longer belonged in the barracks. For the first time since entering the camp, I felt completely at a loss.

Because there was always something to do, I reminded myself. If we'd had any free time, the Drill Instructors would happily have filled it. *But now I am at a loss.*

I lay back on my bunk and stared up at the ceiling. It was hard to summon the energy to do anything, even walk out of the camp - I could do that now - and take the train to Wells. I'd heard a great deal about the city from Joker, including elaborate details about its bars, brothels and other entertainments. Once, I wouldn't have hesitated before heading to the city to drown my sorrows, but now…now I felt as though I didn't belong there.

It was nearly an hour before Bainbridge poked his head through the door. I was surprised to see him. We might have told ourselves that Drill

Instructors spawned in barracks, or were created in test tubes by mad scientists, but we knew they had to have wives and families of their own. It wasn't as if they were *needed* to look after us not-recruits. I sprang to my feet and saluted, hastily. The habit was too ingrained to lose quickly.

Not that you want to lose it, I reminded myself. *There's the Slaughterhouse to come…*

"Stalker," Bainbridge said. "There's an officer from the Imperial Army who would like a moment of your time."

I blinked in surprise. "This recruit…ah, *I* didn't do anything!"

Bainbridge smirked. "A guilty conscience, Stalker? He's not here to arrest you, whatever you might have done, but to offer you a job."

He refused to be drawn any further. Instead, he led me back to the administrative block and into a small interview room. A man wearing a gorgeous uniform - I thought he was a colonel, but it was hard to tell - was sitting on the other side of a small table; he rose to his feet as I entered and held out his hand, rather than saluting. I hesitated - I hadn't shaken hands with anyone since entering Boot Camp - and then shook his hand firmly. It was impossible to be certain, but he didn't *look* like a soldier. I would have placed him as a teacher, without hesitation, if he hadn't been so unpleasantly plump.

"Mr. Stalker," he said. "I've followed your career with great interest."

I was suspicious at once. My career had consisted of little more than six months of intensive training, unless one counted the incident with Viper…and I was fairly sure that counted as a black mark. I *could* have prevented a near-disaster by reporting him to the Drill Instructors…No, I was being flattered…and I knew from experience that flattery was very dangerous. It only grew worse as he poured me a cup of coffee with his own hands. What sort of colonel served a mere recruit coffee?

"Thank you, sir," I said.

"I'm Colonel Weise," he continued. He waved me to a chair, then sat down facing me, resting his elbows on the table. "With your permission, I'll cut right to the chase."

"Of course, sir," I said.

"I represent the 101st Regiment, the famed Earth Guards," Weise explained. "We'd like you to join us. I can arrange for you to be commissioned as a lieutenant as soon as you enter the regiment, with a promotion to captain guaranteed within the first couple of years. There would be a choice of deployments, either on Earth or within the Core Worlds. Some of them will be dangerous, if you happen to crave excitement, while others will give you nothing, but time to catch up on your reading and attend parties."

For a long moment, I was *sure* I'd misheard. I'd known Boot Camp wasn't safe long before Ace's death, let alone the moment Viper had tried to kill me, and I'd had no illusions about combat (even if some of the danger zones did seem safer than the Undercity). I could have gone somewhere else if I'd wanted to be safe, or at least to have a reasonable chance of avoiding combat. It wouldn't have been *that* hard to become an indent, if I'd tried, or a zero-cost colonist...

It took me several seconds to stammer out a reply. "You want me to join you?"

"You're a young man of rare promise," Weise said. "The Earth Guards would be glad to have you, Mr. Stalker."

I stared at him. I'd been warned that it would be at least two years of active service before I was promoted to corporal, let alone lieutenant. Bainbridge had told us that such ranks were technically brevet ranks; they were hard to get, but easy to lose. It wasn't uncommon for a marine to remain a rifleman for his entire career. Why not? A marine rifleman ranked well above a lieutenant in the army.

It would have been tempting, I had to admit, if I'd merely wanted rank. The odds of reaching captain in the marines were low - and, really, I didn't want to rise any higher. No matter how regularly our officers were rotated between combat assignments and desk jobs, senior officers weren't really at the tip of the spear. How could they be?

"There is a signing bonus of ten thousand credits," Weise continued, when I said nothing. "It can be placed in your account as soon as you sign, then you will be entitled to a month's leave before you take your post..."

I wanted to shake my head. It was clear that Weise wasn't serious. He might have been serious about wanting to sign me up - I don't think anyone would have wasted my time or his for a trick - but he wasn't serious about going to war. I knew little about the Earth Guards, yet they were either desperate for trained manpower or intended to have me do the work while their officers partied. And if they were letting me party too…yes, something was definitely rotten in the regiment. I didn't really want to parade around all day, even if the regular uniform was something more reasonable than Weise's sniper-attracting garb.

Somehow, I managed to lean forward. "What else can you offer?"

Weise didn't seem surprised by the question. "Our salary is second to none," he said. "There are a host of other benefits, including access to some of the most well-connected officers in the military. Should you retire at the early age of forty" - twenty-one years in the regiment, I calculated silently - "you will have a splendid pension and the freedom of Imperial City on Earth. Your children, should you have any, will mingle with the children of the aristocracy."

And have a jolly time trying to afford the lifestyle, I thought, sarcastically. The children of gangsters always tended to have more than their friends and I assumed the principle was the same. *No one would want that for their kids.*

"I'd have to think about it," I temporised. Bainbridge would have kicked my ass for not having an immediate answer, but I wanted to see what Weise would do. "When can I get back to you?"

Weise reached into his uniform jacket and produced a business card. "A message sent to this address will reach me ASAP," he said, shortly. "I'd appreciate having your answer within the next couple of days."

"Yes, sir," I said.

He shook my hand again, then even opened the door for me as I left. It was so unlike a *real* officer that I could hear alarm bells ringing in my head. Weise wasn't just interested in my services, he was *desperate*. And yet, what could make him so desperate he wanted me, a very junior graduate from Boot Camp? The offer of being commissioned as a lieutenant *had* to be a joke. Maybe I should have demanded it in writing. *That* would have been harder to deny, later.

Bainbridge was waiting for me, just down the corridor.

"In here, Stalker," he said, leading me into another room. "What did you make of Colonel Weise?"

"It's a joke, sir," I said. "It *has* to be a joke."

Bainbridge smiled, coldly. "And why do *you* think it has to be a joke?"

I took a moment to organise my thoughts. "He offered me ten thousand credits as a signing bonus, as well as commissioning me as a lieutenant," I said. "Sir…it is a joke, isn't it?"

"I wish it was," Bainbridge admitted. "It isn't a joke, Stalker. And if you want to sign up with the Earth Guards, you'd get that bonus and more besides."

I stared. "Why?"

"Your teachers at school weren't allowed to tell you anything that might *traumatise* you," Bainbridge said. "And the precise definition of *traumatising* was made very broad indeed."

"I don't think they could tell us anything more traumatising than having to live in the Undercity and attend an Undercity school, sir," I said, tartly.

"Yes, but you're applying common sense," Bainbridge said. "And common sense is, alas, very uncommon."

He gave me a long considering look. "One of the things they weren't allowed to tell you was how the levers of government actually work," he added, after a moment. "Or, perhaps, how politics overshadow everything outside the Marine Corps and the Imperial Marshals. It isn't an exaggeration, Stalker, to say that you're much more qualified for the Earth Guards than anyone who comes out of their academy. Your training was actually focused on fighting and winning wars."

"I don't understand, sir," I admitted. "What does that have to do with my schooling?"

"The Earth Guards gets a crop of well-connected officers who have the collective military experience of a pea - or a grape," Bainbridge said. I wasn't sure that actually answered my question. "They *need* other officers who actually have some better training, because they're not allowed to train their officers properly. Yes, they *can* commission you as a lieutenant right from the start. They might even be able to give you a higher rank if you prodded. I imagine that Colonel Weise is desperate to ensure he doesn't have to do anything that resembles work."

He shrugged. "Take the offer, if you like," he added. "You'll probably find yourself serving as a captain, perhaps even a major, whatever rank you formally hold. There may well be some excitement. Or you may discover that you're doing nothing more exciting than marching around on the parade ground, watching helplessly as well-connected officers steal all the credit."

"Just like school," I said. "Why don't they teach us these things?"

"Because they're not allowed to teach the truth," Bainbridge said. He shrugged at my expression. "Knowledge is power, Stalker, and those in charge do their level best to keep power away from everyone else. How can you resist if you cannot even understand what is being done to you?"

I thought I understood, then. A punch in the face was blindingly obvious; you might hit the puncher back, or drop to your knees begging for mercy, but you'd know what had happened to you. You could think of ways to avoid it. But a more subtle attack, worked out over generations, might be impossible to comprehend. A primitive tribe, with no knowledge of radiation, might be wiped out without ever understanding a neutron bomb, let alone why one might be deployed against them. They would have no hope of fighting back.

And if someone comes up with an excuse that makes it impossible for you to learn, I thought, *you won't ever be able to stand up for yourself.*

"Shit," I said.

"It's your choice, Stalker," Bainbridge said. "You might find that it's a worthwhile post, if you're lucky. Or you make your own luck."

"I'm down for the Slaughterhouse, sir," I mused.

"Yes, you are," Bainbridge said. He made a show of checking his watch. "You have a week before the next ship leaves for hell. If you want to go, make sure you're here to catch it. Until then…you have a travel warrant, if you want to use it. Go play tourist and see something of the Solar System."

He turned and marched out of the room, leaving me alone. I knew he wouldn't tell me what to do. The corps only wanted people who wanted to be there. If I decided to cash in my chips and join the Earth Guards instead, no one would object. Hell, they'd probably be pleased to have a marine-friendly officer in a position of influence. I could get a lot done while my nominal superiors partied…

But it wasn't what I wanted. I wanted the camaraderie I'd shared with Joker and the rest of the squad. I wanted…I wanted a family.

I felt a stab of envy so strong it shocked me. Joker had a family, people who loved him; Viper, wherever he was now, had a family, even if his father was an asshole. But me? My family was dead. Self-pity was unlike me - there was no time for it in the Undercity - and yet I just wanted to scream at the unfairness of it all. Angrily, I shoved the thought to the back of my mind and locked it away, mentally throwing the key out of the window. The universe wasn't fair and if I wanted to change it, I'd have to keep that in mind.

And...

The thought struck me as I started to walk back to barracks. I could go anywhere within the Solar System, anywhere at all. It wouldn't be hard to see the sights of Mars, or Jupiter, or the giant forests of Venus…but I wanted to go back to Earth. I wanted to see my birthplace through new eyes.

I sat down at the terminal as soon as I reached the barracks, then did two things. First, I accepted the offer of a place at the Slaughterhouse. I'd go there and become a marine or die trying. And second, I booked a ticket to Earth. How much did it say about my education, I wondered, that I would have had problems booking a ticket before I'd gone to Boot Camp? I barely knew anything about the datanet.

And then, reluctantly, I started to pack. There wasn't much; the bedding and everything else belonged to the camp. My towels would be washed, then passed to the next set of recruits. I would have to leave my pistol and rifle behind, but everything else…

I wasn't looking forward to the trip, not really. But it was something I felt I had to do.

CHAPTER TWENTY-TWO

There were, of course, other problems in the military training academies. The toxic combination of political correctness and bureaucracy had practically eliminated anything more than very basic training; by the time a cadet graduated, he or she might only have fired a dozen rounds in training. (By contrast, a marine recruit could expect to fire off thousands of rounds during the first month of Boot Camp.) Grades were assigned on the basis of rank and family connections, not actual ability. The handful of graduates who proved to be genuine military geniuses were heavily outnumbered by the uniformed fops.

-Professor Leo Caesius

Earth *stank*.

It wasn't something I'd noticed, back when I'd been a child. People can get used to anything, if they don't know any better. Now, though, I'd lived on Mars, in Boot Camp. There, the air had been clean; here, it smelled of burning hydrocarbons and too many humans in close proximity.

I hadn't been able to take a marine shuttle, this time. Instead, I'd boarded an in-system ship at Wells, which had transported me to one of Earth's giant orbital towers. It - and the halo of asteroid stations and industrial nodes surrounding Earth - had been impressive, but the interior was a vast disappointment. It was dirty - grime lay everywhere - and the people...*dear god,* the people! They were awful!

The long line of people waiting to pass through customs gave me ample opportunity to observe Earthers from an outside perspective. There were men so overweight that their clothing kept threatening to burst open, escorted by women so thin that they looked suspiciously like beanpoles. One of them had a son who had been surgically modified to look like an elf; beside him, his older sister had breasts so large they couldn't possibly be real. Once, perhaps, I would have stared at her openly; now, all I could do was look away in disgust. But all I saw were more and more examples of the absolute grossest of humanity; men who'd deliberately enhanced their muscles, women who'd enhanced their bottoms until I thought they'd need to sit on cushions and children who had been shaped - and reshaped - to meet current fashion. It was utterly revolting.

You were born here, my thoughts reminded me.

Shut up, I thought back.

The inspector eyed my travel warrant carefully, clearly angling for a bribe. I glared at him when he started making the traditional sign, my eyes promising bloody violence if he even *thought* about delaying my trip. He looked down, stamped my warrant and then waved me through, without even bothering with a close inspection. I rolled my eyes - I could have smuggled several of the more *interesting* weapons through without problems - and headed to the elevator. Maybe if I got drunk fast enough…

I pushed that thought aside, then found a quiet seat and waited for the elevator to start its descent to Earth. I'd never have dreamed of reading in public before - only nerds did that - but now I dug one of my books out of my bag and started to read. If someone had tried something stupid, I could have given them a nasty shock. A girl who would have been pretty, if she hadn't dipped her face in make-up, sat down next to me and tried to make small talk, claiming to be on her first trip to Earth. I had no trouble in recognising a pickpocket when I saw one and glared at her, keeping one hand on my wallet, until she got the hint and sauntered off to sit next to a teenage boy who was remarkably fat. He beamed at such a pretty girl paying attention to him. I just hoped he wasn't carrying too much money.

It only got worse as we reached the bottom of the shaft and walked through the concourse and into the giant CityBlock. There were hundreds of thousands of people all around me, pressing in so tightly that I almost had a panic attack. Small children - some of them with their parents, some learning how to beg or steal from travellers - were running everywhere, getting underfoot. I picked out their masters effortlessly, wishing I could do something about them. It wasn't *right* that children should have to steal to live - and be exiled to various colony worlds, if they were lucky when they were caught. But I knew there was no point in trying to do anything. I could kill every one of the masters within sight and a hundred more would take their place within days.

"Hey, soldier," a girl called. "Looking for a room to spend the night?"

A year ago, I knew I would have accepted. She was pretty enough, with long dark hair that drew attention to her breasts and probably a year or two older than me. It wouldn't be long before she looked old enough to be my mother, begging on the streets after she lost her looks and her pimp dumped her. A combination of drugs and abuse - both physical and mental - would drain her of life well before she actually died. Her pimp wouldn't give a damn. The hell of it was working up here, servicing a dozen men a day, was still better than life in the Undercity.

"No, thank you," I said.

The girl shrugged - she was probably rejected all the time - and turned her attention to the next potential customer, who looked a little more interested. I hoped he was smart enough to use protection - prostitutes tended to pick up all sorts of unpleasant surprises for the unwary - and then shrugged, dismissing the problem. He could probably take care of himself.

Unless she's really luring rich customers into a trap, so they can be mugged, I thought, sourly. I'd seen that game in the Undercity, although it was relatively rare. No one had anything worth stealing. Besides, the cops would take *some* kind of action if visitors to Earth were mugged the moment they stepped off the elevator. *Or would they, on Earth?*

I pushed that thought aside too, then found an airbus heading to my CityBlock. It struck me I could spend my time seeing the sights, such as they were, instead, but the urge to visit my home was overwhelming. Earth's atmosphere looked far more dangerous than Mars, I decided, as I peered through the porthole. Mars might have regular storms that grounded aircraft and even threatened shuttlecraft, but at least it didn't rain acid and pollution on a daily basis. For all the ranting and raving about preventing pollution and cleaning up the Earth, the situation was getting worse and worse by the day.

No one even looked at me as I disembarked from the airbus, then walked towards the shafts leading down to the Undercity. It looked worse, far worse, than the scenes that had greeted me when I left the elevator. We'd *known* that the upper-blockers were wealthy, but I understood now that they weren't much richer than any of us. They'd only been luckier, perhaps, to live in a place where the gangs weren't so strong. They had a slightly more peaceful existence.

At the cost of being raped by the government, my thoughts mocked me. The government dictated the lives of every last person in the upper block. They couldn't buy extra toilet paper without some bureaucrat asking questions. *That's the biggest gang of all.*

I frowned as I saw the gang signs painted in the shaft, marking their territory, then shrugged to myself. It shouldn't really be surprising that they were unfamiliar. Gangs formed, then fell apart with terrifying speed. Every gang I'd feared and hated as a child was probably long gone by now. I kept walking, entering a long corridor that led towards my old apartment and school. The kids were just coming out of the security gates; the nerds running, as fast as they could, in hopes of escaping the bullies, while the stronger ones sauntered along, some clinging to the girls they protected in exchange for sex. I'd known girls who were grandmothers by the time they turned thirty. No wonder, if a strong man was their only hope of protection…but it never actually lasted.

When society breaks down, I recalled from one of the lectures, *women always get the worst of it.*

I didn't want to look at them. Most of them looked beaten, broken, downtrodden…it was horrifying to think that I had been one of them, once. The junior school wasn't much better; the kids were younger, not even entering their teens, yet there was a hardness in their eyes that I had once accepted as normal. Even the ones lucky enough to have a stable family who didn't beat or abuse them had that bitter look, the awareness that their lives were already over before they were born. They'd grow up at the mercy of the gangs…

They could leave, I thought…

...But even as I thought it, I knew it wasn't true. I'd been lucky; I'd found the marines and then planned to join them even before my family died. Everyone else...they'd get killed, or broken, or addicted to drugs, or join the gangs and prey on their fellows. The wolves would eat the sheep, while there wasn't a single sheepdog amongst them. What sheepdog would risk his life for such awful sheep?

I couldn't bear it any longer. Gritting my teeth, I turned and walked towards my former apartment. It had been months, but I knew the way like the back of my hand. I'd half-expected to see the door still open, the bodies still on the floor, even though I knew it was silly. I shouldn't have been surprised to realise that a new family had been moved into the apartment, presumably after the bodies had been removed. They should have been taken to the recyclers, but I knew they might have been dumped down a shaft or simply eaten by whoever had found them. Cannibalism was far from healthy, quite apart from any moral objections one might have, but the Undercity rarely saw fresh meat. My family might have ended their days in someone's stomach. I hoped, bitterly, that they'd given the cannibals indigestion.

There was a sound, just down the corridor. I blinked tears away from my eyes as I saw a door open and a young girl peeking out. She took one look at me, then jumped back and slammed the door closed. I didn't blame her. The Undercity might be infested with rats, cockroaches and other small creatures, but the most dangerous animal of all walked on two legs. No one with the power to do anything about it gave a damn.

"You're a fucking idiot, Edward," I said, as I turned and started to walk back towards the shaft. "What did you *expect* to find down here?"

I'd definitely been an idiot. There wasn't anything for me here, but validation. I'd made the right choice when I'd fled, no matter what Trevor had said. If I'd stayed, I would have compromised and compromised again until I was a monster - or worse. I wished, bitterly, that I'd been able to take my sisters with me, instead of having to watch them die, but leaving had been the right choice. There was no future in the Undercity.

Bainbridge would have kicked my ass. I was so lost in my own thoughts as I walked back past the schools that I didn't realise I was being tracked until five men - boys, really - moved out of the shadows to block my way to the shaft. They looked intimidating enough, to someone who knew no better, but I didn't feel particularly impressed. Three of them were clearly on a cheap battle drug - we'd been warned not to use them - while the other two were carrying makeshift weapons and trying to look tough. I felt a sudden surge of hatred as I pulled myself up into a combat stance, then deliberately overdid it. They'd think I was faking everything…

"Give us your wallet and everything else you're carrying and you can go," the leader said, in a thick accent I hadn't heard for six months. I knew, of course, that they wouldn't let me go so easily. They had a reputation to keep. "Now."

"Come and take it," I said. They were armed, but I was dangerous. I was more worried about the handful of children staring at the impending fight, as if it was a form of entertainment. Watching a beating was always amusing in the Undercity, at least as long as you weren't on the receiving end. "If you think you can…"

I stuck out my tongue, deliberately. One of the druggies snarled and lunged forward, the drug overriding his common sense. His companions followed a moment later. They *do* enhance aggression, true, but they also tend to dampen any possibility of calculated violence. No one in their right mind gives out battle drugs unless they don't give a damn about either their troops or the local population. The last time anyone ever tried deploying a drugged-up regiment, the enemy were brutally slaughtered before the troops turned on the locals and committed enough atrocities to make even the Civil Guard blanch.

"Idiot," I said, coolly. *Viper* had been a better fighter than any of the drug-addled morons. "I can take you like *this*."

I slammed my fist into the leader's throat. He stumbled to a halt, his companions crashing into him and shoving his body aside ruthlessly. I caught the next one as he threw a meaty fist at me, stepping aside and kneeing him in the balls. He doubled over; I kicked him in the head, hard enough to crack his skull, then turned to the third. The drug had overridden his rationality so badly that he seemed to have forgotten his target, his gaze flickering from face to face as if he was trying to decide who best to attack. It was quite possible he'd go after the children…

I didn't give him the chance. I struck him in the chest, then brought my knee up and slammed it into his nose. Bone crunched as he toppled forward and hit the ground. I spun around, just in time to evade a swipe from a makeshift sword. The gangster thought of himself as fast, I was sure, but I'd had six months at Boot Camp and he might as well have been crawling towards me. I caught his arm, applied pressure and smiled as he yelped in pain and dropped the sword. It was easy to snatch it out of the air - the balance was appallingly bad - swing it around and slice it into the side of his neck. I didn't think the blade was particularly sharp either; I'd hit with all my strength, but I hadn't managed to behead him. Still, the fountain of blood was enough to prove he was dead, unless he got immediate attention.

The last gangster, the leader, was sneaking backwards, holding his sword in a suddenly limp hand. I felt a flush of anger and came at him, carrying the sword I'd stolen in one hand. He tried to parry my thrust, but he didn't really have any proper training at all. His sword was so badly designed that it shattered when I slammed my blade against it. I shoved him against the wall, then used my sword to impale him. He let out a gurgle and died.

I felt nothing. My training had sunk in too deeply for me to enjoy what I'd done, even though I'd just carved through five gangsters within minutes. They'd deserved it, I told myself; they'd raped, murdered and looted in the certain knowledge that no one would dare to stand up to them. They were wolves and I was a sheepdog. Killing such vermin was what I was born to do.

And yet I still felt nothing, even when the children started to clap. They knew better than to show anything other than delight; hell, maybe they *were* delighted. I turned to look at them and they started to flee. Maybe they'd go to their parents and tell them that the gangs could be beaten - or, more likely, they'd tell them that a new gang was moving into the CityBlock, one that was utterly ruthless. I took one last look at the gangsters - their bodies would be fodder for the rats soon enough, if the cannibals didn't get them - and then started to walk back to the shaft. No one tried to block my way as I returned to the surface and headed to the nearest elevator. It was high time I returned to Mars.

Once I returned to Boot Camp, I did two things. First, I downloaded a complete guide to the Slaughterhouse, along with a number of books from the recommended reading list. It would take at least two weeks to *reach* the Slaughterhouse, even on a marine transport, and I had no intention of wasting the time. Second, I contacted the personnel department and requested permission to change my name. Two hours later, I had a new set of ID paperwork and it was done.

For reasons I never fully understood, marine nicknames sometimes became official names. I think it was a tradition that dates back to the first foreign legion, but no one knows for sure; I suspect it was intended to draw a line between civilian and marine that would be harder to cross in the future. That, at least, was how it was for me. My old surname no longer fitted the person I had become. As far as anyone would know in the future, I was Edward Stalker.

And the person I had been, the scared Undercity rat, was dead.

CHAPTER TWENTY-THREE

No one can fault Edward for killing the gangsters. As he correctly points out, they were vermin, monsters who made it impossible for anyone to have a decent life. However, his actions made no difference. The dead gangsters were replaced within hours and whatever flickers of hope were sown in the hearts of men were swiftly quenched. It was the whole system, the refusal to bring law and order to the Undercity, that was guilty - and it was quite beyond repair.

The children Edward saw might have lived long enough to sire the next generation. Their children did not.

-Professor Leo Caesius

The Slaughterhouse is the strangest world in known space.

At least in my opinion. It's certainly the most brutal. The first terraforming attempt failed spectacularly - that's only happened twice in all the thousands of years mankind has been exploring space - and the successive attempts to tame the world only made it nastier, more unwelcoming to human settlement. Someone introduced animals from a dozen different worlds and let them fight it out for dominance, just to see what would happen. By the time the Terran Marine Corps bid for the planet - and purchased it for a song - the Slaughterhouse was a mess. No one believed the marines would keep the planet for long.

"Welcome to the Slaughterhouse," Commandant Jeremy Damiani (yes, *that* Damiani) said, once we were escorted off the shuttle and into a large hanger. "Welcome to hell."

I kept my face impassive as he looked us up and down. There were nearly four hundred troopers - we were no longer recruits - in the hanger, men assembled from a hundred Boot Camps scattered over the length and breadth of the Empire. Joker stood beside me, of course, along with four others I knew who'd been selected for the Slaughterhouse. The remainder were strangers. Some of them looked tougher and more capable than I had ever dreamed of being, back when I'd first heard of the marines. Others had the calm professional look we'd been taught to present at all times, even when the shit was hitting the fan. It kept the civilians from panicking.

"You can leave this place in one of five ways," Damiani continued, calmly. I don't think he paid any special attention to me - and really, why should he? I was just one out of four hundred new candidates for the Rifleman's Tab. "You can quit, as you know; you can die, you can commit one of the Headshots, you can join the auxiliaries or you can qualify as fully-trained marines. There aren't any other options."

He paused, studying us all coldly. "We search for four things in our candidates," he said, after a long moment. "We want our candidates to be adaptable, to be smart, to have grit and - perhaps least of all - to have muscle. Many find this unusual, but the truth is that we can use augmentation and genetic engineering to produce any number of muscle-bound morons. The first three qualities are often more important to us. That you are here, on the Slaughterhouse, is testament to the fact we believe you can make it. You would not be here if we thought otherwise.

"The Slaughterhouse is deliberately designed to be a foretaste of hell. Those of you who aced Boot Camp are in for a nasty surprise. You will be pushed right to the limits - and beyond. If you pass, you will have achieved something that no one will ever be able to take from you, whatever happens. And, if you fail, there is no shame in trying."

I wasn't sure I believed him. But then, I didn't *want* to fail. I wanted to be a marine.

"The basic rules have not changed from the days of Boot Camp," Damiani said, slowly. "But there is one difference that needs to be hammered home. This is the first time you will train alongside two very different groups of people. There are those from outside your sector - and those of the opposite sex. You are to keep two things in mind at all times. First, they have passed the same Boot Camp as you; second, sexual contact of any sort between marines - even troopers like yourselves - is still strictly forbidden. We have ways of finding out the truth and I will not hesitate to break anyone guilty of crossing the line. The very best any of you can hope for is a dishonourable discharge that will ensure you never serve in the military again."

I glanced around as best as I could, without making it obvious. Were there women in the group facing the Commandant? I couldn't see any; hell, as far as I could tell, we were all men. But he wouldn't have kept the women segregated any longer, would he?

"I hope to be the one who pins the Rifleman's Tab on your collar, the day you graduate from the Slaughterhouse," Damiani concluded. "Until then, I wish you the very best of luck. You're going to need it."

He returned our salute, then stepped out of the hanger. A grim-faced man wearing another Smoky the Bear hat - this one black as night - stepped up to take his place.

"Greetings," he said. His tone admitted of no weakness whatsoever. "I am Drill Instructor (Slaughterhouse) Larry Southard. For my sins, I have been placed in charge of the latest intake of prospective marines. With me are Drill Instructor (Slaughterhouse) Gaige Mosher" - a thin wiry man with a faint smile, standing next to a short man who seemed to have muscles on his muscles - "and Drill Instructor (Slaughterhouse) Jim Seibert. It is my task to shepherd you through the course and turn you into qualified marines. You heard the rest of the speech at Boot Camp, so I won't bore you with it again."

"Thank God," Joker muttered.

"You are troopers now, not recruits," Southard continued, coldly. "We will not be peering over your shoulders at all times, not like the Drill Instructors did at Boot Camp. You have proved you can be trusted to handle yourselves. However, if you are caught slacking off, you will regret it. This is the one and only warning you will get."

He paused to allow that to sink in, then spoke on. "You will now report to the medics, who will carry out a series of tests before you are cleared to enter the training grounds," he told us, his voice never wavering. "While you are waiting, you should read the documents that will be handed out to you. They will give you a basic introduction to the Slaughterhouse and how we expect you to comport yourselves during training. There *will* be a test on it later."

I groaned, inwardly. I'd had enough of such tests at Boot Camp. Professor had been an expert at drawing information from documents and summarising it for the Drills, but I'd always had problems. Professor had even complained that the person who'd written the documents was an idiot. It wasn't until much later that we'd realised they'd done it deliberately.

"Follow me," Southard ordered.

We marched through the door, across a parade ground and into another medical building. It looked identical to the one on Mars; later, I learned that was deliberate, a way of preparing the recruits for the Slaughterhouse and Marine FOBs. All of our prefabricated buildings were identical, just waiting for us to slot them together. Inside, we lined up, took a copy of the induction briefing from the pile by the door and waited impatiently for our names to be called.

"Stalker," Joker hissed. "Look at her."

I looked. For a moment, I thought Joker might be mistaken. The trooper on the other side of the room didn't *look* very feminine. She had no breasts, as far as I could tell; she looked very much like a thin muscular man. Her hair was shaved close to her scalp, like mine. Indeed, I *would* have taken her for a male if it hadn't been for a faint hint of uncanny valley around the trooper, as if there was something about her that wasn't quite right. She looked up, caught me staring and glared back at me, challengingly. I had been told that Boot Camp was harder on women than men, but I hadn't believed it until that moment.

"Stalker," the medic bellowed.

I nodded as respectfully as I could to the woman, then headed through the door and into the examination room. (Or, as we came to call it, the chamber of tortures.) The doctor ordered me to strip, poked and prodded me in a number of delicate places - I barely managed to keep myself from asking if he was going to buy me dinner afterwards - and then took another set of blood, urine and stool samples. I stayed on the table and waited as patiently as I could until the analyser came back with the results.

"You're clean of anything dangerous or incriminating," the doctor said, gruffly. He didn't seem intimidated by me at all. Like most of the planet's staff, he was probably either a marine or an auxiliary serving a term on the Slaughterhouse before returning to the front lines. He'd seen far worse, I suspected, than a trooper who had a high opinion of himself. "I believe you visited Earth, correct?"

"Yes, sir," I said, automatically.

"Generally not a good place to visit without broad-spectrum vaccines," the doctor said. "Luckily, the jabs you got at the start of Boot Camp covered you against any threats."

"I was *born* on Earth," I protested.

"Some quite nasty bugs loose on the planet will see their chance to strike at you again, if you leave Earth for a few months," the doctor said. "It's the most disease-riddled planet in human space."

I shuddered. I'd had the basics of field hygiene and sanitation drilled into me in Boot Camp and, in hindsight, it made me sick to realise just how badly we'd been fouling our nests in the Undercity. A sewer bursting and releasing its contents into the corridors was seen as a chance to play games, not something to cause a panic; hell, there were places you couldn't visit without stumbling over dead bodies, left where they'd fallen. If we hadn't had some genetic engineering worked into our bodies, most of us would probably have died a long time ago.

"Personally, I blame it on the Nihilists," the doctor added. "They've been looking for a way to slaughter millions of people overnight for years."

He looked me up and down, then nodded. "You're dismissed, trooper," he said. "Go through that door" - he pointed to a door on the other side of the room - "and wait until the Drill Instructors corral you."

"Yes, sir," I said.

Outside, there were a handful of benches and not much else. I sat down next to a couple of troopers I didn't know and started to read through the short briefing document. It wasn't anything like as bad as I had feared; it was a brief outline of the planet's history, a guide to the areas we could visit and a number of stern warnings of precisely what we could expect if we tried to enter any of the high security areas. Joker emerged next, looking obscenely cheerful; I rolled my eyes as he sat down next to me, then leaned over to whisper in my ear.

"I think she likes you," he hissed.

"I think she isn't worth getting the boot," I hissed back.

It was an odd thought. The idea of a woman actually fighting was new to me, let alone a woman joining the marines. In my experience, women either sought protectors or simply gave it up the moment someone pressed. But then, all else being equal, the average man will always be stronger than the average woman. It isn't sexism, just cold hard biological fact…yes, training and weapons can even the odds, but both training and weapons are in short supply in the Undercity, certainly not the kind of weapons women can use without a great deal of practice.

You could clean up the Undercity within days if you handed out pistols to each and every woman above the age of ten, I thought. *But their lords and masters prefer to leave them defenceless.*

It was nearly an hour before the Drill Instructors entered the compartment, by which time all four hundred of us had seen the medics and I'd read my way through the briefing documents twice. The Slaughterhouse had one large island that had been completely terraformed - Liberty Island - and a number of training facilities scattered around the main continent. We would be granted permission to go on leave to Liberty Island every so often - unless we were on punishment duty for one reason or another - but we were expected to abide by the rules while we were there.

Southard explained it to us while we were marching to our next destination. "Every marine - and every auxiliary - has the right to spend his or her retirement on the Slaughterhouse," he told us. "They often bring their families here, to a place where safety is guaranteed and children can be raised without fear of two-legged predators. There is even a Boot Camp facility for any of their children who wish to become marines.

"There are facilities at the lower tip of the island - Liberty Town - for anyone who is not a permanent resident," he continued. "You can visit the brothel, if you wish, or spend the day gambling in the casino. Those facilities, uniquely in the Empire, are owned and supervised by the corps. The safety and security of those who go to visit is guaranteed."

But you'll know who develops a gambling habit, I thought. Everything was a test, we'd been told, and Liberty Town was just another way to see how we behaved. *And who starts treating the whores badly.*

"However, you are not permitted to develop a relationship with the partners or children of serving or retired marines," Southard warned. "I don't care if it is one hundred and fifty percent consensual, I don't care if your lover is well over the age of consent; you're not allowed to have any form of sexual contact with the partners or children of serving or retired marines. Should you graduate, either as a marine or an auxiliary, things will be different."

I puzzled over the restriction for a long time. There had been some girls in the Undercity no one had dared touch, if only because their fathers had been gangsters or strong enough to take bloody revenge on anyone who soiled their daughters. I wouldn't have cared to touch the daughter of a serving marine…or even a retired one, someone who could call on friends and allies if necessary. Later, I learned it was a standard precaution; a trooper might be on the planet one day, then gone the next. We weren't meant to date, let alone marry, until we knew where we stood.

Southard stopped as he reached a building, then started to bark out names. I found myself assigned to a training platoon with Joker and eight other troopers I didn't know, including the woman. She regarded us all impassively and said nothing as Southard informed us that we were the latest Slaughterhouse Training Platoon #37 and that we had a long and proud history of producing marines to live up to. His companions showed us to our barracks, a cramped room that looked even less comfortable than the barracks on Mars, then directed us back outside.

"I'm Joker," Joker said as we waited for the other platoons to assemble, "and this disreputable asshole is Stalker. Who are you?"

I smiled as we were told eight new nicknames. The woman turned out to have been nicknamed Sif, although I had no idea why. Joker kept chatting to everyone, trying to draw them out; it helped, somehow, to cope with our fraying nerves. By the time Southard bellowed for attention, I knew that four of the eight troopers - including Sif - came from the rim and the other four came from a handful of worlds in the Inner Ring. We didn't have much in common, beyond a shared desire to be marines.

"Blackmon," Southard said, as he passed us. "You're the Platoon Leader."

"Yes, sir," Blackmon said.

"And he does have the authority to kick you all in the ass, if necessary," Southard added, addressing us all. His voice was still hard. "You're not in Boot Camp now."

I nodded. Recruits were given ranks within the platoons and told to assert authority, but they rarely had any *real* power. Bainbridge had explained, quoting a very old textbook, that no one ever saluted a recruit-officer unless the lighting was *very* dim. I hadn't understood until I realised that the idea was to develop *personal* authority, rather than *positional* authority. If we couldn't convince our fellows to follow us, we wouldn't be able to assert authority on the battlefield.

But this was the Slaughterhouse. Things were different here.

Southard cleared his throat for attention, an evil glint in his eye. "Are we all having fun, troopers?"

"YES, SIR," we bellowed. I don't think I was the only one thinking *oh shit*.

"Good," Southard said. His voice took on a sweet tone that convinced me that I wasn't going to enjoy what was coming next. "Glad to hear it. Now everything is squared away, it's time for a run. It's five miles to the Chow Hall and if we don't get there in time the food will all have been eaten by the REMFs."

I was right. I didn't enjoy the run at all.

But, compared to what was coming, it was paradise itself.

CHAPTER TWENTY-FOUR

The oddest thing about the Slaughterhouse is that it was technically independent of the Empire, even as it provided the Empire with its greatest warriors. Major-General Carmichael, the effective founder of the Terran Marine Corps, somehow convinced the then-Emperor to grant the planet a charter of perpetual freedom, allowing the development of a marine-civilisation on a very small scale. It was a world where few of the Empire's laws were heeded yet, in many ways, it was the safest place to live.

Unfortunately, few other planets had the means to follow the Slaughterhouse's example.

-Professor Leo Caesius

The first month at the Slaughterhouse went by in a blur. I only half-remember the details, even though I can look back at my personal logbook and see the number of route marches, shooting exercises and other pieces of training I did. It was thoroughly hellish; we were marched until we very nearly broke, carrying more than double our bodyweight as we struggled up mountains and through muddy swamps, then shot at as we carried out a tactical advance to battle (tabbing, we called it.) And then they gassed us, ran us through another set of Conduct After Capture exercises and then shot at us some more. It was not a pleasant time.

It would be wrong to say there wasn't any levity, I suppose. Joker did his best to keep us entertained, cracking jokes at one moment and singing songs the next. (I'd write the lyrics to his version of *Rain, Rain, Go Away*, but then this book would be banned even on Old Earth, where just about anything was considered acceptable.) Southard and his two demonic assistants thought of this as a personal challenge - "if you have enough breath to sing," he'd say, "you have enough breath to walk faster" - and pushed us all much harder. It was a relief when we were finally granted two days of liberty in Liberty Town, with a warning ringing in our ears that it might be the last leave we ever had.

We found out what they meant when we returned to barracks and saw an ancient-looking spacecraft sitting on the launching pad. It was so outdated it actually used rockets to fly, rather than antigravity fields. We were given yet another lecture on what to do if things went wrong, then we were marched into the spaceship and sat down. Moments later, it took off with a roar like thunder and launched itself into orbit. I recalled the aircraft we'd jumped from, back on Mars, and felt a tinge of guilt. Compared to the spacecraft, the aircraft had been perfectly safe.

Disaster struck as we entered orbit. A loud *bang* echoed through the craft, followed by the tell-tale whistle of depressurisation. I felt a flicker of panic, but hours spent jumping from aircraft in increasingly flimsy parachutes - the less said about HAVLO parachutes the better - had taught me to keep my fear under control. We grabbed for our facemasks as the drives cut off, leaving us suddenly weightless. The temperature dropped rapidly as more and more air flowed into the icy vacuum of space.

"This ship is going down," Southard said, quite calmly. "We don't have the fuel to stabilise our orbit or even to hold position long enough for another shuttle to take us off. Ideas?"

I felt numb. It was a test. It *had* to be a test. And yet, I was scared.

"Get to the station," Blackmon said. He was the only one of us who'd been born in space, the child of a spacer father and a RockRat mother. I don't think he'd had a happy childhood, although he rarely spoke of it to us. "We have some EVA packs onboard. It should be possible to fly to the station. If we send a distress signal, they should have someone ready to catch us if necessary."

"We could link them together and use the thrust to push us into a stable orbit," Sif offered, grimly. She was always putting forward ideas, as if she was desperate to prove she belonged amongst us. "They should have enough thrust."

"They're not designed to be linked together," Blackmon countered.

"We could don them, then get to the hull and fire in unison," Bloodnok suggested. "We might just save the shuttle."

"There isn't time," Blackmon said. "We'd have to calculate our trajectory - and if we burned out the packs before we made it into a stable orbit, we would have sealed our fate."

There was a pause. I searched frantically for a better idea, but I couldn't think of anything. I was a brave man on the ground - it isn't easy to sneak forward when some asshole is pinging bullets bare millimetres above your head - but in space...? I wasn't a coward, but space had always left me cold. It was the most hazardous environment I'd experienced since leaving Earth.

"If you're not within reach of life support gear," Bainbridge had said months ago, "pull down your trousers, bend over backwards and kiss your ass goodbye."

Blackmon shook his head. "Get the EVA packs," he ordered, as he checked his datapad. "I think we should have a reasonable chance of making it if we jump in five minutes, when we're closest to the station. I'll transmit the emergency signal."

We nodded, then hurried to strap the EVA packs onto our backs. They had looked fun, when I'd first seen them, although they weren't much good on a planetary surface. The man-portable jetpack wasn't exactly a fantasy, not with antigravity units helping to reduce the mass, but a man wearing a jetpack made a distressingly easy target. I checked my shipsuit carefully, then checked Joker's while he checked mine. They were, in theory, rated for long-term use in space, but no one cared to take chances. Space wasn't exactly safe by a long chalk.

"Check your radios," Blackmon ordered. He waited for us all to sound off, individually, then led us to the airlock. "Get onto the hull, then prepare to boost on my command."

The cold of space seemed to leech through the shipsuit as I stepped through the airlock and out onto the spacecraft's hull. We were tumbling through space; the stars rotating around us, with the Slaughterhouse itself coming into view every forty seconds. It looked surprisingly normal from orbit, just another blue-green orb floating in the interplanetary void. But there was no sign of anything remotely *human* from orbit, nothing like the angry grey-blue Earth with her orbital towers reaching up to low orbit…

"On my mark," Blackmon ordered. "Boost!"

I triggered my EVA pack and jumped off the hull. It was a leap of faith; one of the lights high overhead had to be the station, but which one? Stars don't twinkle in orbit, not when there isn't any atmosphere to create the effect; they looked like pinpricks of light, blazing out against the all-encompassing darkness. There were people who worship the dark between the stars, I knew; now, staring into the darkness, I understood just how they felt. No matter how brightly the stars blazed, eventually entropy would take them and the whole universe would fall into darkness.

"Here she comes," Blackmon said. The station loomed out of the darkness, illuminated by brilliant lights that cast her structure into sharp relief. She looked like a child's set of building toys, a fragile network of cylinders held together by golden framework. "Get ready to latch on…"

I braced myself, then used the last of the propellant to slow down as I closed with the station. Perception shifted; I was suddenly *falling* towards the station, rather than closing in on it. I fought down a sudden wave of disorientation, then caught hold as I hit the cylinder. There was no time to congratulate myself, I knew; I forced myself forward to the nearest airlock and keyed it open. Moments later, I was safely inside the station.

"Well done," Southard said, once we gathered in the station's personnel compartment. "You all managed to survive."

We beamed, even though none of us were particularly pleased about the test. It had been rigged, of course, and there had been no real danger…but it had still been thoroughly unpleasant. A single misjudgement at the wrong time could have sent us spinning helplessly into interstellar space…or down towards the planet below. The former might have been bad enough, but the latter would have been disastrous. None of our shipsuits were rated for re-entry and a shuttle might not be able to catch the faller before it was too late.

"There will not, of course, be any break," Southard continued, as if it had been merely a minor bump in the road. "You're due to spend two weeks on this station and by the time we return to the planet, you will have laid the groundwork for understanding operations in space."

It was, in many ways, both the most fascinating and the most frustrating part of the time I spent at the Slaughterhouse. Space poses a whole new series of tactical problems; your enemy can come from any direction, forcing you to spread your defences thinner than you would prefer. You're completely dependent on the starship, or battlestation, or shuttle; maintenance isn't a luxury, it's an urgent requirement. Decompression or life support failure can become major threats at the worst possible time. And then there is the endless problem of forcing your way into a starship - or an orbiting battlestation - that doesn't want to surrender. A smart enemy, one who knew there was no hope of escape, might just wait for you to land, then trigger the self-destruct.

"Pirates know they have no hope of survival," Southard told us. He didn't sound guilty at the thought of butchering pirates. "But what about their prisoners? Don't they deserve a chance to survive?"

"They're helping the pirates," Bloodnok pointed out. "Shouldn't we be putting them on trial as collaborators?"

Southard pulled himself over to him. "Imagine that you're a crewman on a trader starship," he sneered. "Your father is the commander, you're the chief engineer, your sisters are the crew chiefs, your mother is the medic…imagine you have strong ties to your family. You love them dearly.

"And then you fall into pirate hands," he added. "Your father is killed. You're told that your mother and sisters will be raped to death unless you collaborate. What do you do?"

I groaned inwardly. It was my first introduction to a problem that would bedevil the Empire right up until its fall. Pirates were automatically sentenced to death when they were caught - no one had authority to do anything else - and it made them *very* unwilling to surrender. But blowing their ships out of space ran the risk of killing innocent hostages, while storming them meant risking a marine platoon or two. I had a feeling that most commanding officers - perhaps even including a few marines - opted for the first option. It was, after all, impossible to *prove* that innocent captives were killed.

"I like to think I would resist, sir," Bloodnok said.

Southard was *not* impressed. "Imagine the woman who gave birth to you being raped, time and time again, by pirates," he said. "Imagine your sisters with their teeth knocked out, then raped orally and anally until they died. Would you still resist?"

It hit me, then, that my sisters had died that way. I'd never been offered a choice to do something - anything - that would save their lives. Hell, I wouldn't have trusted the gangsters if they'd offered to spare them in exchange for a service or two. But if there had been the merest hope of keeping them alive and unhurt, I would have taken it.

"I don't know, sir," Bloodnok said.

"No one ever knows," Southard said. He turned so he could see us all. "No one ever knows how he or she will react until they are forced to make the choice. It's easy to say that you will do the right thing, but what *is* the right thing?"

He pulled himself backwards. "Years ago, a howling mob of rebels overran an imperial base on their homeworld," he said. "They captured everyone on the base, including the base commander and his wife, then demanded the commander hand over the codes to open the safe or else. When he demurred, they threatened to rape and murder his wife right in front of him. Do you blame him for giving up the codes?"

I swallowed. It was easy to see why the commander had surrendered. It's a great deal easier to endure physical pain than watch it happening to someone else, particularly a loved one. I couldn't really blame him at all. But, at the same time, his decision might have led to unfortunate consequences down the line. It would be easy to blame him if more lives were lost, even though I understood his dilemma.

"These days, we're very careful about leaving potential hostages in places they can be snatched," Southard said. "Why do you *think* we allow retired marines and their families to live on the Slaughterhouse?"

I felt an odd stab of envy. Joker and I had walked through Liberty Island, admiring the neat houses - so alien compared to the Undercity - and the confident men, women and children who made up the population. They lived without fear, knowing that they were allowed to stand up for themselves - and defend themselves with deadly force, if necessary. The contrast between them and my family, growing up in a nightmare, could hardly be more pronounced.

We completed our stay on the station with the first of many - many - orbital dives. In theory, it was very similar to parachuting - we had jumped from some impressively high altitudes on Mars - but in practice it was quite different. Civilians did orbital jumping too, but civilians tended to use tougher equipment. Marines preferred to remain unnoticed.

"The planetary defences are designed to track objects entering the planet's atmosphere," Southard told us, as we donned the first set of suits. "A marine in a suit is an easy target, if they detect and identify him in the first place. Accordingly, standard procedure is to pretend to be a piece of space junk re-entering the planet's atmosphere. It isn't uncommon for pieces of hullmetal to make it all the way to the ground, even if they're relatively small."

He smiled. "Ideally, we'd want to use a meteor shower for camouflage," he added, "but we so rarely get a perfect storm right when we want it. Pieces of space junk make much better cover."

I cursed, mentally. I'd pretty much overcome the agoraphobia that had plagued my early days at Boot Camp, but I really wasn't mentally prepared to dive through a planet's atmosphere. Not that I had a choice, I knew; there was no way to avoid making the jump if I wanted to be a marine. There was honour, genuine honour, in serving as a marine auxiliary, but it wasn't what I wanted. Besides, I wasn't sure I could offer many skills to the auxiliaries, save shooting. I had trained hard, yet I was no engineer, or medic, or EOD officer...

"One by one," Southard ordered. "Joker; go."

It was my turn to jump next. I walked into the airlock, then braced myself as best as I could as the exterior hatch opened, revealing the Slaughterhouse below me. This time, I didn't allow myself to show any signs of hesitation as I stepped out of the airlock and used my EVA jets to tip myself towards the planet. Unlike parachuting, there was no immediate sense of descent; it would have been easy enough, if I had wished, to remain in orbit. But I kept inching down until the planet's gravity caught hold and *pulled*. My suit started to flash up warnings as the exterior armour heated up. There was nothing I could do, but wait and pray; there was no way to slow my fall until I was in the lower atmosphere.

And if this was real, I thought grimly, *I'd be leaving a flaming trail behind me that a blind man could see.*

I clicked the switch as soon as I reached the right altitude and deployed the parachute. My suit shook violently as my fall slowed dramatically, but not enough to prevent me hitting the surface with enough force to hurt. For a second, I was stunned and then training took over. I pulled the parachute, smouldering slightly after the passage through the atmosphere, away from me, then keyed the bolts on the suit. It shattered, allowing me to jump free, weapon in hand. No one came to greet me as I looked around, taking in a swampy environment that threatened to swallow me if I put my foot in the wrong place. Had I drifted off my assigned course?

We were warned it might happen that way, I thought. *But they will have tracked my descent.*

I was on the verge of striking out for home anyway - despite strict orders to stay as close to the suit as possible - when the helicopter came into view. They picked me up, collected the remains of the suit and then flew me back to barracks. Southard was waiting for us, armed with a copy of the descent records. Half of us, it seemed, had drifted off course quite badly.

"That's par for the course, unfortunately," he said, once he'd finished outlining the results. "It's hard to make any sort of course changes without alerting the enemy to your true nature - and by the time you're under their radar environment, it's too late to make any significant changes. But we will work on it."

I groaned, inwardly. But we worked on it anyway.

CHAPTER TWENTY-FIVE

Again, if anything, Edward effectively understates the case. By the time I was exiled to Avalon, there were enough multi-ship pirate bands operating along the Rim - even within the Inner Worlds - to pose a serious threat to public security. Some of them were even commanded by men who had sensed, however dimly, the fading of the Empire and sought to take advantage of it. Indeed, the pirate group that attacked Avalon, shortly after we were cut off from Earth, was led by a man who believed he could found an empire of his own. He came alarmingly close to success.

-Professor Leo Caesius

"What you have done, so far, fits into two categories," Southard said, two months after we began. The platoon stood to attention, eying him warily. "First, you have refreshed and expanded upon skills taught at Boot Camp; second, you have trained to deal with problems that are rarely faced by regular soldiers. Now, it's time for you to face considerably greater challenges. Your mission is as follows."

We watched him carefully as he projected a map in front of us. "Chesty - a city with a population of over two million souls - is under siege by the Bolshevik Liberation Army," he said. "As you can see, the BLA has managed to cut the city off from its sources of supply in the hinterlands and, after a dazzlingly successful raid on the ports, destroyed most of the fishing boats that might otherwise have brought in enough food to keep the city going. Our most favourable projection suggests that the city will be forced to surrender within two weeks, unless something happens to raise the siege."

Joker raised a hand. "Why not bombard the BLA positions from orbit?"

"Most of their positions are surrounded by innocent civilians, mostly children," Southard informed him. "The Imperial Navy is prepared to consider a bombardment as a last resort; however a successful bombardment will not only kill thousands of civilians, but also destroy the food supplies the city needs. In short, they're up shit creek and sinking fast. Luckily, we believe we have an alternative solution."

He tapped a control. The map focused on a small village thirty kilometres from the front lines. "According to our intelligence, Comrade Li Hamah - the BLA commander-in-chief - is stationed there, directing operations personally. She rose to the post of supreme commander after the previous two commanders were killed in the early stages of the war; since then, she has spent more time playing politics with her fellow communists rather than prosecuting the war. She is something of a mystery; we don't even have a photograph of her. It is no exaggeration to state that removing her might well trigger a faction fight amongst the BLA to nominate her replacement."

"Thus winning time to replenish the city," Joker commented.

"Precisely," Southard agreed. "You will plan and carry out an operation to take her into custody - or, as a last resort, to kill her. Stalker, *you* will be Troop Leader this time."

I nodded, refusing to show any signs of nervousness. I'd been Troop Leader several times - easy come, easy go - but it always worried me. I disliked being responsible for others lives; I knew, intellectually, that it was a giant exercise, yet it was still possible for someone to get killed while under my command. Southard gave me the map, a datachip loaded with intelligence and a list of assets under my command. There wasn't much, beyond the platoon itself. A pair of helicopters, a handful of drones and the promise of fire support if things got too hairy.

"Don't count on it," Southard warned, when he saw what I was studying. "The Imperial Navy is either ruthless, hammering targets so hard they often hit friendly forces too, or completely pusillanimous about firing when they're not sure of the target. It depends on just who happens to be in command at any given moment."

"Yes, sir," I said.

The platoon gathered around me as I placed a printed map on the table. "This is the plan, so far," I said. "We take the helicopters to here, a location five miles from Target Alpha, and hike the rest of the way. The helicopters make their way to a safer place if we can't get some additional security to them, while we attack the village, kill the defenders and capture our target. Once we have her, we either call the helicopters in directly or make our way back to the LZ and link up with them there. Any thoughts?"

We hashed over the details until we were all satisfied with the basic idea. It might seem odd - a military unit cannot be a democracy - but the marines preferred to share ideas, just to make sure that nothing was overlooked. There weren't many points, save for a suggestion from Joker that we didn't take anything heavier than a machine gun with us. Target Alpha - there was no name attached to the village, so we gave it one - didn't look any different from the other villages, a construction of wood and mud rather than stone or anything that would stand up to even the lightest weapons.

"Very good," I said, once we were ready. "Let's move."

The Marine Corps had spent a staggering amount of time and resources on building the Slaughterhouse, more money than I'd ever expected to see in a lifetime, but it wasn't until the exercise began that I started to understand - truly understand - just how much they'd done. It was far more than just a shooting range, or a march over the long-dead volcano on Mars; it was an entire region that had been designed to serve as an exercise ground. Chesty, the city under siege, was practically a *real* city; the only thing it lacked, it seemed, was an actual population.

They pay people to play civilians caught in the middle of a war zone, I thought, as the helicopter swooped low over the jungle. *And they have trained soldiers ready to play the part of our enemies.*

Joker clapped my shoulder. "It's a good plan," he said. "Don't worry about a thing."

I snorted as the helicopters dropped down towards the LZ. "I'm not worried about my plan," I said, shortly. "I'm worried about what will happen when the plan goes to hell."

We jumped out of the helicopters, weapons raised, as soon as they landed and secured the LZ. I was expecting everything from a hail of incoming fire to a flanking attack on the helicopters, but nothing materialised. The helicopter pilots took off, as per orders, while I checked our location manually and then led the way towards Target Alpha. It was hot and muggy the moment we stepped under the jungle canopy, but there was enough noise in the vicinity to conceal our movements from any listening ears. Everything was going well, far too well. I was tense as hell by the time we holed up close to Target Alpha, then dispatched Joker and Sif to sneak forward. They were the stealthiest people in the platoon.

Joker returned, ten minutes later. "Found a place to spy on them," he said. "Coming?"

I nodded and crawled behind him until we reached the overhang. The village was smaller than I'd realised; really, it was more of a hamlet. I wouldn't have suspected anything if I hadn't been close enough to see a handful of guards in various positions, watching for encroaching threats. There weren't any workers in the fields either, which were starting to look suspiciously overgrown. But then, the BLA could have accomplished its objectives by driving away the farmers or forcing them to take refuge within the city.

"Joker, Bloodnok and I will attack the main compound," I said, after I had finished checking the village. I was fairly sure that Comrade Li would be using the smallest building compatible with running an insurgency, but there weren't many to choose from in Target Alpha. "When we're in position, I'll send a signal. I want the remainder of the platoon to lay down a murderous fire against the enemy guards."

"Aye, sir," Sif said.

We sneaked down into position as quickly as we could, doing everything we could to avoid detection. The insurgents didn't seem to be very good guards, but we knew better than to take that for granted. As soon as we were ready, I sent the signal and the platoon opened fire, shots picking off the visible guards before they had a chance to react. I ran forward, trusting to the platoon to cover my back, and slapped a breeching charge against the door. It exploded, blowing the door inwards; I lunged inside, screaming for the inhabitants to drop their weapons and put their hands in the air. A man swung around, trying to draw a pistol; I dropped him where he stood. The other three people in the room, all women, stared at me with defiant eyes. But which one of them was our target?

"Comrade Li," I snapped. "Come here and the others will be spared."

Two of the women glared at me. The third, a younger woman with dark eyes, pulled at her belt. It came undone, allowing her robe to slip to the floor. Her body was scarred, as if she had been whipped badly enough to leave permanent marks; she lowered her eyes the moment she saw I was looking at her.

"Stop that," I ordered. "What are you doing?"

"You're going to rape me," the woman said, pitifully. "There's no way I can resist, so…"

She clutched her breasts, holding them up. "I can make it good for you, if you don't hurt me."

"We're not going to rape you," I said. There was something about the whole act that bothered me, something nagging at the back of my mind. Understanding clicked a second later. Who would look twice at a girl who had been beaten down so badly? "Comrade Li?"

The girl's eyes flashed with hatred. "You…"

"Put your dress back on," I ordered. "If you come with us now, your friends will be left here."

Comrade Li did as she was told. The other two women were searched quickly - one of them was hiding a pistol in a spot that must have been incredibly uncomfortable - and bound with plastic ties, then placed against the wall. I had a feeling they would be in for some trouble when their comrades found them, but at least they would have a chance at life. Maybe I should have killed them both, yet I'd given my word. Ideally, I would have liked to take them with us, but that didn't seem possible.

I searched Comrade Li as soon as she was dressed - she flinched at my touch, which didn't stop me removing a knife and a small pistol from her robe - and then bound her hands before leading her outside. The shooting had stopped; there was no point in trying to conceal our presence any longer, so I keyed my radio and asked for an update.

"The fighters are dead, sir," Sif reported. "We got them all."

"Good," I said. I switched channels as I hurried Comrade Li up the slope towards the rest of the platoon. "Flight, Stalker; come get us…"

I broke off as a hail of fire crashed towards us. For a horrified moment, I thought there had been a ghastly blue-on-blue, then I realised the enemy had had another unit hiding out in the jungle, only a few short minutes from the village. Someone had had enough initiative to march to the sound of the guns.

"Belay that," I said, countermanding my order. We hurried as I tried to work out where the enemy was. Behind us, it seemed. They hadn't had the time to surround the village and then advance from all possible angles of attack. "Hold position."

Joker pointed his rifle at Comrade Li's head. "Call for them and you're a dead woman."

"It won't be enough," I said. I thought I recognised the true fanatic in her eyes. We didn't normally gag prisoners, but I found a piece of cloth and jammed it into her mouth. She glared bloody murder at me; I ignored her as we linked up with the rest of the platoon and exchanged notes. "We're going to have to march out of here."

"Aye, sir," Joker said.

"Blackmon, you and Bloodnok leave a handful of traps behind to upset the enemy," I ordered. If we were lucky, we'd have a chance to break contact before they realised they needed to give chase, but I had a feeling we wouldn't be lucky. "The remainder of us will start moving to the LZ."

"Better keep a sharp eye on her," Sif advised. She gave Comrade Li a sharp look; the insurgent leader glared back at her, seemingly unbothered by captivity. "Better still to carry her."

I nodded. "You and Dodger carry her," I ordered. They could carry her on a branch, which would ensure they each had a hand free. "Let's move."

It was nearly seven minutes before we heard the first booby trap detonate. I cursed inwardly, sharing a look with Joker. Someone might have been injured or killed - at the very least, their day would have been ruined - but they now knew which way we were going. We pushed onwards as fast as we could, leaving a number of traps behind us. They kept detonating with alarming frequency.

"They must know who we've caught," Joker muttered.

"Maybe it was a mistake to leave those women alive," I agreed. I could have killed them, then burned the building to ashes. They wouldn't have *known* their leader had been kidnapped. "I…"

My terminal buzzed. I glanced at it and swore. ELINT - Electronic Intelligence - was warning us that the enemy was sending signals - and picking up replies from locations all around us. The BLA had to have hidden more than one of its armies under the jungle, I realised; they were trying to organise an ambush. And the location of the transmitters might not be where the armies were…

"We could make a stand," Joker suggested.

"We'd be overwhelmed," I said, shaking my head. It was tempting, but we only had a limited supply of ammunition. We'd sell our lives dearly, yet we'd definitely end up dead - or, worse, captured. "We have to keep moving."

I glanced at the map, thinking hard. The enemy wasn't stupid. Sure, they'd made the mistake of leaving their commander in a vulnerable location, but they really hadn't had a choice. A bigger town, crammed with fighters, would be an easy target for orbital bombardment. They would expect us to try to use helicopters to get out of the mess…and they'd know, roughly, where the helicopters would have to land, if they wanted to pick us up. I would be surprised if they didn't have the LZ already targeted, just waiting for us to call the helicopters…

"I've had an idea," I said.

It was risky, but the original plan had been blown out of the water. Staying where we were wasn't an option; we might have been able to sneak clear, if we weren't encumbered by a prisoner, but there was no way Comrade Li could be trusted to come with us. I keyed my radio again, knowing it ran the risk of exposing our position. Moments later, the helicopters were on their way towards us.

"Sif, Dodger, get up the trees," I ordered. "Comrade Li will have to be hauled up."

We'd practiced using ropes to carry a wounded comrade over some distance, but it was the first time we'd ever tried making a net for a POW.

Comrade Li eyed us - for the first time, I thought I saw uncertainty in her eyes - as we bundled her up, then waited for Sif and Dodger to drop ropes down to us. Moments later, Comrade Li was hauled up into the branches and we followed, just as the first helicopter swooped down. We tied Comrade Li to the dangling harnesses, then grabbed hold ourselves. The helicopter lunged upwards as a hail of bullets rose up from below, yanking us into the sky. Moments later, we were safe.

"Made it," I breathed, as we headed back towards the base. If the enemy had had a single MANPAD, it would have been a very different story. "We did it."

"Congratulations," Southard said, when we landed. "You did a very good job of escaping a trap."

"Thank you, sir," I said.

"Leaving the women alive was dangerous, though," Southard added. "You could easily have been wrong about Comrade Li's identity."

I hesitated. *Was* I wrong?

"I didn't feel right about killing them, sir," I said, carefully.

Southard lifted his eyebrows. "Even during a simulated exercise?"

"I was told to treat it as real," I reminded him. "If I had killed them, I would have been guilty…"

"Perhaps," Southard said. "Why *do* you believe you walked away with the *right* Comrade Li?"

"Comrade Li is a woman doing a job that many of her followers believe could be done better by a man," I said. It hadn't been *that* long since I'd held many similar attitudes, shaped by life in the Undercity. "The last thing she would want is to keep a woman so battered down that she takes off her clothes the minute she believes herself to be threatened with rape. It would undermine her position. She really wouldn't want to make her male followers start thinking about weak and feeble women."

I paused, then went on. "It was an act, sir," I concluded. "She acted submissive because it would have made us underestimate her. And it nearly worked."

"So it did," Southard said. He raised his voice, addressing us all. "Grab some sleep, troopers. You're going to Chesty tomorrow."

CHAPTER
TWENTY-SIX

Psychologically, it is fatal for a woman to convince a man that she is weak, emotional, dependent or prone to female tribalism. Any of the above can seriously weaken a woman's position and compromise her authority. Indeed, if the only way to get ahead in a male-dominated environment is to be 'one of the boys,' revealing oneself to be 'one of the girls' can be disastrous. It may not breed hatred, but it can breed contempt.

Ed's reasoning, therefore, was sound. 'Comrade Li' had nothing to gain - and a great deal to lose - from keeping a reminder that women can be broken in her headquarters. Further, her pretence might just have led the troopers to hold her in contempt, which might have led to them turning their backs on her…

-Professor Leo Caesius

"Joker, you're Troop Leader," Southard said, as soon as we landed at the FOB on the outskirts of Chesty. I hadn't realised that several different platoons were being exercised at the same time, but they wouldn't have laid so much on for us alone. "You'll have a somewhat less challenging mission, on the face of it."

We eyed him suspiciously. Less challenging? There had to be a sting in the tail somewhere.

"Thanks to your earlier mission, the BLA is pulling back from Chesty in some disarray," Southard continued. "This gives us an opportunity to ship additional supplies into the city and feed the starving women and children. Your mission is to provide security for the food supplies and oversee distribution. Be warned; local factions will attempt to steal the food for themselves in the hopes of leaving the other factions to starve."

I winced, inwardly. I'd learned a great deal about psychology in the last few months, including how badly humans could behave when they were under pressure. The whole idea of snatching food from starving women and children was horrific, but I had no doubt that some of the local factions would do it, if we gave them the chance. Relying on the locals to distribute the aid was asking for trouble. But trying to distribute the food even-handedly would also cause problems.

"Take the trucks to the distribution point, then start handing the food out," Southard concluded. "Good luck."

I watched as Joker looked down at the map. "We'll take the trucks and four AFVs," he said, after a moment. "The roads should be largely clear, but we'll respond with lethal force if challenged."

We hastily checked the vehicles, then mounted up. Joker sat behind me in the lead AFV as I took the wheel, even though it would probably be the first vehicle to attract fire if we ran into an ambush. I was tempted to tell him he should probably pick another vehicle, but we had practiced what to do if we lost our commanding officer. Bloodnok - Joker's second - would take command at once.

It might still disorientate us for a second, I thought, grimly. There were too many things that could go wrong before Bloodnok assumed command - and let us know that he *had*. *But Joker would think that we would think less of him if he stayed in the rear.*

"Let's go," Joker said.

I gunned the engine, then led the way onto the highway leading down towards Chesty. It was strewn with the rubble of hundreds of vehicles, providing far too many places to hide an IED or stage an ambush, but nothing happened apart from a handful of shots fired from the distant jungle. The machine gunners rotated their guns and searched for targets, finding nothing. I wondered if Joker would order them to lay down suppressing fire anyway, but he said nothing. There was little point in wasting ammunition without clear targets.

Chesty itself was both strange and alien. I'd never seen a true city until leaving Earth - I had had a chance to visit Wells on Mars, where humanity had established its first foothold on another world - but Chesty was in ruins. Hundreds of buildings were pockmarked with bullet holes, showing where the local defenders and the BLA had fought desperately for control. In the absence of heavy weapons, taking a large city is far from easy. Starving Chesty out had probably been their best option, assuming the starships played no further role in the engagement.

And they might have been right, I thought, grimly. *A thousand civilians dead as collateral damage wouldn't play well with the media.*

I pushed the thought aside as we rolled past the defenders - who looked little more organised than the BLA fighters we'd attacked earlier - and headed for the distribution point. Most of the city's menfolk had been press-ganged into one militia or another, leaving the women and children at home; I hoped, numbly, that they were relieved that we'd saved the city from starvation. The fighters would have had the best food, such as it was; everyone else, civilian or not, would have been left to starve. By now, they'd probably started considering how best to cook human flesh.

Joker coughed as I turned the corner. "This is the distribution point?"

"GPS says it is," I said. Once, it had been a nice piece of parkland; now, the trees had been cut down and everything else had been dug up in the city's desperate attempt to find something - anything - to eat. Maybe people *could* eat grass - genetic engineering could work miracles - but it wasn't very tasty, let alone nutritious. "At least we have clear fields of fire."

"So do the tower blocks," Joker muttered.

I followed his gaze and swore. The towers were nowhere near as impressive as Earth's CityBlocks, but they still provided ample room for snipers. We could come under fire quite easily. If we'd had a choice, I would have set up a base in one of the buildings; it might have been more awkward, but at least it would have provided protection...

"Squad Two, secure that warehouse," Joker ordered, keying his radio. "If it's abandoned, we'll use it as the distribution point."

We dismounted, then hastily started to unload the supplies and carry them into the warehouse. Joker would have been in deep shit if he'd been in the Imperial Army, where rewriting orders to suit local conditions was heavily discouraged, but the marines took a different view of things. If he succeeded in his mission, any small revisions of his orders would be overlooked; even if he failed, it might not be enough to end his career. Squad three patrolled the edges, while Sif and Bloodnok scrambled onto the roof to provide top cover. If the militias - or anyone - tried to make a go of it, we'd give them a hot reception.

"Joker's Joke Shop is now open for business," Joker declared, when we had unloaded the trucks and moved them to a safer location. We weren't planning to transport the supplies back *out* of the city. "Let's see who comes calling, shall we?"

Our first customers were a handful of middle-aged women and a number of children, too hungry and thin to care about the possible dangers in approaching strangers. We did our best to look friendly, then passed out ration packs and offered to let them sit in the park - or what was left of it - to eat. Some of them accepted; others, their eyes fearful, took the food and scurried away. I watched them go, understanding their fear more than I cared to admit. We might have been distributing food, but - just like anyone in the Undercity - we could turn nasty or demanding at any moment.

"Got trouble moving towards us," Sif warned, through the radio net. "Five men, carrying weapons. One of them looks to be a boss."

"Copy," Joker said. "I'll meet them in the park. Squad One will cover me."

The newcomers strode into the park as if they owned the place, surrounded by an air of competence and barely-restrained violence that practically gave me flashbacks to the Undercity's gangsters. None of the footsoldiers looked particularly competent, but their weapons and their willingness to use them gave the bastards more than enough power to dominate the city. Their master, who had a rifle casually slung over his shoulder, had a nasty expression on his face. I disliked him on sight.

"Got an ID," someone whispered through the radio net. The FOB was looking through the handful of sensors we'd scattered around the perimeter. "Boss Gordon, leader of the Blue Boys Militia."

Joker opened his mike, so we could all hear, and stepped forward. The boss scowled at him, then glanced at the rest of us, holding our weapons with easy precision. He didn't look up, much to my private amusement; Sif and Bloodnok could have wiped all five of them out before the rest of us had our guns up and ready to fire. We didn't want a fight, but we would win within a second if one started.

"Thank you for bringing us food," Boss Gordon said. If he was aware of just how much danger he was in, he didn't show it. I would have awarded him points for composure if I hadn't been so sure he was too stupid to realise just how badly he was outmatched. "My men will take over distribution. You may hand it over to us and return to your base."

It was, I suspected, a situation that called for diplomacy. Unfortunately, marines are not known for diplomacy.

"Fuck off," Joker said.

Boss Gordon gaped at him. He'd grown too used to being the big man in the city - or one of them, at least. His militia had given him access to everything from food - such as it was - to wine, women and song. No one had dared defy him for a very long time.

"I would ask you to reconsider," he said, lowering his voice. I gripped my weapon, bracing myself. There was no hierarchy keeping Boss Gordon in position, nothing but the threat of superior force. He had no choice; either he made us back down or the spell would be broken and his own people would turn on him. "We control this city. Either you give us the food to distribute or no one will get the food."

Joker slammed his rifle into Boss Gordon's chest. The man doubled over, gagging; we sprang forward and overpowered his four guards before they could even get their weapons up and aimed at us. Joker smacked Boss Gordon to the ground, searched him roughly and bound his hands with a plastic tie. Once we had secured the others, we picked them up and carried them into the warehouse. They could either be carried out to the FOB, once the distribution was over, or just left to the tender mercies of the city's inhabitants. I had a feeling Joker would probably be publically reprimanded and privately congratulated for his coup. The Blue Boys Militia, having lost their leader, would have to decide who would succeed him before launching an attack.

"Watch for incoming threats," Joker ordered, as the trickle of starving citizens turned into a flood. "The militia isn't likely to let this pass."

"No, sir," I agreed.

I kept running security around the edge of the park as the civilians walked through, some concealing weapons; we didn't disarm them as long as they kept their weapons firmly holstered. The Imperial Army would probably have snatched their weapons, on the grounds that they *might* pose a threat, but we knew it was pointless. Everyone who could buy, beg or steal a weapon would be armed, knowing that there was no other defence against the human animals unleashed by the siege. One man started to beat his wife - I have no idea why - only to be shot by one of our snipers. The crowd rustled uncomfortably as we pulled the body out and dumped it by the side of the road, but did nothing. We'd been taught that showing the merest hint of weakness to a crowd was fatal.

And besides, I didn't like wife-beaters. None of us did.

All hell broke loose two hours after we'd arrested Boss Gordon and his men. A large mass of civilians, male and female, appeared at the edge of the park and advanced towards our positions. Very few of them seemed to be armed with anything more dangerous than sticks and stones - which can be very dangerous in the wrong hands - yet sheer pressure alone would eventually overwhelm us. We levelled our weapons, but held our fire. We'd slaughter hundreds, perhaps thousands, if we pulled the triggers. The bullets would slice through the first rank and injure others in the rear before they finally stopped.

"There are people at the end, encouraging the mob forward," Sif reported. "I can slot them."

"Take them out," Joker ordered. "Squad One; deploy shields. Squad Two; prepare to launch gas grenades."

The mob surged forward as we deployed our shields and locked them together. They struck the shields with astonishing force, but we held; I prayed, inwardly, that the mob would start coming apart now the agitators were dead. But a mob has a mind of its own. Someone a great deal smarter than me said, years ago, that a crowd is only as smart as the stupidest person in it; personally, I believe a crowd is only *half* as smart as the stupidest person in it. A person smart enough to run, when faced with deadly danger, would think himself invulnerable if he was part of a mob. I cringed as the surging tidal wave of emotions raged over me, a force threatening to suck me into the mass. There is something in all of us that seeks to be part of a crowd...

"There's more coming," Sif reported, as we fought to hold the line. "Three more groups, including a number of heavily-armed men."

"Shit," Joker said. "Squad Two; grenades. I say again, grenades."

I braced myself as the grenades were hurled over the interlocking shields, landing amidst the crowd. Gas was already spewing from them, a translucent yellow cloud that was meant to knock out anyone who breathed even a tiny whiff of it. We were immune, of course - several of the rioters had the bright idea of hurling our grenades back, which didn't do more than annoy us - but none of the rioters had any defence. Several of them had been smart enough to carry wet cloths with them, which provided a limited degree of protection; the remainder, one by one, started to fall to the ground in front of us. I knew far too many of the rioters would be injured when they landed, or when someone bigger landed on top of them. It was hard to feel sorry for them, but I did. They'd probably been told that we were withholding supplies until we were given control of the city.

"Squad One, drop shields and advance," Joker ordered. "Knock out the remaining protesters."

I swung my shield to the side, then lunged forward. A rioter, his face covered by a wet cloth, tried to jump at me; I knocked the cloth away from his mouth, then watched dispassionately as he sagged and fell to the ground. It was hard to push forward without stamping on someone, but we had no choice. One by one, we picked off the remaining rioters, the ones too stupid to flee while they had the chance. But the other groups were still incoming...

"Drop grenades on the other protestors," Joker ordered. It was a grim decision, all the more so as we had no real control outside the park, but there was no real choice. "Pick up the ringleaders, if you can identify them, and move them back to the warehouse. The remainder..."

He broke off, clearly thinking hard. What did we *do* with the remainder? They were mainly starving civilians, not insurgents or legitimate combatants. There were no legal or moral grounds for mass slaughter.

Leave them to wake up, which they would; the gas wouldn't last forever. Or pick them up, dump them in a makeshift detention camp and put them to work for their food? The briefing hadn't been clear about just who would take control of Chesty once the BLA was driven well away from the city. No doubt the sudden collapse of the Blue Boys would leave a power vacuum for other militias to fight over.

"I'm forwarding this decision to higher," Joker said, reluctantly. I understood. It was *just* possible that Southard expected *him* to come up with a solution. "They can decide what to do with them."

Orders came back, five minutes later. We were to round up the male rioters and dump them in the trucks, then take the poor bastards to a detention camp. The women and children were to be woken and told to go home and behave themselves. We'd finish distributing the food once everything else was done. Hopefully, it would be easier now the main troublemakers were gone.

"What a fucking realistic test," Joker muttered, later. The debriefing had pointed out that he had probably caused the riot, although - as Southard had admitted - there had been no good choices. At least we hadn't faced a major assault. "I keep forgetting."

I nodded. The exercises *were* realistic. They had to be; Bainbridge had said as much, back when we'd started. Hard training, easy mission; easy training, hard mission. And yet, looking around Chesty - and a dozen other training areas - it was easy to forget that it was an exercise. Which was, I supposed, the point. They wanted to see how we behaved when we thought we were in very real danger.

We had the mission into Shithole a week later. But that, I believe, is where I started.

CHAPTER
TWENTY-SEVEN

One very real difference between an exercise, however well designed, and real combat, is that the danger of death is minimised. Not, I should add, removed altogether, but minimised. It is therefore easy to regard the exercise as a game, rather than serious combat. This leads to an attitude that allows the trainees to romp through the exercise, without learning much - if anything. The Marine Corps works hard to make the exercises realistic to convince its recruits that they are in very real danger. It's the only way to test the young men and women before putting them into the fire.

-Professor Leo Caesius

"So tell me," Doctor Juliet White said. "Why did you want to join the Marine Corps?"

I tried hard - very hard - to keep the resentment off my face, but I don't think I succeeded. A week after the exercise in Shithole, the platoon had been rotated back to barracks and we'd been given a truly heroic reward of *three* days of leave. I was less than pleased at being told I had to talk to Doctor White first - and even *less* pleased when I discovered that Doctor White was a psychologist, rather than a medical doctor. Yes, she *had* been a marine auxiliary herself - not that anyone would know it if they looked at her - but I still didn't take her seriously. I had very little respect for *any* headshrinkers.

"Because it was a chance to get away from my former life," I said. It wasn't something I *really* wanted to talk about, but I had a feeling that any evasive answers would be counted against me. (And, by now, I'd practically been conditioned not to be openly dishonest.) "It was an escape from the Undercity."

"After your family was murdered," Doctor White said. "How do you feel about that, after your encounter with another attempted rape?"

I kept my voice as steady as I could. "What happened to my mother and sisters, Doctor, was hardly *attempted*," I said. "They *were* raped and they *were* murdered."

"That doesn't answer my question," Doctor White said. "And please, call me Juliet."

"I still feel guilty about being unable to save them, *Doctor*," I said. I had no intention of calling her by name, not if I could avoid it. Looking at her brought back all the old resentments; she looked middle-aged, warm and protected. It was hard to believe she'd been within a light year of a combat zone. "But I no longer feel helpless."

"That's good," Doctor White said. "And how tempted were you to pull the trigger, when you thought you were witnessing another rape?"

"Tempted," I admitted. I had come within seconds of pulling the trigger. In hindsight, the limiters on the rifle would probably have cut in, saving their lives, but it had still been dangerous as hell. I didn't *like* Young and never would, yet it was hard not to respect him for taking his life in his hands. "But it was more important to take him for trial."

Doctor White smiled. "Do you really believe that, Edward?"

"Yes," I said, honestly. "We aren't angels, *Doctor*. We do have our bad apples. But if we punish them, if we are seen to punish them, we keep our reputation pure."

Bainbridge had said that, nearly a year ago. The Drill Instructors were good at recognising recruits who might go off the handle, but they weren't perfect. Some of the most successful marines had later gone spectacularly bad; not many, not enough to weaken us, yet even *one* marine who went bad would be remembered longer than a thousand dedicated marines who died honourably. Punishing the guilty - and making sure that everyone *saw* the corps punishing the guilty - was one way to save our reputation. Trying to hide everything, the standard practice of the Civil Guard, was pointless. Everyone knew the only real difference between the Civil Guard and the gangsters was that the Guardsmen wore uniforms.

"And yet, it might have been better if you *had* pulled the trigger," Doctor White said. "It would have saved us the cost of a trial."

By now, I had learned to recognise a deliberately provocative statement. Even so, it still made me angry.

"I would have been charged with murdering another marine - two marines," I said. Young and Hobbes *were* full marines, not troopers learning the tricks of the trade. "Even if my superiors believed me, believed that they deserved to die, there would still have been problems. And if they hadn't, I would have been executed myself."

"True enough," Doctor White agreed. "Do you consider yourself ready to be a marine?"

I cursed, inwardly. If I said yes, it would be taken as a sign of arrogance; if I said no, they'd take it into account (and hold it against me) when they considered moving the platoon into the final stage of training. There *wasn't* a good answer.

Or so I thought. "Is there a good answer?"

"There can be," Doctor White said. "But it depends on how you justify your answer."

I took a breath. "I think I am, yes," I said. "I no longer have any connections to the outside universe."

"That seems a sharp answer," Doctor White said. "Do you have no empathy for the civilians? The ones you must fight to defend?"

"I have a great deal of empathy," I said. It was true enough. "But I don't have any connections that would keep me from becoming a marine, or going anywhere in the service of the corps."

It was true - and, in some ways, it *was* a genuine advantage. Bainbridge had told us, before we graduated from Boot Camp, that prospective troopers were not expected to marry, at least before leaving the Slaughterhouse. It was difficult to maintain any sort of relationship with light years between you and your partner, Bainbridge had said, and no civilians were allowed onto the Slaughterhouse unless they were married to marines or auxiliaries. But, at the same time, it cut us off from the rest of the universe.

"An interesting answer," Doctor White said. "How *do* you feel about your brother?"

I refused to allow myself to be shaken by the sudden change in subject. "I think he was a very weak person," I said, curtly. "He had *options* for leaving the Undercity, if he'd been prepared to take them; instead, he intended to work his way into the local gang structure and forge a life for himself. In the end, his ambitions wiped out the entire family, save for me."

Doctor White nodded. "You may go," she said. "There's a shuttle to Liberty Town in an hour, if you want to take it."

I blinked. "Did I pass?"

"Your case is being constantly reviewed," Doctor White said. "That's true of every trooper, by the way. You are far from the only one with potential triggers in your past. We need men who can deal out staggering levels of violence at one moment and then switch instantly to a peacekeeping mode, if necessary. Some troopers are quietly removed from the course every year."

She gave me a faint smile. "You'll have the answer soon enough," she added. "You may go."

I nodded and left the office, my head spinning. Had they devised the test just for me? Or had they come up with a generic test for *every* marine, to see if we would cross the line when we were confronted with the ghosts of our pasts? It bothered me all through the two days I spent in Liberty Town - I wandered through the museum, drank in a bar and listened to some of the stories from the retired marines - and nagged at my mind, even as I boarded the shuttle to return to barracks. Just how carefully did they evaluate us?

Part of the answer came two weeks later, when we were marched five kilometres to yet another anonymous building. Inside, we discovered an examination chamber, just like the ones we had used in Boot Camp. Our normal Drill Instructors stayed at the rear as an officer I hadn't met stood on a wooden box to allow us to see him properly. The fact that someone had written 'explosives' on the box was probably intended to catch our attention. It worked.

"This is one of the most stressful parts of the Slaughterhouse," he said. He didn't introduce himself, unusually; indeed, I never saw him again. "You are going to be writing peer evaluations for each of your platoon mates. There are basic forms provided in the individual terminals, which you will fill out as necessary. *Do not* leave any form unfilled. If you have nothing to say, say so."

There was an uncomfortable pause. "From this moment on, you will not speak to any of your platoon mates until you have completed the peer evaluations," he continued. "We have had too many problems with platoons deliberately trying to rig the system, either to avoid losing anyone or to pick on someone unpopular within the platoon. Any of you who speak from this moment onwards will be given, at the very least, a full week of punishment duty.

"You will enter the cubicles, fill out the forms and then leave," he concluded. "We strongly suggest you do not discuss your answers with anyone else, no matter how flattering - or insulting - you were. There is no formal punishment for post-evaluation discussions, but you *will* have to deal with the consequences. They could severely weaken your team."

They could have warned us, I thought, as we were shown to our cubicles. *But that would have given us time to plan our answers.*

The door banged closed as soon as I entered; I sat down at the terminal, poured myself a glass of water and keyed a switch, bringing up the first peer evaluation form. Joker's name glared out at me, followed by a whole series of penetrating questions. Did I have confidence in this trooper? Did I trust this trooper? Would I share a foxhole with this trooper? What were this trooper's strengths and weaknesses? Did I believe this trooper should be allowed to graduate?

We could have planned our answers, I thought, sourly. *This way, we get honest results.*

I worked my way through Joker's peer evaluation form, then moved on to Sif. Oddly, despite my earlier fears, I *did* have faith in her. Sif might not be the strongest in the platoon, but she plugged on gamely no matter what the Drill Instructors threw at us. Privately, I had a feeling she would have kicked my ass soundly if she'd been a man. And she was easily the best sniper amongst us.

But would I share a foxhole with her?

Yes, I would; I decided. She'd shown no hint of weakness, no suggestion she might break when confronted with *real* bullets. (Or, at least, real bullets fired by people who genuinely wanted to kill us.) I tried to think hard about her strengths and weakness before doing my best to give honest answers. Her main strength was that she never gave up, no matter what happened; her weakness, perhaps, was that she tried too hard. But was that really a weakness? Joker and Bloodnok were just as good at suggesting alternate angles of approach as Sif. More to the point, we couldn't survive as a unit if we always took the direct route to the target. Charging madly into enemy fire would get us all killed.

I was tired and headachy when I finally staggered from the room, having filled out nine separate peer evaluation forms. None of us looked very good when we returned to the lobby; Southard, who seemed to have forgotten that we were allowed to talk, growled at us to shut up as soon as we entered, then told us to sit down. We did as we were told, silently grateful to him. I didn't want to talk about the answers I'd given and I don't think anyone else really wanted to either. We had, after all, been honest.

"The results will be evaluated over the coming week," Southard told us, when we were all gathered in front of him. "Should any of you have *failed* to earn the respect of your platoon mates, you will probably be switched to another platoon or recycled for a second try through the Slaughterhouse. If you fail a *second* peer evaluation, you will be dropped from the course. It is likely you will be offered a chance to join the auxiliaries or transfer to the Imperial Army."

I swallowed, nervously. Who knew what they might have said about me? Joker was a friend…but did he consider me a solid companion in battle? And what about Sif, or Bloodnok, or Blackmon? Did they think I was worth keeping around or had they urged my removal from the course? We'd all be walking on tenterhooks until we knew our fate. None of us, I suspected, wanted to believe that we'd wasted the last eight months.

It wouldn't be a waste, I told myself, unconvincingly. *I could join the army, if I wished, or even the Civil Guard…*

The Drill Instructors, of course, didn't give us time to brood. They gave us several hundred push-ups (I calculated once that I'd done over a million, between Boot Camp and the Slaughterhouse), a whole string of exercises and finally led us into a lecture hall for a talk from another marine professor. This time, it was more focused on our current training phase.

"A society works by certain rules, which can be both written and unwritten," Professor Cunningham said. He was a tall man, with glinting eyes and a war record longer than my arm. He'd literally been there and done that. "You may discover, when you are inserted into a society, that the unwritten rules are more important than the written rules. The person who is formally in charge may not actually hold any power. Determining who *actually* holds power, who can actually make decisions that hold the force of law, is the most important aspect of understanding how a society functions."

He paused to let that sink in. "I was on Jeddah during the deployment," he continued, after a moment. "In theory, the Emir had crushed the tribes and imposed a monarchy on his population; in practice, the tribal influences were still quite strong. A battalion of local soldiers might have a captain in command, but the captain would defer to a lieutenant who had better connections to the tribal power structure than himself. It was often quite hard to determine just who was *actually* in charge of any given unit - and to avoid giving unintended offence by asking the wrong question.

"Just to make matters more complex, the Emir had imposed a draft and conscripted every firstborn son into a giant army. This army had little in the way of training that might have broken down the tribal links; naturally, if the headmen had called, their tribesmen would come running back to the tribe, weapons in hand. It took us longer than it should have done to realise that, apart from a relatively small force from his own tribe, the Emir controlled very little in the way of military force. Whatever might have been said on paper, the reality was quite different.

"This caused us no shortage of problems," he admitted. "The Emir's bureaucrats had very little actual power, particularly when they were deployed to places that hadn't seen the Emir's army. Trying to put them in command was a waste of time without enough power to overawe the local inhabitants. We would go there, discover that none of the people listed as having power *actually* had power, then waste months trying to figure out exactly who *did*. It generally tended to be shared between the headmen and the clerics. The only places that had effective governance were when the bureaucrats and the headmen were one and the same.

"There was, in fact, an odd balance of power between the religious and secular authorities. A headman commanded the loyalties of his tribe, while a cleric looked to their souls. When they worked together, they managed to achieve wonders; when they disagreed, nothing was done. They tended to have limits to their power; headmen couldn't commit themselves to anything without the support of a majority of their followers, while clerics had to be careful not to step too far out of line. *And* they tended to be very careful about committing themselves."

It was an odd lecture, but one that turned out to have practical applications. Living and working inside a community, we discovered, gave us a chance to make friends and scope out who actually wielded power. We worked our way through a set of examples - including several that were obviously fictional, as one was based on a subgroup of humans who possessed magic powers - and prepared ourselves for the coming tests. The next set, I was sure, would be harder.

But, oddly, I no longer doubted that I would pass through the Slaughterhouse and graduate as a marine. I had passed the hump; my confidence was unshakable. Whatever they threw at me, I would take it and carry on.

I was never told just what my platoon mates had said about me - and I never talked about it to anyone, not even Joker. The whole subject was one we avoided talking about, even when it became clear that *none* of us had been switched to another platoon or recycled to a junior platoon. We talked a *lot*, about everything, but not that. None of us really wanted to know what the others had said.

And I never looked it up, even when I had the rank to look at my own records. I still don't want to know.

CHAPTER TWENTY-EIGHT

> Peer evaluations are rare outside the military - like everything from IQ to aptitude tests, they have been deemed unfair. However, they serve a valid purpose. If someone who joined the platoon failed to fit in to the group, it would be better to recycle them to another platoon rather than risk a major incident in a combat zone. That said, it is quite rare for a trooper to fail peer evaluation. By the time they face the test, they have generally mastered fitting in with the platoon, at least during training and deployment. There is no room for lone wolves in the Marine Corps.
>
> -Professor Leo Caesius

We wasted no time in putting our lessons into action. Southard took us from one part of the Slaughterhouse to another, forcing us to march through hot deserts crammed with dangerous animals - I was stung by a tiny scorpion that put me in my bunk for four days, even though the little bastard wasn't any bigger than my finger - and wade through swamps inhabited by man-eating alligators. Flies were everywhere, of course; we searched constantly for ways to kill them before finally giving up and letting them swarm all over us. (I'm sure the flies were genetically-engineered to suck human blood.) And then, still tired after the last set of exercises, we marched back into Chesty and practiced everything from urban combat to organising meetings with local dignitaries.

It was a frustrating experience, I had to admit - and frighteningly realistic. There was no way to hide the fact that we couldn't stay forever, so the locals were reluctant to help us. One man begged me to give him a black eye, giving him an excuse for betraying the local den of insurgents; another came very close to being killed when he visited our FOB, posing as the owner, then used what he saw to call mortar fire down on our position. I kept reminding myself that the locals were merely looking out for themselves, and that I would probably do the same in their position, but it was hard not to loathe them. They were siding with insurgents who would conscript their sons, rape their daughters and take their crops, rather than marines who would die to save them from their enemies. How could I not dislike them…and come to disbelieve everything they said?

We were moved on two weeks later, where we undertook harassment operations against an enemy armoured column that intended to strike our flanks; we fired antitank missiles at the leaders, sniped at the infantrymen accompanying them and bugged out before they found their range and returned fire. It was a better exercise than working with the locals, I decided, although I had my doubts about its value. Would we actually need to know how to fight tanks when they were rarely used by anyone, save the Empire? No one else would risk using them when orbiting starships could pick them out and drop hammers on their heads before they got into attack range.

"You might be surprised," Southard said, when I asked. "You have no idea of some of the shit that goes on out there."

He moved us on, again, a week after a series of sniping exercises. This took us to a large hill, covered in trees and bushes that provided ample cover to an enemy force. We eyed it with tired eyes, wondering just what was waiting for us. We'd seen too much to doubt that we would be pushed to the limits, once again.

"The enemy has occupied the hill and is using it as a base of operations," Southard informed us, shortly. "Higher command has decreed the capture of the hill, rather than pounding it into the dust from orbit. They believe that a show of military skill will lead to the enemy surrendering. Your mission is to capture the hill, capturing or killing every last enemy fighter."

Joker scowled. "Surely pounding the hill into rubble would be a sufficient show of force."

Southard gave him a nasty look. "One; we wouldn't know which of the enemy commanders we killed, so there are genuine military reasons to take the hill by infantry assault," he said. "Two; you will certainly receive orders like this when you go into active service, so it is actually a realistic scenario."

"He didn't give you push-ups," I muttered, as the Drill Instructor turned away. "This *must* be bad."

"Looks that way," Joker agreed.

"You have twenty minutes to plan your offensive," Southard informed us. "And then you have two hours to take the hill. Stalker...*you're* in command."

"I think he heard you," Joker whispered.

"I think I heard you too," Southard said, deadpan.

We shared tired smiles, then I sent Sif and Blackmon to survey the terrain while I read through the briefing notes. For once, there was hardly any data; the only thing we knew for sure was that the enemy had moved a sizable force, at least six hundred men, onto the hill and camped out. Given a couple of weeks, which they'd had, they could have dug trenches, established a network of bunkers, set up communications wires (which are much harder to knock out than radios, as they don't emit detectable signals) and taken any number of precautions. They wouldn't have lasted long if someone had ordered an orbital bombardment, but that seemed to be off the table.

"We have no helicopters or aircraft," I said. It didn't look as though the operation was considered very important. A single platoon against *six hundred*? We'd be outnumbered so badly I doubted our training would make much difference. "Merely a handful of long-range guns."

"Maybe you should request reinforcements," Joker said. Bloodnok nodded in agreement. "It could be part of the test."

But Southard disagreed. "You have only a platoon, Stalker," he said. "Make the most of it."

I looked back at the hill and swore. The reports from the snipers were coming back and they didn't sound good. Enemy forces - the BLA seemed to be a hydra; no matter how many heads we cut off they kept coming back - were dug into the hillside, daring us to advance against them. It didn't look as though there were any weak points, save one…and it was so blatantly obvious it practically *had* to be a trap. Maybe I *was* meant to demonstrate moral courage and refuse the mission. Technically, I *did* have that authority…

…But it would be too much like giving up.

"Very well," I said, finally. There were only five minutes left to sort out the plan, but with some fiddling I could make arrangements while we moved into position. "This is what we're going to do. The gunners are going to plaster the hill with shells, aimed at disrupting as much of the enemy position as possible. Sif and Blackmon will take up sniping positions and pick off any enemy who shows his face. The rest of us are going to advance forward under cover of shellfire, taking out any surviving enemy positions as we pass. If we need additional fire support, we'll call it in from the reserve gunners. Any questions?"

None of them looked enthusiastic, I had to admit. I didn't feel very enthusiastic either. If we'd had reinforcements, we might have been able to take the hill without hammering it with the guns; if we'd had helicopters, we might have been able to drop down to the hillside under cover of darkness and capture or kill the enemy leadership. But all we had was a battery of guns, our rifles and a number of grenades. It didn't seem like enough, somehow.

"The guns may run out of shells," Bloodnok pointed out. "They have only a few thousand rounds."

"Then we may have to pull back and admit defeat," I said, grimly. It would get me in deeper shit than simply refusing the mission, but at least we would have tried. "We move in five minutes."

I couldn't help feeling nervous as we slipped as close as we dared to the hill. There was no sign that the enemy had deployed a line of pickets, or even a handful of sensors, but it worried me. If they were good, they might even be watching us through telescopes; low-tech, impossible to detect and next to impossible to stop. Sif and Blackmon *might* see the watchers and take them out…or they might not. The more I looked at the operation, the less I liked it - and it was my plan.

Fuck it, I thought.

"Fire," I ordered.

The gunners opened fire. We hit the deck as the shells screamed down and exploded, peppering in the hillside with giant explosions. It seemed unlikely that *anything* could survive, but we knew from bitter experience that even a relatively small degree of protection could save the targets from anything less than a direct hit. The ground shook madly as the first hail of shells hammered the hill, a handful of incendiary shells setting light to the undergrowth and creating a problem I should have thought of: smoke. Flames roared through the undergrowth, stripping the enemy positions of cover.

"Go," I ordered, as the gunners walked their shells up the hill. It would hopefully keep the enemy too busy to notice us as we slipped forward. "Don't stop for anything."

We ran forward; Squad One taking the lead, with the other two squads taking the rear. I watched carefully as we reached the bottom of the hill, then advanced rapidly up the remains of a stream that had run down from high overhead. It wasn't a perfect trench, but it would give us some cover if - when - the enemy launched a counterattack. Sif and Blackmon kept up a running commentary in our ears as they sniped enemy soldiers, making it harder for them to see us coming. I saw the opening of a bunker, ideally positioned within the hillside, and tossed a grenade inside. The resulting explosion set off a chain of secondary explosions that blew the bunker to pieces and threw debris everywhere.

"Must have been some shells stored in there," Joker commented.

I shrugged. There was no time to talk, not now. We kept running forward, shooting enemy soldiers wherever we saw them, until we threw ourselves down as a machine gun opened fire on our position. Bullets splashed down around us, tearing up the mud; I cursed as Sif reported she couldn't see the gunner to take him out. He was keeping his head down, which was lucky; he could have wiped us out if he'd adjusted his position by a handful of millimetres. Still, we couldn't rely on him staying where he was indefinitely. I called the gunners and told them to load a seeker round while Joker illuminated the machine gun nest with a laser pointer. The resulting explosion wiped the machine gun out of existence, but triggered two more. I called down more fire as I hastily reassessed the situation. If there had been more of us…

...But there weren't.

"Squad One, take the left," I ordered. I might have blundered badly, but the situation was not beyond repair. "Squad Two, take the right. Let them think they have us pinned down."

Bloodnok snorted. "They don't?"

I ignored his sally as I issued orders to the gunners, then crawled to the left, keeping my head in the mud. A handful of enemy positions were smashed as a new wave of shells crashed down, giving us a moment to inch forward and seize the heights. Moments later, I saw a line of enemy soldiers emerging from yet another hidden bunker; they'd hidden underground when the shelling had begun, then returned to retake the positions before it was too late. And they were too closely intermingled with us to risk calling down more fire…

"Grenades," I snapped. There was no point in trying gas - by now, the BLA would have secured immunisation jabs for themselves - but HE would make their lives miserable. I threw one into the mass of soldiers while Joker and Moriarty hurled two more further into the bunker. In confined spaces, the effect would be even more devastating. "Get a lid on that bunker, now!"

Joker ran forward…and fell, under a hail of fire from high overhead. I didn't have more than a second to mourn his loss before the unseen gunners swept their weapons over me. Squad One was wiped out moments later, leaving Squad Two the sole target of enemy fire. And there weren't enough of them to push forward before it was too late.

My radio buzzed. "END EX," Southard said. He sounded calm, too calm. I'd have preferred him shouting at me. "I say again, END EX. Return to deployment zone."

"Aye, sir," I acknowledged, as I rose to my feet. I'd been pinged, all right; I'd 'died' before, but this was particularly humiliating. I had a feeling I was in *very* deep shit. "We're on our way."

Southard was waiting for us as we returned to the deployment zone. "Perhaps you could tell me," he said, "just what went wrong?"

"I screwed up," I said.

"And did I ask you to talk?" Southard asked. "Sif. What went wrong?"

Sif hesitated, noticeably. "We attacked with insufficient force," she said, after a moment that was really too long to escape Southard's attention. "And we didn't have the power to keep the enemy suppressed before it was too late."

I felt a glimmer of pity. Southard had deliberately placed her in a nasty position, giving her the choice between backing me up, which would have made her look like an idiot, or betraying me. I really wouldn't have complained - I certainly *couldn't* have complained - if she'd blamed everything on me. It had been my fault, after all.

"So," Southard said, after a chilling moment. "Stalker. Do you agree with her?"

"Yes, sir," I said. "I made a set of mistakes that lead to our defeat."

"And to the loss of an entire platoon of troopers," Southard said. "Defeats are one thing Stalker; they do happen, even if the propaganda department tries to convince people they don't. But having an entire platoon wiped out takes it from *defeat* to *debacle*. Where did you go wrong?"

I had a nasty feeling I knew the answer. "Sir," I said. "I should have refused the mission."

Southard's eyebrows quirked upwards. "You would have defied an order from the highest commanding officer on the planet?"

"The order was impossible to carry out," I said. I knew that now; hell, even before, I'd known the mission would be very difficult. "We needed more firepower, more deployable forces and more...well, more *everything*. A full company could have attacked from several different directions, forcing the enemy to spread their defences wide; a flight of drones could have called down fire on the bunkers, targeting them for precision missile strikes that would have saved the advancing forces from being surprised."

I paused. "Or we could just have flattened the hill from orbit."

"Yes, we *could* have done," Southard said. He stepped back, as if he were addressing us all, but I knew he was speaking to me. "There are two forms of courage in this world. It takes a certain kind of courage to advance against enemy fire, true, but it takes another kind to refuse orders that will lead to certain defeat. You should have refused your orders, Stalker; indeed, you had a *duty* to refuse those orders.

"We're very capable soldiers, but we are not gods. Nor are we superhuman. You could not have won the battle with the forces you had on hand, no matter what you did. In hundreds of years of operations, *no one* has ever won. The only winning move, as the saying goes, was not to play."

I wasn't sure I believed him, at least not at first. I hated the idea of giving up; there was a part of me that believed, despite everything that had happened, that there *was* a solution. And yet, I knew I'd blundered badly. It wasn't until much later, really, that I came to terms with the idea that some battles were unwinnable and the only realistic option was to go to ground and reform for the next round.

"You will, of course, be expected to discuss - fully - the reasons for your failure," Southard added, after his words had sunk in. "Why *didn't* you refuse your orders?"

"Because…because I thought we could do it," I said. It wasn't a complete answer; we'd been told, time and time again, that disobeying a legitimate order was a court martial offense. And yet, a suicidal order…was it really legitimate? Would there come a time when we might have to hold a position against impossible odds to save the rest of the force? "And I was wrong."

"Yes, you were," Southard said. I *knew* he knew what I'd been thinking. "You were wrong, Stalker, and your troops paid the price."

He looked at the rest of the troops. "You were free with your opinions," he added. "But the opinion you *didn't* put forward was a suggestion that the mission was impossible. You're not being trained to be dunderheaded guardsmen, but marines. You should have raised objections if you believed it was an impossible task."

I winced. It wouldn't have been easy for anyone to stand up and say so, not in front of the rest of us. But that too, perhaps, required a special form of courage.

"You'll all be tested," Southard said, quietly. "And I hope you will learn something from this experience. Because the next time may not be *quite* so obviously unwinnable."

And, with that, he marched us back to the tents.

CHAPTER
TWENTY-NINE

> The Marine Corps was, perhaps, the only military service where refusing orders, no matter how suicidal, was seen as acceptable. No other service would tolerate open insubordination; a CO who refused to carry out an operation would be rapidly relieved of command and earmarked for an immediate field court martial. The sentence, of course, would be death. It would not matter, indeed, if the operation failed spectacularly; the accused would probably take the blame, even though he had tried to stop the operation.
> This may not explain all the problems facing the Empire in its final decades. But it certainly explains why the military was so unable to handle them.
> —Professor Leo Caesius

No one gave me a hard time over my failure.

Well, no one apart from myself. I was *mad*. I'd screwed up; my mistake had led to the death of everyone in my platoon. Never mind that the deaths were simulated; the exercise had been stunningly realistic and they would have died, for real, if we'd been in actual combat. I *should* have declined the mission, or requested reinforcements; instead, I'd lacked the courage to admit that the mission was impossible.

Time went by, of course; we had hundreds of other training sessions, some designed - as we had been warned - to be impossible with what we had on hand. Learning to recognise those was difficult; we ended up appointing a trooper to serve as a devil's advocate and enumerate all the reasons we shouldn't attempt the mission. It didn't always work, but at least it prepared us for the tasks facing us. By the time we geared up for the Crucible, we thought we were as close to ready as possible.

"This is the final obstacle before you earn your Rifleman's Tab," Southard said, as we gathered outside the gate. It was dark - they'd woken us at 2am - and the gate was lit up, the only source of light in sight. Some wag had written 'abandon all hope, all ye who enter here' above the gate, warning us that we could expect nothing but hell inside. "It defeats half of the platoons who step inside, forcing them to either break up and reform or recycle the individual platoon members to newer units. Some of you may die inside. Is there any of you who wants to back out at the final hurdle?"

We shook our heads. We'd spent nearly a year on the Slaughterhouse and any quitters had been lost long ago. None of us wanted to back out now, even though we were guaranteed careers in the auxiliaries. It would have wasted a year of suffering, bleeding and experiences that most civilians would unhesitatingly have termed cruel and unusual punishment. I still had nightmares - when I wasn't too tired to dream - about the last set of Conduct After Capture drills. They'd been truly unpleasant.

"Good," Southard said. "You have had ample opportunity to read about the Crucible, so you know what to expect - apart, of course, from the tests that aren't written down." He smirked as our faces dropped. "I won't bother to go into details. If you're too stupid to read the briefing notes, that's your problem not mine. All that matters is that you will emerge as marines, or quitters, or in a body bag. We'll graduate any dead troopers as marines and grant them burial on the Slaughterhouse."

There was a long pause. "You each have your emergency beacons," he added, darkly. "As always, there are no accidents. You trigger them; you get hauled out. Any of you can leave at any moment, but bear in mind that every one of you who leaves weakens the overall team and may make completing the assault course impossible. Your weakness may doom everyone."

I scowled, inwardly. We'd talked, more than once, about refusing to carry the emergency beacons, but the one time we'd asked if we could leave the beacons behind we'd been told that carrying them was yet another test. The corps had no room for quitters; if we had the grit and determination to complete the course, we'd resist the temptation and complete it even while carrying the beacon. And he was right. If I quit - if any of us quit - we'd weaken everyone else's chances of graduating. We might break, if we were the only ones on the course, but it was harder to quit knowing that everyone else would be brought down, too.

We don't fight for the Empire, I recalled Bainbridge saying, months ago. *We fight for the jarheads on either side of us.*

"Good luck," Southard finished. He pointed to the gate. "When you're ready, you may enter."

I met Joker's eyes, just for a second. None of us had been designated as leader; as far as we knew, we were all equals. Who should go first? I hesitated, just for a second, then hefted my pack and strode forward through the gate. Everyone else fell into line behind me. Nothing happened as we passed the line, but I couldn't help feeling a tingle of excitement. We'd complete the course or die trying.

I'd like to give you a blow-by-blow account of the Crucible, but the memories just blur together. I know what I did - I know what I must have done - yet everything is a hazy blur in my mind. We marched for hours, following a path laid down for us, then assaulted an 'enemy' position without even a second to catch our breath. As soon as we captured it, we were split up and told to make our own way to the RV point before the enemy caught up with us. We made it there, somehow, only to be told that we had to carry on; the helicopter that was meant to pick us up had been cancelled by someone in high command. I thought about quitting there and then, but I couldn't let the others down. We marched onwards, the enemy snapping at our heels…

We reached the next testing station, which seemed a normal shooting range right up until we stepped inside. Holographic enemies, all incredibly hard to see even with night-vision gear, appeared all around us; we shot our way through them, trying hard not to hit the civilians they were using as human shields. There *was* a casualty allowance, an unspoken understanding that there *would* be civilian deaths in a point-blank gunfight, but we knew we would be marked down for every non-combatant we hit. We completed the shooting range, only to discover that three of us had been 'injured.' And so we carried them umpteen miles to the *next* waypoint, whereupon they 'recovered' in time to help us storm another building, rescue several hostages and kill a dozen terrorists.

There were roughly four hours of sleep - if that - and then we were on the move again, this time advancing towards an enemy target. We climbed a mountain, crossed a fast-flowing river using a makeshift rope bridge, then crawled through a disgusting swamp, holding our weapons above our heads, before reaching the target. None of us were in any state for a prolonged offensive, so we just charged forward the moment it came into view. The enemy must have been surprised, because they wilted almost at once and never recovered before we took the complex and wiped them out. It turned out to be a trap; the moment we thought we'd won, several large enemy formations counterattacked. We were forced to use enemy weapons and ammunition to hold the line long enough for our relief to arrive.

And then we were launched into space, put through a whole series of nasty decompression exercises, then dropped back into the atmosphere. Warned that the enemy was on the prowl, we struggled - again - to the waypoint, whereupon we were told to set up camp for the night and prepare ourselves for the following morning. We were so tired that we almost set up there and then, but when we considered the location it became clear that a half-assed enemy force could wipe us out with ease. Somehow, drawing on reserves we hadn't known we had, we moved the tents to a safer location, then organised a watch schedule. Staying awake for even a single hour was very - *very* - difficult. I found myself dozing off twice before I heard the faint hints that *someone* was poking their way towards us., Cursing, I woke the others - what they called me was so thoroughly unprintable it would make a Drill Sergeant blanch - and we stood to, ready to defend our position. The enemy launched a flare into the air, casting an eerie light over the surroundings, then sniped at us until the sun started to appear over the distant hills. Their shooting wasn't very good - none of us were hit - but it was quite enough to keep us from getting much sleep. Who knew when we might have to move again?

It was a tired and utterly shattered platoon that finally made it to Drill Instructor Bridge, on the far side of the Crucible. The bridge probably looked thoroughly unsafe, at least to the handful of civilians who had set foot on the Slaughterhouse, but to us it looked like the gateway to paradise. We stumbled forwards, our arms and legs aching in places we hadn't known we had, then stopped dead as Southard appeared on the far side and walked across the bridge.

"There's a final forced march to undertake," he said, casually. Too casually. At that moment, I think he was the most hated man on the Slaughterhouse. "Turn to the right and follow the marked path for ten kilometres."

I stared at him. There was a part of me, a very large part of me, that wanted to tell him to shove his orders somewhere unmentionable and stalk past him onto the bridge. I wasn't sure I had the energy to keep going, not when the bridge was in sight. We could just push him aside; sure, he *was* a Drill Instructor, but there were ten of us…

…And it would mean failing.

I turned, somehow, and started to walk. Behind me, everyone else followed.

"Belay that order," Southard said. "About face and cross the bridge."

If I'd thought I'd hated him before…a test, another damned test. And one so simple that it had damn near overwhelmed us. Did we have the guts to keep going even when the end was in sight? I turned, stumbled across the bridge automatically - and crossed the finish line. A statue of a dozen marines, holding weapons at parade rest, peered down at me. My legs buckled, but somehow I kept going until I reached the medical centre. The medics barked orders, practically cut off our uniforms and went to work. Many of my aches and pains faded away under their tender ministrations…

…And the overwhelming sensation that I had succeeded, that I had completed the final requirement to become a marine.

Naked, we stumbled out of the medical centre and into a lobby. Southard stood there, waiting for us; ten small piles of clothes rested on the table behind him. He was wearing his dress uniform, I realised; he must have changed while we were being poked and prodded by the medics. His gaze flickered over us - I'd been through too much to give a damn about my nakedness - and then he waved to the clothes.

"Find yours, then get dressed," he said. He sounded more friendly now - although *that* wasn't hard. He'd never been as aggressive as

Bainbridge and his comrades, but he had always maintained a reserve. "And congratulations."

I found my clothes and pulled them on, one by one. We'd been told that only full marines could wear dress blacks - the black uniform we wore during parades, or whenever protocol demanded we dress formally - and the fact they'd given it to us, now, was a sign we'd made it. I turned, looked at myself in the mirror, then reached for the cap and placed it firmly on my head. Perhaps trying to fight in dress blacks would be a pain in the ass - actually, there was no doubt about it - but for the moment I just felt tired delight. I was a marine.

"Follow me," Southard ordered, after we were all dressed. "The chefs have laid on a special buffet."

There's a joke about military cooks that dates back to somewhere long lost in the mists of time. They're the most lethal part of the military; they've killed thousands of men, mostly by poisoning them. I didn't think it was actually true - I learned later that there were quite a few cooks in the Civil Guards who were responsible for outbreaks of disease, mostly by using substandard meat - and it definitely wasn't true of the marine cooks. The food was normally bland, but it was edible and filled us up. This time, however, they'd laid on a dinner of steak and eggs. If Southard hadn't reminded us to use napkins, we would have ruined our new uniforms within seconds. As it was, it was a pretty close shave.

Once we were finished, Southard led us into the armoury. "You'll find your dress swords in the drawers," he said, once we were all inside. "Strap them on, then collect your weapons from the desk outside. The Commandant wants to see you in the parade ground."

Swords had struck me as old-fashioned when they'd first started teaching us how to use them in combat, but I had to admit they were snazzy as hell. (And besides, swords, knives and batons didn't make a sound or emit any betraying radiation.) I pulled mine from the drawer and examined it, carefully. They'd written a serial number on the blade, but my name wasn't visible. It didn't matter, not really; the serial number was good enough for the marines, while having your name on your weapon is a serious security problem. Who knew *what* the enemy could pick up from your droppings?

Well, *we* did. We'd watched as post-battle assessment teams and sensitive site exploitation teams worked over our campsites, learning far too much about us from what we'd left behind when we'd departed. Sherlock Holmes - a detective from an era few outside the corps knew had ever existed - would have been astonished at just how much they'd deduced about us. It hadn't taken us long to learn how to sanitize our campsites, but even so it was hard to prevent them from learning *something*.

"It's a great weapon," Joker said, giving his sword an experimental swing. "I could use this in combat."

I nodded in agreement. The weapons were far from ceremonial. There were no shortage of stories about marines who'd used their swords in combat, when the bullets ran out - or when they'd been barred from bringing firearms into the building. Most people, used to the fancy soldiers in fancier uniforms they see during parades, assume that their weapons are plastic fakes. It's worked in our favour more than once.

"Put it away," Southard ordered. "Draw your weapons from the desk and then prepare for the parade."

My rifle didn't feel *right* when I picked it up, although it took me several minutes to work out precisely what was wrong. They'd removed the nametag I'd been so proud of, a year ago, leaving only the serial number in place. I felt a pang I couldn't quite explain. My name on a rifle, just like my name on a sword, could be far too revealing, yet I felt as if I'd lost something very dear to me. I stared down at it for a long moment, then checked the pistol instinctively. My name was gone from its butt too.

"Draw ammunition," Southard reminded us. "You're *marines* now. We trust you with live ammunition."

I nodded. We'd fired off thousands upon thousands of rounds as we'd made our way through the Slaughterhouse, but we'd never been allowed to keep our weapons loaded when we weren't expected to use them. Now... now, I could carry my weapons locked and loaded, ready to fire, whenever I pleased. Once I had the permit, I could even carry a weapon on Earth, although I knew it would be best to keep it out of sight. Civilians would start screaming if they saw a *real* weapon, while the police might assume the worst and engage with deadly force. They were not particularly well trained.

"There isn't long before the parade," Southard said, once we were assembled in the antechamber. "I want you to know I'm proud of you. You didn't lose a single member to the Crucible."

They'd hammered the statistics into us, time and time again. Only one in ten Boot Camp attendees went to the Slaughterhouse, while half of the troopers would quit, or claim a medical discharge, or die. The best of platoons sometimes came apart when faced with the Crucible, perhaps through sheer bad luck. A handful of early injuries could ruin the entire platoon. The thought of having to go through it all again was horrific.

"What you forged, over the last year, will not last," he added. "Some of you will start advanced training, others will be classed as Combat Replacement Of War - CROWs - and slotted into units in need of new marines. But you will *remember* each other as more than just buddies. None of you would have made it through without all of you."

We'd been lucky, I knew. There were platoons that just failed to get any traction at all, even though all of their members had passed Boot Camp. And others that had dissolved into mutual recriminations that had forced the Drill Instructors to break them up and start again, perhaps even discharging the worst of the offenders…

But we'd made it. And that was all that mattered.

CHAPTER THIRTY

> The Slaughterhouse is the event that binds marines - and even their auxiliaries - together and the bonds it forges can last for life. Ed told me that he stayed in touch with his platoon mates until his final assignment to Avalon. For older marines, their training platoon can serve as the building block of a chain that works its way through the entire corps. It isn't uncommon for platoon mates to help each other out after their graduation…
>
> -Professor Leo Caesius

I'd never seen the parade ground before, not even when we were practicing marching up and down - or prancing around looking pretty, as Southard had put it. Troopers simply weren't allowed into sections of the complex reserved for marines, not until we'd earned the right to enter. Now, we marched through a gate and into a parade ground dominated by a reviewing stand, a large set of seats for the witnesses and the two 'enemy' companies that had harried us throughout our training. I would later command one of them, at Officer Candidate School, but for the moment all I could do was admire them. They'd been formidable foes.

Commandant Jeremy Damiani himself, surrounded by a handful of older men in dress uniforms, gazed down at us as we marched past him, while the crowds cheered. They were mainly dependents - it was a point of honour for the marine dependents to attend each graduation parade - although there were a handful of retired marines amongst them. There were no auxiliaries, as far as I knew; they rarely cared to attend graduation ceremonies. They were reminders of what they'd been unable to achieve. Very few people made a fuss about it.

"Present arms," Southard bellowed, as we marched once around the field and then stopped in front of the stand. "And...*relax!*"

We relaxed slightly, *very* slightly. I don't think anyone could have told we were doing anything, but standing fully to attention. The Commandant, who presumably *could* tell what we were doing, smiled as he stepped forward. I couldn't help noticing that he was holding a small leather bag in one hand.

"Let me start by saying," he said, "that it is a very great honour to be here, watching as these troopers take the final step to become marines. They have undergone the most feared training course in the history of warfare, shedding all those who could not make it along the way. I offer you my most sincere congratulations on your success. Please join with me" - he looked up at the watching crowd - "in giving a hearty round of applause for these new marines."

There was a roar of applause. I felt...*odd*. I'd felt jealous, somewhat, at Boot Camp, when families and friends had been welcome to attend. Here, there was no one who didn't have a strong link to the corps. I felt almost as if I had a new family...no, I *did* have a new family, one that would always be there for me. Joker and the others were my brethren now, but so were the rest of the marines.

"These are hard times for the Empire," Damiani said. "The established order that we have fought so hard to defend, over the last three thousand years, has been badly weakened. New challenges are springing up everywhere, while recruiting for the armed forces is at an all-time low. Our society is decaying in front of us. You have embarked upon a career that will be marked by hundreds, perhaps thousands, of thankless tasks. You will be, at best, perpetually misunderstood by those you defend. There will be times when you will ask yourselves if it is worth it. All I can tell you is that your work, your determination - and, at times, your sacrifices - is geared towards protecting the civilians of the Empire. It is to *them* that we owe our allegiance. "

He was blunt, perhaps too blunt. If the speech became public knowledge, he might well be forced to resign. But he went ahead anyway, showing the moral courage I'd been taught to develop on the Slaughterhouse. It was only with the benefit of hindsight - after Damiani exiled me and my company to Avalon - that I realised he must have known the Empire was doomed, no matter what we did. He was planting seeds for a post-Empire universe that wouldn't fall into barbarism.

"You will see the very worst of humanity," he said. "You will watch helplessly as the darkness falls over countless worlds. But you will also see brave men and women, pinpricks of light, fighting desperately to hold back the darkness. We exist to support them, to help them, to make it possible for them to save us all from chaos.

"You - the poor bloody infantry - are the heart and soul of the Marine Corps. I salute you."

He saluted. We saluted back.

Damiani reached into his bag. "Marine Kehormatan, come forward."

Sif stepped forward to a roar of approval from the crowd. She was the only one whose name I remember - and only then because I thought it was unusual. It wasn't until much later that I realised her entire family had been serving with honour for hundreds of years. Damiani pinned a badge on her collar, then shook her hand. Sif looked overwhelmed, almost, as she stepped back into line.

It was my turn soon enough. "Marine Stalker, come forward."

I found it hard to walk up to the Commandant, who was holding a dull gunmetal-grey box in his hand. I'd inched forward against overwhelming fire, but this was harder...somehow, I stepped up to him and stared as he opened the box, revealing a golden badge. The Rifleman's Tab glowed faintly against the metal; he picked it up, gently pressed it against my collar and secured it in place. I was a marine.

There are a whole series of myths surrounding the Rifleman's Tab, mostly nonsense. The only important detail is that they're made for each marine individually and the only way to get one is to graduate from the Slaughterhouse. If a marine dies, on active service or in bed with his wife, the badge is returned to the Slaughterhouse and added to the memorial for fallen comrades. Humans being humans, a single Rifleman's Tab is worth billions of credits on the black market, but very few are available at any price. The corps has a legal right to seize any stolen badge without warrant or compensation.

And it was mine. No matter what happened, no matter what I did, it couldn't be taken from me until the day I died.

Damiani shook my hand. It was the last time we met, face-to-face, until I was stationed on Earth. Maybe he saw something special in me, maybe he didn't; it doesn't matter. He would go on to become Commandant of the Marine Corps - and, perhaps, the *last* person to bear that title. And he was a good man.

"You are dismissed," Damiani said, when every last one of us had received their tab. "There is now two days of leave, after which you will be given your first assignment."

The rush from the parade ground - also traditional - was probably best described as undignified. Somehow, we ended up in the bar, where we found ourselves being congratulated by dozens of current and retired marines; they bought us hundreds of drinks, but none of us got drunk. (I was relieved to discover that one of the treatments we were given negated the effects of alcohol and hard drugs; sadly, I think I was very much in the minority.) The rest of that leave passed in a blur; two days later, feeling oddly unhappy to be bored, I found myself being shown into another office.

"Stalker," Captain Garfunkel said. I'd met him, briefly, during one of the psychological tests we'd undergone. "Please, be seated."

"Yes, sir," I said.

"Call me Sam," he said. "We're both marines now."

I doubted it. I'd developed the habit of looking the instructors up on the datanet, when I had a free moment, and Sam Garfunkel had a combat record longer than my arm. If he hadn't suffered a major injury, judging by his file, he would probably have stayed on the front lines and left evaluating new-minted marines to others. The idea of considering him to be anything other than my superior was absurd.

"You were assessed thoroughly as you passed through the course," Garfunkel said. "Your Drill Instructors agreed that you showed definite signs of leadership potential, although you would also make a good NCO. You were quite good at taking the lead and equally good at offering ideas to your superiors, when you weren't in command. However, we cannot send you to OCS until you have had at least five years in the field."

"Yes, sir," I said. I'd known as much. Every marine is a rifleman first; there was no way I'd be given a command assignment without first having served as a lowly rifleman. It wasn't something I could argue, either. A person without field experience in command is asking for trouble. "Am I going to the field?"

"We believe there is no room for you to develop a more focused MOS" - Military Occupational Speciality - "at the moment," Garfunkel said. "You were not interested in serving as a combat medic, a combat engineer or an EOD officer. Therefore" - he made a show of consulting his datapad, although I was sure he had it memorised - "we would like to offer you a posting to 453rd Company, otherwise known as Webb's Weavers. They've lost several men on deployment recently and are in desperate need of CROWs."

"Yes, sir," I said. Whatever he said, I knew I wasn't really being offered a choice. "When do I ship out?"

"There's a supply ship leaving for Moidart in two days," Garfunkel said. "You and the other CROWs will be on it. Once you arrive, you will be integrated into the Weavers as soon as possible. Captain Webb may wish to have you flown out to join them or have you wait at the base until the Weavers are rotated back behind the wire. Dare I assume you wish to accept this assignment?"

"Yes, sir," I said.

"Very good," Garfunkel said. He tapped his terminal, then produced a datachip. "You'll report to the ship by 0800, Tuesday. There's a list of everything you're expected to bring on the chip; if you're having problems finding any of them, talk to the supply sergeants."

He took a breath. "Make sure you don't miss the deadline or you will be in deep shit," he added. "At the very least, the cost of arranging transport will be taken out of your pay. Trust me, that's enough money to rent an apartment in Imperial City for a month. You can report now, if you wish, or spend some more time in Liberty Town. I'd advise taking the leave, myself. You'll find yourself wishing you had once you depart."

I took the datachip when he held it out to me. "Thank you, sir."

"Thank me when you get back," Garfunkel growled. He cleared his throat. "Do you want a word of advice?"

"Yes, sir," I said.

"There's a good chance that some of the CROWs travelling with you will be from your platoon," he said. "We do try to jumble platoons up as much as possible, but that isn't always easy. In the event of that happening, I advise you to spend time with the other CROWs too. You may end up serving with them on the surface."

"Thank you, sir," I said. I'd learned how to get along with my fellows, even if we cordially disliked one another. "I'll do my best."

"Just make sure your best is good enough," Garfunkel said. "Good luck, *marine*."

I stepped out of the office, torn between two different sets of emotions. On the one hand, I was finally going to get a chance to put my training to work; on the other, I was going to go into very real danger. There wouldn't be any Drill Instructors rigging the tests to make the prospect of a deadly accident less likely, not on a real battlefield. There wouldn't be any simulated enemy soldiers or IEDs that blasted out ink, rather than terrifying explosions. And an injury might be real…

"Hey," Joker said. He was waiting outside. "What did you get?"

"Moidart," I said. I knew nothing about the planet, save for its name, but it sounded like excitement, adventure and deadly danger. Could it beat the Undercity? I rather doubted it; I'd checked and even Terra Nova, humanity's first colony world, didn't have anything like the crushing population density of Earth. "Want me to wait for you?"

"Sure," Joker said.

As a child - or a teenager - I would have leaned against the wall, but as a marine I stood at parade rest and waited. Everyone who passed greeted me as *marine* - I doubted I would ever get tired of it - and saluted, formally. I had to salute back, every time. By the time Joker emerged, grinning from ear to ear, I was getting tired of *saluting*. But it had to be endured, at least as long as we were in safe territory.

"Moidart," Joker said. "They want me as a CROW."

I nodded. "Did he give you the warning about befriending the others too?"

"Yup," Joker said. "Be nice to our fellow CROWs - or else."

He shrugged. "Do you want to get our supplies now, then go back to Liberty Town?"

It was easy to get our supplies; we presented the supply sergeants with the list and ten minutes later we had a pair of knapsacks, carefully packed with everything we wanted. I checked mine anyway, just in case; the Drill Instructors had told me to make sure of everything for myself before I signed for anything. And they'd even issued the wrong gear from time to time, just to make sure we knew to check. This time, everything was in order; we stowed the bags in lockers, then headed for Liberty Town. I could hear the siren call of wine, women and song, perhaps not in that order, calling for me.

Two days later, we boarded the shuttle and were duly shipped up to MTS *Walter Gold*, a huge Marine Transport Ship. The officer who greeted us when we stepped through the hatch pointed us to our quarters, warned us to stay out of restricted sectors and not to try to leave the ship without authorisation. We agreed, walked to our quarters and discovered that they were nothing more than another set of barracks, complete with bunks, shared facilities and little else.

"Terrible conditions," Joker said, deadpan. "I'm totally writing them up online."

"They'd sue to get you to take down the review," I said. Actually, it looked better than some of the apartments I'd seen in the Undercity. Marines are clean and tidy, after all, and none of us would have *dreamed* of leaving the barracks in a mess. "And it beats hiding in a hovel while Snowstorm Elsa rages overhead."

Joker shivered, dramatically. Spending three days in the midst of a howling snowstorm had been the low point of the Slaughterhouse - or it *had* been, until the Drill Instructors found something worse to throw at us. The corps was good at preventing bullies from becoming Drill Instructors, but there were times when it was hard to tell the difference. We'd wound up huddling together, sharing heat, as the temperature plummeted rapidly. And it had been hard to prepare our weapons to fire afterwards.

"They couldn't sue me," he pointed out. "What do I have for them to take?"

"Your salary," I countered. Actually, I had a feeling the corps would ensure our salaries remained firmly with us, at least until we decided to spend our money, but it wasn't something I wanted to test. "And your life, if there is nothing else to give."

The hatch opened, revealing two more newly-minted marines. They rapidly introduced themselves as Hatchet and Sawdust, both from a different training platoon. We introduced ourselves, shook hands and spent the next hour swapping lies about our experience in the Crucible. (Actually, we *then* spent the next couple of hours arguing over who'd had the worst experience (it was us, of course), but the ship's departure from orbit interrupted before we could start trading blows.) By then, we had been joined by Trajan and Whisper, a female marine.

"I meant to ask," I said, when Whisper and I were alone together. "What is Boot Camp *like* for women?"

She gave me a cross look, which relented slightly as she realised I was honestly curious. "It's pretty much the same as the one for men," she said. "We just get additional training in dirty fighting and dire warnings about what might happen to us if we fell into enemy hands. But we lose more recruits than you."

"So we get told," I said. "Why did you join?"

Whisper shrugged. "I grew up with an uncle who liked to touch me," she said. "It was one of those shitty little planets where everyone knows everyone else, so there wasn't anyone who'd believe me if I complained. My parents had died when I was six. One night, I hid a knife in my sleeve and stabbed him when he came to my bed, then ran. The corps was the only place I could go."

"At least you killed him," I pointed out.

"Yes, I did," Whisper said. "And you can bet your ass they would have executed me, if they'd grabbed me before I was shipped off-world. It wasn't a good place to grow up without a family."

"You have a family now," I said. I couldn't help being impressed. "Coming to spar?"

CHAPTER
THIRTY-ONE

Whisper's story was not, alas, unusual. The Empire took a dim view of any of the peons engaging in self-defence, preferring instead to urge anyone under attack to scream for help from the police. Earth's staggeringly high rate of theft, rape and murder sprang from a simple inability to protect eighty billion (at least) inhabitants, a reluctance to punish criminals who were caught and a refusal to tolerate any form of self-defence. Those who did try to defend themselves often discovered that they were prosecuted for trying.

The net result was, perhaps, inevitable. For the last fifty years before the Fall of Earth, no female candidates from Earth made it through Boot Camp. Indeed, the rate of men passing through Boot Camp was also dropping. The only women who made it through - and then took on the Slaughterhouse - were women raised on worlds that took a more sensible attitude towards self-defence.

-Professor Leo Caesius

Moidart was a planet that should have worked.

According to the briefing notes, it had been founded three hundred years ago by a wealthy nobleman who'd invested in a great deal of development before the first colonists had landed on the surface. The combination of settlement opportunities - including interest-free loans from a local bank, rather than one of the interstellar corporations - and the prospects for skipping a couple of colonial developmental stages attracted thousands of settlers, all of whom eagerly pledged allegiance to the nobleman, who crowned himself King Henry I. By the time Henry died, leaving a controlling interest in the planet to King Fredrick (the son he'd considered most like him), Moidart had a growing population, a handful of major industrial estates and even a handful of tiny asteroid mining operations.

And then disaster had struck. A routine survey mission had found traces of a dozen rare elements - including several used to make Phase Drives - under populated farmland. Fredrick, in need of money for various reasons, sold mining rights to one of the interstellar corporations, which promptly landed a large number of miners and displaced thousands of farmers from their fields. The farmers didn't take it calmly and began a revolution, aided and abetted by Prince George, Fredrick's older brother, who bitterly resented being passed over by his father. King Fredrick, feeling the noose tightening around his neck, had screamed for help from the Empire, which had responded by dispatching a regiment of imperial troops to back up the locals. Just to complicate matters, the Hammersmith Corporation, which had bought the mining rights, also shipped in a vast number of mercenaries, which promptly made themselves even *less* popular than the royal troops.

Fifty years of intermittent warfare later, the planet was a horrendous mess. King Fredrick controlled his capital city (and very little outside it,) Hammersmith controlled the mines, the Imperial Governor (appointed after Fredrick had failed to pay back his loans) claimed to control the entire planet and the warlords, operating outside the capital, controlled everywhere not heavily garrisoned by the off-worlders or the royal troops. The briefing notes had concluded with a grim observation that Hammersmith, which was getting tired of being unable to carry out its mining operations in reasonable safety, had urged the Grand Senate to do something. After a considerable number of bribes had exchanged hands, the Grand Senate had detailed two companies of marines to reinforce the Imperial Army.

"Looks a right fucking mess," Joker commented, as the starship approached Moidart. "Are you sure we're on the right side?"

It wasn't a pleasant thought. King Fredrick had betrayed his people, Hammersmith had forced them to leave their farms (while poisoning the land for miles around), but the warlords weren't any less brutal. Fifty years of warfare had left a mark; they were quite prepared to do anything,

anything at all, to win. There were reports of entire villages and towns wiped out for refusing to send men and supplies to the rebel armies, women kidnapped and sold into sexual slavery to fund the war (and keep the soldiers entertained) and far worse. Whatever ideals the warlords had started with, they'd lost them long ago.

I wasn't surprised. We'd studied the subject intensely at the Slaughterhouse. The longer a rebel faction had to fight, the greater the chance its leaders would become ruthless men (or were replaced by ruthless men). By the time they won, if they won, they no longer had any respect for the rule of law; indeed, they'd lost sight of why they'd started the war in the first place. They tended to impose dictatorships rather than democracies.

And the Governor's forces weren't much better. The orders they'd been given were masterworks of contradictory mealy-mouthed evasion. I wasn't a JAG - there were hardly any JAGs in the corps - but no matter how I looked at the orders, they seemed written to allow the Governor to suggest that the outcome, whatever happened, was what he'd been ordered to do all along. On one hand, he was to suppress the rebels and support the corporation; on the other, he was to create the framework for a lasting peace. (It took me some time to realise that Hammersmith's enemies had helped write the Governor's orders, as any lasting peace would involve Hammersmith being kicked off the planet.) Faced with such indecision, the Imperial Forces had occupied most of the remaining towns and cities, then tried to exterminate the rebels. So far, they were failing miserably.

Not that you would have known it, I realised, from the official news bulletins. The contrast between the marine briefings and the Governor's bombastic statements could hardly be more pronounced. *He* claimed that hundreds of thousands of rebels had been killed, or brought over to support the royal forces; the *marines* claimed that, if anything, the rebellion was growing stronger. The warlords might have disliked each other just as much as they disliked King Fredrick, but the prospect of being snuffed out by off-world forces pretty much condemned them to work together.

"They can't win the war, but they don't dare lose either," Whisper commented. I'd come to know her pretty well over the three weeks we'd spent in transit, along with the others. She had a cynical view of the universe that was pretty close to my own. "So they keep spinning every little engagement as a victory and hope they get relieved before it's too late."

I suspected she was right, but before we could continue the discussion we were called to the shuttlebay. Us CROWs - and a number of engineers who had been summoned to Moidart - were going to be the first down to the surface. Judging from the reports of rebels launching HVMs - which they shouldn't have had - at shuttlecraft, I had a feeling it wasn't really a honour at all. I considered, briefly, suggesting we jumped through the atmosphere, then dismissed the thought. We didn't have the equipment that would make a jump possible.

"When you get down, move into the nearest hardened shelter," the crew chief told us. *That* didn't sound encouraging. "You'll be collected as soon as possible."

We exchanged glances, checked our weapons and boarded the shuttle. The flight down to the surface was hellishly unpleasant, although not as bad as some of the flights on the Slaughterhouse. I think the pilots must have known the dangers, because they kept jinking from side to side and launching flares every time their sensors squealed an alert. We didn't come under fire - a HVM might have killed us before we knew we were being attacked - but we didn't miss any of the experience. By the time the shuttle crashed to the landing pad, we were feeling unwell *despite* our training.

The hatch banged open, allowing us to take our first step onto Moidart. I took a breath and shuddered as I tasted strange - and unpleasant - scents in the air. Hammersmith *claimed* its mining operation wasn't polluting, but the marine briefing had made it clear that they *were* causing untold amounts of ecological damage. They *could* have cut down on the pollution, simply by shipping in more expensive equipment…if, of course, someone had thought the long-term investment was worthwhile. Given the situation on the ground, I rather doubted that *anyone* would consider Moidart a decent investment opportunity. Chances were the corporate sharks running the operation were among the worst of the worst, sent to Moidart merely to get rid of them.

We sprinted for the nearest shelter as alarms howled over the spaceport, announcing the arrival of a hail of mortar shells. Laser defence units opened fire, swatting most of the shells out of the air, but a handful made it through and struck the runway. The damage seemed to be minimal, from what I could tell - the runway was designed to soak up a great deal of damage and be easy to repair - yet it was only a matter of time until the rebels got lucky and hit a moving aircraft. I'd learned enough about logistics to be sure there was no way to replace any helicopters without shipping them in from out-system.

"I don't think much of their security," Joker said, as the alarms finally wound down. A pair of attack helicopters passed overhead and out of sight, but I didn't hear them launching any weapons. The rebels might just have preset the mortars to fire - the spaceport was large enough that the shells would be bound to strike home - and then legged it. "In fact, I feel rather exposed."

"There's only one major spaceport on the planet," Hatchet pointed out. In the distance, I saw an explosion rising into the air. "Everything we need to maintain ourselves has to be shipped through here."

We paused to contemplate the problem. There was no shortage of shuttles that could land without a dedicated spaceport, but the heavy-lift craft that carried most of our supplies needed a proper set of landing facilities. If the spaceport happened to be overrun, the forces on the ground would find it much harder to call on reinforcements and eventually run out of ammunition. Moidart *could* produce simple ammunition - the factories were heavily guarded, according to the briefing notes - but anything more complex than a simple RPG was beyond them. I could easily see the royal forces deserting the moment they ran out of ammunition.

"Fuck me," Joker said, finally.

"Not on duty," a new voice said. We straightened to attention as a newcomer, wearing the combat uniform of a Command Sergeant, strode into the shelter. "Welcome to hell. I am Command Sergeant Singh, Webb's Weavers. I understand that three of you are bound for the Weavers and the other three are assigned to Robertson's Rangers?"

"Yes, sir," we said.

"The Rangers are currently on deployment to Kilkenny," Singh said. In all my career, I never learned his first name. It should have been in his file, but when I looked it turned out that it was marked as restricted. He'd probably served in one of the more secretive units before transferring back to a conventional company. "You three" - he looked at Hatchet, Sawdust and Whisper - "will be assigned to perimeter security until they return. The others will start their service as soon as we reach the FOB. Follow me."

He turned and strode out of the shelter, heading straight for a large armoured car. We followed him and, at his command, climbed into the rear of the vehicle. It was uncomfortably cramped with six marines and their gear, but I had a feeling it was better than trying to walk to the FOB. Singh started the engine and drove past a set of hangers onto a throughway, then right past a man in a red uniform who shook his fist at our retreating backs.

"Traffic warden," Singh said. I thought he was joking at the time. It wasn't until later that I realised he was deadly serious. "They have a habit of bitching when we drive past the speed limit."

The spaceport grew more crowded as we reached the gates. Armed soldiers watched, nervously, as a convoy entered; they waved us through without hesitation, clearly more concerned about anyone trying to get into the spaceport. A long line of local workers were being searched before they were allowed to enter, their faces set in expressionless masks that told me they were as resentful as hell. I didn't blame them - some of the guards were clearly enjoying themselves - but what choice did we have? A single suicide bomber who got through the gates could cause a great deal of trouble if he blew up the right building.

"We're based some distance from the regulars," Singh said, as he gunned the engine. "Their security sucks shit through a straw. Don't trust anyone who isn't a marine and you might just stay alive long enough to learn what you're doing."

I nodded, keeping my eyes on the environment. The fields surrounding the spaceport might have been pretty once, but someone had cut down every last tree and bush within five miles, just to prevent them being used for concealment. It looked very much as though they'd followed up by spraying the area with something that had killed the plants, leaving it barren even at the height of summer. Or maybe it was just the pollution drifting through the air. The road itself was solid workmanship, easily wide enough to take three tank transporters running abreast. I doubted anyone could place an IED in position without it being noticed. It would be much harder to see them once we got off the roads.

Whisper leaned forward. "Do they have a habit of getting close to the spaceport?"

"They fire off mortars every time a resupply ship arrives," Singh grunted. "No HVMs so far, although it's only just a matter of time. They have the local system command network thoroughly penetrated, even though it's run by Hammersmith. Many of the local bureaucrats are interested in keeping on the good side of the monarch and the rebels, so they kiss the ass of the former and slip information to the latter. Expect them to know what we're doing as soon as we do it."

Joker had a different question. "How reliable are the royal troopers?"

"Some units are good; mostly, the ones that have good reason to fear the worst if the rebels win," Singh said. "Others just crap their pants and run away when the shooting starts. There isn't any sort of vetting procedure for recruits, so the rebels manage to slip quite a few moles into the forces. They're so desperate for manpower that they don't even carry out basic checks."

He refused to be drawn any further until we reached the FOB. It had started life as a warehouse on the edge of Charlie City; now, it was surrounded by barbed wire, murder holes and prefabricated protective shields. It looked flimsy, but I knew from training that the shields could soak up anything short of an HVM. On the roof, there was a mounted radar set and a laser defence system, covered by a set of sniper hides. The rebels might be able to storm the FOB and kill us all, but they could be sure we'd sell our lives dearly. Like the spaceport, the ground around the FOB had been cleared; dozens of buildings had been knocked down, just to make it harder for anyone to sneak up on us. I couldn't help wondering just how popular that had made us with the locals.

Probably not at all, I thought. I wouldn't have been too pleased if someone knocked down my home either. *But what choice did we have?*

The FOB was far more secure than the spaceport, thankfully. A guard checked our fingerprints before allowing us to enter; Singh ordered us out the vehicle and pointed us right into the warehouse. Inside, the hard concrete floor was covered with sleeping pallets; dozens of marines, trying to catch a few hours of sleep, lay everywhere. I couldn't help feeling as if I didn't belong, not really. They had months, perhaps years, of experience, while I had almost none.

"The Rangers are to report to Corporal Little," Singh said, gruffly. He glanced at the sleeping marines, then nodded to himself. "The rest of you, with me."

Captain James Webb didn't look like someone who had stepped out of a recruitment poster, to my private disappointment. He looked short, with brown hair an inch or two longer than the haircuts inflicted on us at regular intervals. Indeed, I would have mistaken him for a doctor or a bureaucrat if he hadn't had a muscular body, sharp eyes and mannerisms I'd seen on several other senior marines. Singh saluted - we copied him, quickly - and withdrew, leaving us alone with our new commanding officer.

"Welcome to the Weavers," he said, without preamble. His voice was warm, but there was no hint of weakness. I'd read his record and it was clear he had over two decades of experience. "You're replacing popular men, I'm afraid; one dead, two badly wounded. You won't have an easy time of it. However, we expect you to cope with it. We're going to be going back into the field in four days, unless we get called forward early. You have that long to fit into your new platoons.

"You've had a chance to read the briefing notes, so you know what to expect. The war is stalemated at the moment, without any real chance of either side making a breakthrough, but we will keep the pressure on until the enemy cracks. Or until we get pulled out and sent elsewhere."

He looked at each of us, one by one. "Sergeant Singh will see to your combat assignments," he concluded. "Welcome to Moidart."

And that was our introduction to our new commanding officer.

CHAPTER THIRTY-TWO

Moidart was, of course, a classic example of an ongoing problem. The local forces couldn't take the burden of security from the outsiders, the outside forces didn't have the numbers to impose peace and the rebels didn't have the ability to actually win. Without something that changed the balance of power, the war was doomed to stalemate. There was no hope of coming to an agreement to end the war because the different sides were simply too far apart; the royalists wanted a return to a monarchy, the corporations wanted to rape the land and the rebels wanted to destroy the monarchy and evict the corporations. How could anyone propose a workable compromise?
-Professor Leo Caesius

Captain Webb had been correct, I discovered, as I worked to integrate myself into 3rd Platoon. (Formally, 3rd Platoon, 453rd Company.) Rifleman Yates, who had been killed in an IED strike two months ago, had been popular, very popular. I was a newcomer, a CROW; I knew it would take them time to warm to me, but it was still disheartening. The week I spent prepping for operations with the platoon was, perhaps, the most depressing week of my life.

"You're not too bad, for a cherry," Singh conceded, after we ran through a series of exercises in teamwork. "Could do with a little more refinement, but Moidart will knock the edges off you soon enough."

I nodded. I'd been in danger before, of course, but I'd always known it wasn't quite real, that precautions were taken to minimise the risks of serious injury. Now, everyone pointing a gun at me would have murderous intentions…and the bullets would be real, rather than pulses of laser light or deliberately aimed to miss (but only by a few inches). The fire team - Singh had assigned me to his own team - was good, very good. But Yates had been good too.

"Remember to watch for anything out of place," Singh warned, as we marched out to the muster ground. "The locals have bugger all in the way of services, so there are piles of rubbish everywhere. Expect the rebels to use them to conceal IEDs."

"Yes, Sergeant," I said. I'd called him 'sir' once and had been forcibly reminded not to do it again. Sergeants were rarely addressed as anything other than 'Sergeant' outside Boot Camp or the Slaughterhouse, where there were few officers for us to practice on. "Do they snipe at us on patrol?"

"Sometimes," Singh warned. "Charlie City is supposed to be secure, but there are gaps in the defences everywhere. Watch your back."

I nodded to myself as the gates opened, allowing us to march out and into Charlie City. I'd seen some of the city when we'd been driven from the spaceport, but this was different; a number of buildings looked abandoned, while others were heavily guarded by private security forces. The mercenaries looked tough, but nervous; they knew they were perhaps the most hated soldiers on the planet. I'd heard that the rebels maintained a special hatred for them and any mercenary who fell into their hands could expect a slow and unpleasant death.

"They're not good for anything, but defending their bases," Rifleman Lewis told me, as the platoon spread out. "Don't expect them to come to your aid if we get into shit."

"Understood," I muttered. Lewis hadn't been bad to me - none of them had been *bad* - but he hadn't warmed up to me yet. I had a feeling I'd been assigned to Singh's team to make sure the sergeant could step on me if I turned out to be a weak link. "Is there any *good* news here?"

Lewis snorted. "Not really, Stalker," he said. "The locals either hate us or are too scared to do anything to help us. Either way, we're screwed."

He had a point, I realised, as we walked onwards, into a housing estate. The locals, many of them clearly too poor to buy new clothes, watched us warily, too listless even to get their women and children out of the line of fire. I couldn't believe just how poor they were, not when they were surrounded by land and boundless opportunity. But a combination of bad government and endless war had made investment impossible, trapping countless civilians before they could make something of themselves. I found my heart going out to a handful of children who were kicking a tin can around, laughing in the midst of hell. They didn't deserve to be caught up in a nightmare.

"That's probably a good sign," Lewis told me. "If there was an ambush planned, they would have gotten the children out of the way."

I nodded in agreement. Terrorists - and insurgents - liked using women and children as human shields, but the locals tended to take a dim view of it. Even the most listless population - the most *terrified* population - would turn on the terrorists if they weren't allowed to protect their young. Smart terrorists gave them the chance to remove their children before the shooting started.

A young man - probably around fifteen, although it was hard to be sure - glowered at me as we passed, his dark eyes challenging me. Judging from his skin colour, he was probably a bastard son, perhaps the child of a miner and a local woman. I'd never quite understood the point of racism - in the Undercity, there are all shapes and colours - but I had a feeling the locals probably treated him as a pariah. Someone like that would have a burning urge to prove himself. No doubt, if things had been different, he would have made an excellent marine. Instead, he was probably trying to decide if he could get away with shouting insults or squeezing off a few rounds at us. The pistol concealed under his shirt wasn't invisible to me, not after months at the Slaughterhouse. I'd seen people conceal weapons in far more awkward places.

It was his lucky day. He lowered his eyes, then turned and walked away. I knew from the notes that turning one's back was regarded as a local insult, but I didn't feel offended. The pistol he'd carried might not pack enough punch to break through our body armour, yet the shirt and jeans he'd worn wouldn't offer any resistance to our bullets. He would have been killed before he could get off a second shot, throwing away his life for nothing.

"Move to the right," Singh ordered, quietly. "That pile of rubbish looks suspicious."

I shook my head in disbelief as we gave the pile a wide berth. It wouldn't have been hard to pick up the rubbish, transport it to a disposal centre and feed it into a disintegrator (if it couldn't be recycled) but the locals didn't seem interested in cleaning up their city. The sheer number of shootings, bombings and kidnappings probably made it hard for them to do anything; the files had warned, in great detail, that civil servants - even garbagemen - were targeted for elimination.

And besides, a pile of rubbish *was* an easy place to hide an IED.

I tightened my grip on my rifle as I heard an explosion in the distance, followed by a handful of shots. The radio net buzzed with brief updates - a patrol on the other side of the city had been hit - but we weren't directed to go to their aid. It was a relief, I felt; if we'd made a beeline there, we would probably have been sucked into a second ambush. Even so…I glanced around, watching the handful of visible locals. One of them was quite probably a dicker, reporting our movements to his superiors.

We walked past the remains of a building - it looked as though someone had slammed an antitank rocket into it, blowing the interior into charred debris - and into the next housing estate. It was like crossing an invisible line; I couldn't help thinking of the gang territories back in the Undercity and the places where one gang's control was replaced by another's, where few dared cross without permission from both sides. But the locals looked as poor and hopeless as the first set of locals. A handful of young women eyed us, their older mothers scowling at them fiercely. Below them, sitting on the sidewalk, a number of young men glared. It made no sense to me at all.

"They're hoping for an Exit Permit," Lewis commented, quietly. "If they happen to marry one of us, an off-worlder, they can get permission to leave this shithole and set up a home somewhere else. There isn't much for them here, beyond marrying an unemployed lout, bearing his children and turning into a carbon copy of their mothers. The young men, of course, don't like us threatening to take their women."

I blinked. "We don't…do we?"

"*We* don't," Lewis said. "There are strict orders against fraternising with the local women - or men, if your tastes swing that way. But the regulars often do start relationships, not all of which end well. And the local men *hate* it."

I remembered some of the lessons in applied psychology from the Slaughterhouse. Sex is one of the driving urges of human civilisation; sex… and the urge to procreate. Men wanted to spread their genes as widely as possible, so they felt the urge to impregnate as many women as they could; women wanted a man who could protect them and, in exchange, offered themselves to one man. But men also wanted to make sure the women *only* bore their children, hence the historical fact that female adultery was treated as more serious than male adultery. It didn't seem fair, but it made a certain kind of sense.

"A person has a *rational* brain," Professor Tomkins had said, "but he also has an *emotional* brain. The average man is perfectly capable of adopting, and loving, a child…provided that he understands, *rationally*, that the child isn't actually his. However, discovering that he has been caring for a cuckoo in the nest, another man's child, leads to outrage directed against the child, even though the child is obviously blameless. The emotional brain overrides the rational brain."

It wasn't a pleasant concept. But it might explain why my mother, who had had four different children with four different men, had never found a husband. And there had been no pressing *need* for her to find a husband either. She'd been fed and watered by the state as she churned out children and waited to die.

I pushed the thought aside as we walked through the rest of the estate - it didn't look any better - and took a detour through what had once been a football pitch. The grass had been removed, somehow; it didn't look as through anyone was trying to grow food, even though it would have helped solve the problem of feeding the city's population. We kept a wary eye on a pair of tall buildings, both easily capable of hiding snipers, as we walked past them, weapons at the ready. And then a small child - a girl, wearing a frilly pink dress and carrying a knapsack - came into view. She was running right towards us.

"Get down," Singh snapped.

I hit the deck at once, training overriding the part of my mind that didn't see a real threat. A girl barely old enough to walk couldn't threaten us, could she? I was wrong. Seconds later, there was an explosion…it took me several seconds to realise that the girl had been carrying a bomb, which someone had detonated via remote control. There was nothing left of her…the sound of bullets cracking down around us snapped me out of my horrified trance as Singh barked orders, directing the fire team to lay down covering fire.

"There's a sniper up there," Lewis snapped.

"Take him out," Singh snapped back.

I covered Lewis as he snapped a grenade launcher into place on his rifle, then launched a contact grenade towards the sniper's location. There was a sharp explosion and the sniper fire stopped abruptly. Pieces of debris crashed down around our position, but luckily none came within metres of actually hitting us. I let out a sigh of relief as we searched for more targets, finding two more enemy fighters hidden within abandoned buildings. Singh snapped orders; one fire team provided cover while our fire team inched forward, then crashed into the building. Inside, three enemy fighters died before they recovered from the blast we'd used to blow down the door.

"Three tangos down," Lewis reported. There was a shot from overhead which narrowly missed Rifleman Atwell. I snapped up my rifle and picked the terrorist off, sending his body crashing down to the concrete floor. "Correction; four tangos down."

We searched the building, but found nothing else. The other fire team, which had attacked the other enemy position, reported that the terrorists had fled, leaving behind an IED which hadn't been set up properly. There didn't seem to be any point in taking it back to the FOB, so Singh ordered them to blow the IED in place and then leave the building alone. The remaining bodies were left where they'd fallen.

I looked at Singh. "Sergeant, shouldn't we be calling in an SSE team? Or a WARCAT unit?"

Singh shook his head. "If we were in command of the war effort, Stalker, that would be a good idea," he said. "But as it is, no one really gives a damn."

I wanted to argue, to point out that we'd been schooled in gathering intelligence to use against the enemy, but it wasn't the time or place.

Instead, we rejoined the rest of the platoon, did a quick check for injuries and then resumed our patrol. I couldn't keep myself from looking at where the girl had died, unable to comprehend such evil. Even the Undercity hadn't been so vile...

...But that wasn't really true, was it? I'd known parents who'd sold their children into slavery - or worse. They'd justified it to themselves, no doubt, by believing that the children would have a better life, although there was no way in hell that was true. The lucky ones would be shipped out to a colony world, where they would be assigned to adoptive parents; the unlucky ones...I didn't want to think about it. At least the girl had died instantly, probably without ever knowing what had happened to her.

I ground my teeth in cold hatred. Someone had given her the knapsack. Someone had loaded it with a bomb and a remote detonator. Someone had told her, a girl too young to understand the danger, to run towards us and...and do what? Hug us? It didn't matter; the only thing that mattered was that they'd pushed the detonator as soon as she was close enough and blown her to hell. They'd killed an innocent child, for nothing. The worst we'd suffered was a handful of bruises.

"That happens a lot," Lewis said, grimly. "The local religion frowns on suicide, so the rebels use children or mentally-disabled people to carry bombs. Or drivers who don't know what they're carrying...I saw a woman pass into a checkpoint, as cool as you please, then die when the bomb under her car exploded. We later found out that she hadn't known that she was a suicide bomber."

I felt sick. Who could *do* that to an innocent child?

When war is fought to the knife, I reminded myself, *the rules of war go out the window.*

We heard the shouting and screaming as we kept moving forward; Singh ordered two fire teams to provide cover, while leading his fire team forward to see who was making the noise and why. I covered him as we entered an alleyway; a woman was leaning against the wall, blood dripping from her nose, while a man was leaning over her, shouting something about having to keep his head down. The woman opened her mouth to say something and he punched her, right in the chest. She spewed up blood as she doubled over.

Singh didn't have to say anything. We lunged forward, as one, and took the man down effortlessly. He cowered at once; it wasn't enough to save him from a series of punches that didn't inflict permanent harm, but hurt. I knew they hurt, all right. I'd been on the receiving end at Boot Camp. We swung him over and tied his hands while Rauls - the team medic - attended to the woman. She was babbling something about her daughter…

It struck me as I looked at her. "Sergeant," I said, "do you think she's the mother of the girl…?"

"Perhaps," Singh said. The woman seemed scared of us, but there was something in her eyes…a spark of anger that overrode fear. "If we take her back to the FOB…"

He spoke to Rauls, then to the woman. I couldn't hear what they said, but when they were finished he produced a plastic tie from his belt and secured her hands behind her back. Her husband was hauled to his feet, a gag was stuffed in his mouth, and then he was shoved forward. The woman followed him, looking downcast.

"They'll be watching," Lewis said. "It would be better for both of them if the rebels think they weren't taken willingly."

We headed back to the FOB, watching carefully for additional surprises. An intelligence officer was already waiting for the prisoners; the man was marched off to the makeshift brig, while the woman was taken elsewhere. Singh told us to grab some rest, then headed off to report to Captain Webb. I didn't envy him the discussion he was about to have…

"You did well, Stalker," Lewis said. Rauls and Atwell, the other fire team members, nodded in agreement. "Welcome to the Weavers."

Despite myself, I glowed.

CHAPTER THIRTY-THREE

> As I have discussed before, it is unlikely in the extreme that insurgent movements will shrink from breaking the laws of war. There is little for them to gain by challenging a vastly superior force to an open battle, even though it would allow them to claim the moral high ground. Using children as suicide bombers is far from the worst tactic; they've done worse, far worse. The Empire's flat refusal to consider that the early insurgents might have a point only ensures that the later insurgents use any means necessary to win.
>
> -Professor Leo Caesius

They didn't give me any time to brood, which wasn't a bad idea. I'd known horror - or so I'd thought - but using an innocent child as a suicide bomber? The Undercity dwellers, at least, had the excuse of being raised in the Undercity; here, where there was more than enough land to spare, there should have been no call for *any* war. But that was hopelessly idealistic, the result of long-buried envy for the upper-blockers. They had their own reasons to fight.

We chattered briefly, sharing notes about our lives, then got about two hours of rest before we were summoned into the briefing room. It wasn't much - a handful of chairs, a table, a paper map of the city hanging from the wall and a computer terminal that was switched off - but it was better than I'd expected. I later learned that the computer terminal was only used when the brass turned up to demand briefings on just how many insurgents we'd killed in the last month or so. But we couldn't kill our way to victory…

"We may have had a lucky break," Webb said, once we were seated. "3rd Platoon took a woman into custody, a woman whose daughter was used as an unknowing and unwilling suicide bomber. The woman was quite happy to tell us where the bomb-maker is hiding out, although he may no longer be there. They presumably know she was taken into custody."

I nodded. It might have *looked* like we were taking prisoners, but the insurgents would assume the worst. The woman wouldn't have had any treatments designed to neutralise truth drugs; willing or unwilling, she'd talk within a few minutes of being cuffed to a chair and shot with something designed to make her talkative. But as long as the rebels thought she was an unwilling captive, they *might* not punish her for daring to betray them.

"We're going to raid the complex and take everyone into custody," Webb continued. He pointed to the paper map, where a building was marked with a red flag. "2nd and 3rd Platoons will carry out the raid itself, while the other platoons will take up positions here, here and here" - he pointed to a number of crossroads on the map - "and block any line of retreat. No one, and I mean *no one*, is to leave without permission. Once we have the site secured, I'll call for an SSE team to go through the building and recover what they can."

I frowned. Why not have a team on alert right from the start?

"Prisoners will be shipped back here for interrogation," Webb said. "We need to take the bomb-makers alive, so use minimum necessary force. These people are classed as High-Value Targets and I don't want any of them to enter the local POW camps; if someone turns up and demands that they're handed over to the locals, tell them to piss off and direct any further complaints to me. Any questions?"

There were none. "I'll be calling for mobile fire support once the raid gets underway," Webb told us. "Good luck."

I caught Singh as we headed outside, checking our weapons as we moved. "Sergeant," I said carefully, "why *not* have the SSE team on alert now?"

"They're not based here, Stalker," Singh said. He sounded irked; asking questions wasn't discouraged, at least not when we weren't under fire, but I was dangerously close to questioning his commanding officer. They'd served together for several years. "To call them, Captain Webb would need to speak to General Gordon, perhaps even Governor Pritchett. By the time they came to a decision, the entire planet would know we were planning a raid on a sensitive site. The bombers would put two and two together, guess they were the intended target and bugger off."

"Shit," I said.

"Quite," Singh said. He gave me a leer. "And for every one of the bastards we kill, capture or otherwise put out of business, another one will spring up to take his place. Now, grab your gun and get ready to move."

I'd been wondering how Captain Webb intended to keep the enemy from realising that we were on the way. An entire company of marines - a hundred men - was hard to miss, certainly in the middle of a crowded city. But Webb had developed a habit of running random patrols through our Area of Responsibility, just to keep the rebels on their toes - and, more importantly, to keep from building up repetitive patterns they could use to hit us. They wouldn't see anything particularly surprising in ten platoons making an advance into the city, ready to provide mutual support if necessary. Indeed, unless they were feeling particularly reckless, they'd be likely to batten down the hatches and stay well out of sight.

"Keep your eyes peeled," Singh ordered. "There's no shortage of idiots around here."

Should try to get them to fight for the royalists, I thought sourly, as a bunch of young men came into view. What would these young men have made of themselves if they'd had half a chance? They could hardly have ended up in a worse place than Charlie City, where the opened sewers stunk of piss, shit and decomposing flesh and disease was rampant. *But why would they risk their lives for their king?*

The young idiots in question shouted a handful of taunts, which we ignored, and then fell behind as we crossed from one housing estate to the next. This one looked a little neater - the rubbish, at least, had been piled up in one place - and the private security guards seemed a little more professional. But I had a feeling the enemy had feelers everywhere, even inside the secure housing estate. And who lived there, in any case?

"God knows," Lewis said. "But they have money."

I pushed the thought away as we turned and headed down the street, towards the bomb-maker's hideout. It looked like every other house; a cold concrete block, utterly soulless, without even a pretence at a garden in front. Officially, such houses were normally intended to serve immigrants who would then move on to something better, but in reality they'd long since become permanent dwellings. I saw eyes peering down at us, half-hidden behind curtains, that vanished as the owners realised I could see them. It was the kind of place where everyone knew everyone else's business, which raised the question of precisely how the bomb-makers had managed to remain there for so long. But I knew the answer; the locals either hated the government or were terrified of the insurgents. And they had good reason for both.

"On my mark," Singh ordered, very quietly. "Lewis, I want you to take the lead."

"Aye, sergeant," Lewis said. He'd told me he had a badge in EOD, as well as a number of other awards. "We could go through the wall…"

"Too much chance of causing a disaster," Singh said. "We go through the door…*mark*."

We moved as one; Lewis reached the door and checked it carefully, then picked the lock with a tool from his belt and kicked it open. There was a shout from inside, but no explosion; the bomb-makers must not have realised that the woman knew where they lived. We crashed inside, weapons at the ready; I opened fire with the stunner as soon as I saw three men, spraying their bodies with stun pulses. Civilians think that stunners work perfectly, but the truth is that even a thin layer of clothes can provide a certain degree of protection. The men collapsed; I shot them again, just to be sure, as Singh pushed past us and charged into the next room.

"Four more in here," Singh said.

I followed him inside, my rifle raised. It looked like a schoolroom, one more fascinating than anything I'd seen on Earth. A handful of commonly-available household products lay on a large table, ready for conversion into IEDs; behind them, there were a number of military-grade detonators and a box of plastic explosives, thankfully not prepped for detonation. My instructors had had their doubts about the crap the Imperial Army used for its weapons - apparently, it was so hard to make it explode that it was sometimes impossible - but it might have worked in our favour. There hadn't been any time for the terrorists to blow the building and kill us, as well as their students.

"Get upstairs," Singh ordered, as we heard someone rattling overhead. "Hurry!"

We ran up the stairs, abandoning caution. I unhooked a gas grenade from my belt and threw it into the room, then followed; the terrorists started to choke at once as yellow gas billowed through the room, in no condition for a fight. One of them managed to get to his feet; I slammed my rifle butt into his head, knocked him down and stunned him. The others were still puking helplessly as we stunned them, called it in and moved to the next room.

"Fuck me," Lewis said, as he peered inside. "If I'd done this in training…"

His voice trailed off. I peered past him and swore. The room was a safety violation that would have had Bainbridge screaming, let alone a safety inspector from the Imperial Army's Inspectorate General. He'd probably have a heart attack the moment he saw the collection of detonators, makeshift explosives and a number of highly-unpleasant chemical compounds. A spark in the wrong place and the entire building would have gone up like a baby nuke. There was no number of push-ups that could make up for such an error, although Bainbridge would probably have invented some new numbers. Anyone stupid enough to get through Boot Camp and *then* store explosives so carelessly would be discharged through an airlock, rather than merely kicked off the training course.

"You would probably have been summarily strangled by the instructor," I said. "Is it safe for the moment?"

"I wouldn't count on it," Lewis said, grimly. He shook his head in disbelief. "If the acid had melted through the containers and dripped onto the detonators…they'd have killed themselves without ever knowing what hit them."

I keyed my radio. "Sergeant, we have a Code Black here," I said. "We need to evacuate the building until it can be made safe."

"Understood," Singh said. "Lewis?"

"I'd prefer not to stay here any longer than necessary," Lewis said. He ran through a brief outline of what we'd found. "This isn't a fixed IED, Sergeant. There's no way to disarm it by removing the detonator or the explosives."

"Snap the scene, then grab the prisoners and get them outside," Singh ordered, after a moment. "We'll call in additional EOD experts before proceeding."

"Aye, Sergeant," I said.

Lewis took a number of photographs as I checked the rest of the upper floor, then returned to the first room and began to secure the prisoners. One of them looked to be halfway to choking to death on his own vomit; I hesitated, just for a second, before slapping him on the back to clear his throat. There *was* a need to interrogate them, after all. Lewis joined me after a moment and together we carried the bastards downstairs and dumped them in the street. 2nd Platoon had secured the surroundings and started bellowing warnings for the locals to stay inside and away from the windows. I had a feeling everyone would heed their commands.

"Got crowds forming on the edge of the perimeter," a voice said, through the intercom. "I think they're being stirred up."

"Snipers, deal with the agitators," Webb ordered. "Helicopters are inbound."

I looked down at the prisoners as the remainder of the EOD officers appeared. The prisoners looked young, save for a couple who were clearly older, if not wiser. Their scarred hands suggested that they'd spent *years* working with dangerous compounds. Probably the bomb-makers, I decided, here to teach the youth of Charlie City how to make bombs and blow up a few of their enemies. Their students looked around fifteen to nineteen; I was surprised, despite myself, to recognise that two of them were definitely young girls. The locals didn't have any cultural history of treating women as second-class citizens, according to the files, but they'd definitely developed a habit of protecting their wives and daughters from everyone else.

Except that rat bastard sent his daughter to become an unwilling bomber, I thought, fighting down the urge to vomit. *Did he give her up willingly or was he taking his helplessness out on his wife?*

The helicopters swooped overhead as we started to load the prisoners into armoured vans. By the time they woke up, they should be in the POW camp; if they woke up sooner, if they had time to realise what had happened to them, I really didn't care. We searched them carefully, removed a number of weapons and tools, then dumped them inside. I caught sight of Joker - he'd been sent to 2nd Platoon - and nodded as he picked up one of the terrorists and carried him into the van. He nodded back. We hadn't really had time to catch up since we'd arrived on Moidart, but we'd have a chance once we returned to the FOB.

"This place is as safe as it is ever going to be," Lewis said, over the radio. "We've separated the detonators and acid from the batteries and explosives, but none of it is particularly *safe*."

"Hold the building until the SSE team arrives," Captain Webb directed.

The devil - and Sergeant Singh - makes work for idle hands. I was directed to join the convoy transporting the prisoners back to the FOB, then to return, escorting the SSE team along the way. They looked professional, something that surprised me; I'd heard too many horror stories about the regulars. And they looked surprisingly enthusiastic. Between the royalist incompetence and the sheer number of moles in the government, they rarely had a chance to work their magic.

I watched as boxes upon boxes of material - some explosive, some not - were carried out of the building and loaded into the vans. The SSE team were *good* at searching for evidence; they went over the building quickly, missing nothing. I hadn't realised just how much crap the terrorists had moved inside until I saw it moved out. Weapons and explosives weren't the only thing they found, too. There were records, a number of ciphers and detailed information on a hundred possible targets. I wasn't too pleased - and nor was Singh, judging from the explosion - to note that they had a set of plans for our FOB. Only our defences had deterred them from attacking in force.

"The building is clear," Captain Graham reported, finally. I was pulling guard duty near Captain Webb's makeshift command post when he appeared. "I think we're not going to be able to pull anything else out of here."

"Then we can get back to the FOB," Captain Webb said. "Does the building need to be sanitised?"

"I'd advise sending a clean-up crew," Graham said. "There were a *lot* of dangerous chemicals in there, sir, and some of them are poisonous."

Webb snorted, bitterly. "There's small hope of that happening, Tom."

"I know," Graham said. "All we can really do is post warnings and hope the locals pay heed."

I knew, too. The royalists wouldn't bother to clean up the house, not when they barely had the resources to hold the line against the rebels. It was far more likely that some of the hundreds of homeless people in the city would move into the house, only to find themselves poisoned. Maybe we should have simply destroyed the house…but that would have earned us more enemies. The locals wouldn't have thanked us for destroying perfectly good housing.

"Mount up," Singh ordered. "Time to move."

There was no attempt to keep us from returning to the FOB, somewhat to my surprise. The rebels had hit a couple of positions on the other side of the city, but otherwise they'd cut their losses and kept their heads down. I couldn't help feeling that it boded ill for the future. The enemy commanders had recognised a losing prospect and backed away, rather than trying to save their people. It suggested they were smarter than their royalist counterparts…

And, as it turned out, they were.

The woman? She was sent into a witness protection program and, after much bureaucratic wrangling, was granted an exit permit. I have no idea what happened to her after that, but the corps does take care of those who help it. Her husband was sent to a hard labour camp, where he was presumably worked to death. Webb told us his fate two days after the raid, just so we knew. None of us felt particularly sorry for him.

And really, why should we? He'd sold his daughter to the rebels, who'd turned her into an unknowing bomber and killed her. They wouldn't have taken her without his permission, not when it would have alienated the civilians. He didn't deserve any sympathy at all, certainly not from us. We were the ones trying to *stop* the bombers.

I just wish I'd had the chance to pull the trigger myself.

CHAPTER THIRTY-FOUR

Social breakdown, as I have noted elsewhere, leads to a collapse in what might be considered civilised standards of behaviour. Certainly, there is always an upsurge in looting, rape and murder as the threat of punishment recedes, but there are also darker forms of behaviour that suddenly become permissible. Selling one child to have the food to feed others, for example, suddenly seems a justifiable form of behaviour.

And, once you get used to justifying horror, it's a short step to justifying something worse.

-Professor Leo Caesius

"Show a leg," Singh ordered, the following morning. "Captain's giving a briefing in twenty minutes."

We cursed, grabbed our weapons and hastily stuffed ration bars in our mouths. It had to have been arranged hastily or we would have been given more warning. I just hoped it wasn't a combat jump or something that required careful preparation. As much as I was starting to like my new teammates, we weren't ready to switch from ground patrols to orbital insertions without more practice. I swallowed pieces of my ration bar - I'm sure the flavours get worse every year - and hurried into the briefing room. It didn't look to have changed overnight.

"Intelligence reports that we have managed to discomfit the rebels," Captain Webb said, shortly. The Imperial Army might operate on a strict need-to-know basis (with senior officers determining who needs to know) but the marines take a more sensible policy of sharing everything with the troops. "The bomb school we found and knocked out yesterday was their principle training zone for Charlie City. Right now, there's a shortage of bombs in the vicinity."

"Oh, what a pity," Lewis said, deadpan.

Webb smiled, rather dryly. "Indeed it is, Lewis," he said. "No doubt you'll be pleased not to have to disarm so many unpleasant surprises over the next two weeks."

He looked back at us. "Unfortunately, the rebels - feeling the urge to keep their operational tempo - have started moving more bomb-makers and their kits into the city," he continued, his voice hardening. "I don't think I need to tell you what *that* means. Higher command wishes to intercept the transports before they arrive. We're going to be taking over the checkpoints along the ring road and searching every vehicle entering or leaving the city."

I looked at the map. Charlie City was surrounded by a highway that, in more peaceful times, allowed the population to drive rapidly around the city without having to pick their way through the middle of the town. There were twenty-one junctions where cars and trucks could leave the ring road or drive in from the outlying towns. Each of them would have to be secured…I cursed, under my breath. There were only a hundred marines assigned to the company. We couldn't send a single fire team to each potential point of entry.

"The Rangers will be joining us," Webb said. "They're going to take responsibility for junctions one to ten, we'll be taking responsibility for junctions eleven to twenty. Junction twenty-one will be closed. This means spreading ourselves a little thin, but a regiment of imperial soldiers and several battalions of royalist troops will be in position to back us up if necessary."

I couldn't help noticing that no one seemed particularly pleased to hear that. The imperials were something of a mixed bag - their units ranged from very good to appallingly bad - but no one had had anything good to say about the royalists. As far as I could tell, the general consensus was that they would either run from the battlefield as soon as the shooting started or turn their guns on their supposed allies. We neither liked nor trusted them and they were quite happy to return the favour.

"Follow the standard procedures for searching vehicles," Webb concluded. "And take prisoners, if you can. We need more intelligence."

I wanted to ask what they'd learned from the bomb-makers, but I kept my mouth shut. The briefing ended shortly afterwards and we hurried outside to our vehicles. Singh was in a right temper, checking everything time and time again; it took me several minutes to realise that he was annoyed because a handful of marines were being held back to defend the FOB. We were paring our defences right down to the bone. If the enemy realised we were dangerously exposed, we might come home to find the FOB in ruins.

This is a hell of a war, I thought, as the driver started the engine. It was dark outside, but the sun was already glimmering over the horizon. *We can't trust our friends any more than we can trust our enemies.*

The drive to the checkpoint was shorter than I'd expected, largely because there was almost no military traffic on the ring road. (Civilians had one lane out of four; someone had helpfully separated their lane from everyone else with barbed wire.) The junction itself looked remarkably simple; a pair of exit lanes, a concrete bridge and a road leading into the distance. A handful of cars were already making their way past the checkpoint, which didn't look particularly secure. The royalist guards seemed more interested in smoking and patting down pretty girls than actually searching for high explosives and detonators.

I sucked in my breath as I saw the royalists for the first time. They were called redshirts by the marines, but I hadn't realised that it was *literal*. The blood-red uniforms they wore would make them incredibly obvious targets to anyone with a sniper rifle, while the way they carried their weapons suggested they didn't have much practice on the shooting range, let alone firing at moving targets. Maybe red uniforms *would* stop the blood from showing, thus not demoralising the troops, but I suspected it was wasted effort. A man dropping to the ground after being shot does tend to be rather disconcerting.

"Get your men to the roundabout and stop the flow of traffic," Singh snapped, as he dismounted from the AFV. A redshirted officer looked astonished to be given orders and started to puff up like a balloon. "Don't argue with me, just *move!*"

"Watch your back," Lewis warned, as we dismounted. "And watch the sergeant's too."

I nodded. The other two fire teams hastened to set up a proper checkpoint, including prefabricated barriers to redirect the force of an explosion, while we covered the sergeant and kept a wary eye on the redshirts. I hoped, as the sergeant's iron will worked its magic, that he would just order them to return to their barracks and take the rest of the day off. It would be better to be outnumbered than have soldiers behind us who might easily take shots at us as well as the enemy.

No such luck. The redshirts gathered at the far end of the bridge, doing as little as they could, while we finished setting up the checkpoint. A handful of cars and trucks appeared, horns honking loudly as they were told to wait; I prayed, inwardly, that none of them were manned by terrorists. They could have blown themselves up and taken a dozen other vehicles with them. As soon as we were ready, Singh placed a large sign at the roundabout, warning drivers that there was a checkpoint ahead, then walked back and waved for us to open the gate. Moments later, the first car drove into the killing zone and stopped.

I watched, from my position, as the driver and his two companions - he claimed one of them was his sister and the other was his sister-in-law - were searched by the fire team, who then searched their vehicle as thoroughly as possible. They complained, loudly, using words I hadn't heard before, even at Boot Camp. The fire team ignored them, completed the check and waved the car onwards. I shook my head in grim disbelief as the next car rolled into the killing zone; if it took five to ten minutes to be reasonably sure there was nothing dangerous inside the vehicle, there were going to be tailbacks stretching back for miles.

We rotated positions after thirty minutes; Singh supervised as we searched the vehicles, then waved them onwards. I swiftly got used to the torrent of abuse - they weren't as unpleasant as some of the Drill Instructors - and did my best to ignore the humiliation clearly written over the faces of the women and children I had to search. Several of them were carrying weapons, but we ignored anything smaller than an assault rifle. Too many people wanted to defend themselves to make confiscating weapons a viable option…although that hadn't stopped the Governor from decreeing a zero-tolerance approach to weapons in private hands.

"This is going to cause too many problems," Lewis predicted, as we rotated to the back and took the opportunity to drink some water. "Bet you this just makes everyone *madder*."

I couldn't disagree. The line of waiting vehicles stretched back for miles, as I'd expected, and countless people were hopelessly late for their appointments. Several cars were even reversing course and heading back to their homes, their drivers probably concluding that it wasn't worth the time to wait. My ears were ringing; the drivers just kept blowing their horns, as if that would make the checkpoint magically vanish. And to think I'd thought that live rounds were bad.

A car passed through the checkpoint and screeched to a halt in front of me. I looked up, alarmed, as the driver jumped out and glared at us. "Hey," he shouted, as we jumped to our feet. "Who's going to pay for my spoiled produce?"

I looked at him. "What produce?"

His glare deepened; he opened the side door, revealing a number of crates containing fruits and vegetables. I was no expert, but it definitely looked like at least half of them had turned rotten. On the other hand, they did look better than the slop we were served in Boot Camp, when they weren't feeding us ration bars. (I was told that there are regiments of the Imperial Army where the soldiers are deliberately fed something horrible, just to make them mad enough to kill their enemies and anyone unlucky enough to be standing close to their enemies when the shit hits the fan. Unfortunately, it sounds quite plausible.) I exchanged a look with Lewis, then shrugged.

"I can't sell these," the driver protested. "I'll be lynched!"

I keyed my radio. "Sergeant," I said, "we have a situation."

There was a pause. "Give him a compensation chip," Singh ordered. "And tell him to present it and his produce at the garrison to have it honoured."

"They always underpay," the driver complained, when I gave him the chip. "I grow these fruits myself and…"

"It's that or nothing," I said, tartly. I understood his feelings, but it was hard to care. He wasn't the one wondering if the next vehicle that entered the killing zone would be the one with the bomb hidden underneath the driver's seat. "Go to the garrison and they'll give you *something*, at least…"

The ground shook violently as something exploded on the bridge. I cursed and ran for cover, while the driver - showing remarkable presence of mind, if not common sense - hastily closed the rear doors, jumped into the cab and drove off. There was no time to worry about him; I peered past the cover and saw a handful of flaming vehicles on the bridge. The enemy must have realised that destroying the checkpoint was futile, so they'd settled for weakening the bridge instead. Idiots; if they'd waited, they could have taken out three marines and weakened us quite badly.

"Incoming fire," Lewis snapped, as bullets started to ping off the walls. "They've taken up position on the other side of the highway."

I nodded, already searching for targets. There wasn't much concealment on the other side - the royalists had cut down all the trees year ago - but the enemy had had plenty of time to prepare themselves. I fired a round at an enemy fighter who showed himself for a second, yet I don't think I actually hit him. The first RPG round soared in a moment later and spent itself harmlessly against the checkpoint. A second, fired from a different position, overshot and came down inside the city itself. I hoped no one was hurt, but there was no time to check.

"Hah," I said, as another enemy fighter appeared. This time, I saw him fall as my bullet struck him. "Scratch one tango."

"Scratch two," Rifleman Parker said. "There are too many civilians in the area…"

The skirmish rapidly turned into a stalemate. We couldn't get to them, but they couldn't get to us. Hundreds of civilians, caught in the middle of a firefight, stayed as low as they could, praying they weren't hit by one side or the other. We watched them carefully, knowing that some of them could be dickers…and that there was nothing we could do to help the wounded. If we'd sent medics out, they would have been targeted too.

"Helicopters inbound," Singh said. "Brace yourselves…"

Two helicopters, their stubby wings loaded down with weapons, swooped overhead, their machine guns opening fire on enemy positions.

The enemy, undeterred, fired a handful of RPGs at the helicopters, then melted away into the undergrowth. Singh snapped orders and we abandoned our position and ran forward, searching for targets. I saw an enemy fighter running for his life and shot him in the back, then ducked as a bullet snapped over my head and vanished somewhere behind me. The remaining enemy fire slackened off and came to an end, leaving us alone…with the civilians. A number of cars were burning brightly, their occupants either lying by the roadside or dead in their vehicles. Others were turning and heading away as fast as they could.

"I've called for medics, but they're not going to be here for hours," Singh warned, over the radio net. "Parker, set up a triage station; fire team three will hold the checkpoint while the other fire teams collect the wounded."

Over a year ago - it felt like *decades* ago - I'd been told that anything could be healed, as long as it wasn't immediately fatal. Now, those words seemed like a sick joke. We'd been taught how to triage the wounded, how to separate the dying from those who could be healed quickly, but I'd hoped never to have to do it. I carried a dying girl to the roadside - her father was already dead - and left her there to die, then helped a nine-year-old boy to where Parker was providing emergency treatment. His burns looked nasty, but they were purely superficial. The girl, on the other hand, was doomed unless she was shipped to a modern hospital and I knew it wasn't going to happen.

"This is all your fault," an elderly woman raged, as I carefully pulled her adult son from his car. He'd taken a bullet in the side of the head. "If you weren't here, this wouldn't have happened."

I shrugged - the planet's problems had started a long time before the Grand Senate authorised military intervention - and placed the body by the side of the road. The elderly woman kept shouting at me until I walked off, leaving her behind. What else could I have done? Nothing I said to her could have made the slightest bit of difference. Her son was dead, his children - if he had any - were fatherless, his wife was a widow…what could we do to fix it?

And the redshirts were completely useless. They'd hit the ground as soon as the shooting started and stayed there, even though they hadn't drawn any fire. I couldn't blame the enemy for not shooting at them, not when they posed absolutely no threat at all. Now the fighting was over and the enemy had retreated, the redshirts got to their feet and started pushing the civilians around, as if they could make up for their cowardice by mindless arrogance and brutality. We eyed them with increasing anger; indeed, if a regiment of soldiers hadn't arrived to take over, I think something nasty would have happened.

"Sergeant," Lewis said as we made our slow way back to the FOB, "wouldn't it be easier if something bad happened to the bastards?"

"There's plenty more where they came from," Singh said. The bastard didn't even sound tired, somehow. Everyone else looked as though they would collapse if the wind blew a little harder. "Kill every currently-serving Redshirt and there would be hundreds more tomorrow."

He was right, I suspected. The Redshirts didn't serve for love of king or country; they served for money and the chance to push their helpless fellows around as much as possible. Maybe they weren't *quite* as bad as some of the more extreme rebels, but they were still quite nasty enough. Give a coward and bully a taste of power and he'll turn into a monster. And, like most cowards and bullies, he'll run when he comes face to face with someone who can actually fight back.

And that, unfortunately, is what is so badly wrong with the Civil Guard.

"What a day," Lewis said. He sounded no better than I felt. "And just *think*! Tomorrow we get to do it again and again and again. Isn't that just swell?"

"Fuck it," I said. The thought seemed unbearable, somehow. I'd killed men for the first time and it was getting to me. And I'd seen innocents caught in the crossfire and cut down by one side or the other. "Maybe I should just call in sick tomorrow."

I didn't, of course. Like everyone else, I went back out and did it again.

CHAPTER THIRTY-FIVE

The Civil Guard - and the Redshirts were counted as Civil Guard units on the muster rolls - was always a mixed bag. On some planets, they were a tough and professional volunteer force, with the unspoken purpose of defending those worlds against the Empire if necessary, while others were nothing more than thugs, as dangerous as the insurgents they faced. As always, strong leadership and political structures made the difference between viable military units and cannon fodder.

For the Empire, though, they did have one great advantage. They were cheap.

-Professor Leo Caesius

I'd like to say things got better after that, but it would be an outright lie.

We went out each day for a month, patrolling the streets, manning checkpoints and carrying out the occasional raid on an enemy target. It didn't get any easier. The population hated us, the insurgents hit us regularly and then faded away before we could catch them and we grew more and more frustrated. Two marines were badly wounded by an IED and a third was killed when a sniper managed a lucky shot before we could drive him away. By the time we were finally rotated back to the spaceport for some leave - or what passed for leave on Moidart - we were pushed right to the limit.

"I want you to go in pairs, even when you're inside the wire," Singh ordered. "Make damn sure you have loaded weapons with you, because you can't trust anyone who isn't a marine."

We groaned, but he was right. The spaceport was supposed to be secure, but between the number of locals working various roles and the poorly-paid security forces, it wasn't too hard for the rebels to slip men and weapons through the wire. A bar had been blown up last week, we'd heard, killing a dozen REMFs. No doubt our combat efficiency had improved enormously. It would do them good, Lewis had said, to actually feel the war…and no one else had disagreed.

The armoured cars drove us back to the spaceport. I couldn't help thinking it was even less welcoming than the FOB, although that could have been because I knew how poorly it was guarded. The FOB might have been more uncomfortable than an Undercity school, but at least it was heavily defended by competent soldiers. We clutched our rifles tightly as we passed through the first set of checkpoints, Singh chewing out a couple of local guards who wanted to take our weapons before we entered the spaceport. I couldn't believe the sheer stupidity of the guards - and the officers who oversaw the defences. If the spaceport was vulnerable, wouldn't it be better to arm everyone so that any threat could be countered as quickly as possible?

"The brothel isn't bad here," Lewis said, as the armoured cars passed through the second checkpoint and parked beside our barracks. "Or you can go gambling, if you like, but remember the golden rule."

I nodded. We weren't allowed to gamble with more than half of our salary. It stopped us getting into debt, first to gambling houses and then to loan sharks. Unlike the army, the marines saw to it that we were housed, fed and watered; there wasn't a real chance of getting into debt with anyone else. The army, on the other hand, found itself acting as a collecting agent far too often. Bastard loan sharks lend money to soldiers at high rates of interest because they can rely on the army to collect their money for them.

"Keep your weapons with you," Singh said, again. He'd harped on it throughout the trip, even though none of us really needed the reminder. "And don't try going into any of the secure zones."

Lewis smirked. "They had us raiding the base to test the defences," he said. "We practically waltzed through them."

We scrambled out of the armoured cars and looked around. The barracks were designed for marines on leave and were the very height of luxury; the showers were private, there was *real* paper in the toilets and there wasn't any requirement for one of us to stand watch. (We did anyway, as Singh's warnings had sunk in.) Beyond the inner fence, we saw the spaceport strip; a line of bars, brothels and entertainment complexes, broadcasting loud music in all directions. I'd seen something like it on Mars - Liberty Town on the Slaughterhouse was surprisingly demur in comparison - but an air of desperation hung over the whole complex, as if everyone knew it was just a matter of time before they had to leave.

"Hey," Joker called. "Coming to explore with me?"

"Definitely," I said, grateful. We really hadn't had much time to exchange more than greetings since joining the company. The policy of putting CROWs in separate platoons had seen to that. "Let's see what we can find, shall we?"

"Food first," Joker said. "And then we can see what else there is."

I grinned and followed him through the gate. The music grew louder as we walked past a bar, clashing horribly with music from a different bar. I looked inside; my eyes widened as I saw three women dancing around a pole, wearing nothing but their hair. A crowd of uniformed men - and not a few women - were watching the dancers, their faces glazed with lust. A terrorist squad could launch an attack and kill half of them before the rest realised they were in danger. I shook my head in disbelief, then followed Joker to a fast food place displaying giant pictures of burgers, fries and hot dogs. Joker had better taste than me - the Undercity isn't the place to be snobbish about food - and I was happy to let him take the lead.

"I'll get the burgers," Joker said, as we stepped through the door. "You find a place to sit."

"Sure," I said. It was quieter inside, much to my relief. "Get me a" - I scanned the menu quickly, then gave up - "get me something you think I would like."

Joker nodded and hurried towards the counter at the front. I looked around, saw a plastic table firmly bolted to the floor and hurried towards it. An officer in a uniform that hadn't seen a day of combat in its life stared at me, as if I were a wild animal that had just walked up to him and sniffed his crotch. In no mood to put up with nonsense, I stared at him until he turned and staggered away, looking pale. I knew I was wearing my BDUs instead of dress blacks, but I'm pretty sure I didn't look *that* bad.

I sat down and studied the patrons…and realised, to my growing horror, that I truly was out of place. Most of the eaters wore clean uniforms and looked snappy, too snappy. We'd been taught that we could either look good or *be* good - that it was impossible to be both - and I was looking at the proof. The uniforms they wore marked them as REMFs, definitely; they certainly weren't combat troops. And none of them carried any weapons. Hell, a handful of them were even staring at the rifle on my shoulder as if it were a spider crawling up my back.

REMFs, I thought in disgust. *Don't they know there's a war on?*

I'd heard stories, but I'd never quite believed them. One man was boasting, loudly, about being in a building when it had come under attack - apparently, a bullet had missed him by centimetres - while another was complaining that the refectory had a shortage of ice cream. Ice cream? We'd been eating ration bars and drinking water in the FOB and we'd been glad to have them both. A third man had a girl perched on his knee and was feeling her up in public, marking his territory in a way I hadn't seen since the Undercity. The girl was wearing a uniform also, one that marked her as a data-entry clerk. I couldn't help noticing that it was carefully tailored to display her ample charms.

No doubt she wants protection too, I thought. *And she doesn't give a damn about her professionalism.*

"If there's anyone here who's actually been shot at," Joker said as he sat down facing me, "I can't see him."

"Me neither," I said. It was true enough that the spaceport was mortared on a regular basis, but it didn't really count. Thankfully, the insurgents didn't have the warheads they'd need to punch through the hardened shelters. "Put them on the streets and the rebels would win in an afternoon."

The burgers tasted remarkably good after weeks of nothing but ration bars. I gobbled mine down as fast as I could, then drank the milkshake Joker had thoughtfully purchased for me while I nibbled the fries.

Someone said something about us not having any table manners, which was probably true; I didn't see any particular value in using the *right* knife or the *right* fork while dining, certainly not in a greasy diner. Besides, a part of me took a perverse pleasure in shocking the REMFs.

"That girl keeps looking at me," Joker said. "You think I have a chance?"

I rolled my eyes. "She's on that fat bastard's lap," I pointed out. "I think she's just a little nervous around us."

"She shouldn't be," Joker said. "That asshole will drop her the moment it suits him."

I shrugged. I never really understood why some REMFs regard us - and *real* soldiers from the army - as monsters, people worse than the terrorists and insurgents we fought. If they hadn't understood that war means fighting and fighting means killing, they should never have joined the army in the first place. But the Imperial Army is a colossal bureaucracy and her bureaucrats, no matter where they serve, rarely see actual fighting. They certainly never risk their lives in combat. I rather doubted they even knew how to handle a gun.

It sounds absurd, I know, but Bainbridge had explained why. Every last round fired off during training had to be accounted for, somehow. Think about that for a moment; every…last…round. We burned through hundreds, perhaps thousands, of rounds when we carried out live-fire training; logically, the army should have aimed to do the same. But logic and bureaucracy come from two different worlds. Their training sergeants were so overwhelmed with paperwork that they preferred simply not to offer training at all. The results were inevitable.

"Don't worry about it," I said. "There's a brothel just up the road."

Joker shrugged. We were just slurping down the remains of our milkshakes when a trio of armed military policemen - the dreaded Shore Patrolmen, or SPs - arrived and glared down at us, trying to look intimidating. Neither of us were particularly impressed. Bainbridge had had more intimidation in his little finger than all three of them had put together. Besides, their uniforms were clean, their boots were shiny and they weren't even ready to draw their weapons and use them. We could have taken them before they had a chance to remedy that problem.

"We've had a complaint about you intimidating others," the leader said. She sounded as though she was trying to be firm, but she didn't have the nerve to pull it off. Sif would probably have bawled her out, then told her to go grow some ovaries and woman up. "I'm afraid I'm going to have to ask you to leave."

"All right," Joker said, leaning back on his stool. "Ask us to leave."

The woman blinked in surprise. "What?"

"You said you would have to ask us to leave," Joker said, with the air of someone explaining a punchline to a person without a sense of humour. "So do so. Ask us to leave."

"Very well," the woman said. Her hand rested on her stun baton. I'm sure it was *meant* to be intimidating, but she still didn't have a hope of drawing the weapon before we knocked her down. "Please leave."

"No," Joker said. He spoke on before the woman could say a word. "You *asked* us to leave and we said no."

"Barracks-room lawyer," I muttered.

Joker smirked at me, then winked at the woman. "Can I ask for your com-code?"

Her face purpled and she started to splutter. "Leave this place now and I won't have to arrest you."

I felt a flash of white-hot rage. We'd done nothing…and yet some of the REMFs had found our mere presence intimidating? If it wasn't for us, the losers staring at the confrontation would be captured, tortured and killed by the rebels! I rocked forward, hands clenching into fists, before I could stop myself. There was nothing to fear from a few hours in the glasshouse - the spaceport's brig - but Singh would be pissed if we started a fight. And the sergeant was *not* someone to anger.

"I suppose that means you won't give me your com-code," Joker said. I'm not sure if he was trying to defuse the situation or make it a great deal worse. "I have it on good authority I'm great in bed."

"Yeah," I said, as I rose to my feet. "My right hand doesn't have much to say to me either."

All eyes were on us as we stalked out of the diner. I hated them all in that moment; the bastards who did nothing while we fought, bled and died on the streets. If a gunman had appeared and opened fire…I knew I would have stopped him, but I would have regretted it afterwards. The SPs followed us at a distance, their faces relieved. They'd known they would have come off worst if we'd started a real fight.

"Stupid bitch," Joker muttered. "Sif would have had her for breakfast."

"Her back-up wasn't much good either," I agreed. "What do you think Nordstrom would have said if we'd clowned around like that?"

"He wouldn't have said anything," Joker said, after a moment. "He'd just have dragged us into the pit and beaten a few lessons into us."

I smiled in fond recollection. None of us had ever managed to land a real punch on the Drill Instructor, even when three of us had tried to gang up on him. Now, even after the Slaughterhouse, I wasn't sure I could have taken him. Nordstrom had been an absolute master of *Semper Fu*.

The other eating places didn't look any more welcoming. I shook my head at a place that boasted of fresh lobster - I hoped they'd caught them in the ocean, although only an idiot would eat something pulled from Earth's polluted waters - and sighed as I saw the senior officers clogging the tables. It looked very much like a demented birthday party; I'm sure several of them were rat-assed drunk. One of them staggered outside, threw up in the gutter and then bellowed thankfully incoherent orders at a waitress. She looked revolted - she hid her feelings well, but I could tell - as she helped him back inside.

"If she wasn't a rebel before coming here," Joker muttered, "she sure as hell is now."

I looked into the entertainment complex as we walked past, but there was nothing to catch my interest. A handful of gambling machines, a collection of primitive gaming consoles and a giant projector for watching flicks; I rolled my eyes at the cartoon on display, then walked past. There were just too many people on Earth who remained glued to the viewscreens, no matter what happened. The lives of virtual people on the display were more important to them than their partners and children. My mother had done that too, when she hadn't been banging random men. I had no intention of wasting my life away like her.

"This looks promising," Joker said. "A brothel. Coming?"

I looked at the building. A long line of men, mainly REMFs, stretched out of the doors and around the block. The signs advertised male as well as female prostitutes, but there didn't seem to be many women standing in line. I supposed the female personnel found it easier to pick up a partner for the night without going to a brothel. Just for a moment, I was tempted to wander through the bars and see what I could find...

"They'll probably try to get you off quickly," I said. I'd seen brothels on Mars; the pimps worked hard to keep customers moving, threatening the girls to force them to hurry up. "Sure you want to go here?"

"We can find someone else tomorrow," Joker said. He dragged me into the back of the line, behind a pair of actual combat soldiers from the army. "But for tonight, I just want to get laid."

"Good idea," one of the soldiers said. He looked tough; not as tough as us, of course, but tough enough to earn respect. "Ask for Mary, if she's available. She's ugly, but damn if she isn't good in bed."

"She'd have to be," Joker said.

"Just don't go for Bella," the other soldier said. "She just lies there and takes it."

"Probably doesn't want to be here," I said.

I never found out, but I was fairly sure that was the answer. The prostitutes were mainly women who'd managed to get into debt, then discovered that the only way to get out was to sell their bodies. And the debts would be carefully managed to ensure they never got out of debt, no matter how hard they worked. The pimps wouldn't hesitate to brutalise any whore who started demanding her freedom...or kill her, if she pushed too hard. There was no shortage of others where she came from.

Yes, it *was* a shitty war. And all we'd really done was make it worse.

CHAPTER THIRTY-SIX

As always, Edward understates the situation. It is hard to be sure, but during the fifteen years of imperial involvement with the Moidart Civil War, over twenty thousand young women were press-ganged into service as waitresses, cleaning women, maids and prostitutes. Horrific as it may seem, this was one of the better situations; there were a number of worlds where the entire population was effectively indentured in payment of their debts to the Empire. Indeed, the (limited) involvement of the imperial military helped prevent worse atrocities. Even so...

It is perhaps not surprising, therefore, that prostitutes turned out to be one of the better sources of information available to the rebels.

-Professor Leo Caesius

The remaining three days of shore leave really seemed far too long. It was almost a relief - despite picking up a sweet filing clerk in a bar on the second day and spending almost all of the third day in bed with her - to be heading back to the FOB. The enemy welcomed us with a handful of mortar shells, then rocketed out of town before our counter-battery fire could take them out. As always, when we reached the mortar sites, we found nothing apart from a handful of IEDs.

It was an even bigger relief, therefore, when Captain Webb called us into the briefing room.

"We're being redeployed," he said, once we assembled. "General Gordon has determined that Warlord Douglas, a former clan chief whose father was evicted from his lands when the corporations arrived, has grown far too powerful to be tolerated. Accordingly, he has decided to reinforce our bases in the Western Hills and then start operations to prune the warlord down to a more manageable size."

I winced, inwardly. Urban combat had its dangers, but it tended to favour us; rural combat, on the other hand, gave the insurgents a considerable number of advantages. It was going to be nasty, all the more so as we'd be offering a challenge to the warlord he couldn't refuse. He would *have* to come after us if he didn't want his allies to start slipping away. But, on the other hand, there would be fewer civilians to get caught in the crossfire.

"The General has assigned us, and five companies of imperial troops to the operation, which he's termed Operation Rampaging Lion," Webb continued. "I'm sure you know what this means."

There was a collective groan. Operation Rampaging Lion - honestly, I couldn't imagine what idiot had come up with that name - would be known to the rebels already, before we or the imperial troops had been told what was expected of us. And six companies…if the route wasn't already determined, it wouldn't be hard for the enemy to guess. We'd be better off flying in, but I already knew we were alarmingly short on helicopters or transport aircraft.

"We're going to be heading up the main highway," Webb warned. "The General wants to prove that his forces can go anywhere, while the insurgents can do nothing to stop us. I expect you all to remember that the enemy knows which way we're coming…and will go all-out to stop us. They won't be any match for our firepower, but that may not matter when they have ample time and warning to set ambushes."

It wasn't a cheerful bunch of marines that headed out to prep the vehicles for deployment, even though the Rangers looked envious at our departure. We all knew it was going to be dangerous; hell, we would have preferred to carry out the operation ourselves. There might be some advantage in displaying our ability to go where we please to the rebels - and to everyone sitting on the fence - but I doubted it would be decisive. The rebels would melt away from us, after firing a few shots for honour's sake, and then pressure the locals to refuse to have anything to do with us.

After all, I thought sourly, *we'll be leaving soon enough and the rebels will be ever-present.*

An hour later, we drove over to the regimental HQ...and waited. H-Hour was 1000 precisely, but it was 1300 when we finally left. Someone, I gathered later, had been finagling readiness reports; two of the five companies that were meant to be backing us weren't remotely ready for a deployable operation. Their training was poor, their vehicles were nether fuelled nor properly maintained and their ammunition stocks were low. And their commanding officer - I never caught his name - stormed backwards and forwards, wearing himself out screaming at his men. I wouldn't have been surprised to discover he was the one playing games with the readiness reports.

"Move out," Webb ordered, finally.

General Gordon was *determined* that the rebels should have no opportunity to miss our advance, I realised, as we crossed the ring road and headed into the countryside. There were fifty AFVs and light tanks, a hundred trucks transporting men and supplies and a dozen attack helicopters hanging overhead, just searching for targets. I was grateful that we were at the front, even though it was fairly certain we'd come under fire first. Everyone else got a shitload of dust in the backwash as we churned up the roads.

"Keep your eyes peeled for IEDs," Singh ordered. "They're very good at hiding them."

I'll say one thing for the planet's government; they knew how to build highways. It would have been hard for someone to conceal one on the road itself, while there wasn't much concealment to either side of the tarmac. Even so, we spotted a handful of suspicious objects and halted the whole convoy while Lewis and his fellow EOD officers inspected the devices, then blew them in place. There was no point in trying to disarm them. I scanned the horizon as the mountains grew closer, a cold wind blowing down towards us. We were moving outside territory controlled by the planetary government, whatever they (and the General) claimed. This was warlord country.

A handful of shots rang out. Parker swung the machine gun around and fired a short burst towards the shooter's position. I don't know if the shooter was killed or not, but there weren't any more shots from that position. One of the helicopters broke off and swept over the countryside, searching for additional trouble; nothing, as far as anyone could tell, appeared to threaten our passage.

"Could be worse," Lewis said. "Maybe they're just waiting for us to reach the base and then split up."

It was possible, I agreed. The local government had managed to maintain control of a number of firebases - mainly through superior firepower - but the warlord held the rest of the countryside in an iron grip. We wouldn't be remaining together for long, either. He'd know that we'd be splitting up, once we reached the FOB. Smaller units would make easier targets...

A missile lanced out of nowhere and slammed into the lead helicopter, which exploded in a colossal fireball. Moments later, mortar shells started crashing down around us, taking out several trucks and badly damaging an AFV. I cursed and knelt down for cover as bullets pinged off the AFV, the driver picking up speed to get us out of the ambush. But behind us, all hell had broken loose. Several of the drivers had hit the brakes - precisely the wrong thing to do - and other vehicles had crashed into them. Another helicopter vanished in a ball of fire, pieces of flaming debris crashing down around us. The enemy had somehow got their hands on HVMs!

Either that or they saved them for the best possible moment, I thought, as I searched for targets. The enemy *had* prepared well; the only way to see them was through picking out the muzzle flashes. Parker opened fire, sweeping bullets across the side of the road, as the helicopters turned and started to launch missiles from a safe distance. But it wouldn't really be safe if the enemy had more HVMs...

"Dismount," Webb ordered, as the machine guns chattered away. A third helicopter was blasted out of the sky, forcing the others to retreat. "We're going to have to push them away, now!"

"Prep grenade launchers," Singh added. "Fire on my command."

I glanced at the rest of the column as I snapped the launcher onto my rifle and loaded a grenade. It was absolute chaos; the better soldiers had taken cover, while the undertrained and underprepared had thrown themselves to the ground or were running in all directions, screaming their heads off. At least one idiot had been run over by an AFV; he clearly hadn't recognised the danger until it was far too late. It would definitely have gone better if we'd been the only ones involved; hell, we hadn't even had time to work together.

(Later, I found out that the General was under a great deal of pressure from the Governor, who was in turn under a great deal of pressure from the Grand Senate, which was itself being pressured - confused yet? - by Hammersmith Corporation. He wanted to produce something that could justify the immense cost of the military deployment to Moidart. I don't think he got what he wanted, but that explains why the whole operation was launched with literally less than a day's notice.)

"Fire," Singh snapped.

We fired, then ran forward under cover of the explosions. The enemy had dug a network of trenches, half-hidden by the undergrowth; they popped out and opened fire as we appeared, only to be cut down savagely. A number threw grenades of their own, then turned and ran for their lives. Someone was screaming over the command net about no mercy, about killing them all, but we did our best to ignore them. The handful of prisoners we took were dragged off to the AFVs, where they would be held until we could hand them over to the intelligence staff.

"Move the rest of the convoy up the road," Webb ordered. He seemed to have taken over command - or, at least, everyone obeyed his orders without question. The nominal commander kept his head well down. "Can the damaged vehicles be repaired in five minutes?"

"No, sir," Lieutenant Spook said. With a name like that, he really should have been in intelligence, but he was too clever and thus overqualified. "They're beyond repair, unless we get them to a workshop."

"Blow them," Webb ordered.

"But captain," one of the army officers objected. "They're expensive."

"And right now they're a goddamned liability," Webb snarled. "There's no point in leaving them here and no point in trying to ship them home, not when we just don't have the time to handle them. Strip them of anything useful, then toss a grenade into the cabs and get rid of them."

I stood guard as the damaged AFV was stripped, then fused. An AFV doesn't have the solid armour of a Landshark tank, yet it's still damn difficult to destroy without heavy weapons. I half-expected the captain to order us to take it out with an antitank missile, but he settled for removing everything of value and burning out the control circuits. In theory, a clean-up team would pick up the remains and ship it home for recycling, but in practice it was probably stuck there until doomsday. We pushed the wreckage off the road, then abandoned it. There was no point in trying to do anything else.

"We could set an IED," Lewis suggested. "Give the enemy a nasty surprise when they come to call."

"Too much chance of killing children," Webb said, as we mounted up again. "All we can do is remove everything that might be of value and abandon the rest."

I glanced up as the helicopters swooped back over us, as if the pilots hadn't been too damn scared of HVMs to do their goddamned jobs. Everyone says that pilots live lives of luxury and that their uniforms are made of silk…and while that isn't true, they do tend to put their aircraft ahead of everything else, including supporting the forces on the ground. It didn't make much sense to me - Moidart should have been capable of turning out attack helicopters, AFVs and an infinite supply of ammunition - but we had to ship most of it in from out-system. Someone, somewhere, had probably won the contract for supplying the military forces on Moidart and had no intention of allowing any local competition.

And to hell with the military necessities, I thought, coldly. At least the locals should have been able to supply their own requirements, although it didn't look as though they were even doing *that*. *What's the point of using simple vehicles and basic weapons if we can't even have them produced locally?*

The drive from Charlie City to the FOB shouldn't have taken more than a couple of hours, but - thanks to the rebels - it ended up taking over ten. They didn't set another ambush, thankfully; they settled for sniping at us, setting the occasional IED and trying to wear us down with constant alerts. We had a *very* nasty moment, as the sun was setting, when we practically stumbled over a *huge* IED some enterprising bomber had concealed right next to the road. Lewis told us, afterwards, that it was easily big enough to wipe out most of the convoy if it had detonated at the right time. By the time we rolled into the FOB, which was surprisingly large for its location, we were all tired and in desperate need of sleep. Even Singh was starting to look a bit wan.

"Get the trucks into the hardened shelters," he ordered, "and then get into the makeshift barracks."

The company guarding the FOB showed a level of skill and professionalism I hadn't come to expect from the imperial army. Even the handful of Redshirts attached to them seemed remarkably competent (naturally, I resolved to sleep with one eye open; they were just *too* competent to be trusted.) They'd organised a giant hanger - the FOB was a former airbase, built for some purpose that had been long forgotten - into sleeping quarters and provided a handful of blankets and other pieces of bedding. It was better than we'd expected; luckily, we'd brought our own bedrolls along as well as ration bars. I didn't hear any grumbling about the food as we lay down, closed our eyes and went to sleep. They told me the FOB was shelled twice in the night, but I wasn't even remotely aware of it.

We wiped ourselves down the following day - there were showers, but water was strictly rationed - and prepared ourselves to drive out again. This time, there were just three platoons of marines; we'd be badly outnumbered, but at least there wouldn't be any imperial army troops getting in the way and screwing up when we came under attack. Webb took command at once, then ordered us back through the gates and onto a dusty road leading north. It looked far nicer than the highway, yet it was much more oppressive. The enemy could easily bury a pressure plate IED under the road and wait for us to drive over it. And the farmlands closed in, providing no shortage of cover for the enemy.

It was a surprise, at least to me, when we didn't take any fire at all. We drove though a couple of tiny hamlets - the inhabitants eyed us warily, but didn't show any interest in talking - and onwards towards Kristin, a small town to the north. The sweat started to trickle down my back as the sun rose higher, shining down on our position. It was almost a relief when a handful of poorly-aimed shots cracked over my head and vanished somewhere in the undergrowth. I swung around, looking for the shooter, but saw nothing. The only thing I could do was hold my fire and wait.

"Probably a local yokel," Lewis said, when no further shots were incoming. "He wouldn't have stuck around for a fight."

I nodded, slowly. A local yokel - a piece of marine slang - is a local inhabitant who refuses to do the smart thing and stay out of a firefight, either because he thinks it's a challenge to his manhood or because he's trying to impress someone. He's rarely directly connected to the insurgents, but he serves their purpose and wastes our time. We'd studied the many different types of insurgent at the Slaughterhouse and I think the local yokel is the most infuriating and frustrating. There was no way to get anything through his skull, save by the most extreme measures. He normally got himself killed comparing dick-sizes with highly-trained soldiers.

And then his family has a grudge against us and a reason to go to the insurgents, I thought, as we rolled onwards. *We kill an idiot who fires at us and wind up with a dozen new enemies.*

"Keep a sharp eye out for trouble," Singh warned, as we approached the town. The farmland was slowly replaced by grasslands, where a number of cows and sheep chewed contently, untouched by human wars. I smiled when I saw a sign, clearly designed by a child, advertising PENNY'S STY. A large pig hid behind it, watching us with beady eyes. "This is a prime spot for an ambush."

We rolled past the final farmhouse, weapons at the ready. A small girl stared at us, then turned and ran inside. An older woman watched our vehicles expressionlessly; behind her, a man who looked old enough to be my grandfather ignored us, as if he could deny our very existence. I didn't really blame him. We'd brought war to his town.

No, it wasn't really our fault. The planet's king had sold his people out, twice. But it was only human of him to blame us...

...And besides, it was much easier to blame the off-worlders for the nightmare that had consumed his world.

CHAPTER
THIRTY-SEVEN

Humans are, of course, social creatures. There is an understandable reluctance to believe the worst of one's own society, no matter its flaws, while being willing to believe the worst of every other society. (Certain worlds throughout history have reversed that trait, but they rarely lasted longer than a generation; no one would fight to defend a society they had been taught to hate.) On Moidart, most of the population did blame Hammersmith Corporation, the Empire's military or the Grand Senate…choosing to ignore King Fredrick's role in selling mining rights to off-worlders. It suited their social obligations to believe as much.

-Professor Leo Caesius

Kristin was a ghost town.

No, not entirely, but the closer we got to the firebase, the fewer people we saw on the streets and the more buildings that were clearly abandoned. A number showed the tell-tale signs of bullet marks, others had been destroyed; no one had bothered to clean up the rubble, let alone try to replace them. The firebase itself had started life as a school, but the windows had been removed and covered with metal netting, the walls had been augmented by prefabricated barriers and a dozen murder holes had been cut through the stone. It looked like the old FOB, I reflected as we were escorted through the gates, but worse.

"Captain Webb," a newcomer called. He wore a dirty uniform, suggesting he was actually a fighting officer. "Welcome to Firebase Gamma - or, as we call it, Hell."

Webb grinned. "It's good to see you again, Bill," he said. "How long has it been since Tarbush?"

"Too long," Bill - Captain William Thompson, Imperial Army - said. "We've been stuck here for the last six months."

"You poor bastards," Webb said. He and Thompson had served together before; indeed, Thompson had once had quite a high reputation, for all that he was a soldier rather than a marine. "Do you have a briefing prepared?"

"Stow your gear, then join us in the schoolroom," Thompson said. "I'll meet you down there in twenty minutes."

We checked our sleeping quarters - we were expected to sleep under the desks, it seemed - and then headed down to the schoolroom. It looked surprisingly like *Webb's* briefing room, right down to the large map pinned to the wall. Kristin was larger than I'd realised and, more awkwardly, was surrounded by a dozen satellite towns. Thompson was expected to patrol fifty square miles with…with what? How many men were assigned to the firebase?

"Thank you for coming," Thompson said, as he strode into the room. "I'll give it to you straight. We've been pinned down here for the last month and we've come frighteningly close to running out of supplies more than once. Last time, we only got one truckload of ration bars from the FOB, thanks to the enemy hitting the convoy with antitank rockets. I actually recommended the firebase be abandoned. We're not achieving anything here."

Webb frowned. "It's that bad?"

"Worse," Thompson said. "I have four platoons under my direct command, thanks to constant attrition and…and higher command stealing some of my subordinate formations for other firebases. Suffice it to say that we have no control at all outside the range of our guns and we come under heavy attack whenever we leave the base. The townspeople hate us, the entire area is seeded with IEDs and there's very little we can do to change it."

He sounded…broken. Later, I discovered that Thompson had managed to embarrass his commanding officer and he'd been punished by being dispatched to Kristin, along with half of the men under his command. His superiors hoped, I think, that he'd either defeat the rebels or lose so badly he could be dishonourably discharged from the army. Caught in a bind, he'd settled for pulling in his horns and holding the firebase against all comers.

"The base itself has been attacked too, several times," Thompson added, slowly. "We've come close to running out of ammunition completely twice; it took all of my powers of persuasion to convince higher command to make emergency shipments of weapons and ammunition. I don't think I need to tell you what *would* have happened if the enemy had managed to overrun us. They came far too close to succeeding last time."

I swallowed. Running out of ammunition hadn't seemed a reasonable possibility in Charlie City - we weren't far from the spaceport, where millions of rounds were stored - but here? I could see it happening. So could the rebels, if they had eyes and ears in the FOB. They'd have to know just how close the firebase had come to running out of ammunition…and they could shape their attacks to force Thompson and his men to expend their limited supply. I knew precisely what would happen if the firebase *did* run out of ammunition; the rebels would overrun the base, kill everyone inside and walk off with thousands of credits worth of useful equipment. It would be, at the very least, a major embarrassment to the governor.

Webb stood. "We will commence patrols tomorrow," he said, firmly. "I want us to make our presence felt throughout the town, then we can start extending our control into the farmlands."

"That won't be easy," Thompson warned. "The warlord controls everywhere outside our guns."

"We can but try," Webb said. "If nothing else, at least we have some additional firepower."

The enemy, as it happened, had plans of their own. We were woken up in the middle of the night by a salvo of incoming fire, followed by a series of gunshots as enemy snipers probed our defences. Thompson's men rationed their fire carefully, only shooting back when they had a clear target; Corporal Stevens and his mortar platoon were more enthusiastic about firing off shells, but the enemy mortars refused to be silenced. We stood to, preparing to repel an offensive, as the enemy fire intensified and then faded away. Our night-vision gear allowed us to identify a number of men watching us, but we couldn't engage them unless we actually saw weapons in their hands. I was starting to understand just why Thompson and his men were so demoralised.

"We don't *know* they're dickers," Singh pointed out.

"They're out and about in the midst of a firefight," Lewis said, coldly. "They're either dickers or idiots."

We didn't get any more sleep that night, even as the sun slowly appeared on the far side of the mountains. There was no sign of any enemy bodies, no proof we'd hit anything…I gritted my teeth as I surveyed the wrecked buildings, realising just how easy it would be for the enemy to slip close. As long as they were careful, and they quite evidently were, they wouldn't have any trouble getting into firing range without being detected. We stuffed ration bars into our mouths, then prepared ourselves for our first foray out beyond the walls and into Kristin. Thompson's men called out all sorts of pieces of advice as we checked and rechecked our weapons and body armour. None of it seemed particularly helpful.

"I should be commanding this march," Singh said, as we prepared to depart. "Captain…"

"I need to get a feel for the terrain," Webb replied, firmly. "There isn't any other way to do it."

I smiled. It did seem foolish for the captain to put his life at risk, but he didn't really have a choice. Terrain is rarely what it seems on the map, something I hadn't understood until I'd been issued a map that was both completely accurate and remarkably misleading. Given the dangers caused by a REMF trying to micromanage operations from the rear, I supposed we should be damn grateful that Captain Webb wasn't anything of the sort. Besides, we admired him all the more for sharing the risks.

The gates opened, slowly, and we inched outside, weapons at the ready. It was already warm, but I wasn't sweating because of the heat. The deserted and ruined buildings had looked sinister enough in the darkness, yet they somehow managed to look worse in the cold light of day. I wondered, absently, just what had happened to the owners as we walked past them, careful to keep our distance from anything suspicious. The enemy would have to be mad to plant IEDs in a populated town, but they'd already shown a frightening lack of concern for civilian casualties.

"There's too much rubble around," Webb noted, as we kept moving. I was sure we were being watched by unseen eyes. "Stay well away from it."

"They could be counting on that, sir," Lewis said. "If they're using it to store weapons as well as cover…"

"Something to bear in mind," Webb agreed.

We inched our way down to the market, which was already coming to life…if a torpid kind of life. A handful of old men were sitting at one end, playing a game that looked like an odd combination of chess and risk; several younger children were running around, kicking a football from place to place. They looked old enough to be on the farms, I noted; I wasn't sure why they were here, unless they were waiting to go into school. Where *was* the school now we'd taken the building and turned it into a firebase? A handful of other children were sitting against the wall, half-hidden in the shade. I peered at them and realised, to my horror, that they were some of the casualties of the war. A young boy was missing his legs, a young girl had an arm that ended in a stump, a teenage male had a cloth wrapped around his eyes…

"Davidson, offer to help them," Webb ordered, quietly. "See if we can do something to make their lives better."

The younger children vanished as soon as Davidson approached, while the blind teenager shook his head, keeping his mouth firmly closed. I wondered, absently, just what had happened to blind him. It couldn't have been our fault, could it? But there were some riot control weapons that *caused* blindness, if pushed to maximum. It wasn't meant to last, yet some victims were unlucky. We'd been told not to use it except as a last resort.

"We move on," Webb ordered.

The sensation of being watched grew stronger as we made our way through the market, passing a dozen stalls. Shopkeepers watched us nervously - half of their trades were probably illegal, under the king's law - but we didn't attempt to interfere. Webb tried talking to a couple of them; a couple looked as though they wanted to talk, yet didn't quite dare. I expected Webb to order us to take a couple prisoner, giving them an excuse for talking to us, but he merely told us to walk on. By the time we reached the end of the market place, I had the uncomfortable feeling that we were walking inside an invisible bubble. Hardly anyone would acknowledge our presence.

"Makes the city look cheerful," Lewis said.

Webb stopped outside a large house and tapped on the door. A middle-aged man appeared - he looked as if he'd once been fat, although he'd lost a great deal of weight - and stepped out, closing the door behind him. I couldn't hear what Webb said to him at first, but he practically shouted his answers to the entire town, denying knowing anything about the rebels and flatly refusing any help we might offer the townspeople. It took me a moment to realise he didn't want to leave any room for doubt about his answers. The town was infested with rebel contacts, who would happily tattle on him if he did anything else.

We finally bid goodbye to the headman and returned to the firebase. As soon as we arrived, Singh led a second patrol out while we checked and rechecked the defences. Lewis and a handful of others were sent to start checking the piles of debris for unpleasant surprises, then left a handful of their own behind. Webb wanted to clear the piles of debris away, but we couldn't spare the manpower to do it ourselves or hire anyone from the town, no matter how much money we offered. Singh suggested forcing people to work at gunpoint, but Webb overruled him, pointing out that it would only make them hate us more. Personally, I was starting to think it was a lost cause.

That night, we were startled by an explosion as one of Lewis's IEDs exploded, alerting us to an enemy presence. We launched flares at once, spotted a handful of enemies as they crept towards us and picked them off. The enemy sniped at us again from a distance, then bombarded us ruthlessly with makeshift rockets and mortar shells. They didn't seem to be short of ammunition, unfortunately. The bastards even smuggled a colossal bomb up towards the walls that would have flattened them, if we hadn't seen them coming and opened fire from a safe distance. Whatever they'd used to make the bomb, it exploded with immense force - the ground shook so badly it did more damage to our positions than hundreds of mortar shells - and put a stop to the attack, at least for the rest of the night. My platoon caught up on its sleep while the other two platoons watched the darkness warily, waiting for the enemy to return.

The following day, we discovered that the entire town had been abandoned. There was no one in the market; every home was empty, completely deserted. We searched a couple of them, but found nothing. Even the injured children were gone. We were in the midst of checking several other houses when we heard an explosion; Rifleman Pablo had stepped on the wrong place and detonated an IED, right under his leg. He survived, thankfully, but he had to be placed in stasis until he could be shipped back to the spaceport, where the doctors removed the remainder of his leg and grafted a cloned replacement in its place. And there was still no sign of the enemy.

We found the clue in the final house we searched, half-hidden under a pile of women's clothing. (It's astonishing, we were taught at the Slaughterhouse, just how many people assume the underwear drawer is a safe place to hide something. Yes, we felt awkward picking through panties and bras, but that didn't stop us.) A letter, written in an unknown hand, warning the inhabitants to leave or die. Someone had distributed them, we guessed, while the firebase had been attacked. We checked the rest of the town, just in case, then returned to the firebase. If the warlord was warning people to leave, it could only mean we were going to come under heavy attack.

I was right. The enemy infiltrated the town shortly after night fell and opened fire as soon as they got into weapons range. This time, they were determined; they sniped for hours, launching so many mortar shells that we almost overlooked the *real* threat. A handful of vehicles drove up towards us, their drivers hidden behind plates of metal shielding. Webb ordered them taken out, fast; we hit them with antitank rounds and they exploded with thunderous force. They'd hoped to get the VBIEDs close to our walls, then detonate them there, wiping us out in a single blow. I had to admire their determination as we held them back, even if they were trying to kill us. There was something about them that was far more admirable than the Redshirts.

Of course there is, I thought, sourly. *They're prepared to fight for what they believe in.*

The fighting didn't stop when the sun rose, not this time. They'd taken over a number of deserted buildings and were using them as firing positions, while trying to slip more teams closer to our walls. Webb called for air support, and finally, three helicopters arrived from the FOB. Their pilots were reluctant to go too close to the town - clearly, the threat of enemy HVMs had sunk in - but they rained missiles into the occupied buildings, blowing them into piles of rubble. *That* wouldn't make us popular, I was sure, yet there was no choice. Clearing them manually would have taken too long, exposed us to too much risk. We pressed out of the firebase, covered by the helicopters, and swept the town. The bastards had mined half the buildings before they finally slipped back into the countryside.

"Detonate them," Webb ordered. "There isn't time to dismantle them all."

It didn't seem fair, I thought, as I watched the IEDs detonated, one after the other. The townspeople who owned the buildings would be mad, but what choice did we have? And yet, we were wiping out their investments, sending them back to poverty…I shuddered as I remembered the prostitutes, women (and men) who had debts to pay and no other way to do it. We were dooming some of the townspeople to the same fate.

And then we discovered we'd been lucky. Five other firebases had come under attack and one had been overwhelmed. The marines had fought their way out of a deadly trap - losing five men along the way - but the Redshirts had been caught and tortured to death. Hell, the FOB itself had come under attack; the enemy had destroyed two helicopters on the ground before the base security force had driven them away. General Gordon's grand plan was in deep trouble and sinking fast…

He didn't give up, of course, and neither did we. Every day, we cleared the town and patrolled the countryside; every night, the enemy came back, placed a handful of IEDs in various places and attacked the firebase. The war, once again, had stalemated. It didn't look as though there was any way to actually win…

And then, thanks be to God, we got a lucky break.

CHAPTER
THIRTY-EIGHT

Edward was right to worry about the effects of the war on the civilians, none of whom wanted to be caught up in the fighting. Quite apart from the hundreds of thousands who had been displaced by Hammersmith, there were thousands of civilians who lost everything they owned to one side or the other; their houses turned into strongpoints, their male children taken to serve as fighters or imprisoned to keep them from joining the rebels, their daughters sold into sexual slavery…

…There was not, of course, any hope of compensation. The rebels offered none, the king offered none and the Governor, who did have the power to offer compensation, preferred to use the funds earmarked for this purpose to enrich himself.

-Professor Leo Caesius

It was a surprise when we were pulled out of Kristin - we'd only been there a week - and driven back to the FOB, where two heavy aircraft sat on the runways. We were rushed into the hanger, fed a collection of ration bars and bottles of water and then waited (hurry up and wait is practically the military life in microcosm) while Captain Webb and Sergeant Singh spoke to the higher-ups. It definitely seemed like we'd been earmarked for something more important than holding an isolated firebase in the midst of an abandoned town, but there was no way to know for certain. All we could do was wait.

Singh called us to attention thirty minutes after we arrived. "All right, marines," he bellowed. "Listen up!"

We stood as Webb unrolled a paper map of the surrounding hills and pinned it to the concrete wall. "We've had a stroke of luck," he said. "Through various ploys, our intelligence staff have located Warlord Douglas's main base, a camp established here" - he tapped a location in the midst of the Western Hills - "firmly isolated from everywhere else. Douglas is using the camp to train new recruits, including many newcomers, before turning them on us. The camp also serves as a major storage dump for the rebels. Apparently, a number of weapons stolen from the spaceport or the garrison in Charlie City have made their way there."

There was a long pause as we considered the implications. The Imperial Army was paranoid over heavy weapons, unsurprisingly; the HVMs that had blown a dozen helicopters out of the air had shown what they could do. It was quite possible that the intelligence staff had attached a transponder to a weapon that was later stolen - or, more likely, allowed the rebels to steal it to see where the weapon ended up. I didn't like the thought of them *deliberately* handing weapons to the enemy, but I had to admit it should work.

"There's no way to get there overland without being detected," Webb continued. "The handful of possible access routes have probably been mined, while the enemy will have ample time to redirect their forces to harass us or simply abandon the base and slip into the undergrowth. An airstrike would obliterate the camp and everyone in it, but we'd never know who we killed or how much material we wiped out. We'd certainly lose the chance to track it back to the bastard who sold it to them in the first place. Accordingly, we're going to make a combat jump and come right down on their heads."

His eyes swept the hanger. "As far as anyone outside the FOB knows, this is a routine redeployment of our forces and you're all going back to the spaceport for some Intercourse and Intoxication," he warned. "The remaining forces on the ground will be alerted once we make the jump, but it will take them some time to get anywhere near the camp. We'll be on our own for several hours, assuming the best."

And we were taught to always assume the worst, I thought. General Gordon was unlikely to refuse us permission to launch the offensive, but he'd run it past the uniformed lawyers, civilian lawyers - including the Governor - and the locals before authorising the attack. By then, the enemy would have ample time to either prepare for an attack or simply evacuate the camp. *Webb's taken his career in his hands.*

"We'll be leaving under cover of darkness," Webb concluded. "Grab some sleep; take-off is at 1900."

I glanced at the clock, firmly fixed to the wall. 1500. Four hours of sleep didn't sound like very much, but it was heavenly to us. The FOB hadn't been rocketed for the last two days - the enemy had taken a beating the last time they'd tried - and if they held off for another five hours or so, we'd be able to give them a very nasty surprise. Singh ordered us back into the hanger, where we lay down on the floor and closed our eyes. Sleep came slowly, and - as always - it felt as though I hadn't slept at all when we were woken. We checked our weapons and supplies, ate a couple more ration bars each and marched out to the planes. They looked in even worse state than the aircraft I'd seen on Mars.

"It's clear air," someone said, as we settled into position. The engines were already warming us, a dull rumble echoing through the aircraft. "Should be a nice easy flight."

Someone - probably a civilian bureaucrat - had written a regulation that insisted all aircraft leaving the FOB had to do so under cover of darkness. It wasn't particularly clever - the enemy had night-vision gear and HVMs, which didn't care about the time of day - but I had to admit it worked in our favour. The aircraft took off, rattling worse than a shuttle that had been holed several times by enemy fire, and climbed rapidly. Our planned course should take us right over the enemy base...

We should try to do it with gliders, I thought. Parachutes weren't so flexible, even in darkness, but Webb presumably had his reasons for deciding against them. Gliders wouldn't allow us to abort the mission so close to the target, if necessary. *The last thing we want is to come down on an alerted enemy camp.*

"Five minutes," Singh said. "Check your chutes."

I did, again. HAVLO parachutes can be dangerous; by the time the emergency parachute realises it's needed, the parachutist might have already slammed into the ground and gone splat. Mine looked fine; another marine reported, grimly, that there was a problem. The jumpmaster checked his pack, agreed it needed to be replaced and shoved another one at the marine. He barely managed to get it on in time before the hatch opened.

Should have double-checked before we left, I thought. *Shit happens, far too often, but there was a reason we were taught to check and recheck everything. Singh won't let him get away with nearly jumping out of an aircraft with a faulty parachute.*

The lights dimmed. I snapped my NVGs into place and checked them. The world turned eerie; the marines were dark shadows, while the plane itself looked oddly alien, as if it wasn't quite part of the world. NVGs worked better when there was more ambient light around and here, there was none. I stood and joined the lines forming near the hatch, ready to take a dive. My heart was pounding so loudly I was convinced the others could hear it.

"Go," the jumpmaster ordered.

Webb was first out of the aircraft, a tradition that took no account of the need for the commanding officer to remain in reasonable safety. (His second, Lieutenant Roscoe, would be the last to jump.) Singh followed, then we jumped platoon by platoon. Darkness enfolded me as I jumped, plummeting down towards the enemy base. No lights appeared below us, nothing to mark the location of the camp. Had we been tricked? But then, the enemy camp would have been spotted long ago if they'd shown lights; the high orbitals belonged to the navy, with dispassionate sensors peering down on Moidart 24/7. It would be easy to determine that there shouldn't be anything in the forest…

My chute popped, right on schedule. The fall slowed, dropping me through a patch of camouflage netting and into a full-sized enemy camp. A handful of men stared at me and the other marines, then grabbed for weapons. We opened fire, taking them out, as we released ourselves from the chutes and ran towards the buildings. The doors opened, revealing a handful of bunks, rather like the barracks we'd used on Mars. I unhooked a grenade from my belt, checked the yield and threw it into the first barracks. A colossal explosion blasted through the building, wiping out its inhabitants. Moments later, two more barracks caught fire, the enemy fighters roasted before they had a chance to fight back.

"They're trying to set up a defence," Singh bawled through the radio net. One set of guards had apparently managed to hold off a handful of marines, just long enough for the remaining inhabitants to grab weapons and start pouring fire through a handful of murder holes. "That has to be the command building."

He barked orders as we assembled, then crawled forward as another platoon provided cover to keep the enemy from spotting us. We grabbed gas grenades, tossed them through the murder holes and watched, moments later, as the enemy came staggering out of the building, choking or puking helplessly. They were in no condition to resist as we grabbed them, knocked them to the ground and secured them. Hopefully, we'd bagged a few enemy commanders among the fighters.

The ground shook as a building exploded, sending a colossal fireball reaching up towards the stars. Someone had blown the armoury, although there was no way to know if it had been an accident or deliberate malice. The remainder of the camouflage netting caught fire and started to fall from overhead, threatening to set the entire camp on fire. I was grateful for my mask as Singh directed us onwards, checking a handful of other buildings for stragglers. One of them held a small unit of enemy women, armed to the teeth. They probably had good reasons to hate the Redshirts too. We ended up throwing stun grenades into their building and storming it while they were twitching helplessly. I was silently relieved that none of them had died, even though they were the enemy. We carried them out, bound their hands and feet, then finally placed them with the other captives.

Another hail of shots burst out as a small enemy party returned to the camp. I was surprised they'd come at all - that damned fireball must have been visible for miles around - but we engaged them, using our NVGs to best advantage. The enemy traded shots for several minutes, then faded back into the darkness. I wanted to give chase, but Singh overruled me.

"There's no way to know what's waiting for us out there, lad," he said. "Check their defences instead."

We did. The rebels had been quite determined to make anyone who came for the camp pay dearly, although they hadn't anticipated a parachute assault. (Maybe they'd thought their spies would provide more than ample warning, as Webb had clearly assumed.) There were several trenches, all quite professionally done, and a number of weapons emplacements that would have been nasty, if we'd been assaulting from the wrong side. 4th and 5th Platoons took over the task of manning the defences, in case the enemy decided to launch a counterattack, while the rest of us were detailed to either make another sweep for prisoners or check the remaining weapons supplies. The armoury that had exploded hadn't been the only one.

"Much better safety here," Lewis observed, as we removed a large crate of mines from the storage compartment. "They must have skipped those lessons for the people they sent to Charlie City."

"Or it's just a different group," I said. "The rebels don't have a simple command structure, do they?"

"No," Lewis said. "They know what we'd do to them if they did."

I nodded. A military hierarchy is relatively simple, with orders flowing from senior officers all the way down to the grunts at the bottom; the chain of command, and the difference between a legitimate and illegitimate order, is easy to follow. An insurgency, on the other hand, is a distributed network of cells, operating semi-independently...or it isn't long for this world. The average fighters we captured simply didn't know anyone higher up the food chain; the senior fighters, the ones who *did*, were careful not to allow themselves to be taken prisoner. We could crack an insurgent cell, capture or kill every last one of its members...and get nowhere. The rebels would still be out there; we'd have to start again, breaking a whole new cell.

"They'd try to cut all the links from here to the rest of the warlords," I said. "But we should be able to learn more from the captives."

We finished moving out the supplies - the insurgents had an alarming number of weapons, including several dozen pinched from the spaceport - and piled them up near the defence line, where we could put them to use if necessary. The prisoners were recovering slowly, glaring at us; I shivered, despite myself, at the hatred written over one young girl's face. I could practically see her life story in her snarl...and bitter helplessness, now she was a prisoner. If things had been different, it might have been my sister looking at me like that.

"Douglas is missing," Webb was saying, as I carried another box of supplies over to the marines guarding the prisoners. "He wasn't among the dead or wounded."

"He might have been killed in the fires," Singh suggested.

"We couldn't count on it," Webb said. "No, he's still out there somewhere."

I heard the frustration in his voice, but I wasn't sure I shared it. Yes, we'd missed our prize - and that was irritating - yet we'd also wrecked one of Douglas's bases, removed or destroyed a great many supplies that would take him years to replace and captured a number of his senior personnel. He'd have to assume they'd talk - perhaps they would, when the intelligence staff got their hands on the prisoners - and relocate every other base, no matter how small, for fear of us dropping a hammer on them. His reputation would take *years* to recover.

"Yes, sir," Singh said. "Do you want to call for a pick-up now?"

"Do it," Webb ordered. "See if we can get out of here before the sun rises."

Singh made the call, then directed us on yet another search of the remaining buildings. The rain started to fall moments later, quashing the fires and drenching the prisoners. Their guards did their best to give the prisoners some shelter, although it didn't look as if any of them were grateful. The best they could expect, I suspected, was a hard labour camp - or, perhaps, a detention camp on an isolated island. I doubted any of them would be freed, unless Douglas was prepared to shell out millions of credits in bribes…

"The flyboys are refusing to fly in this mess," Singh said, over the radio net. "There's a storm moving in from the north and they're saying it's too dangerous to fly until it passes overhead and vanishes. We're going to have to hold out here."

"Wimps," Lewis snarled.

Singh cleared his throat. "The enemy hasn't launched a counterattack yet," he said firmly, before anyone else could interrupt. "Put the prisoners in the cleared barracks, then mount guard on all possible angles of approach. We should be able to hold the line until the flyboys finally stop sipping their tea and get into the air."

I cursed inwardly as we worked hard to strengthen the defences. The enemy might have scattered - no doubt someone as cunning as Douglas had contingency plans for the fall of his main base - or they might have decided to regroup and prepare a counterattack. There was much to gain, if they successfully forced us to expend our ammunition and then overran the camp. We'd take a black eye that would damage the reputation of the entire corps…

…And kill us all, of course.

We checked the enemy crates, then removed machines guns and hundreds of thousands of rounds of ammunition we could fire from our own weapons. Not for the first time, universal standardisation had worked in our favour; I smiled, remembering the lesson Bainbridge had taught us, years ago. There *were* advantages to keeping everything firmly standardised, even if it also meant keeping them simple.

"You're smiling," Lewis said. "What's so funny?"

"I think I'm just enjoying myself," I admitted.

Lewis gave me an odd look. "I sometimes think about taking up a less dangerous MOS," he said, flatly. "And then I recall that I'm good at it and decide…hell, at least it isn't picking pieces of metal out of a sucking chest wound."

"True," I agreed. EOD officers are the bravest men and women in the military and I'll fight the man who says it isn't so. "Do you enjoy your job?"

"Sometimes," Lewis said. "I just wish I wasn't fighting here, where… where there isn't a *real* good side."

"I know what you mean," I said. The rebels weren't very nice people, but the Redshirts weren't any better and the off-worlders were only making things worse. "Maybe we should try to clean up Earth one day."

"Not a hope," Lewis said. He shook his head. "Deploy the entire corps to that cesspit and it wouldn't make any difference, even if we had half the army in support."

I had a horrible feeling that he was right.

Chapter Thirty-Nine

The refusal of the pilots to fly in (admittedly) bad weather was a direct result of the bureaucratic malaise that weakened (and eventually killed) the Empire. A squadron of helicopter pilots would be blamed for any losses they suffered, no matter what they were trying to do. There was no sense of the overall big picture when officers and bureaucrats could focus, instead, on the smaller issues.

And, on something the size of the Empire, there was literally no one who could see the big picture.

-Professor Leo Caesius

The attack started twenty minutes later.

I dived for cover, of course, as the first wave of mortar shells screamed down from all directions, smashing through what remained of the camp and triggering a dozen secondary explosions. Thankfully, between the trenches the enemy had dug and the foxholes we'd prepared ourselves, there was enough room for everyone, even the prisoners. But a direct hit would still be enough to kill anyone hiding in a foxhole.

The enemy threw in a ground attack shortly afterwards, at least three dozen men inching forward under cover of long-range mortar fire. We waited for them to come close, then opened fire, picking them off one by one. The first attack faltered, then the bastards settled down to sniping at us from a distance while we shot back. Dawn was starting to rise when they launched a second attack, this one carried out with a great deal more care. They were digging new trenches of their own and using them as cover, while they sneaked forward and into weapons range. We rapidly ran through our supply of grenades as we threw them back; if we hadn't recovered a number of weapons from the enemy stockpiles, we might have been in some real trouble.

"They're attacking from all sides," Rifleman Dudley reported.

"Splendid," Singh said, trying to boost morale. "They can't get away from us now."

I smirked - *that* was a saying older than the entire corps - and took a shot at an enemy fighter who'd sneaked too close. He darted back, not fast enough to save himself from a bullet through the head. One of his compatriots, who'd managed to remain out of sight, caught hold of his leg and dragged the dead body back into the undergrowth. Their determination to make sure we didn't take any of their bodies was touching, but it also served a practical purpose. It made sure we couldn't trace the bodies back to their families,

Not that it will stop the Governor printing wildly inflated kill-counts, I thought, sourly. If every claimed kill had been real, we would have exterminated the entire population several times over. *Why hasn't anyone noticed that so far?*

But I knew the answer. Moidart was important to the locals, because it was their homeworld, and important to us because we'd been sent there, but it was one tiny world set against the immense vastness of the Empire. The Grand Senate didn't really give a damn about Moidart - no one would give a damn, if the planet hadn't been a potential source of raw materials - and they wouldn't bother to check the reports. One day, I was sure, we'd be pulled off the planet, having accomplished absolutely nothing. And I was right.

The fighting only intensified as the sun rose in the sky, an endless fusillade of shells crashing down amidst us while the enemy sniped at us from the forest. We gritted our teeth and tried to endure, hoping the flyboys would get off their asses and come to our rescue. They could have flown now, but who knew how many HVMs the enemy had ready to turn on our attack helicopters? There was no hope of any relief, either; Webb kept a platoon back as a reserve, but it was no comfort...

I swore as the ground shook, then exploded. They'd actually dug *under* our position while forcing us to keep our heads down. 5th Platoon was in deep shit…the reserve ran forward to secure the lines, while the remains of 5th Platoon struggled to extract themselves from the remains of their trenches. It didn't look good for them.

"Four KIA, two WIA," Singh reported, grimly. "Three more MWIA."

The enemy, scenting victory, lunged towards the weak point in our defences. My fire team was plucked out of the trenches and directed to cover the crater, pouring fire into the oncoming enemy fighters. I marvelled at their dedication, at their willingness to throw their lives away just for a chance of killing one of us; maybe, just maybe, they thought they had nothing more to lose. It didn't matter, I told myself firmly, as I kept firing. It was them or us right now.

"Got something here," Ferris reported, as we were pulled back to serve as a reserve. He was our ELINT officer, charged with monitoring enemy communications, what little there were of them. "There's a place nearby which seems to be serving as a command post."

"Douglas must be there," Singh said. He looked at Webb. "Sir, I request permission to take my fire team and attack the enemy position."

Webb didn't hesitate. "Granted," he said. We had been taught to take the offensive at all times, even when we were pushed to the limits. "Good luck."

Singh hastily reorganised his fire team, sending Lewis - the EOD expert - to 2nd Platoon while stealing Joker from Lieutenant Roscoe. I winked at Lewis - at least we were doing something more than sitting in the remains of an enemy base, fending off attack after attack - and then again at Joker as we prepped for action. The four of us - Singh in the lead, Bellman and me in the middle, Joker at the rear - headed to the rear of the base, where the tempo of attack had slackened off, crouched down low and sneaked through the network of muddy trenches. Once, I would have hesitated to crawl through the mud; now, I knew it was the only way to be safe. Better to be covered in mud than to be shot through the head.

I froze as Singh made a quick signal with his hands, then waited as he crawled forward and sprang. An enemy fighter, either slacking off or watching for a breakout, had no time to react before Singh snapped his neck, one hand covering the fighter's mouth as he breathed his last. I glanced at him as we resumed our crawl - a young man, barely old enough to join the military - then left him behind. There was no time to hide the body.

"Keep very low," Singh signalled, as we crawled onwards. "They're patrolling intensely."

He was right. We had several close encounters with enemy patrols as we made our way away from the base, including staying very low as a line of enemy fighters headed towards our comrades. The temptation to just stand up and start shooting was overwhelming, but I managed to keep it in check. Singh paused as we reached a stream running down from the upper hills - it looked small, but the rainfall had made it stronger - and then led us up the stream, keeping very low. The enemy didn't seem to be watching the tiny gully.

We paused at the top, hunting for the enemy command post. It was hidden in a small shack, some distance from the main base. I wondered absently why the enemy had chosen to use it, then realised that Douglas probably hadn't had a choice. He had made a deadly mistake when he'd allowed us to locate his main base; now, his only hope of remaining a warlord was to retake the base or - at the very least - destroy the marines who had been imprudent enough to capture it. I had a feeling he was throwing everything he had at us, up to and including the kitchen sink.

"Take him alive, if possible," Singh signalled. He was eying his wrist terminal. "He's in the building. Get in, grab him, get down."

We signalled our agreement, then prepared ourselves. The enemy hadn't thrown up any real defences, but there were a number of men on guard. Douglas really *had* to be desperate, or he wouldn't have been using a radio. No matter how low-power the signal, it could be detected and tracked from orbit.

"Go," Singh signalled.

We rushed forward, weapons at the ready. The guards yanked their own weapons up, too late; we gunned them down and ran onwards, without even breaking step over their falling bodies. Singh crashed through the door, then grunted in pain as someone inside impaled him with a knife. Douglas didn't have an opportunity to take a second stab at it as Singh slammed him to the ground, breaking his arm.

"Lie still or I'll fucking break the other one," he snarled. Blood was dripping from his wound - the knife had managed to slip through a chink in his body armour - but he was holding himself together. "Don't you dare shout for help."

Douglas glared at him as we searched the rest of the tiny shack. It must have belonged to a hermit, I decided; there didn't seem to be much in the way of amenities. Hell, I wasn't even sure how the owner had managed to survive. Perhaps he'd been given treatments that allowed him to eat anything, even grass and bark. Or perhaps he merely carried food from the nearest town, seventy miles away. There was a *reason* Douglas had placed his main camp here, after all. It was a long way from any civilians.

"Check his radio," Singh ordered. He turned his attention to Douglas. "Order them to surrender."

"Fuck you," Douglas said.

Singh picked the knife up from the ground and held it against Douglas's throat. "I suggest you reconsider."

"Fuck you," Douglas repeated.

I was morbidly impressed. I'd been told that many terrorist leaders were cowards, but Douglas didn't seem to be willing to betray his people to save his skin. It might not have mattered, in any case; there was absolutely no chance the locals would let him live. Douglas would be given a show trial and then executed, probably by public hanging. Normally, I wouldn't have cared, but I felt an odd degree of kinship with the man.

And he's carried out dozens of atrocities, I reminded myself, sharply. I'd seen the wounded children in the town, after all, and I'd heard of worse. *You should know better than to feel any respect for him.*

"No doubt," Singh said. He glanced at the radio, then smiled thinly. "They won't get any more orders from you in any case. They'll just keep hurling themselves against the defences and get killed."

He tied Douglas up, then patched his wound with a quick-seal pack. I stepped outside with Joker and looked around, half-expecting to run into another enemy force. Who knew *what* the enemy would do now? We wouldn't let Douglas return to their side, not now. Yes, someone else would probably take his place, but at least *he* would be dead. In the distance, I could hear the sound of shooting growing louder. The enemy was still pressing the rest of us hard.

"There are helicopters inbound, finally," Singh called. "One of them is being diverted here, with orders to pick us up. The others are heading for the base."

I froze as I saw someone step out of the forest. "Incoming, sir," I sub-vocalised, keying my radio. There was no point in trying to hide, not when the dead bodies were easy to see. "One tango visible; I say again, one tango visible."

"Hold your fire," Singh ordered. "Fire the moment you believe yourself to be at risk."

Now, of course, I thought. I was seventy miles from the nearest safe place, surrounded by an unknown number of enemy fighters…of course I didn't feel safe! I resisted the temptation to point that out and watched the enemy fighter warily. He looked back at me, then raised his hands and faded slowly back into the forest. I had a feeling I should have shot him right there and then.

"They won't have any radios any longer, not unless they're complete idiots," Singh said shortly, when I reported what had happened. "Remain alert. The helicopters should be here in ten minutes."

I scowled. If we'd told the flyboys we might need - no, that we *would* need - a pick-up, they might have been prepared to fly in the storm. Or perhaps not. I'd never liked flying through turbulence and it was hard to blame the pilots for being nervous. Maybe we should have held off on the raid…

And then they would have a chance to prepare for us, I thought, grimly. *This way, at least they know they got hammered.*

"Incoming," Joker said, quietly.

I tensed, again, as a fighter appeared, waving what looked like a piece of white cloth in the air. Joker sniggered, briefly; it took me a second to realise that the fighter was waving a pair of panties in the air as a makeshift white flag. I pushed my amusement to the back of my mind and stepped forward, ignoring Joker's frantic hissing. Up close, the fighter looked middle-aged, perhaps prematurely aged by the war. He was far from the only person on Moidart who was much younger than they seemed. Experience had worn him down.

"Hello," I said, carefully.

"We have this place surrounded, along with our former base," he said, without bothering with any pleasantries. "You can and you will be wiped out, if we charge."

"Debatable," I said.

"It will happen," he insisted. "Hand our leader over and we will let you go, without further interference."

I keyed my radio and updated Singh. He and Webb would have to make the call, but I was fairly certain they'd tell him to go to hell. There was nothing to be gained by letting Douglas go, not when it would give them a propaganda victory...assuming, of course, they were telling the truth. They might be planning to attack again, with overwhelming force, once their leader was safe. The only upside was that the insurgents clearly didn't have a second-in-command who intended to kill his boss and take the post for himself.

"Tell him no," Singh said, firmly.

"No," I said, relaying the message. "We're not interested in any deals."

His eyes went wide. "But you'll be wiped out!"

"No, we won't," I said. "Go!"

Maybe I should have shot him, there and then. But he *had* come under a flag of truce and I was *damned* if I was going to do anything that would give us a reputation for treachery. I watched as he stumbled off, then hurried back to the shack. If they really wanted Douglas back alive, they couldn't use any heavy weapons...

Unless one of his subordinates is an ambitious toad who thinks he can kill his boss and make it look like an accident, part of my mind whispered. *A single mortar round would kill all five of us.*

I told that part of my mind to shut up as I entered the shack, then closed and bolted the door behind me. Joker could take one side of the shack; Bellman and I could take two more...Singh, thankfully, didn't seem to have been slowed down by being stabbed. He took the final side, then waited. It wasn't long before we saw the first enemy fighters come into view and opened fire.

"They're being careful," Singh said. He glanced at Douglas, lying bound and gagged on the floor. "Your men are quite admirably loyal."

I shrugged as I fired at two men, who seemed reluctant to fire back. The shack, of course, was deterring them; they could riddle the walls with bullets, if they wished, and quite probably accidentally kill their leader. Actually, he was the safest person in the building, as he was lying on the floor. Luckily, they didn't know where we'd stowed him.

"Two minutes until the helicopter arrives," Singh said. A handful of bullets cracked through the window - they'd taken aim at Bellman - and then vanished somewhere on the other side of the shack. "We can keep them off for that long."

I nodded, understanding the unspoken words. Whatever happened, Douglas could not be allowed to return to his people. If nothing else, the faction fight over who should succeed him might just buy General Gordon time to slip more reinforcements into the Western Hills and, perhaps, find a political solution to the war. Douglas would have his throat cut if it looked like we were losing…

And the General couldn't find a political solution if one was spray-painted in front of him, I thought, bitterly. *He can't even find his own bollocks without a satellite fix and a team of expert navigators helping him.*

And then the helicopter swooped down like the wrath of god, firing missiles into the surrounding forest. I watched in glee as the enemy melted away, running for their lives. The next few minutes became a blur as we grabbed Douglas, kicked the door open and ran into the helicopter, which was hovering just above the ground. As soon as we were inside, the pilot yanked the craft back into the sky, a handful of shots following us.

"Chain him to the seat," the co-pilot called. "Regulations!"

"Fuck regulations," Singh swore. He glared at the co-pilot, who flinched back. "He's bound and gagged…"

"Incoming," the pilot screamed. The helicopter lurched so violently I lost my footing and fell forward, hitting the bulkhead. Joker shouted something obscene, but I barely heard it; my head was spinning badly, so badly I was sure I was concussed. "Brace…"

Something exploded, far too close to us, and we dropped like a rock.

Chapter Forty

There was, of course, no hope of a political solution. Moidart cost the Imperial Army over nine hundred lives - the Marine Corps lost fifty-seven - but it simply wasn't worth it. By the time the Grand Senate finally pulled the plug, the local government was losing power even in its own capital city, while the final governor was issuing edicts that touched on everything but fighting and winning the war. The rebels, including Douglas's successor, surged forward in the wake of the Empire's departure and overran the Redshirts in one final battle.

Neither their victory nor the brutal civil war that followed were noticed by the Empire...

-Professor Leo Caesius

I was barely aware of anything as the helicopter slammed down into the forest, rolled over twice and finally came to a halt. My head took several minutes to clear, even after I managed to retrieve the booster capsule from my belt and press the injector tab against my skin. It was a risk - we'd been warned that the drug could have unpleasant side effects, up to and including death - but there was no choice. I had no idea just how far we'd flown from the enemy positions before we'd been blown out of the sky.

Not quite, my thoughts advised me, as I staggered to my feet, almost tripping over the remains of my rifle. I felt a sudden pang as I realised it was beyond repair, then dragged my thoughts back to the matter at hand. *If the HVM had struck the helicopter, we'd all be dead.*

Singh *was* dead, I realised to my horror. I honestly hadn't thought that *anything* could kill him, but his neck was quite clearly snapped. Bellman had been thrown forward, straight into the co-pilot; they were both dead too, the latter still bleeding even through life had gone from his body. I couldn't see the pilot at first; dark suspicions ran through my mind until I spied his corpse lying outside the helicopter. His upper body had been completely separated from his lower half. I gagged - the drug was affecting me more than I'd realised - then hunted for Joker. He, at least, was alive.

"My legs aren't working," he complained, after I injected him with the booster. "Did you get the number of the shuttlecraft that hit us?"

I snorted - he was always cracking jokes, despite endless push-ups - and checked his legs quickly. Both of them were broken; one might be salvageable, with a proper hospital, but the other would need to be replaced. I checked myself as best as I could - the booster blocks pain, so there was no way to tell where I was hurting - and didn't find anything worse than cuts and bruises. But the booster might be concealing interior damage that might bring me down.

"We have to get out of here," I said. The hatch had jammed, forcing me to consider blowing it open before I finally managed to hit the emergency release and send the dented piece of metal falling to the ground. "I'll carry you out."

"I can walk," Joker protested. "It's only a flesh wound."

"No it fucking isn't," I said. In my damaged state, I was midway through a resolution to kill the person who'd shown that stupid flick to Joker when I realised it had probably been Nordstrom. No one else would have dared. "I'll have to carry you."

I hefted him up, somehow - it was so much easier on the Slaughterhouse - and half-carried, half-dragged him out into the sunlight. The helicopter seemed completely dead, thankfully; there didn't seem to be anything on fire or threatening to explode. I glanced upwards, hoping to see another helicopter, but saw nothing. The sky was empty. Webb would have ordered a search, wouldn't he? We don't leave anyone behind.

The thought came unbidden. *But what if they believe the helicopter was completely destroyed*?

I shuddered. The HVM had detonated close to the helicopter - it must have done, or it wouldn't have swatted us into the ground - and anyone watching from a distance might have concluded that we'd been wiped out. If so, there would be no point in looking for bodies…Webb might *want* to come looking, just in case, but his superiors would probably refuse him permission. Why risk move lives for a handful of dead bodies?

A thought struck me. I placed Joker on the ground - he sounded more coherent, thankfully - and hurried back into the helicopter. Douglas was lying there, his body so badly injured that there was no point in taking his pulse. I cursed myself under my breath - I should have checked him at once - and scooped up the emergency pack before stepping back out of the helicopter and rigging a nasty surprise from the remaining grenades. No doubt the enemy would be along soon, looking for their leader and whatever they could pull from the wreckage. It would put them off chasing us.

"It's just the two of us," I said, as I checked the compass. By my reckoning, there was no point in trying to return to the enemy base - they'd have overwhelmed it now Webb and the others were gone - but if we headed south, we would eventually cross the road leading to the FOB. "Just like it was in the old days."

Joker chuckled. "You want to use the emergency beacon?"

"Too much chance of being picked up by the wrong person," I said. The rebels might be reluctant to use radios, but they could certainly track them. Besides, the flyboys had already lost at least one helicopter and wouldn't want to risk any more, the bastards. If I ever had anything to say about it, I'd make damn sure that *every* marine unit deployed with its own helicopters and assault transports. "We'll have to walk."

I picked him up, made sure he had a weapon in hand just in case and then started to walk, heading south. The helicopter rapidly vanished in the undergrowth; I forced myself to keep moving, even when the trees closed in and passage became almost impossible. Joker seemed to be growing heavier by the minute; I reminded myself, sharply, that I'd carried heavier weights before remembering the booster. If it was already wearing off, the aftermath was going to be thoroughly unpleasant for both of us.

"I keep hearing insects," Joker said, softly. I wondered if he too was concussed. If so, there was nothing I could do about it beyond disarming him. "I swear they're everywhere, all around me."

"It's an illusion," I said. "I…"

An explosion, loud enough to make me jump, blasted out from behind us. The IED I'd set had been triggered…and presumably detonated the remaining fuel cells as well. I prayed the enemy had had a nasty fright; hell, while I was praying, I prayed they were all dead. Not a nice thing to ask, I knew, but it would keep them away from us. Hopefully, any survivors would assume that everyone on the helicopter had been killed, including us…

"They'll know the area," Joker muttered. "If you left any tracks…"

I swore. I'd been taught to move without leaving traces, but it was hard to do that when I had Joker slung over my shoulder. I'd be heavier…crap. No matter what I did, I'd probably left a trail of footprints leading right to us. I put Joker down, rigged up a second IED with my final grenade, then scooped him up again and walked on. Ten minutes later, I heard an explosion.

"Put me down," Joker said. "I'll stay here and sell my life dearly."

"I'm not leaving you," I said. I thought frantically. What else *could* I do? Leaving him was unthinkable and *not* leaving him was certain death? "Maybe we can find a place to make a stand."

"Trigger the emergency beacon," Joker urged. "They're on our trail. It can't possibly make matters worse."

I smiled - we'd been told not to say that at Boot Camp - and then did as he suggested. A signal started pulsing out, alerting the watching satellites to our location. But would they believe we were a *real* pair of marines? Or would the higher-ups think we were terrorists, trying to lure a rescue helicopter into an ambush? I groaned inwardly, then kept moving onwards as fast as I dared. If I hadn't had Joker with me, I might have doubled back and tried to outsmart them, but there was no chance to do anything of the sort. All I could do was hope I stayed ahead of them until help arrived.

"Crap," Joker said. He fired, once. "They're here."

I ducked down, dumping him on the ground. He cursed in pain as I rolled over, drawing my own pistol. I could hear something crashing towards us, yelling loudly to summon assistance. He came into view, dashing my hopes he might be part of a rescue party. We fired together, taking him down. I crawled forward and checked his body, removing a small pistol and several magazines of ammunition before crawling back. For once, the ammunition wasn't compatible with any of our weapons.

"Well, there are worse places to die," Joker said. We could hear the enemy approaching now, even though they were trying to be quiet. "And worse people to die besides."

"Really?" I said. "Name one?"

But he was right, I knew. The Undercity would be a far worse place to die. If I'd been killed there as a child, my life cut down in an instant, no one would care. Even my family wouldn't be too upset, not when it meant more food for everyone else. And if I'd died with the rest of them, I wouldn't even have been a footnote in history. Now, at least, I would die trying to save my friend's life.

"My older sister's husband," Joker said, after a moment. It took me a moment to remember what he'd said. "Complete coward, if ever there was one. I have no idea why she married him."

"Maybe he made her feel good," I guessed. "Is he a decent person?"

"Fucked if I know," Joker said.

"We know you're there," someone shouted, half-hidden in the trees. "Surrender now and you will live."

"Fuck off," Joker shouted.

I shouted something ruder. There was no way I was allowing myself to be taken prisoner, not when I knew what would happen to me. We'd sell our lives dearly…

"Crawl backwards," Joker whispered. "I'll hold them off."

"No," I said, flatly. My answer hadn't changed. I was damned if I was abandoning my first real friend. "I'm not going to leave."

I lifted my pistol, bracing myself for the final onslaught. Two magazines left…eighteen bullets, more or less. I could make them count. Beside me, Joker lifted his own weapon…

It happened very quickly. There was a flurry of shots, then a loud explosion, as a helicopter flew overhead. The rebels fired a handful of shots back at the craft, before turning and running deeper into the forest. I let out a sigh of relief as the helicopter came to a halt, then lowered itself to the ground. Joker laughed out loud; I stood, picked him up and carried him towards the opening hatch.

"Hey," the door gunner called. "You want a hand with him?"

"He ain't heavy," I said. Joker snickered and joined in. "He's my brother."

Yes, it's a cliché. But damned if it isn't true…

…And damned, too, if it doesn't encompass what it means to be a marine.

There isn't much more to tell, really.

We made it back to the FOB, where Captain Webb debriefed us carefully, then warned us to expect to be questioned heavily by the higher-ups. Douglas was dead, after all, and there were hopes it would put an end to the war. Maybe the other warlords would see the futility of resistance… we answered their questions as best as we could, but whatever came of their ideals I don't know. The company was redeployed to another world shortly afterwards, once we'd held a funeral for those who had died on Moidart. Their deaths, I suspect, were for nothing.

Moidart was a classic example of just what was wrong with the Empire in the final decades, before we were exiled to Avalon. The local government was incompetent, the off-worlders were more interested in stripping the planet bare than investing and the rebels were just too brutal to forge a lasting peace. Each side had different aspirations, while the political gulf between them was just too wide to be bridged easily. I promised myself that if - when - it was *me* in command, things would be different. But I had to wait until Avalon to put my theories into practice…

…And if I'd still been accountable to the Empire, who knows what *would* have happened on Avalon?

I don't think of my family very often, not really. It's odd, but I think sometimes that there are two Edward Stalkers, that one died with his family while the other went to Boot Camp and emerged a marine. There's such a sharp line drawn between the hellish existence of the Undercity and life as a Terran Marine that, perhaps, they truly *are* two different people. I know it's absurd, but the thought is impossible to avoid. All that matters is that I - we - kept the ideal of the corps alive even as the Empire fell into dust.

(Yes, I *know* there was that incident on Tarzana, but that's another story.)

And now I'm being far too maudlin. It's a bad habit.

Edward Stalker, Colonel of Marines, Avalon
Semper Fi!

The End

Colonel Stalker And His Marines Will Return In:

THEY SHALL NOT PASS

Coming Soon

AFTERWORD

Training for war is not an easy task.

(It's also the title of a free essay by Tom Kratman, which is available on Amazon and well worth a read.)

It's also not an easy subject to write about, particularly if one hasn't served - and I haven't. There is a tendency to fall into the trap of believing that your conception of military training is the correct one, even if my beta-readers do include several people who are either currently serving or have served in the past. There is also the awareness that something that *seems* absurd, discriminatory or simply wrong-headed may be rooted in military realities that I, a civilian, simply do not grasp. So this essay itself may be completely wrong-headed and should be treated with extreme caution.

There were times, in fact, when I seriously considered not writing this book at all. I had created a background for *The Empire's Corps*, including the dreaded Slaughterhouse, that some of my readers wanted to hear about…and yet, I feared not being able to live up to their ideas. Some training books - or books based around training, like *Starship Troopers* - have done very well, but could I match them? Or, if I was writing about Captain Stalker's early life, could I create a child who would grow into the man everyone saw in *The Empire's Corps*? It was only because I like a challenge that I started sketching out what eventually became *First To Fight*.

The Terran Marine Corps is not the United States Marine Corps, nor is it the Royal Marines or the French Foreign Legion. It does draw from them, of course, but it isn't intended as a direct transposition of their formations into the future. In some ways, it has more in common with the Royal Marines than the USMC; a small, elite force, intended for everything from rapid deployment to handling peacekeeping in enemy towns. However, it is its own entity.

(This is, of course, my excuse for anything I get wrong - <evil grin>)

The concept of military training has changed over the last two centuries, when warfare became far more complex than merely giving aggressive young men weapons and pointing them in the direction of the enemy. The French Revolutionary/Napoleonic Wars saw the rise of the 'nation in arms,' of mass armies directed to war; the Franco-Prussian War saw the deployment of heavily-professional armies that crushed their opponents in brutal warfare and the use of railways to move troops from place to place at unprecedented speed. Advances in defensive technology led to the ghastly stalemates of the First World War (foreshadowed in miniature during the Russo-Japanese War); advances in *offensive* technology led to the tank battles that shattered the German lines, the Blitzkrieg of World War Two, the bombing offensives, D-Day and - eventually - the Fall of Bagdad in 2003.

It is easy, in 2015, to look back at the Fall of Baghdad and see it as a new kind of war. Shock and Awe, it was called, and indeed in one sense it was unprecedented. The combination of army, marines, air force and naval power that rolled through a much larger (on paper) Iraqi military in less than a month was new. However, in another sense, it was merely the continuation of an old tradition: a small, numerically inferior, military force carving its way through the local defenders through superior firepower and better training. Operation Iraqi Freedom was the successor of the British wars in India, the French wars in Africa, the American push to the west…none of those wars would have been winnable - and there were quite a few hitches along the way - were it not for training and technology.

However, the concept of military training has come under fire, recently, from Social Justice Warriors and Politically-Correct Brigades.

There is, I feel, an odd degree of respect for military training among the Social Justice Warriors. (Yeah, I know; bear with me a little.) By any reasonable standard, the American military has been head and shoulders ahead of everyone else in breaking down racial barriers in American society, at least in the combat arms. At the same time, however, there is a complete lack of understanding of the *ethos* of military training. One can become a Green Beret, but one cannot become a *black/white/yellow* Green Beret without fatally undermining the whole concept and (re)introducing the curse of racial diversity.

But *wait*, the SJW might say. No one can ignore the fact that there are *black/white/yellow* Green Berets!

Yes, that's true. But there are also blond-haired Green Berets and dark-haired Green Berets and bald Green Berets…and no one gives a damn. Differences in hair colour are completely immaterial. If we are to rid ourselves of racism, we must refrain from taking race into account. We cannot claim to live in a post-racial world when President Obama is lauded as the first black president. To let ourselves draw lines between white soldiers and black soldiers (and every other kind of soldier) is to reintroduce tribalism into military society and undermine the whole concept of the military team.

This is potentially disastrous. Humans are *tribal* creatures. To allow recruits to think of themselves as belonging to the *white* tribe, or the *black* tribe, or the *homosexual* tribe, or the *female* tribe, rather than the *military* tribe will lead to conflicts between those tribes within the military. The military has the odd problem, therefore, of treating its soldiers as individuals and, at the same time, as part of an overall unit. It cannot take the risk of adding a *tribal* layer without risking internal collapse.

Why? If humans accept the existence of tribes, each tribe will start jockeying for position against the other tribes. Outsiders will see those tribes as single entitles; insiders will see outsiders as enemies, rather than allies or neutral observers. Bad apples within the tribes will smear the rest; the tribes will rally round their own, rather than give them up to the judgement of outsiders. (This has been amply demonstrated by the Catholic Church's reaction to child sexual abuse by priests, among other matters; the Church was more interested in defending itself than rooting out the offenders.) Society will be ripped apart as tribes become the dominant powers, eroding a single unifying faction.

Pressure from the SJWs, therefore, has done a considerable amount of damage to the military.

Speaking as an outsider, I see no problems with having women, homosexuals or even transgendered individuals within the military, *provided* they meet the criteria and act in a professional manner. There are aspects of military training that require very high qualifications; lowering those requirements for a specific *tribe* undermines the overall effectiveness of the military. If women can be declared Army Rangers (for example) while completing a course only half as difficult as their male counterparts, it should not surprise anyone that the men regard women with deep suspicion. *Can they carry their weight in a real combat zone?*

This isn't sexism; this is sheer practicality. Take a look at some of the deployments handled by Special Forces in the War on Terror. None of them were scripted by exercise controllers, or designed to allow those who wanted to give up to quit. Shit happens in combat zones; you might find a ten-mile hike becoming a twenty-mile exercise in staying ahead of a hunting enemy force. Or you might find yourself carrying the body of your wounded comrade for miles, trying to keep him out of enemy hands.

There's a milder problem that should also be remembered. Men - as a general rule - respect people who come up with new ideas. If a female soldier comes up with a loophole that anyone could use (at least until it is closed by higher authority) she will earn a considerable amount of respect from her male comrades. On the other hand, if she uses an advantage given to her because of her gender, she will earn nothing but their contempt. If she decks someone making sexist remarks, she will earn respect; if she complains to her superiors, she will earn a reputation as a sneak. And, because humans are inherently tribal, a pathetic female soldier will prejudice every male soldier she meets against every other female soldier.

Tom Kratman's article on women in the military had a rather pithy observation that should be born in mind. The price for being a woman in the military is sacrificing your right to act in a feminine manner. The same could easily be said for homosexuals.

As I see it - and again, I speak from the outside - the American military made a critical mistake when the issue surfaced (and re-surfaced, etc). It should have been simple enough to point to the requirements for Ranger School (which couldn't have been *that* strict, because *soldiers* were passing them) and invite women to try to pass the requirements. (The British Paras allow women to run through the course, although to the best of my knowledge none have passed.) The Pentagon could have argued that *lowering* the requirements for women was inherently sexist, as it implied that women couldn't pass the complete requirements, and therefore invited female soldiers to *try* to pass. It would, at least, have driven a wedge into the SJW camp. And who knows? They might have gained a few full-fledged female Rangers out of the deal.

Such a requirement would have focused on the individual, not women as a tribe (and, as such, separate from the *male* tribe). It would have made it much easier to handle the problem - and, later, any disciplinary issues that might have arisen. If a soldier happens to be in trouble, it is very dangerous to raise the spectre that he/she is being charged because he/she happens to be the wrong gender, or the wrong colour, or the wrong sexual orientation. Such spectres undermine military discipline to the point it will eventually collapse. This is not, alas, unprecedented.

Military training is - and will always be - an ongoing project. We have learned a great deal from our wars in Afghanistan and Iraq, incorporating the lessons into our training programs for soldiers who are on the verge of being redeployed. It is vitally important that we keep honing our soldiers, because our superior training and technology is an inherent part of our military edge over the rest of the world. To weaken it for political reasons - whatever they may be - is to undermine the security of the entire Western World.

Does this seem true? The average Arab recruit, for example, is rarely told anything more than he needs to know. Basic maintenance is beyond him, let alone the complexities of the fine military hardware purchased by his country's rulers. His superior officers are often prepared to work him as a slave; he is punished for showing initiative (as are they.) Those who are recruited for terrorist/insurgent operations may have more enthusiasm, but they are rarely any more technically skilled.

But they do tend to have the numbers.

Military training is one of the factors that gives us the edge. There are others, of course, but training is the bedrock. Weakening it in the middle of wartime is very - very - dangerous.

Christopher G. Nuttall
Edinburgh, 2015

PS - you can download Tom Kratman's essays from http://www.tomkratman.com/

Printed in Great Britain
by Amazon